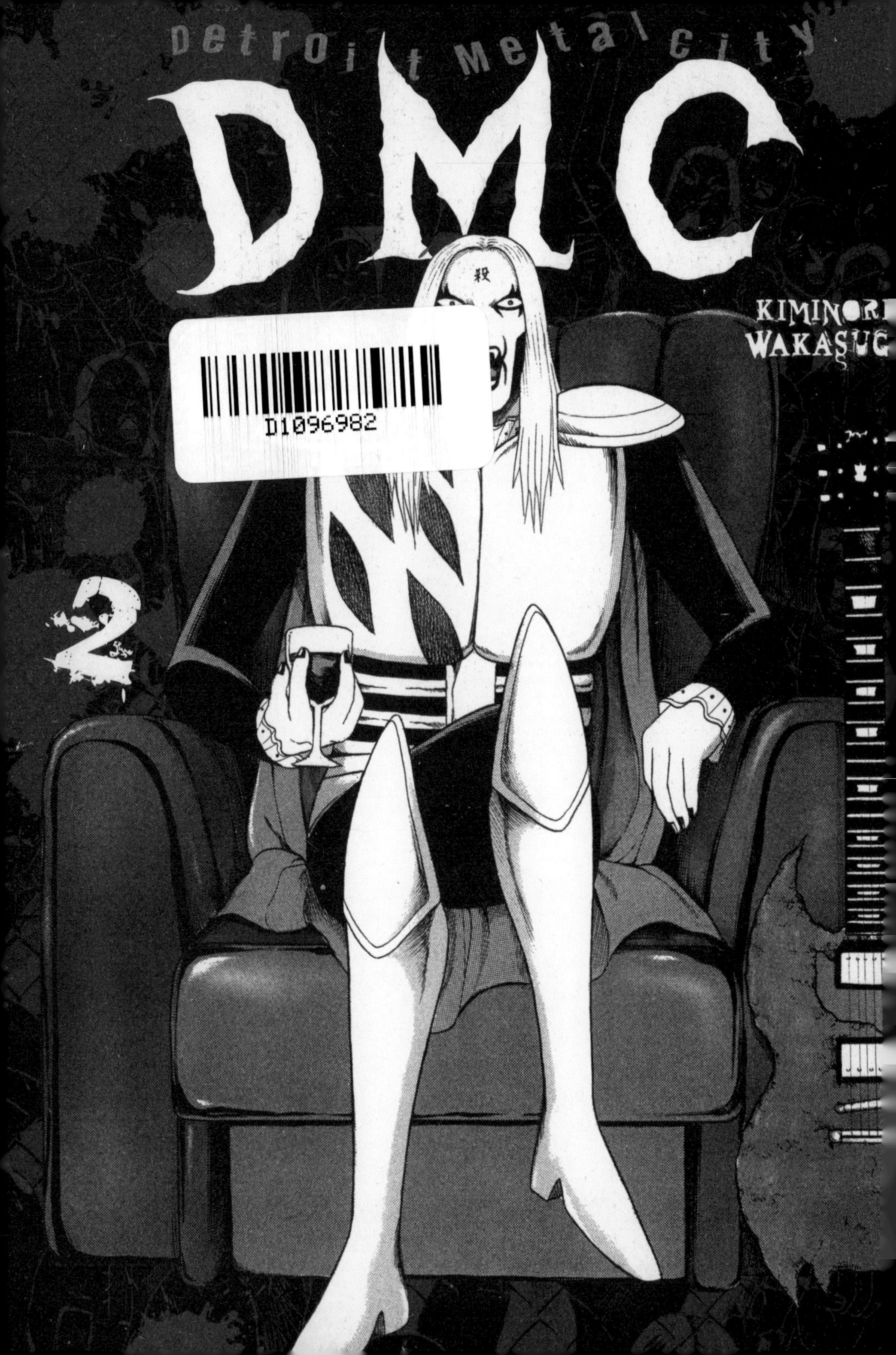
Detroit Metal City
DMC
2
KIMINORI
WAKASUG

DETROIT METAL CITY IS
KRAUSER II (LEAD GUITAR, VOCALS) CAMUS (DRUMS) JAGI (VOCALS AND BASS)

WARNING!
THIS ALBUM
CONTAINS
NOTHING BUT THE
MOST PROFANE
OF PROFANITIES!
LISTEN AT THE
RISK OF YOUR
IMMORTAL SOUL.

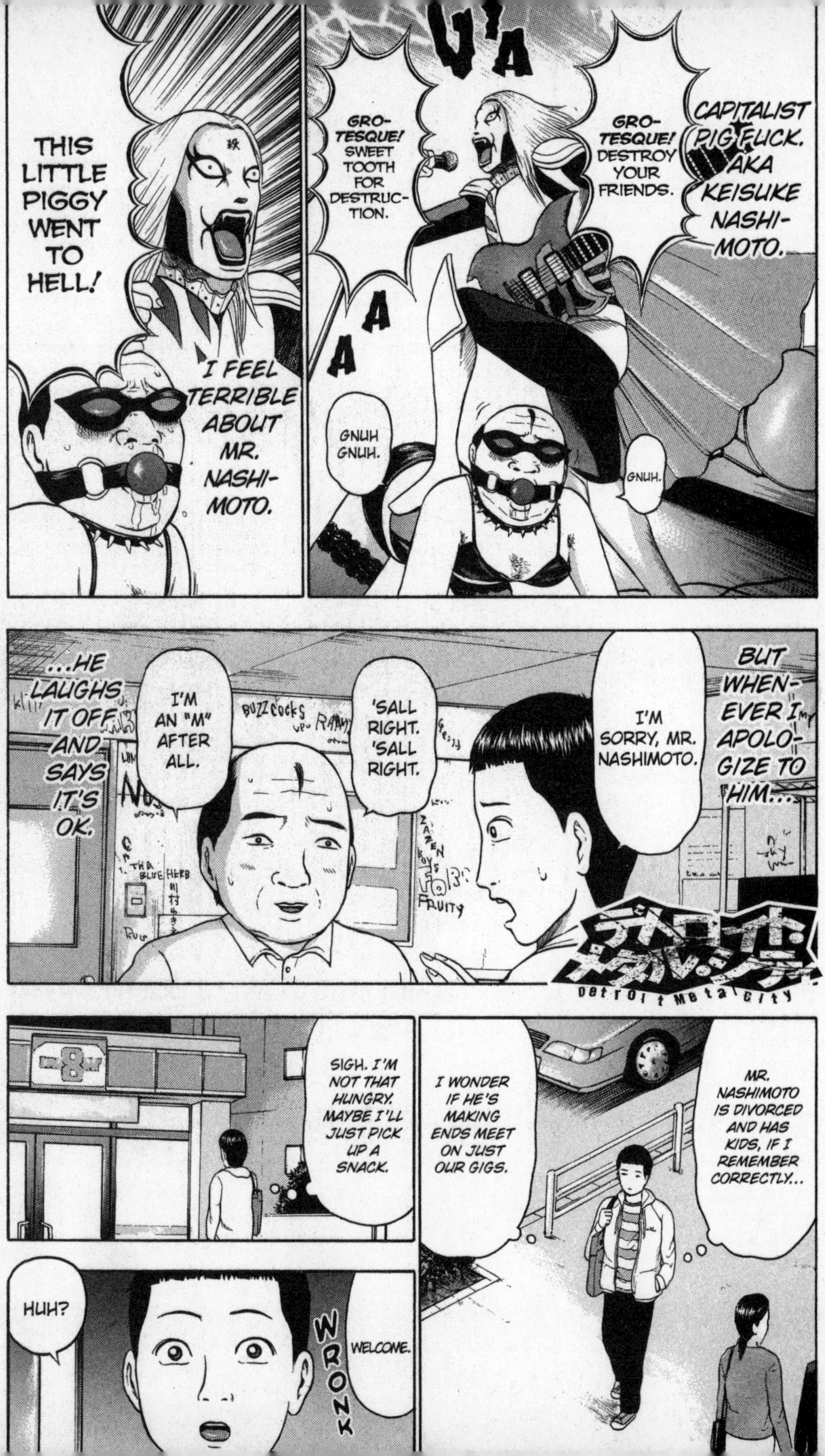
CAPITALIST PIG FUCK. AKA KEISUKE NASHIMOTO.
GROTESQUE! DESTROY YOUR FRIENDS.
GROTESQUE! SWEET TOOTH FOR DESTRUCTION.
A A A
GNUH.
GNUH GNUH.
THIS LITTLE PIGGY WENT TO HELL!
I FEEL TERRIBLE ABOUT MR. NASHIMOTO.
BUT WHENEVER I APOLOGIZE TO HIM...
I'M SORRY, MR. NASHIMOTO.
'SALL RIGHT. 'SALL RIGHT.
I'M AN "M" AFTER ALL.
...HE LAUGHS IT OFF AND SAYS IT'S OK.
BUZZCOCKS
ZAZEN BOYS
THA BLUE HERB
FRUITY
Detroit Metal City
MR. NASHIMOTO IS DIVORCED AND HAS KIDS, IF I REMEMBER CORRECTLY...
I WONDER IF HE'S MAKING ENDS MEET ON JUST OUR GIGS.
SIGH. I'M NOT THAT HUNGRY. MAYBE I'LL JUST PICK UP A SNACK.
WELCOME.
WRONK
HUH?

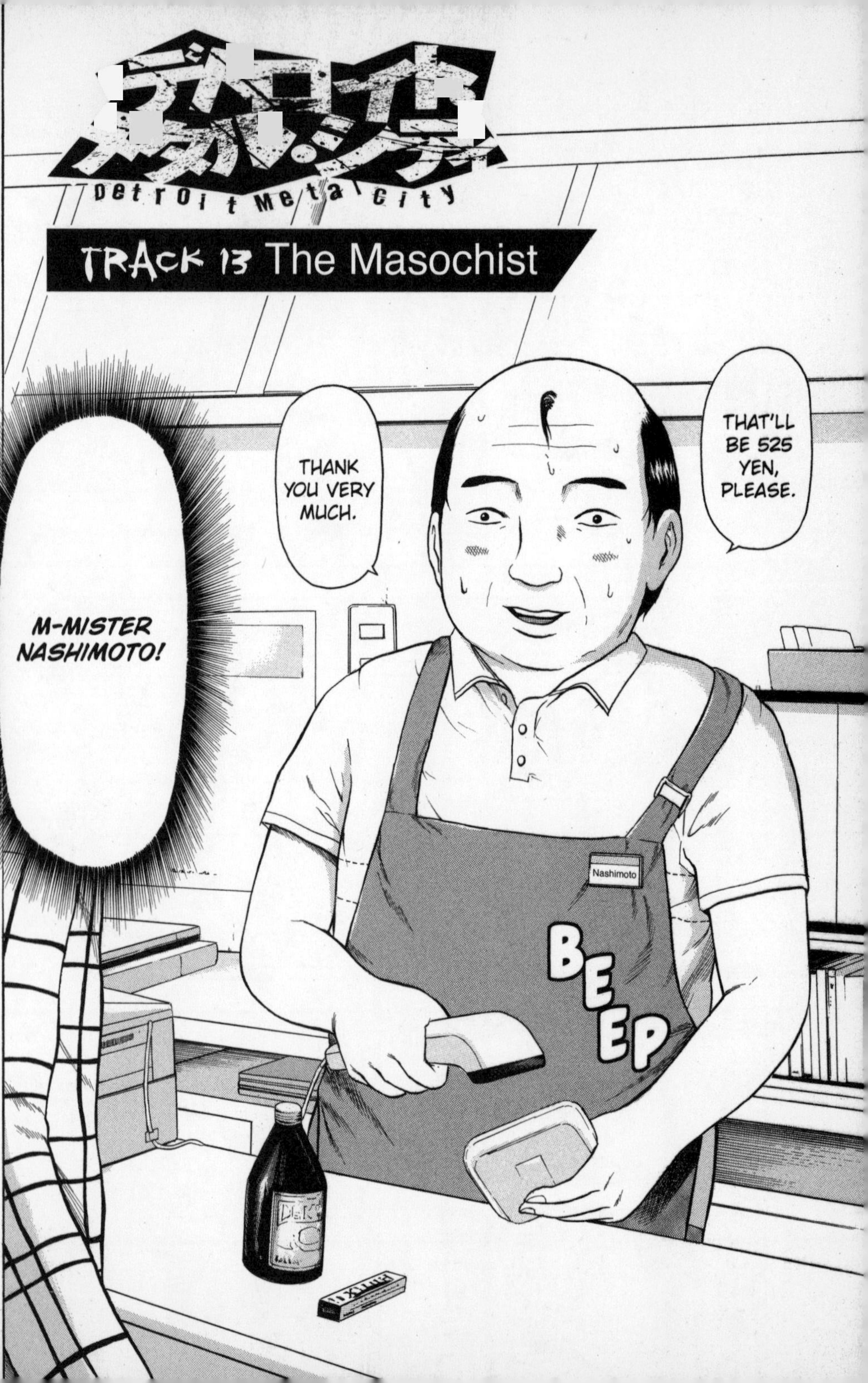
Detroit Metal City
TRACK 13 The Masochist
THAT'LL BE 525 YEN, PLEASE.
THANK YOU VERY MUCH.
Nashimoto
BEEP
M-MISTER NASHIMOTO!

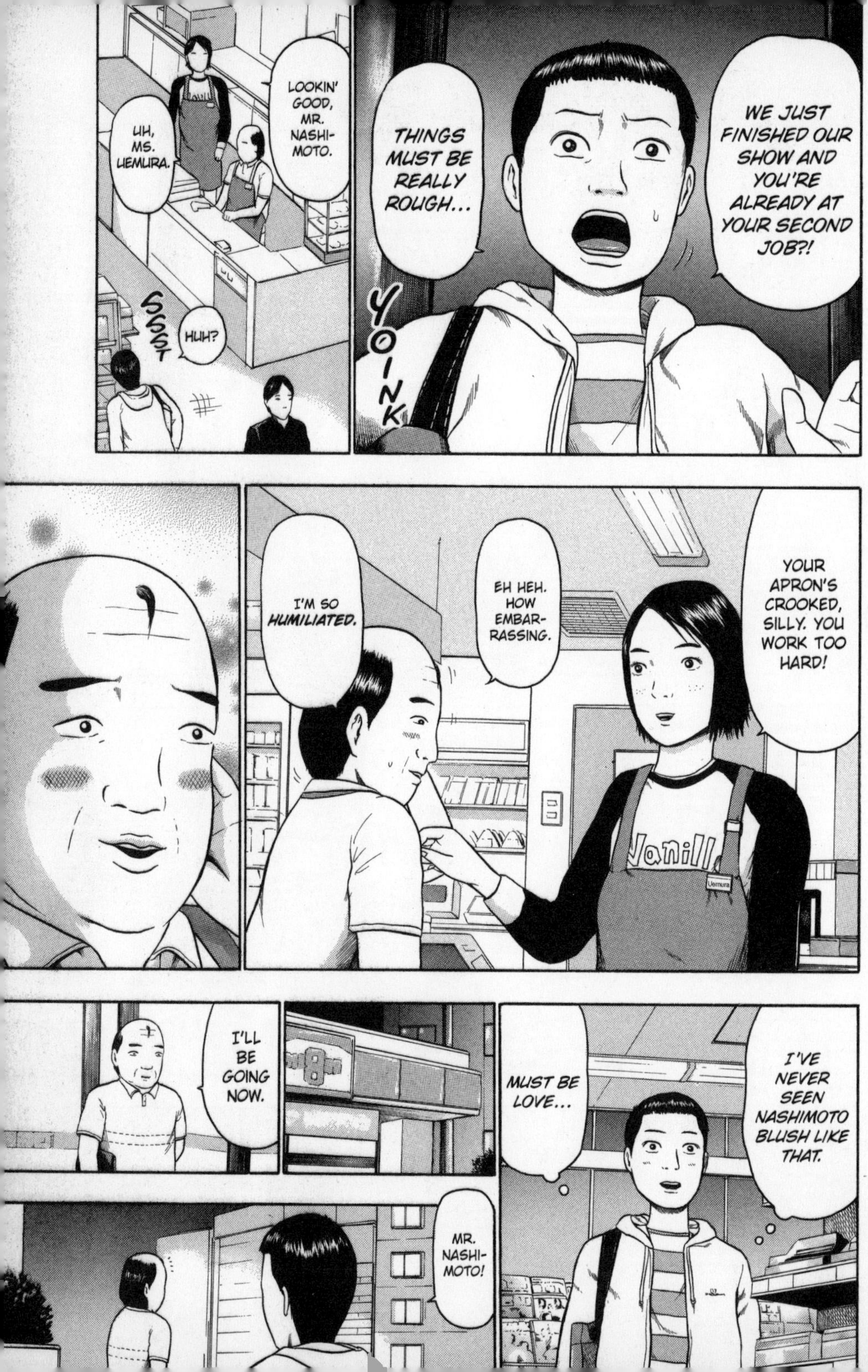
WE JUST FINISHED OUR SHOW AND YOU'RE ALREADY AT YOUR SECOND JOB?!
THINGS MUST BE REALLY ROUGH...
YOINK
LOOKIN' GOOD, MR. NASHIMOTO.
UH, MS. UEMURA.
HUH?
SSST
YOUR APRON'S CROOKED, SILLY. YOU WORK TOO HARD!
EH HEH. HOW EMBARRASSING.
I'M SO *HUMILIATED.*
Uemura
I'VE NEVER SEEN NASHIMOTO BLUSH LIKE THAT.
MUST BE LOVE...
I'LL BE GOING NOW.
MR. NASHIMOTO!

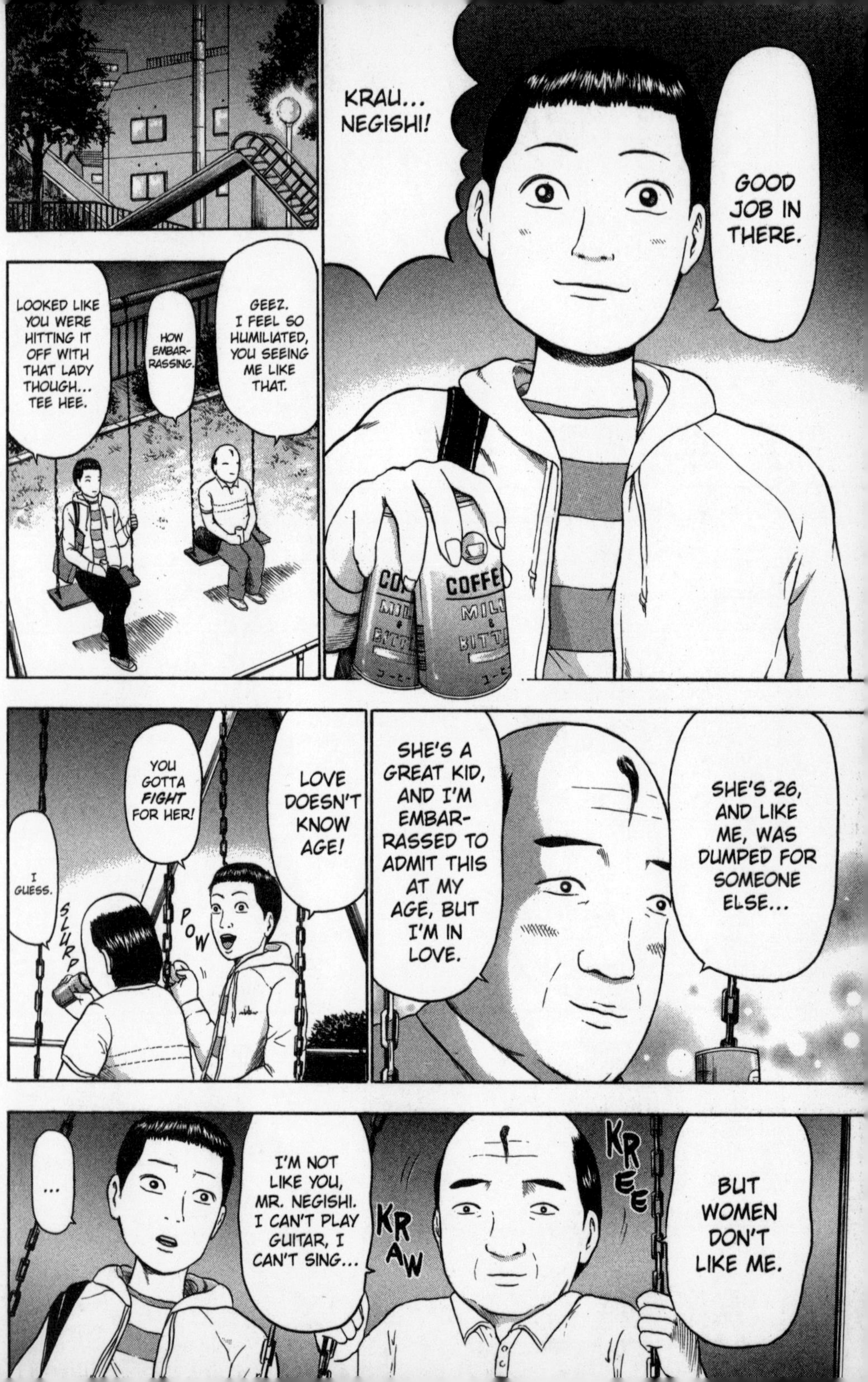
KRAU... NEGISHI!
GOOD JOB IN THERE.
GEEZ. I FEEL SO HUMILIATED, YOU SEEING ME LIKE THAT.
HOW EMBAR-RASSING.
LOOKED LIKE YOU WERE HITTING IT OFF WITH THAT LADY THOUGH... TEE HEE.
SHE'S 26, AND LIKE ME, WAS DUMPED FOR SOMEONE ELSE...
SHE'S A GREAT KID, AND I'M EMBAR-RASSED TO ADMIT THIS AT MY AGE, BUT I'M IN LOVE.
LOVE DOESN'T KNOW AGE!
YOU GOTTA *FIGHT* FOR HER!
POW
SLURP
I GUESS.
BUT WOMEN DON'T LIKE ME.
KREE
KRAW
I'M NOT LIKE YOU, MR. NEGISHI. I CAN'T PLAY GUITAR, I CAN'T SING...
...

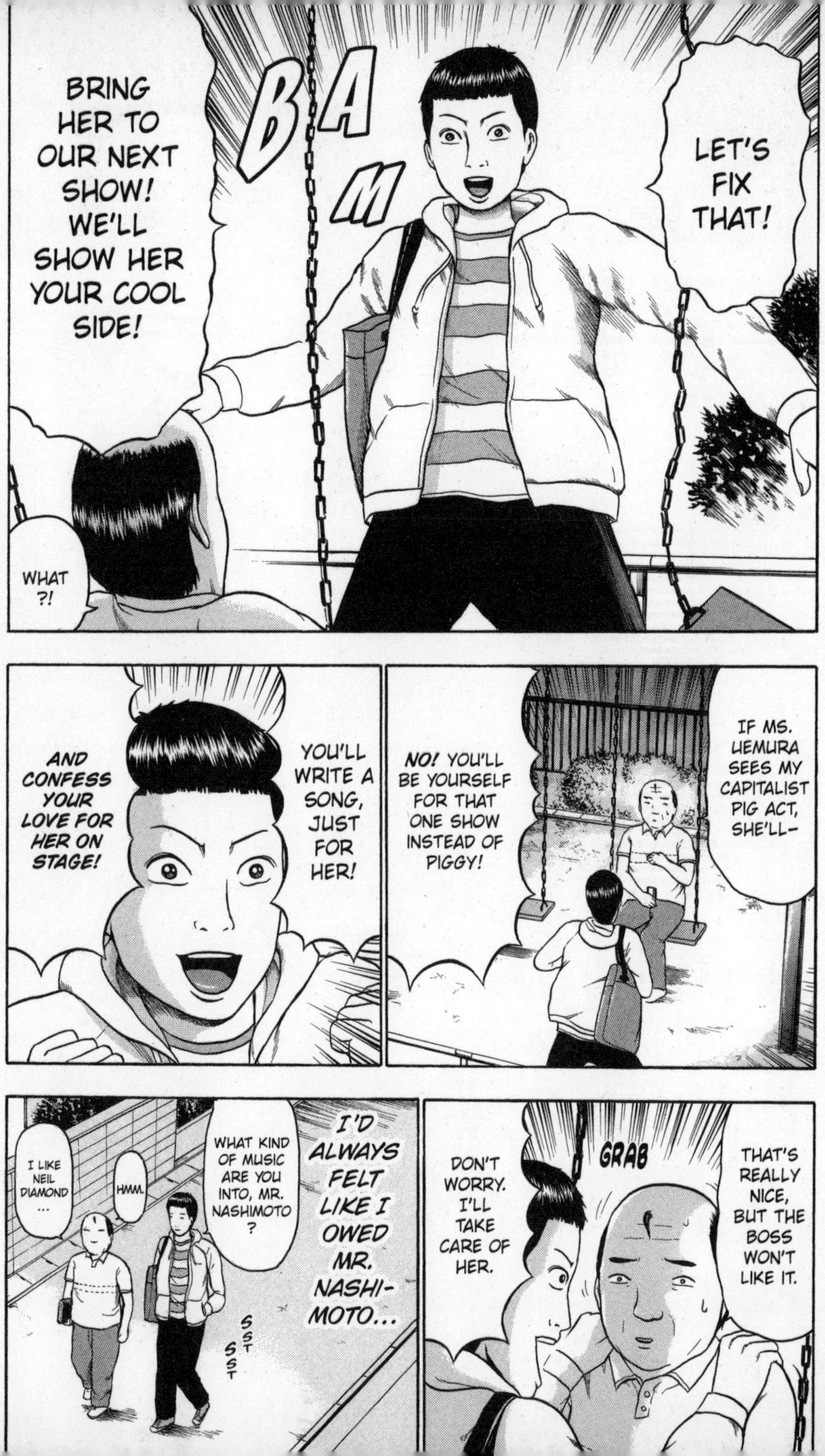
LET'S FIX THAT!
BAM
BRING HER TO OUR NEXT SHOW! WE'LL SHOW HER YOUR COOL SIDE!
WHAT ?!
IF MS. UEMURA SEES MY CAPITALIST PIG ACT, SHE'LL–
NO! YOU'LL BE YOURSELF FOR THAT ONE SHOW INSTEAD OF PIGGY!
YOU'LL WRITE A SONG, JUST FOR HER!
AND CONFESS YOUR LOVE FOR HER ON STAGE!
THAT'S REALLY NICE, BUT THE BOSS WON'T LIKE IT.
GRAB
DON'T WORRY. I'LL TAKE CARE OF HER.
I'D ALWAYS FELT LIKE I OWED MR. NASHIMOTO...
WHAT KIND OF MUSIC ARE YOU INTO, MR. NASHIMOTO?
HMM.
I LIKE NEIL DIAMOND...
SST SST

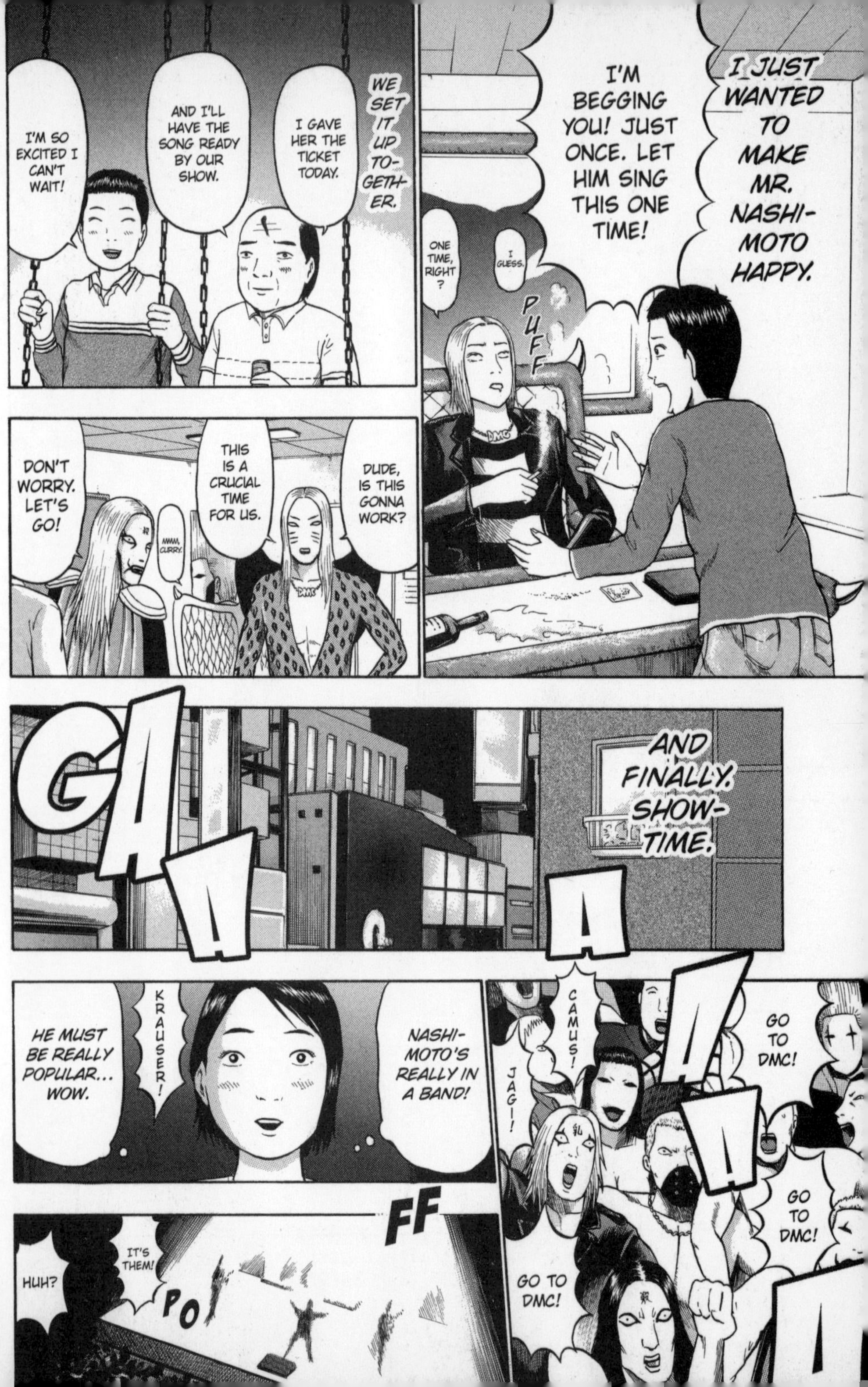
I JUST WANTED TO MAKE MR. NASHIMOTO HAPPY.
I'M BEGGING YOU! JUST ONCE. LET HIM SING THIS ONE TIME!
I GUESS.
ONE TIME, RIGHT?
PUFF
WE SET IT UP TOGETHER.
I GAVE HER THE TICKET TODAY.
AND I'LL HAVE THE SONG READY BY OUR SHOW.
I'M SO EXCITED I CAN'T WAIT!
DUDE, IS THIS GONNA WORK?
THIS IS A CRUCIAL TIME FOR US.
MMM, CURRY.
DON'T WORRY. LET'S GO!
AND FINALLY. SHOWTIME.
GAAAAAA
GO TO DMC!
CAMUS!
JAGI!
GO TO DMC!
GO TO DMC!
NASHIMOTO'S REALLY IN A BAND!
KRAUSER!
HE MUST BE REALLY POPULAR... WOW.
FF
IT'S THEM!
HUH?
PO

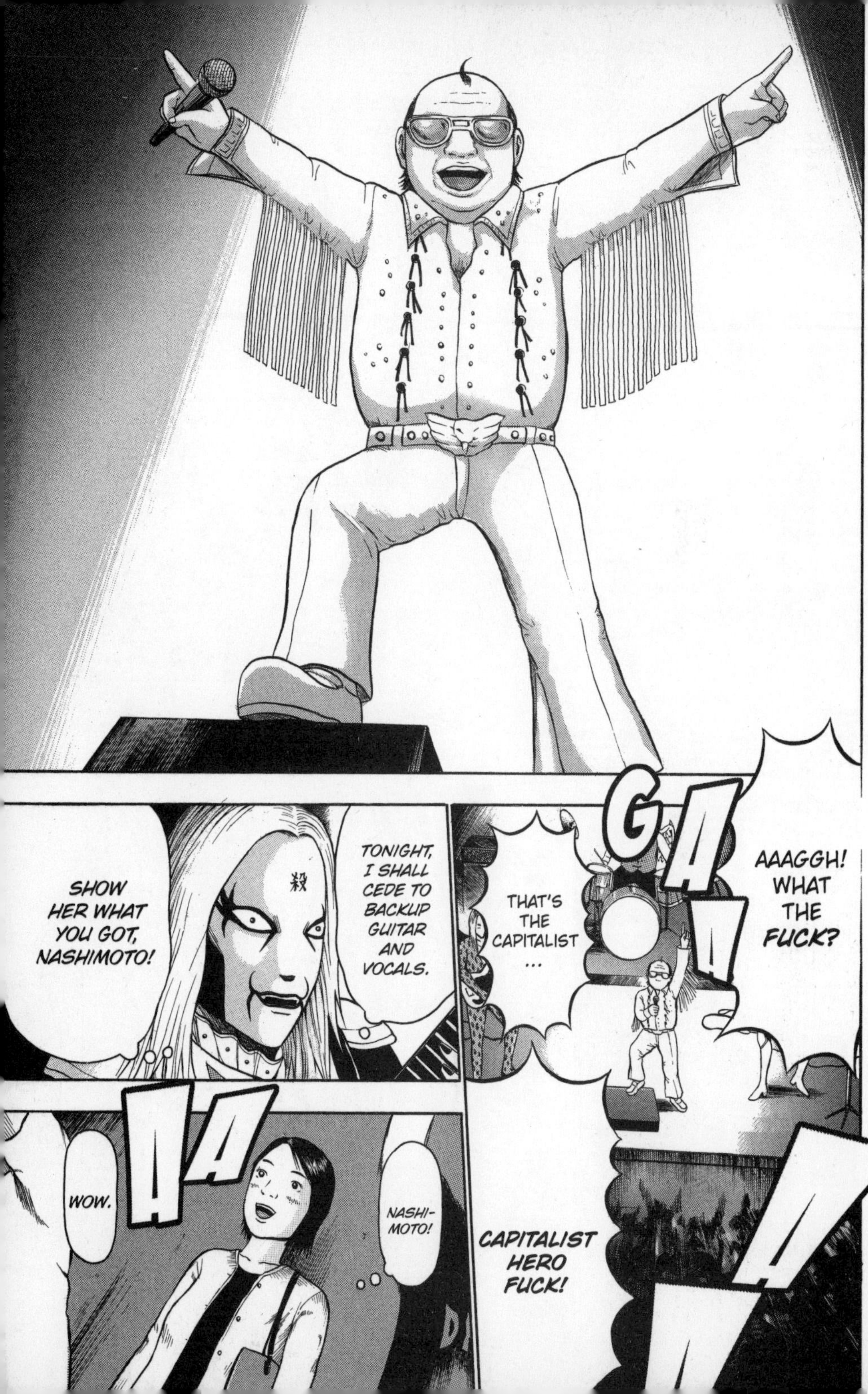
GAAA
AAAGGH! WHAT THE FUCK?
THAT'S THE CAPITALIST...
TONIGHT, I SHALL CEDE TO BACKUP GUITAR AND VOCALS.
SHOW HER WHAT YOU GOT, NASHIMOTO!
AA
CAPITALIST HERO FUCK!
NASHI-MOTO!
AA
WOW.

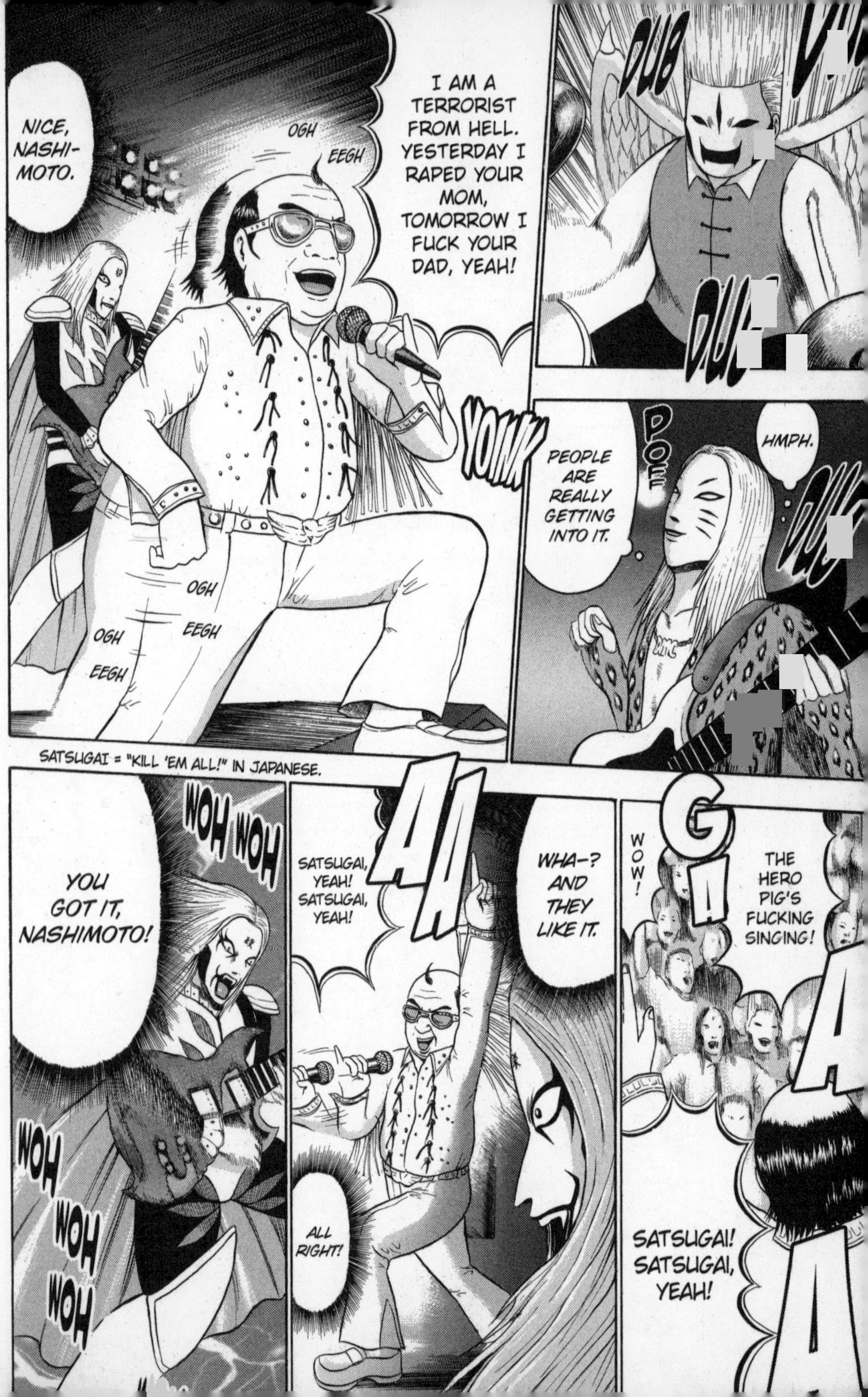

DUB
DUB
HMPH.
POFF
PEOPLE ARE REALLY GETTING INTO IT.
YOINK
I AM A TERRORIST FROM HELL. YESTERDAY I RAPED YOUR MOM, TOMORROW I FUCK YOUR DAD, YEAH!
OGH EEGH
NICE, NASHI-MOTO.
OGH EEGH
OGH EEGH
SATSUGAI = "KILL 'EM ALL!" IN JAPANESE.
G A
WOW!
THE HERO PIG'S FUCKING SINGING!
SATSUGAI! SATSUGAI, YEAH!
WHA-? AND THEY LIKE IT.
AA
SATSUGAI, YEAH! SATSUGAI, YEAH!
ALL RIGHT!
WOH WOH
YOU GOT IT, NASHIMOTO!
WOH WOH WOH

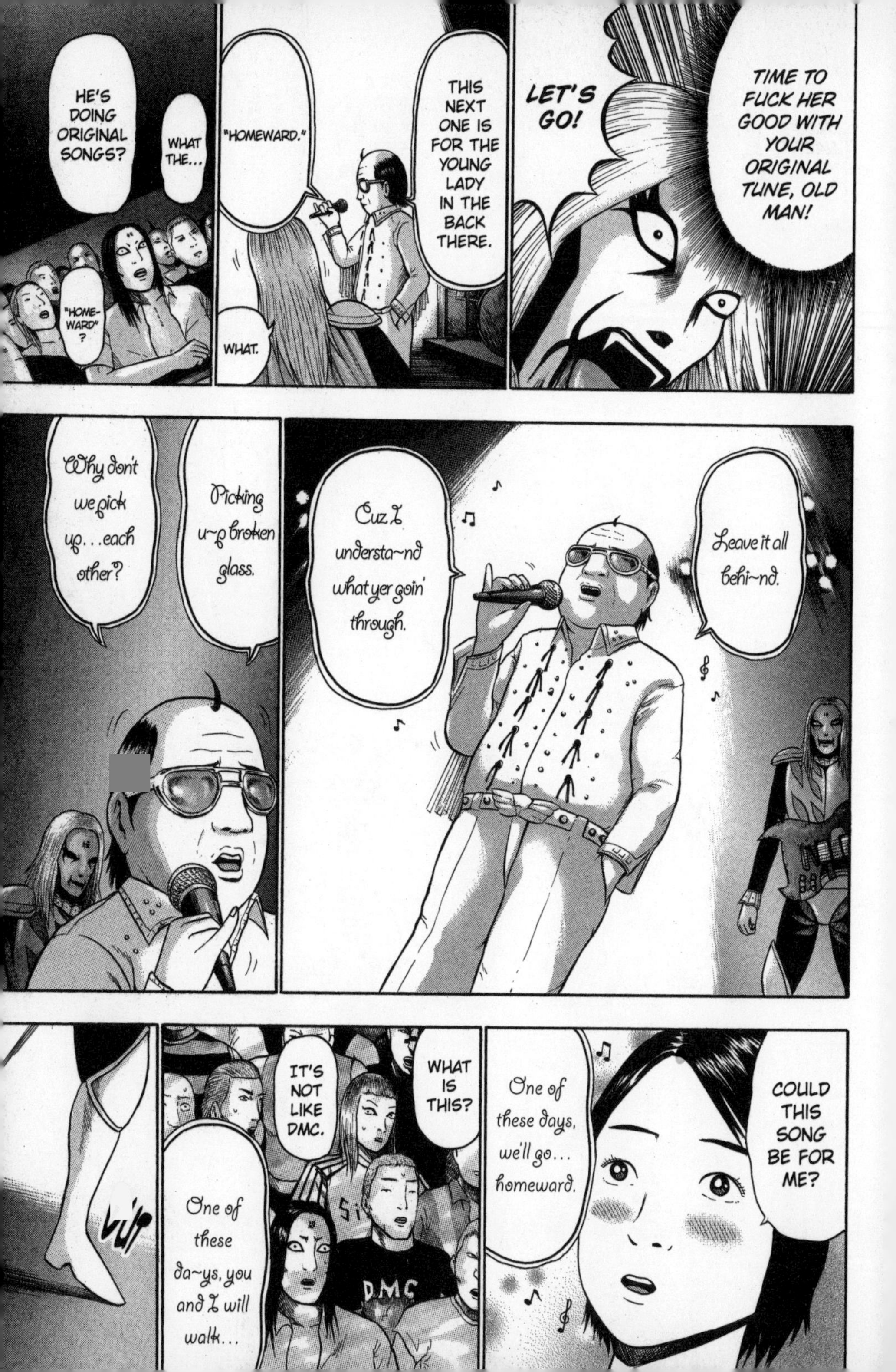
TIME TO FUCK HER GOOD WITH YOUR ORIGINAL TUNE, OLD MAN!
LET'S GO!
THIS NEXT ONE IS FOR THE YOUNG LADY IN THE BACK THERE.
"HOMEWARD."
WHAT.
WHAT THE...
HE'S DOING ORIGINAL SONGS?
"HOME-WARD"?
Leave it all behi~nd.
Cuz I understa~nd what yer goin' through.
Picking u~p broken glass.
Why don't we pick up...each other?
COULD THIS SONG BE FOR ME?
One of these days, we'll go... homeward.
WHAT IS THIS?
IT'S NOT LIKE DMC.
One of these da~ys, you and I will walk...

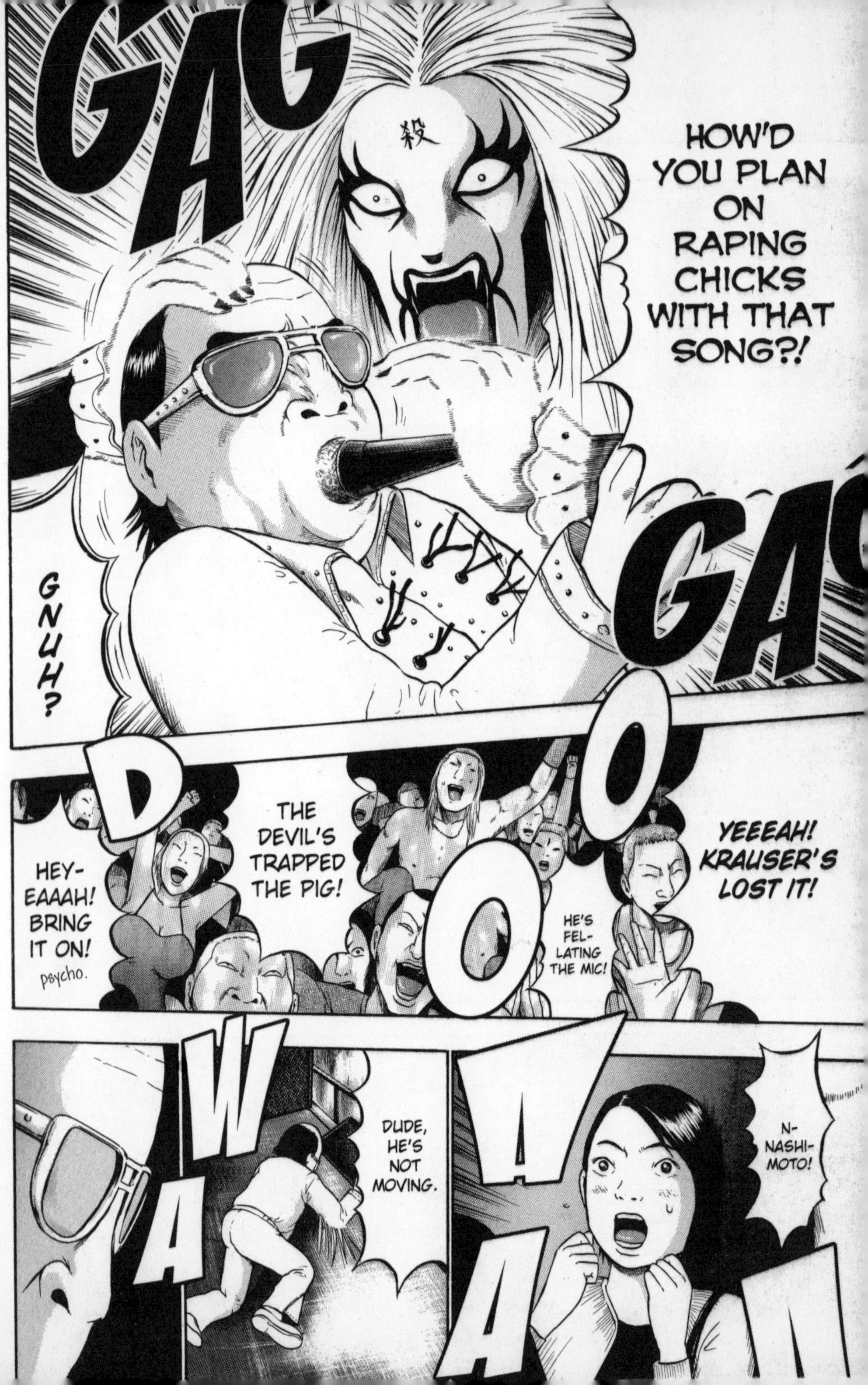

HOW'D YOU PLAN ON RAPING CHICKS WITH THAT SONG?!
GAG
GAG
GNUH?
DOOO
YEEEAH! KRAUSER'S LOST IT!
HE'S FEL-LATING THE MIC!
THE DEVIL'S TRAPPED THE PIG!
HEY-EAAAH! BRING IT ON!
psycho.
N-NASHIMOTO!
DUDE, HE'S NOT MOVING.
GWAAAA

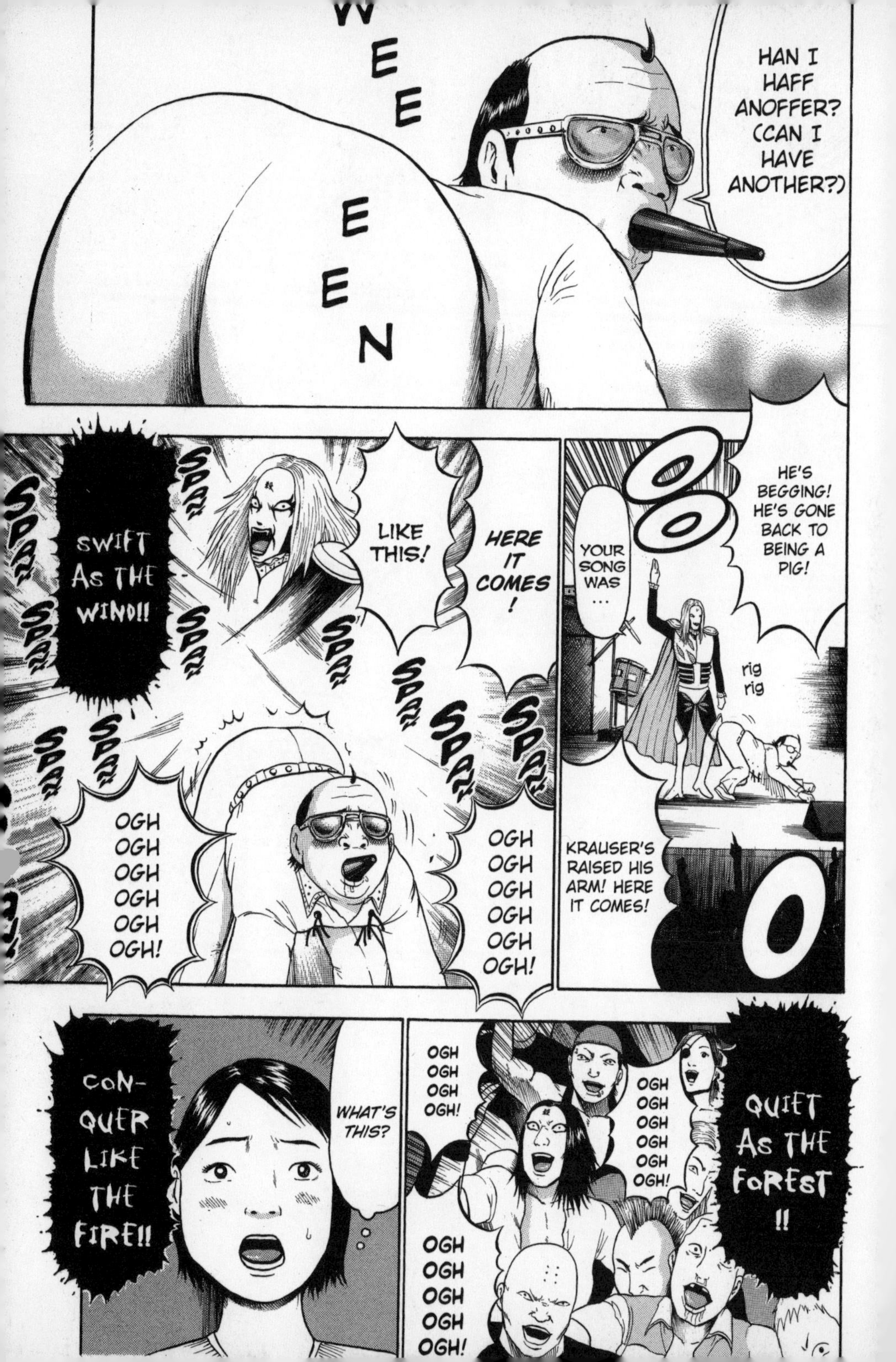
HAN I HAFF ANOFFER? (CAN I HAVE ANOTHER?)
WEEEEN
OOO
HE'S BEGGING! HE'S GONE BACK TO BEING A PIG!
YOUR SONG WAS...
rig rig
KRAUSER'S RAISED HIS ARM! HERE IT COMES!
O
HERE IT COMES!
LIKE THIS!
SWIFT AS THE WIND!!
OGH OGH OGH OGH OGH OGH!
OGH OGH OGH OGH OGH OGH!
QUIET AS THE FOREST!!
OGH OGH OGH OGH OGH OGH!
OGH OGH OGH OGH!
OGH OGH OGH OGH OGH!
WHAT'S THIS?
CON-QUER LIKE THE FIRE!!

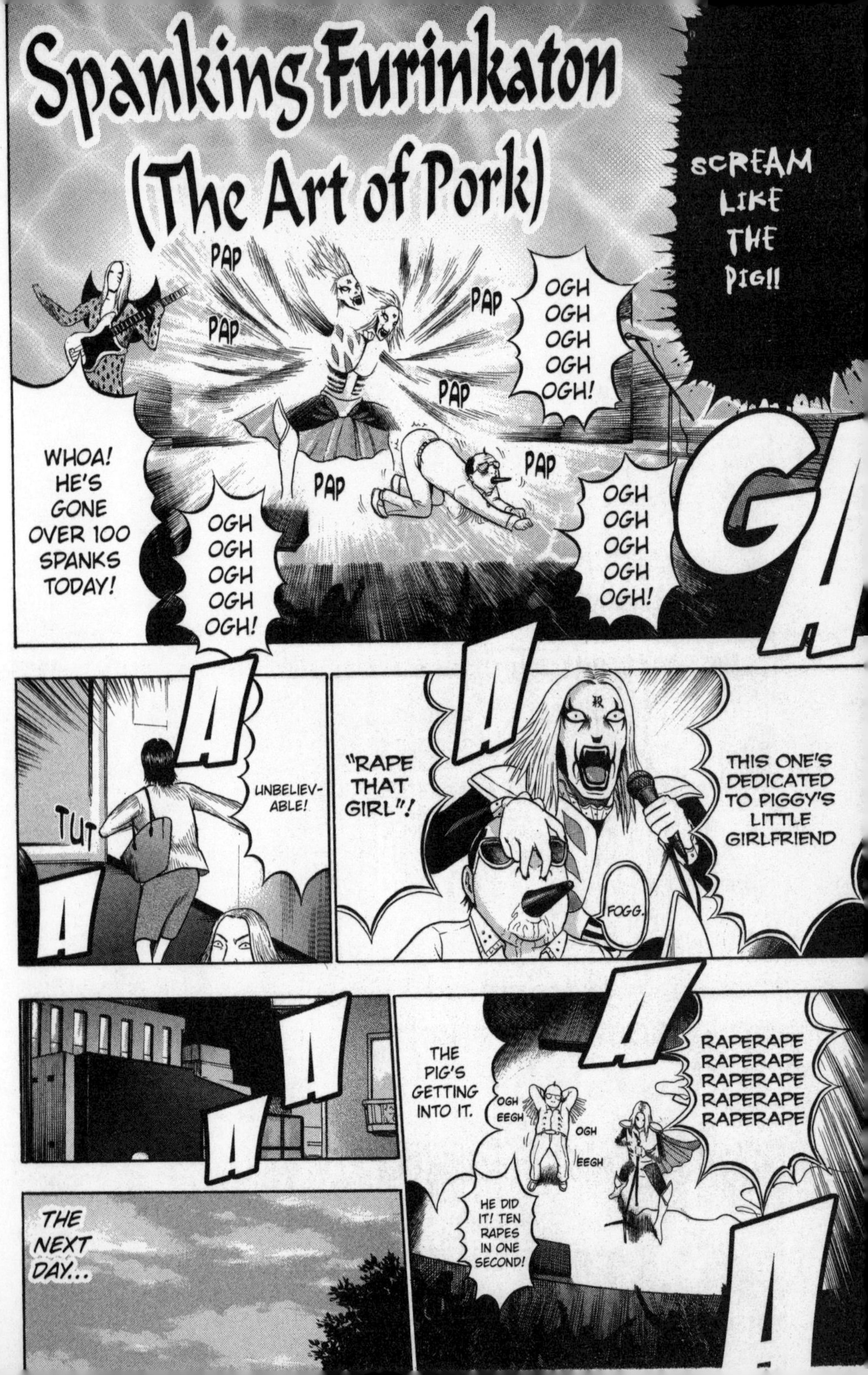
SCREAM LIKE THE PIG!!
Spanking Furinkaton (The Art of Pork)
PAP PAP PAP PAP PAP PAP
OGH OGH OGH OGH OGH!
OGH OGH OGH OGH OGH!
WHOA! HE'S GONE OVER 100 SPANKS TODAY!
OGH OGH OGH OGH OGH!
GAAAAA
THIS ONE'S DEDICATED TO PIGGY'S LITTLE GIRLFRIEND
"RAPE THAT GIRL"!
FOGG.
UNBELIEV-ABLE!
TUT
RAPERAPE RAPERAPE RAPERAPE RAPERAPE RAPERAPE
THE PIG'S GETTING INTO IT.
OGH EEGH
OGH EEGH
HE DID IT! TEN RAPES IN ONE SECOND!
AAA
THE NEXT DAY...

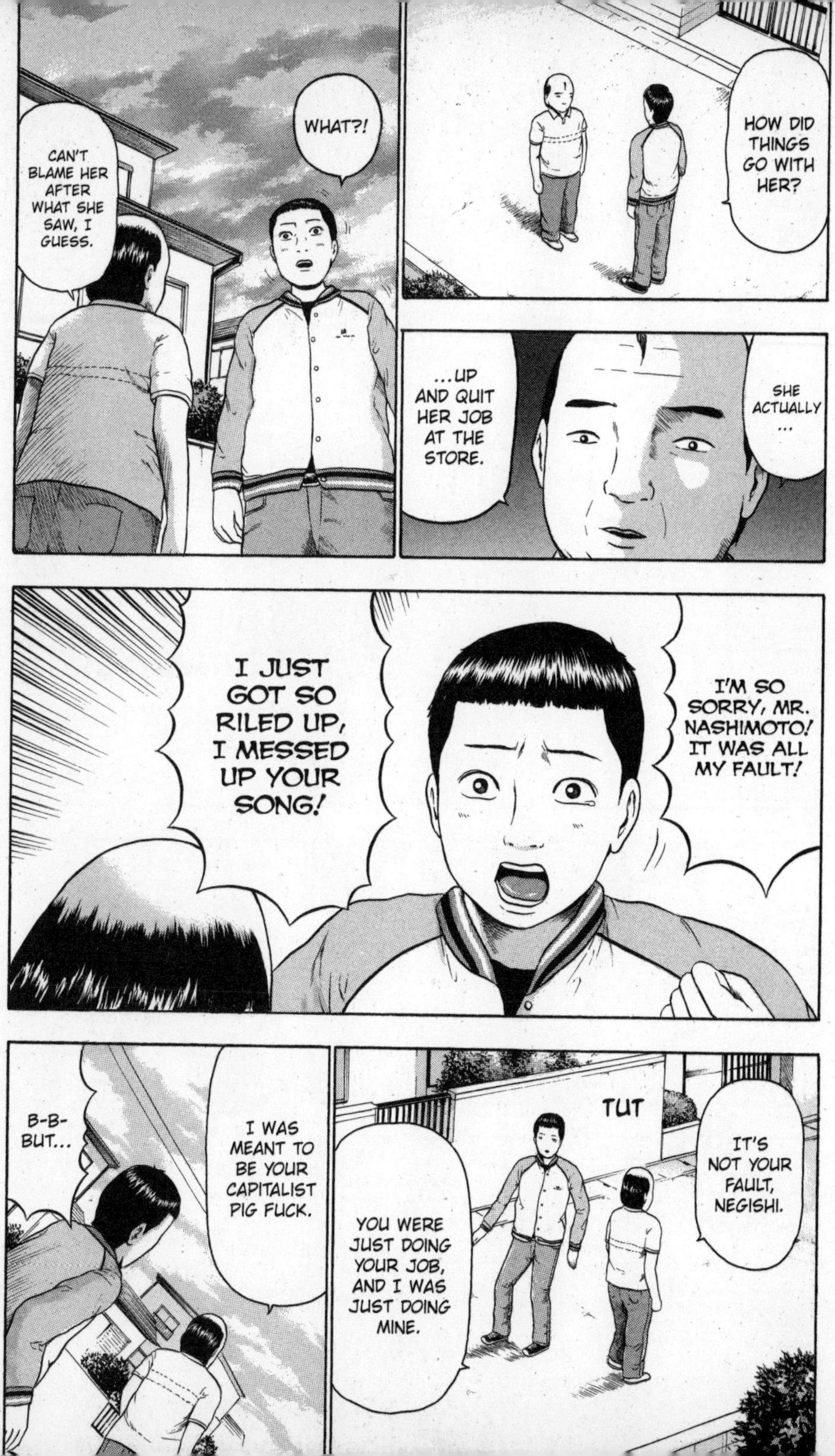
HOW DID THINGS GO WITH HER?
SHE ACTUALLY...
...UP AND QUIT HER JOB AT THE STORE.
WHAT?!
CAN'T BLAME HER AFTER WHAT SHE SAW, I GUESS.
I'M SO SORRY, MR. NASHIMOTO! IT WAS ALL MY FAULT!
I JUST GOT SO RILED UP, I MESSED UP YOUR SONG!
IT'S NOT YOUR FAULT, NEGISHI.
TUT
YOU WERE JUST DOING YOUR JOB, AND I WAS JUST DOING MINE.
I WAS MEANT TO BE YOUR CAPITALIST PIG FUCK.
B-B-BUT...

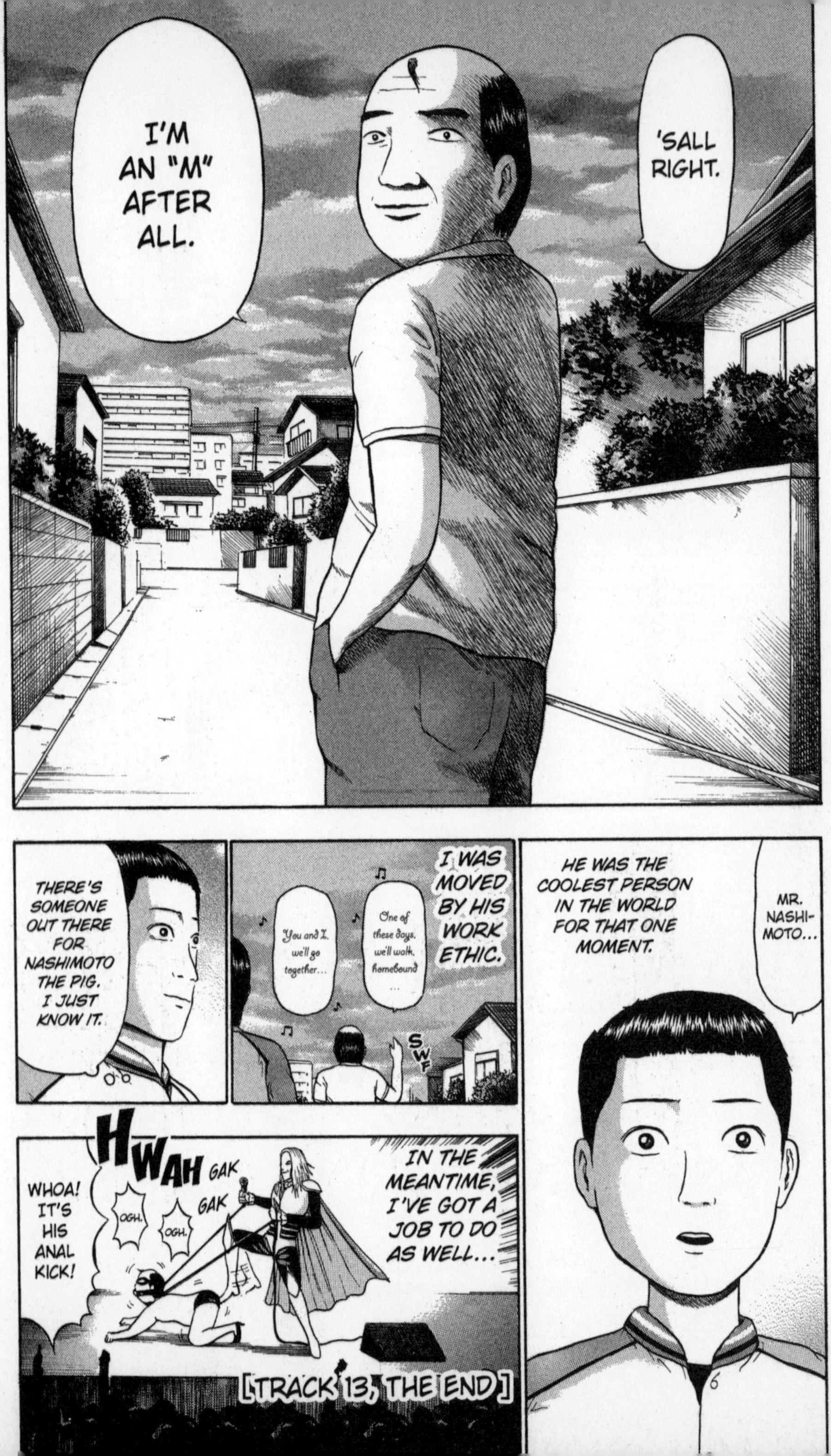
'SALL RIGHT.
I'M AN "M" AFTER ALL.
MR. NASHIMOTO...
HE WAS THE COOLEST PERSON IN THE WORLD FOR THAT ONE MOMENT.
I WAS MOVED BY HIS WORK ETHIC.
One of these days, we'll walk, homebound...
You and I, we'll go together...
SWF
THERE'S SOMEONE OUT THERE FOR NASHIMOTO THE PIG. I JUST KNOW IT.
IN THE MEANTIME, I'VE GOT A JOB TO DO AS WELL...
HWAH
GAK
GAK
OGH.
OGH.
WHOA! IT'S HIS ANAL KICK!
[TRACK 13, THE END]

DMC LEXICON

♥ FURINKATON

The "M" (masochist) dogma. The term originates from its predecessor, furinkazan, which was borrowed from Sun Tse's The Art of War and was coined by the renowned daimyo Shingen Takeda, an out-and-out "S" (sadist). Furthermore, the traditional story says that in their fourth battle for Kawanakajima versus Kenshin Uesugi, Shingen used a fan to capture Kenshin's sword, but rumor is he actually used a training whip. Historians are close to discovering a link between the famous horse-riding battalions of the warring states period and the practice of suspension bondage.

Usage: He's doing it! Our shogun is performing spanking Furinkaton!

デトロイト・メタル・シティ
Detroit Metal City

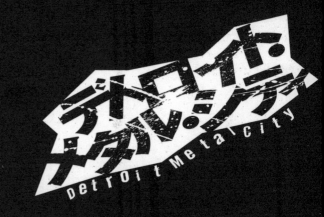

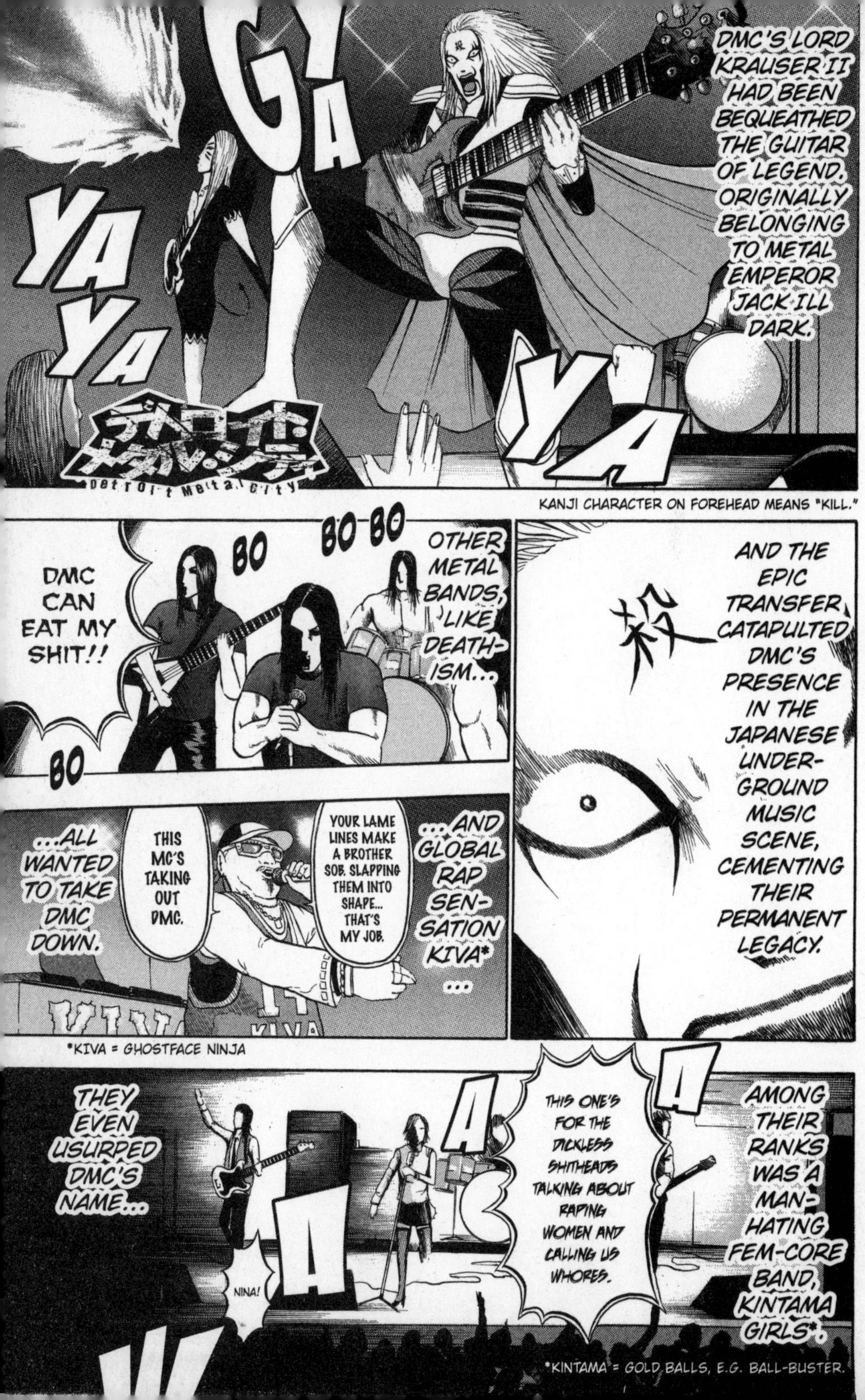

DMC'S LORD KRAUSER II HAD BEEN BEQUEATHED THE GUITAR OF LEGEND. ORIGINALLY BELONGING TO METAL EMPEROR JACK ILL DARK.
GYA
YA YA
YA
YA
Detroit Metal City
KANJI CHARACTER ON FOREHEAD MEANS "KILL."
AND THE EPIC TRANSFER CATAPULTED DMC'S PRESENCE IN THE JAPANESE UNDERGROUND MUSIC SCENE, CEMENTING THEIR PERMANENT LEGACY.
殺
OTHER METAL BANDS, LIKE DEATHISM...
BO-BO
BO
DMC CAN EAT MY SHIT!!
BO
...AND GLOBAL RAP SENSATION KIVA* ...
YOUR LAME LINES MAKE A BROTHER SOB. SLAPPING THEM INTO SHAPE... THAT'S MY JOB.
THIS MC'S TAKING OUT DMC.
...ALL WANTED TO TAKE DMC DOWN.
*KIVA = GHOSTFACE NINJA
AMONG THEIR RANKS WAS A MAN-HATING FEM-CORE BAND, KINTAMA GIRLS*.
A
THIS ONE'S FOR THE DICKLESS SHITHEADS TALKING ABOUT RAPING WOMEN AND CALLING US WHORES.
A
A
NINA!
THEY EVEN USURPED DMC'S NAME...
*KINTAMA = GOLD BALLS, E.G. BALL-BUSTER.

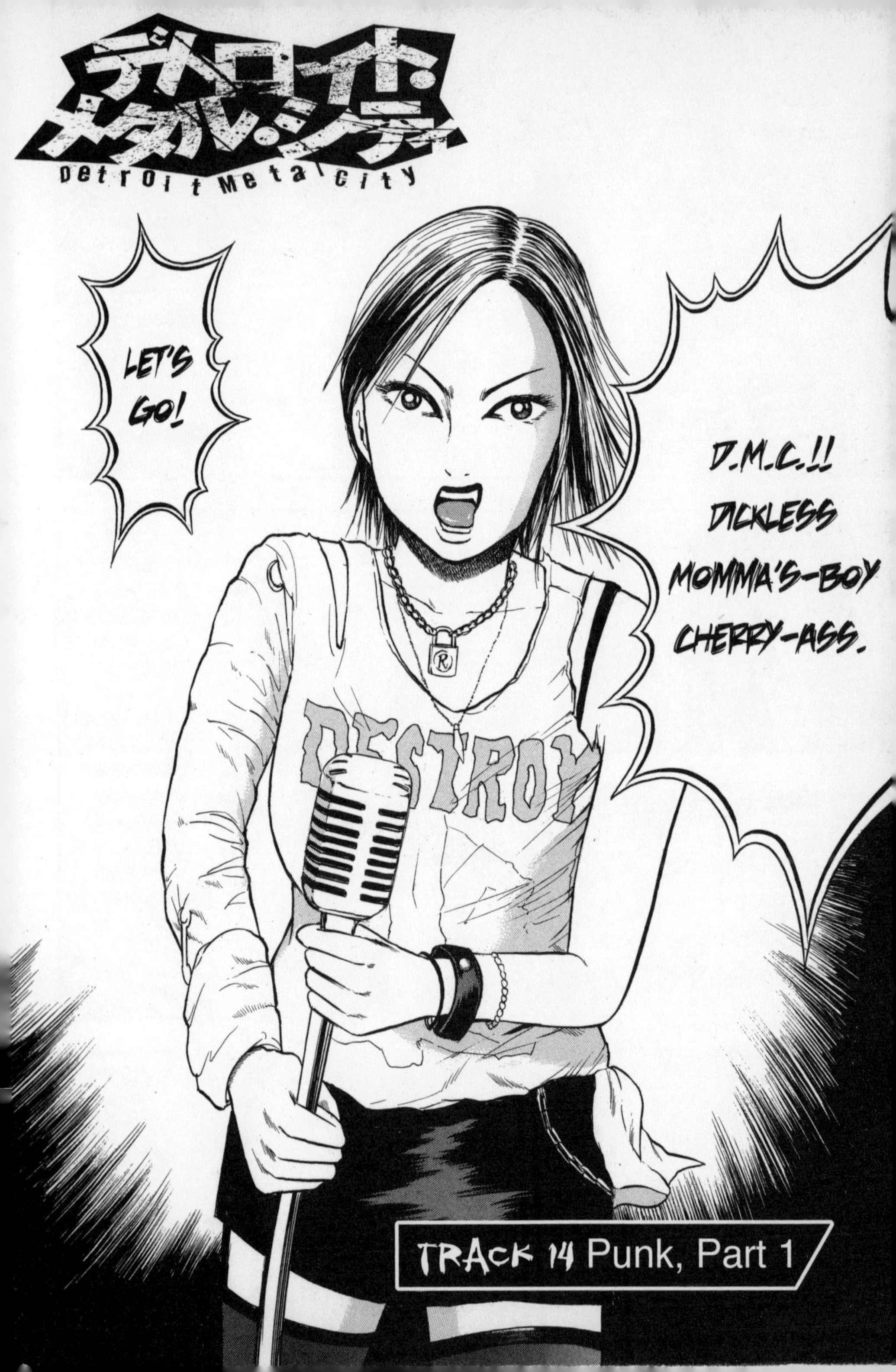
デトロイト・メタル・シティ
Detroit Metal City
LET'S GO!
D.M.C.!! DICKLESS MOMMA'S-BOY CHERRY-ASS.
DESTROY
TRACK 14 Punk, Part 1

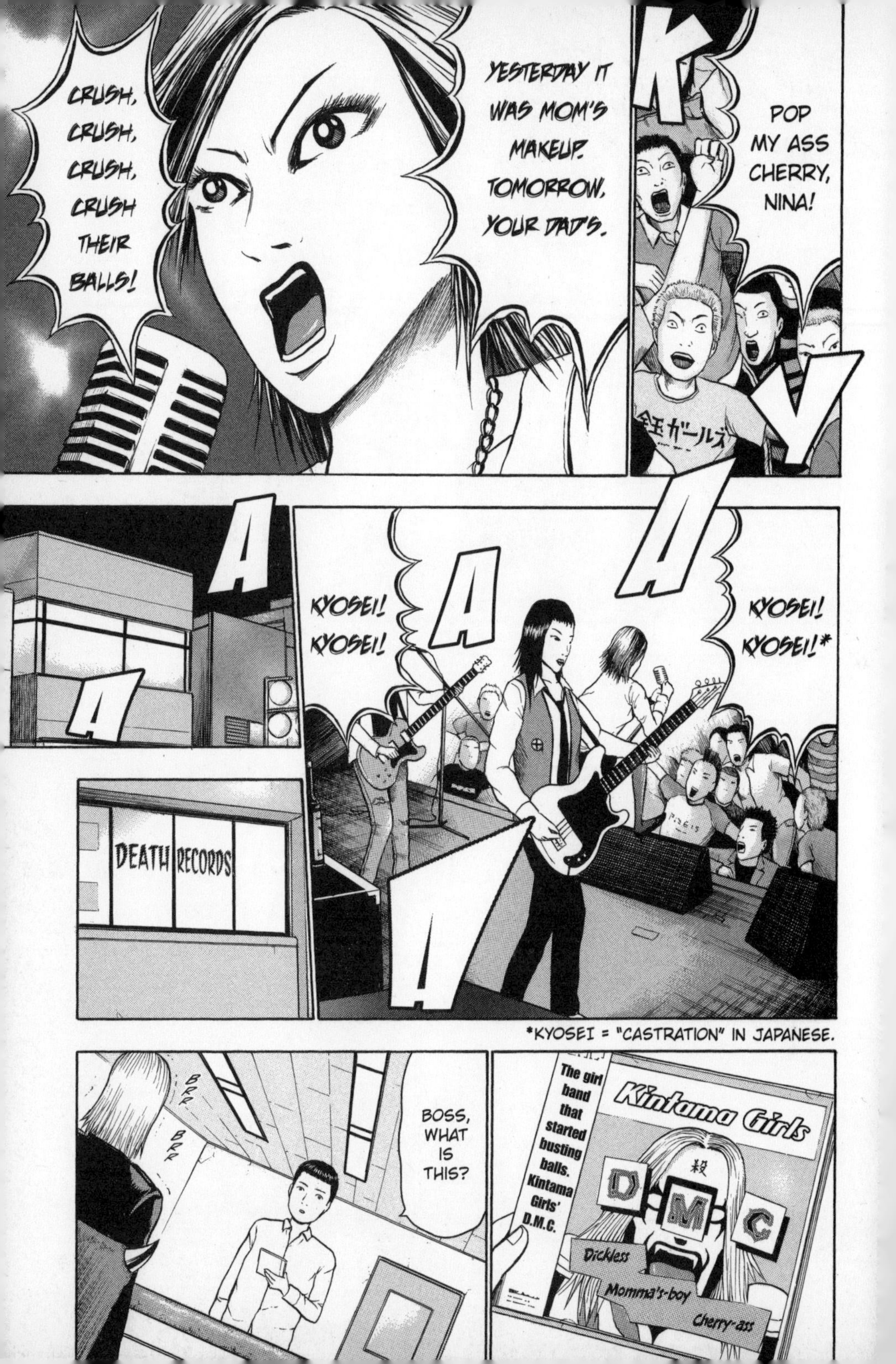

K
POP MY ASS CHERRY, NINA!
Y
YESTERDAY IT WAS MOM'S MAKEUP. TOMORROW, YOUR DAD'S.
CRUSH, CRUSH, CRUSH, CRUSH THEIR BALLS!
A
KYOSEI! KYOSEI!*
A
KYOSEI! KYOSEI!
A
A
A
DEATH RECORDS
The girl band that started busting balls. Kintama Girls' D.M.C.
Kintama Girls
D M C
Dickless
Momma's-boy
Cherry-ass
BOSS, WHAT IS THIS?
BRR
BRR

*KYOSEI = "CASTRATION" IN JAPANESE.

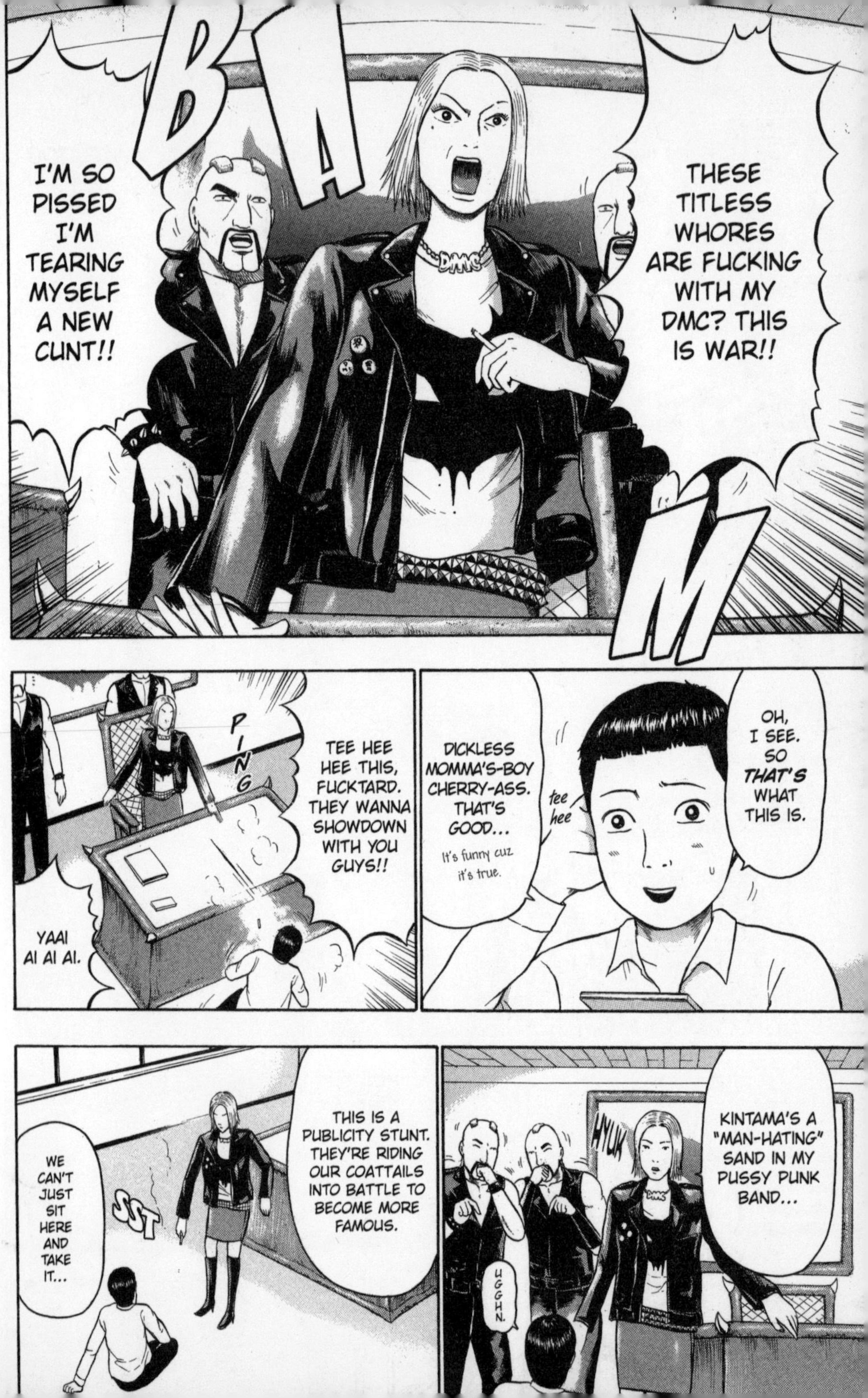
BAM
THESE TITLESS WHORES ARE FUCKING WITH MY DMC? THIS IS WAR!!
I'M SO PISSED I'M TEARING MYSELF A NEW CUNT!!
OH, I SEE. SO *THAT'S* WHAT THIS IS.
tee hee
DICKLESS MOMMA'S-BOY CHERRY-ASS. THAT'S GOOD...
It's funny cuz it's true.
PING
TEE HEE THIS, FUCKTARD. THEY WANNA SHOWDOWN WITH YOU GUYS!!
YAAI AI AI AI.
KINTAMA'S A "MAN-HATING" SAND IN MY PUSSY PUNK BAND...
HYUK
UGGHN.
THIS IS A PUBLICITY STUNT. THEY'RE RIDING OUR COATTAILS INTO BATTLE TO BECOME MORE FAMOUS.
WE CAN'T JUST SIT HERE AND TAKE IT...
SST

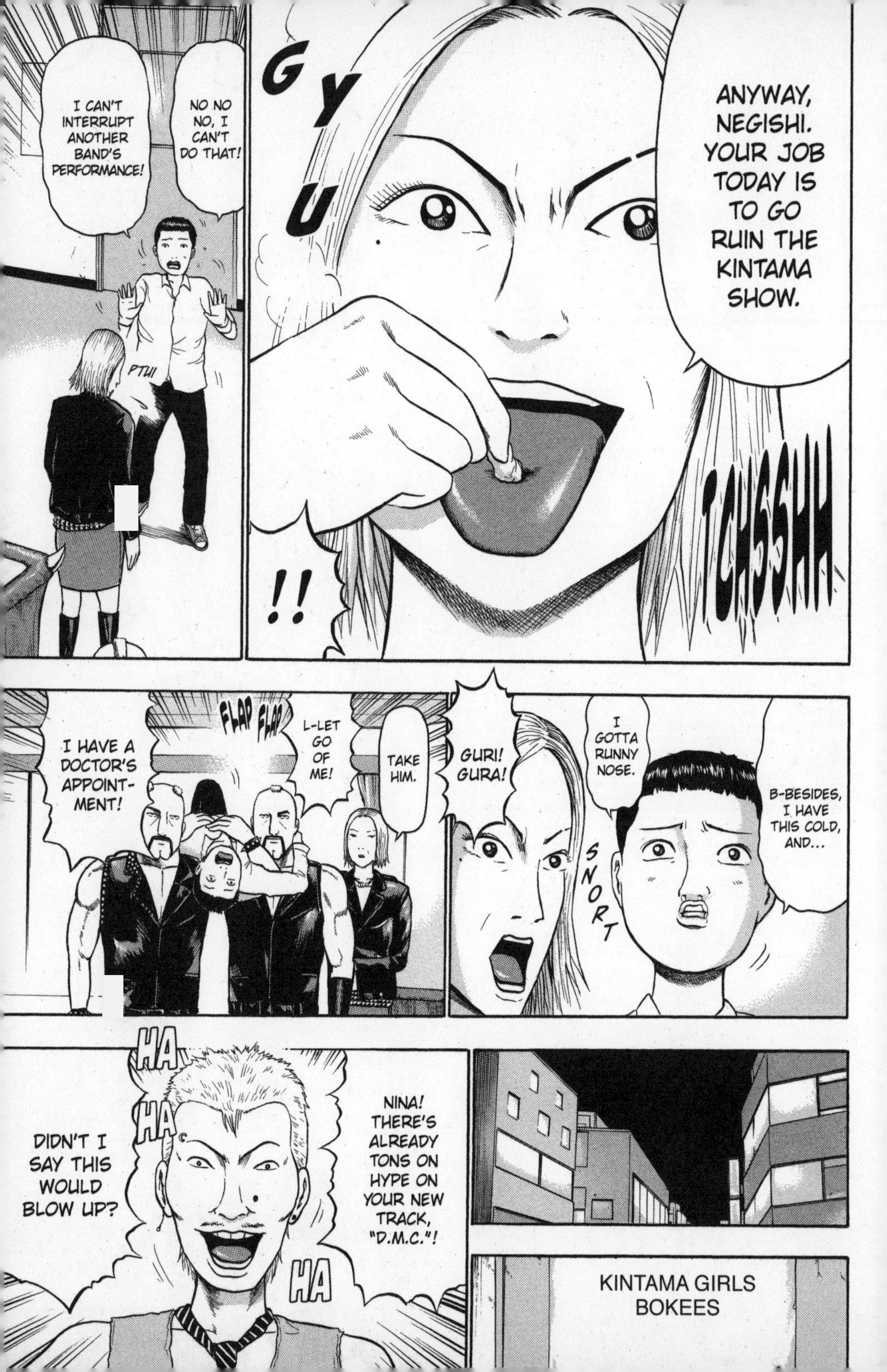
ANYWAY, NEGISHI. YOUR JOB TODAY IS TO GO RUIN THE KINTAMA SHOW.
GYUU
!!
TCHSSHH
NO NO NO, I CAN'T DO THAT!
I CAN'T INTERRUPT ANOTHER BAND'S PERFORMANCE!
PTUI
B-BESIDES, I HAVE THIS COLD, AND...
I GOTTA RUNNY NOSE.
SNORT
GURI! GURA!
TAKE HIM.
L-LET GO OF ME!
FLAP FLAP
I HAVE A DOCTOR'S APPOINTMENT!
KINTAMA GIRLS BOKEES
NINA! THERE'S ALREADY TONS ON HYPE ON YOUR NEW TRACK, "D.M.C."!
HA
HA
HA
DIDN'T I SAY THIS WOULD BLOW UP?

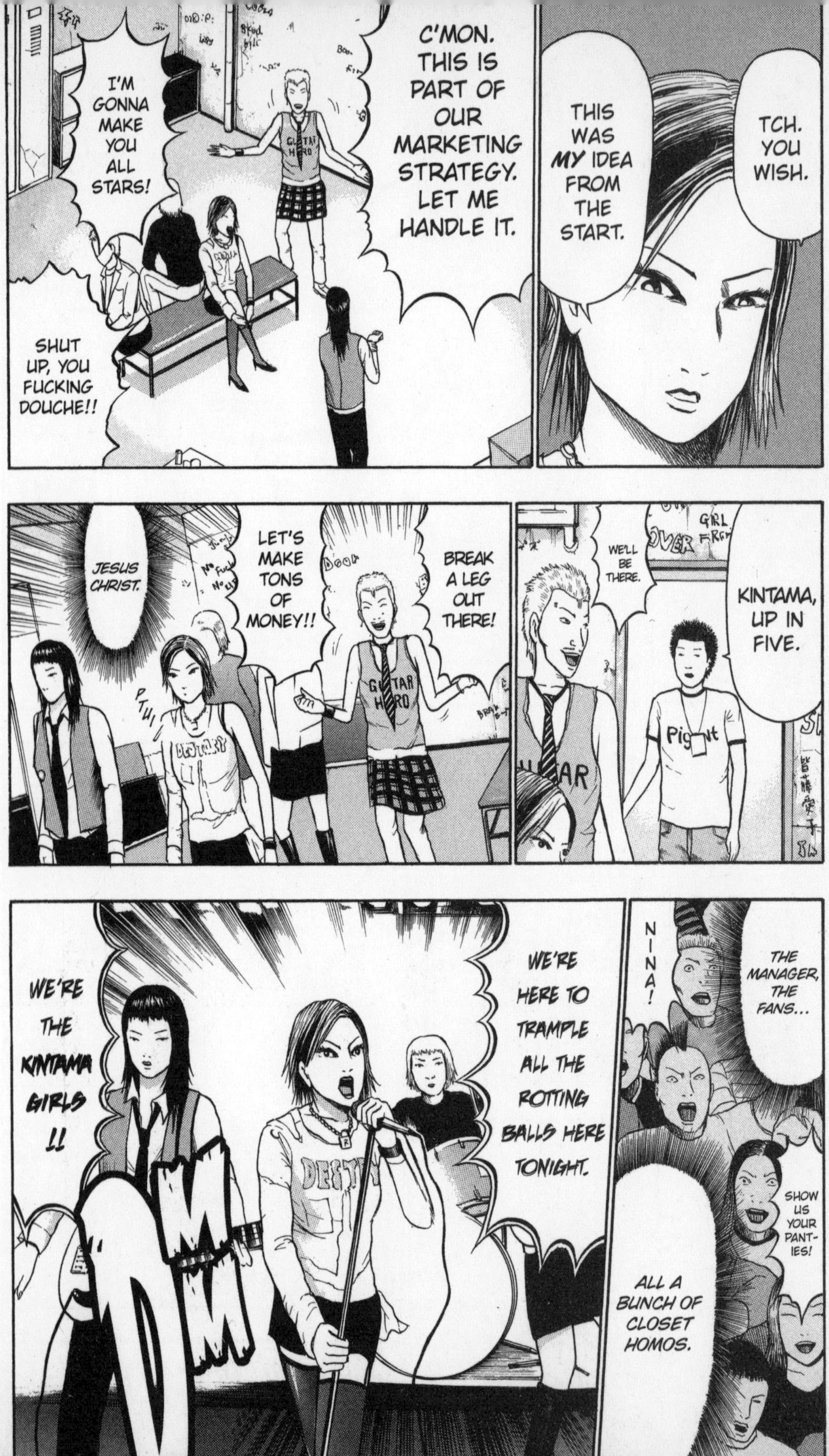
TCH. YOU WISH.
THIS WAS MY IDEA FROM THE START.
C'MON. THIS IS PART OF OUR MARKETING STRATEGY. LET ME HANDLE IT.
I'M GONNA MAKE YOU ALL STARS!
SHUT UP, YOU FUCKING DOUCHE!!
KINTAMA, UP IN FIVE.
WE'LL BE THERE.
BREAK A LEG OUT THERE!
LET'S MAKE TONS OF MONEY!!
JESUS CHRIST.
PTUI
THE MANAGER, THE FANS...
NINA!
SHOW US YOUR PANTIES!
ALL A BUNCH OF CLOSET HOMOS.
WE'RE HERE TO TRAMPLE ALL THE ROTTING BALLS HERE TONIGHT.
WE'RE THE KINTAMA GIRLS!!

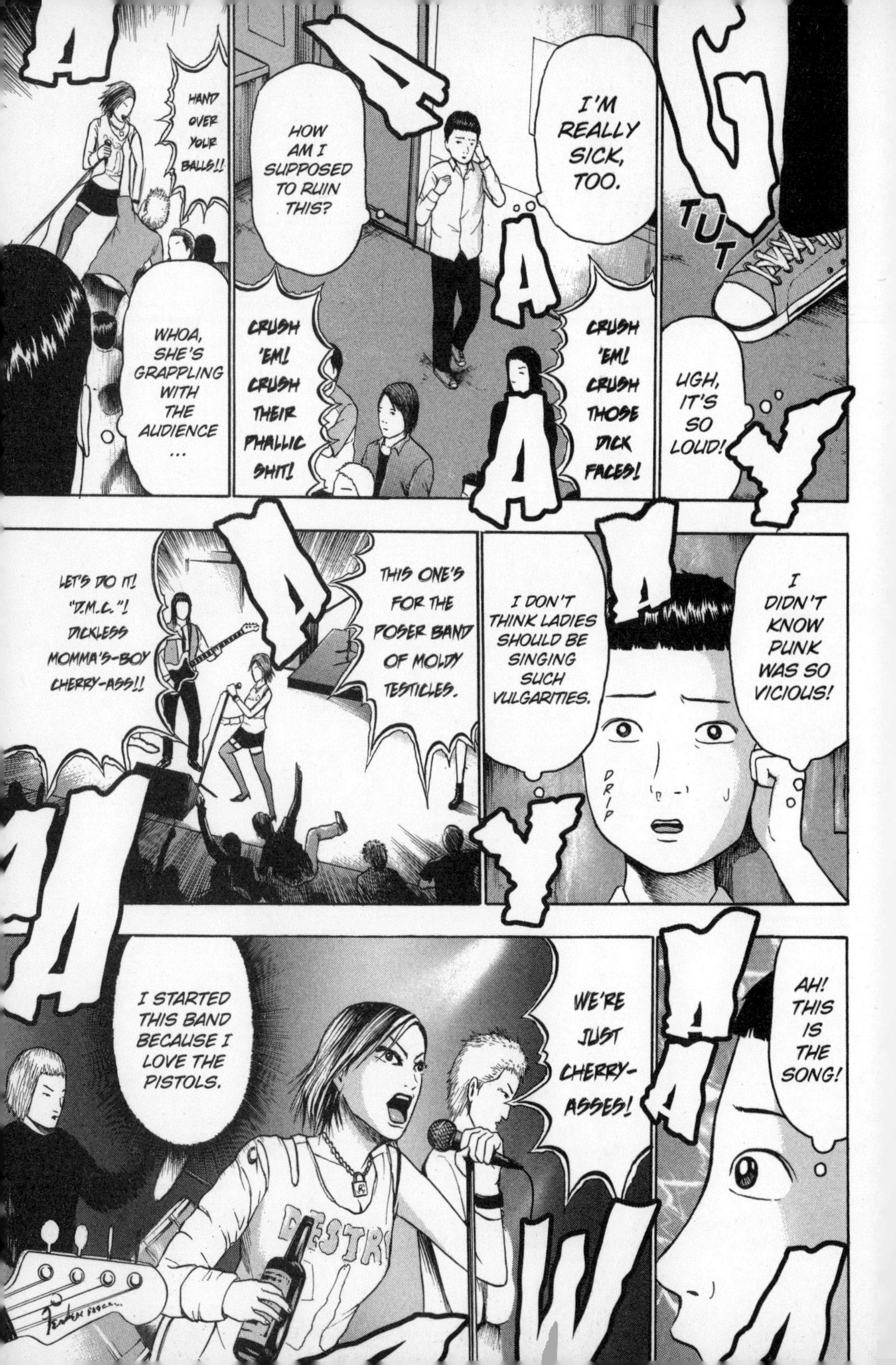
TUT
UGH, IT'S SO LOUD!
I'M REALLY SICK, TOO.
HOW AM I SUPPOSED TO RUIN THIS?
CRUSH 'EM! CRUSH THOSE DICK FACES!
CRUSH 'EM! CRUSH THEIR PHALLIC SHIT!
HAND OVER YOUR BALLS!!
WHOA, SHE'S GRAPPLING WITH THE AUDIENCE ...
I DIDN'T KNOW PUNK WAS SO VICIOUS!
I DON'T THINK LADIES SHOULD BE SINGING SUCH VULGARITIES.
DRIP
THIS ONE'S FOR THE POSER BAND OF MOLDY TESTICLES.
LET'S DO IT! "D.M.C."! DICKLESS MOMMA'S-BOY CHERRY-ASS!!
AH! THIS IS THE SONG!
WE'RE JUST CHERRY-ASSES!
I STARTED THIS BAND BECAUSE I LOVE THE PISTOLS.

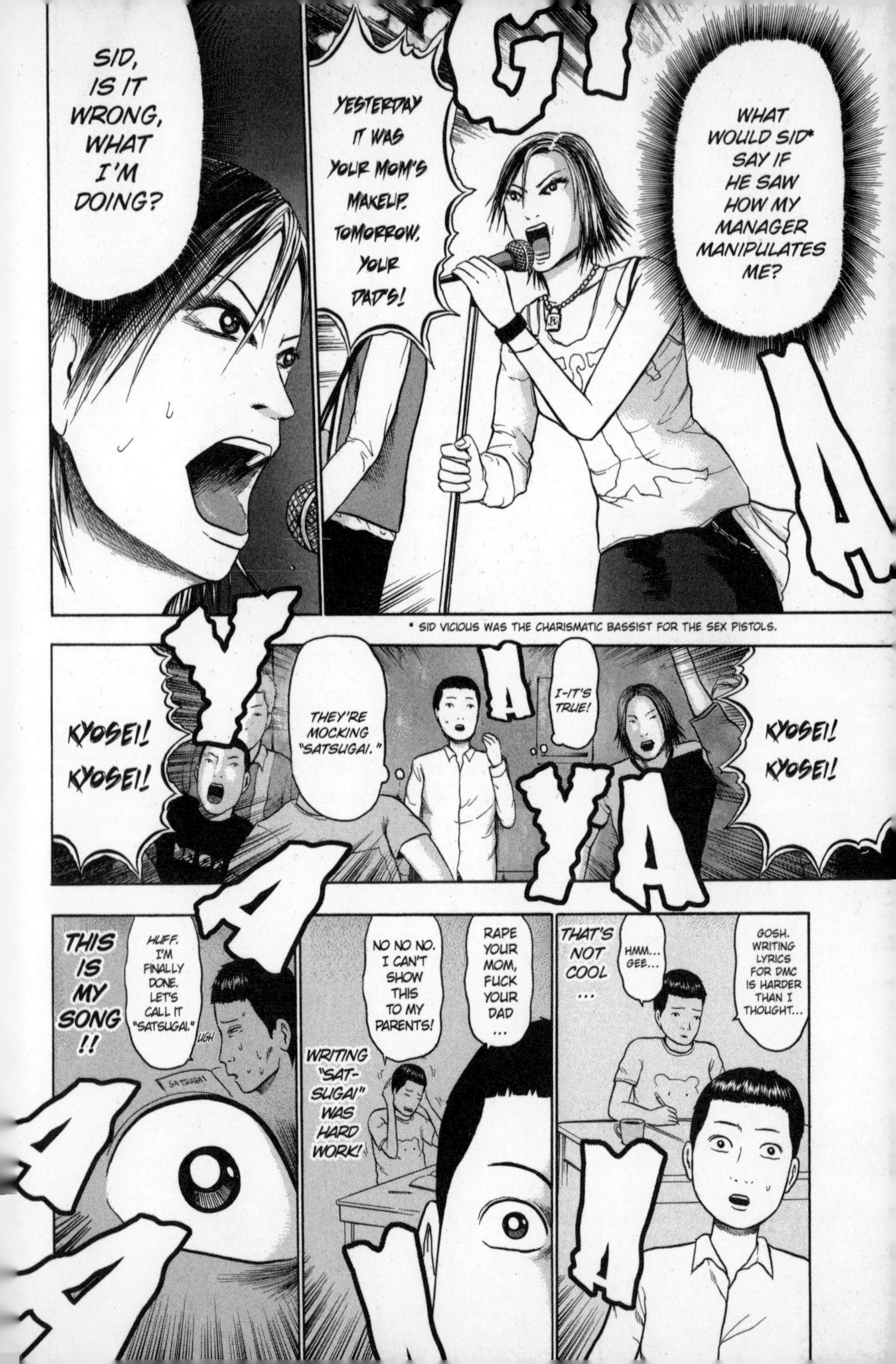

WHAT WOULD SID* SAY IF HE SAW HOW MY MANAGER MANIPULATES ME?
YESTERDAY IT WAS YOUR MOM'S MAKEUP. TOMORROW, YOUR DAD'S!
SID, IS IT WRONG, WHAT I'M DOING?
KYOSEI! KYOSEI!
I-IT'S TRUE!
THEY'RE MOCKING "SATSUGAI."
KYOSEI! KYOSEI!
GOSH. WRITING LYRICS FOR DMC IS HARDER THAN I THOUGHT...
HMM... GEE...
THAT'S NOT COOL ...
RAPE YOUR MOM, FUCK YOUR DAD ...
NO NO NO. I CAN'T SHOW THIS TO MY PARENTS!
WRITING "SAT-SUGAI" WAS HARD WORK!
HUFF. I'M FINALLY DONE. LET'S CALL IT "SATSUGAI."
UGH
SATSUGAI
THIS IS MY SONG !!

* SID VICIOUS WAS THE CHARISMATIC BASSIST FOR THE SEX PISTOLS.

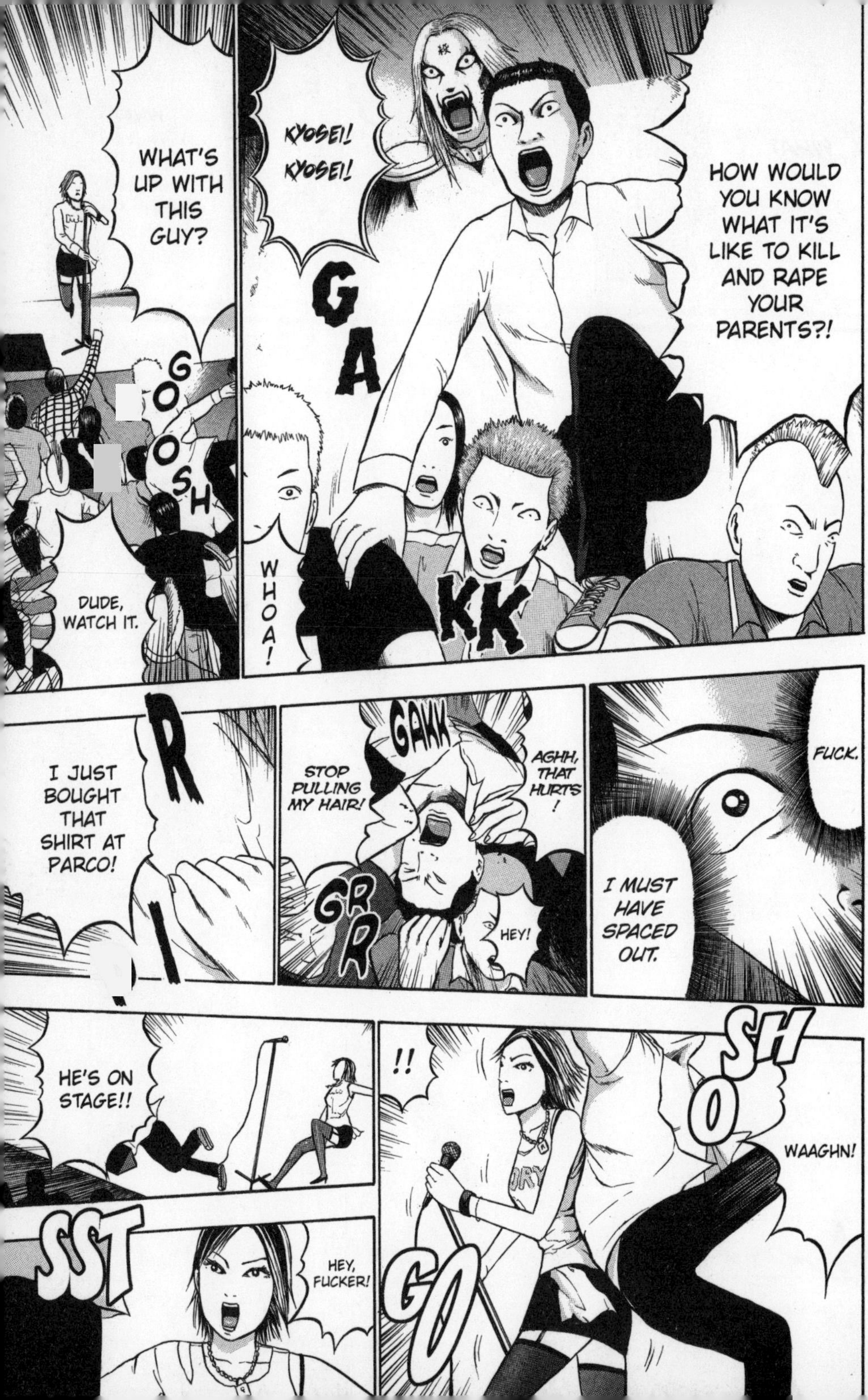
HOW WOULD YOU KNOW WHAT IT'S LIKE TO KILL AND RAPE YOUR PARENTS?!
KYOSEI! KYOSEI!
GA
KK
WHOA!
WHAT'S UP WITH THIS GUY?
GOOSH
DUDE, WATCH IT.
FUCK.
I MUST HAVE SPACED OUT.
GAKK
AGHH, THAT HURTS!
STOP PULLING MY HAIR!
GRR
HEY!
R
I JUST BOUGHT THAT SHIRT AT PARCO!
I
SH
O
!!
WAAGHN!
GO
HE'S ON STAGE!!
SST
HEY, FUCKER!

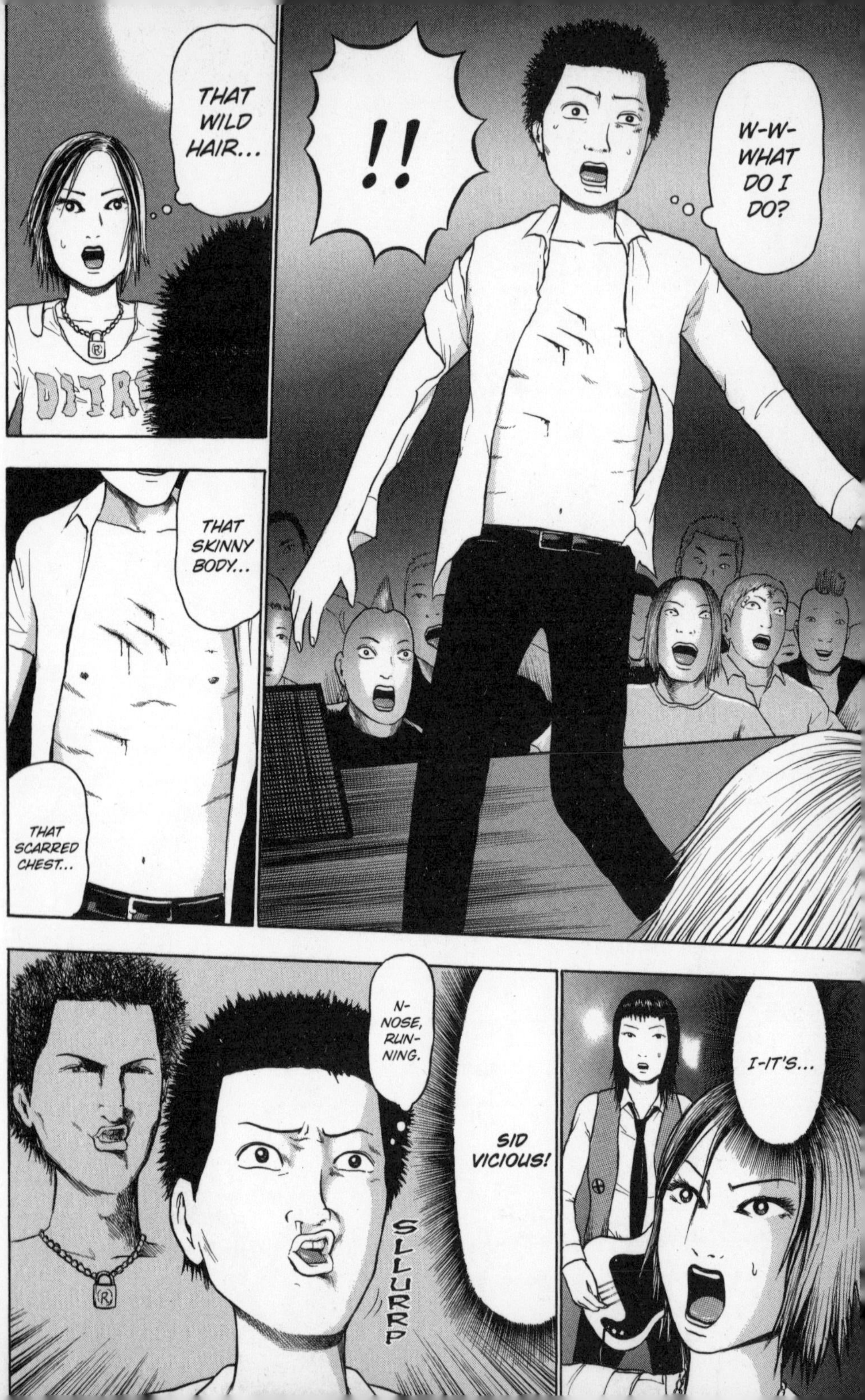
W-W-WHAT DO I DO?
!!
THAT WILD HAIR...
THAT SKINNY BODY...
THAT SCARRED CHEST...
I-IT'S...
SID VICIOUS!
N-NOSE, RUN-NING.
SLLURRP

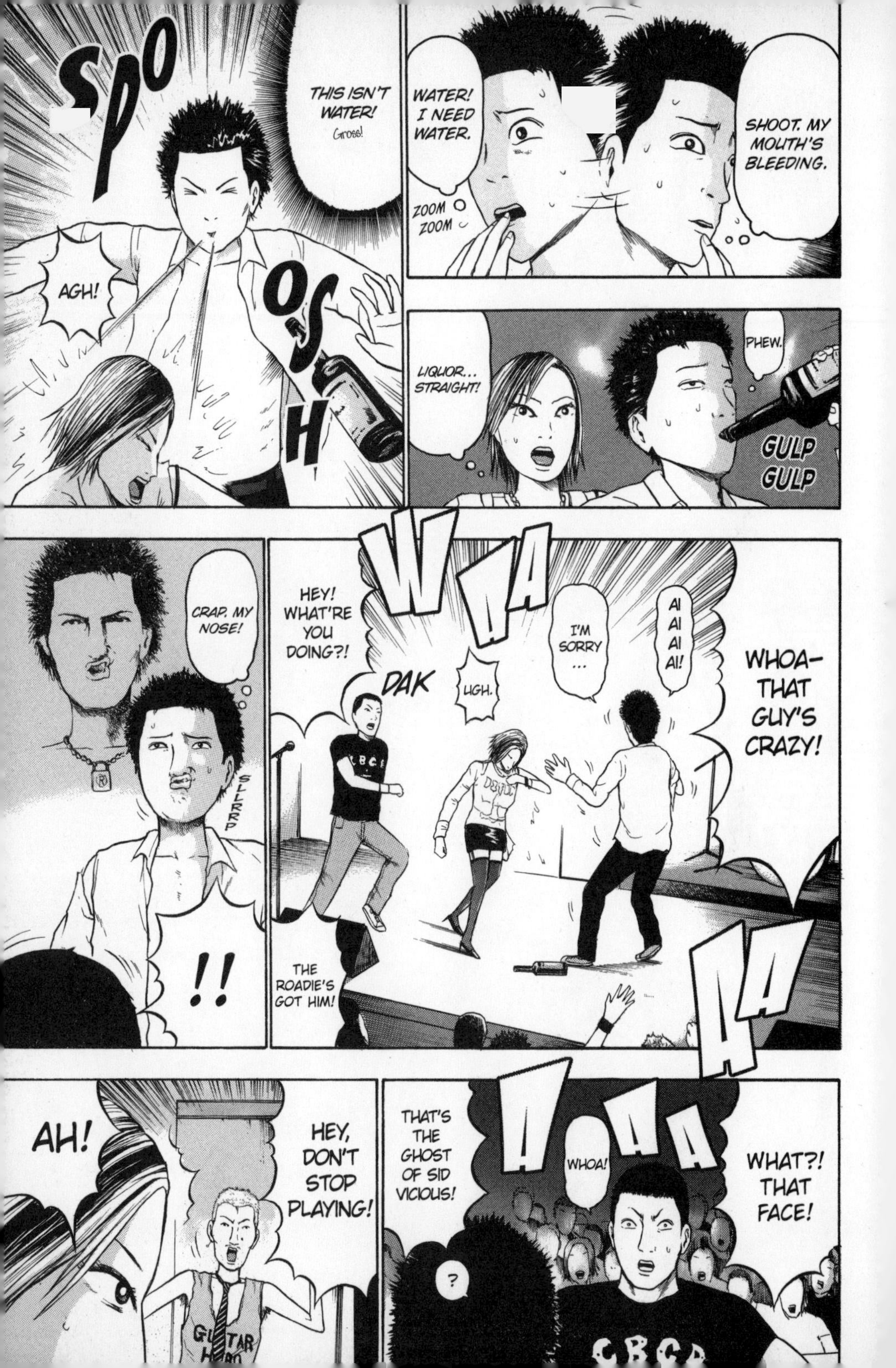
SHOOT. MY MOUTH'S BLEEDING.
WATER! I NEED WATER.
ZOOM ZOOM
PHEW.
GULP GULP
LIQUOR... STRAIGHT!
THIS ISN'T WATER!
Gross!
SPOOSH
AGH!
WHOA-THAT GUY'S CRAZY!
AI AI AI AI!
I'M SORRY...
WAAA
UGH.
HEY! WHAT'RE YOU DOING?!
DAK
THE ROADIE'S GOT HIM!
AAA
CRAP. MY NOSE!
SLLRRP
!!
WHAT?! THAT FACE!
AAA
WHOA!
THAT'S THE GHOST OF SID VICIOUS!
?
HEY, DON'T STOP PLAYING!
AH!

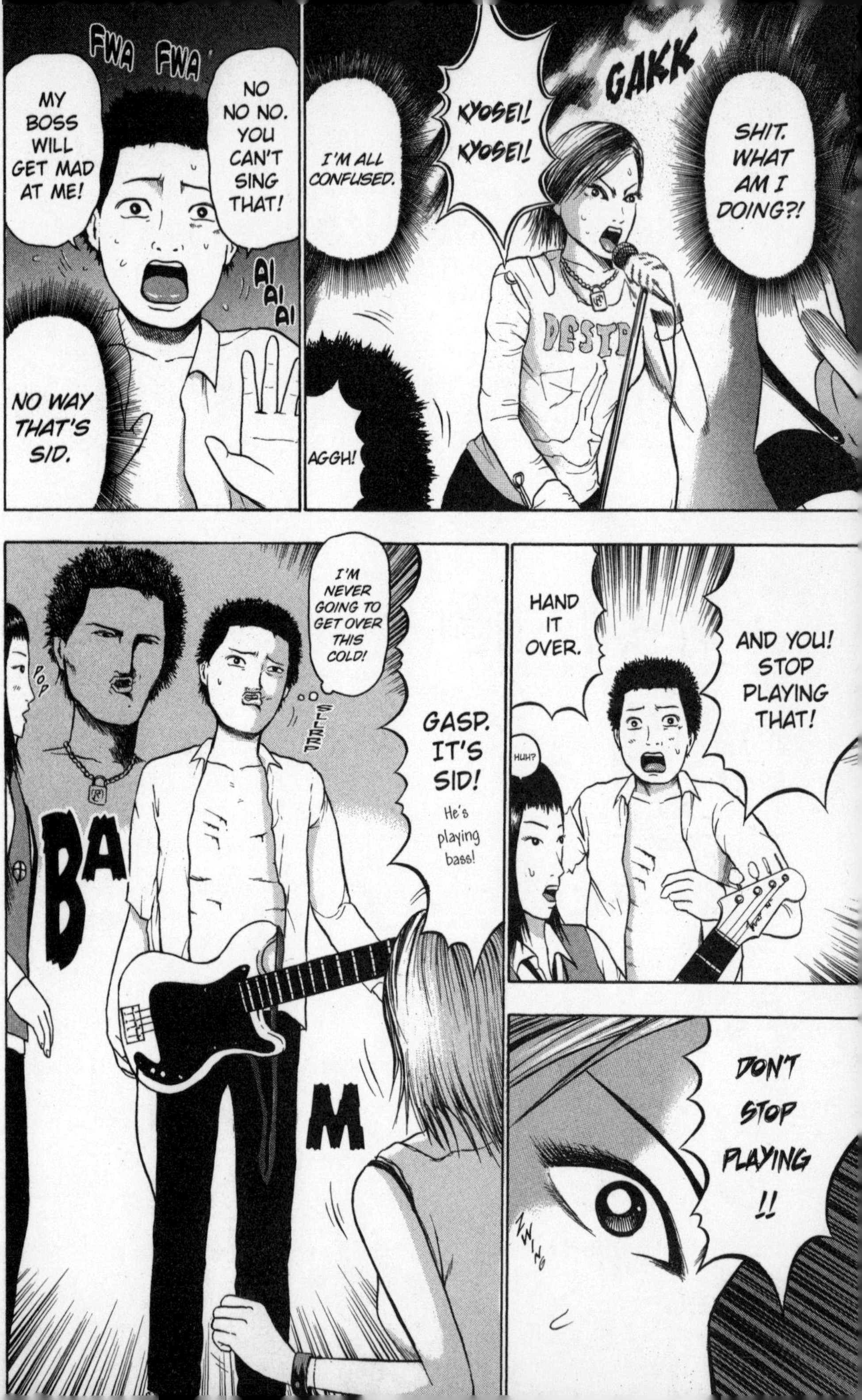
GAKK
SHIT. WHAT AM I DOING?!
KYOSEI! KYOSEI!
I'M ALL CONFUSED.
AGGH!
NO NO NO. YOU CAN'T SING THAT!
FWA FWA
MY BOSS WILL GET MAD AT ME!
AI AI AI
NO WAY THAT'S SID.
AND YOU! STOP PLAYING THAT!
HAND IT OVER.
HUH?
DON'T STOP PLAYING!!
I'M NEVER GOING TO GET OVER THIS COLD!
GASP. IT'S SID!
He's playing bass!
SLURP
POP
BAM

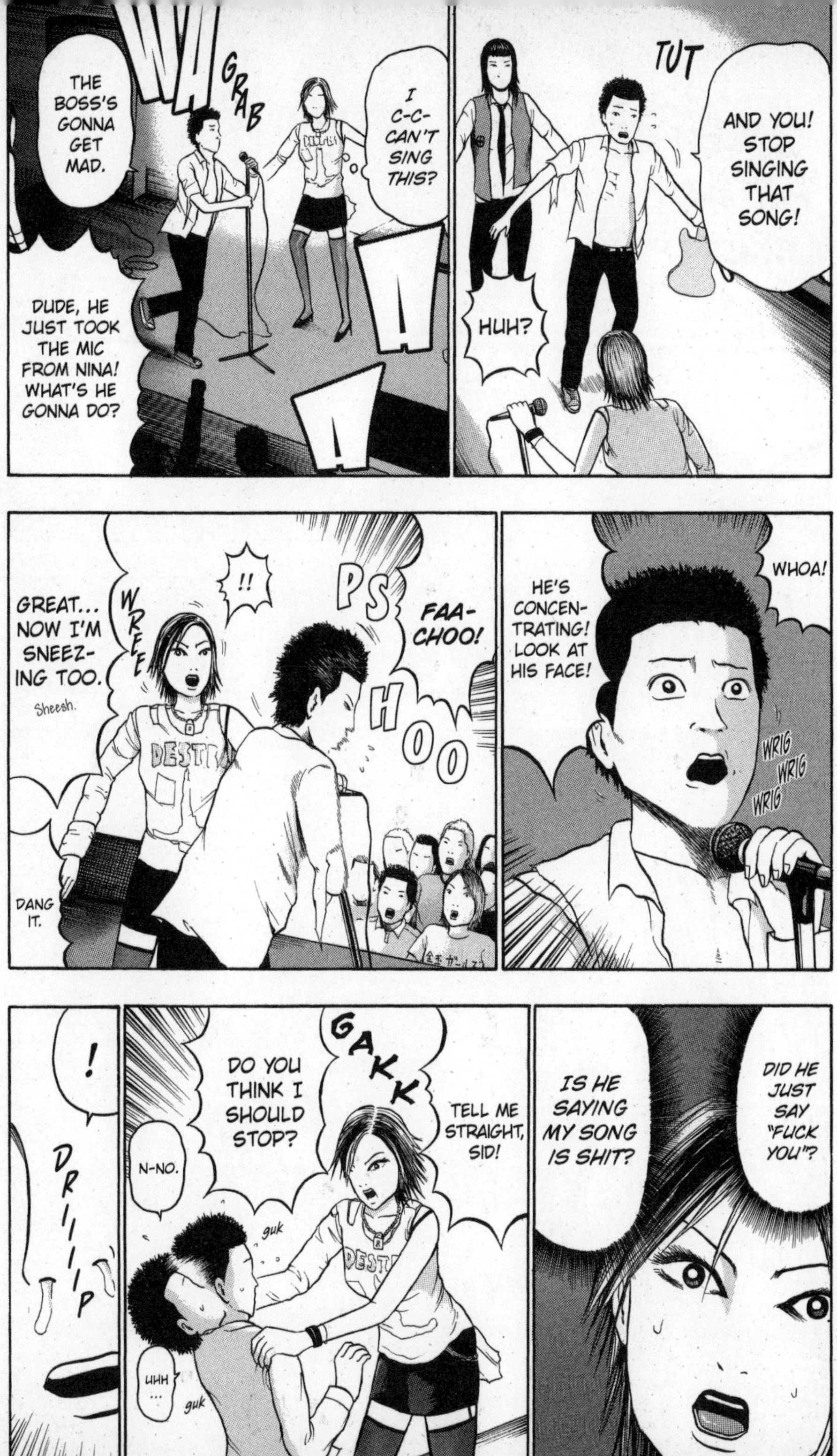
TUT
AND YOU! STOP SINGING THAT SONG!
HUH?
I C-C-CAN'T SING THIS?
GRAB
WHAAA
THE BOSS'S GONNA GET MAD.
DUDE, HE JUST TOOK THE MIC FROM NINA! WHAT'S HE GONNA DO?
WHOA!
HE'S CONCEN-TRATING! LOOK AT HIS FACE!
WRIG WRIG WRIG
PSHOO
FAA-CHOO!
!!
WREE
GREAT... NOW I'M SNEEZ-ING TOO.
Sheesh.
DANG IT.
DID HE JUST SAY "FUCK YOU"?
IS HE SAYING MY SONG IS SHIT?
TELL ME STRAIGHT, SID!
GAKK
DO YOU THINK I SHOULD STOP?
N-NO.
guk
UHH ...
guk
!
DRIIIIP

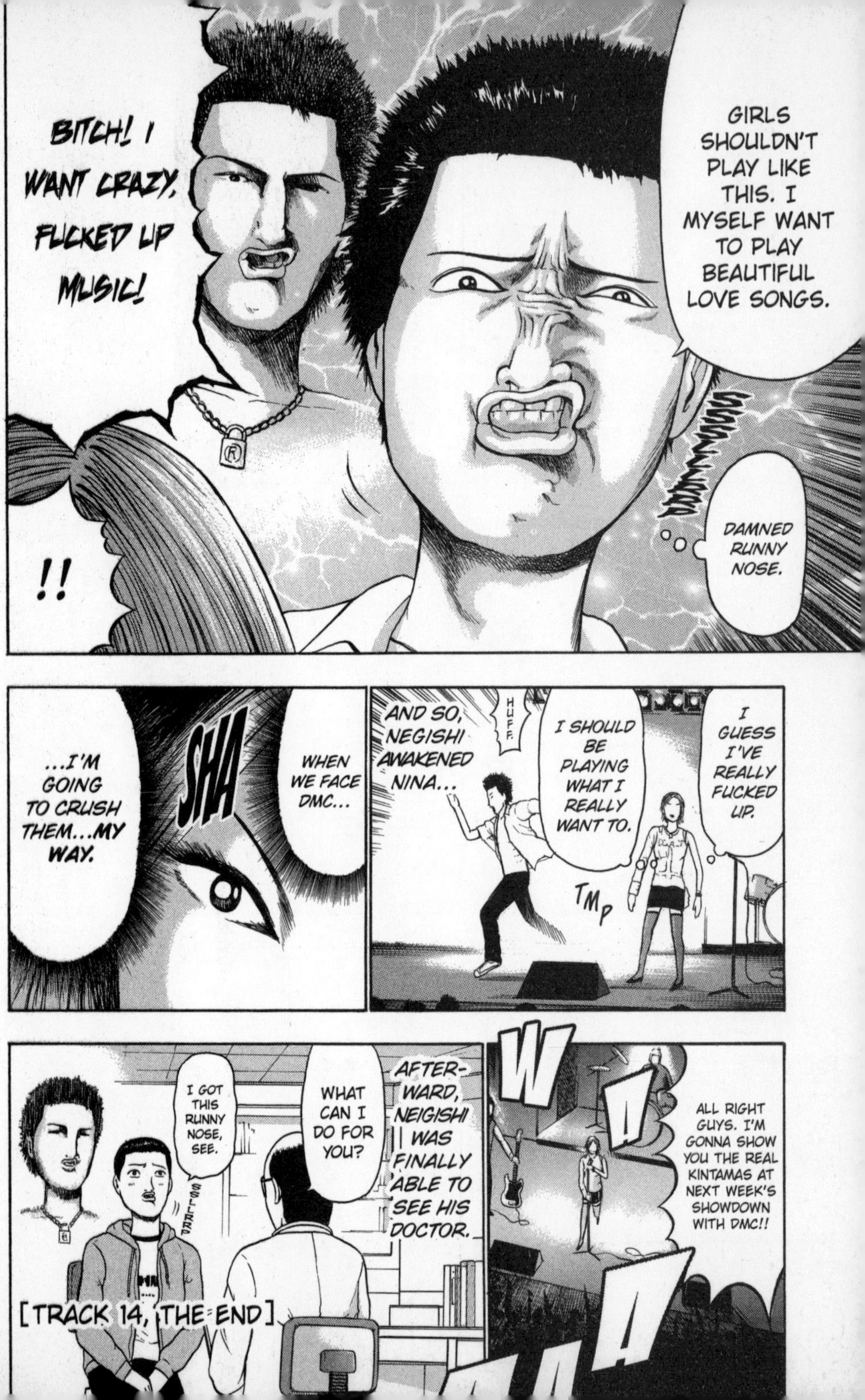
GIRLS SHOULDN'T PLAY LIKE THIS. I MYSELF WANT TO PLAY BEAUTIFUL LOVE SONGS.
BITCH! I WANT CRAZY, FUCKED UP MUSIC!
DAMNED RUNNY NOSE.
!!
I GUESS I'VE REALLY FUCKED UP.
I SHOULD BE PLAYING WHAT I REALLY WANT TO.
HUFF
AND SO, NEGISHI AWAKENED NINA...
TMP
WHEN WE FACE DMC...
SHA
...I'M GOING TO CRUSH THEM...MY WAY.
WAAAA
ALL RIGHT GUYS. I'M GONNA SHOW YOU THE REAL KINTAMAS AT NEXT WEEK'S SHOWDOWN WITH DMC!!
AFTERWARD, NEIGISHI WAS FINALLY ABLE TO SEE HIS DOCTOR.
WHAT CAN I DO FOR YOU?
I GOT THIS RUNNY NOSE, SEE.
SSLLRRP
[TRACK 14, THE END]

DMC LEXICON

♦ DICK FACE

A face resembling a penis. Term can be used to refer to anyone who has a penis-like facial expression, specifically when they are laughing or concentrating. People with that penis-look lurking in the depths of their souls are generally not to be trusted.

Usage: It'd be one thing just dating one, but I'd never marry a dick face.

デトロイト・メタル・シティ

Detroit Metal City

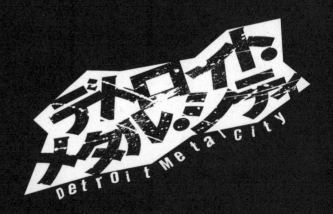

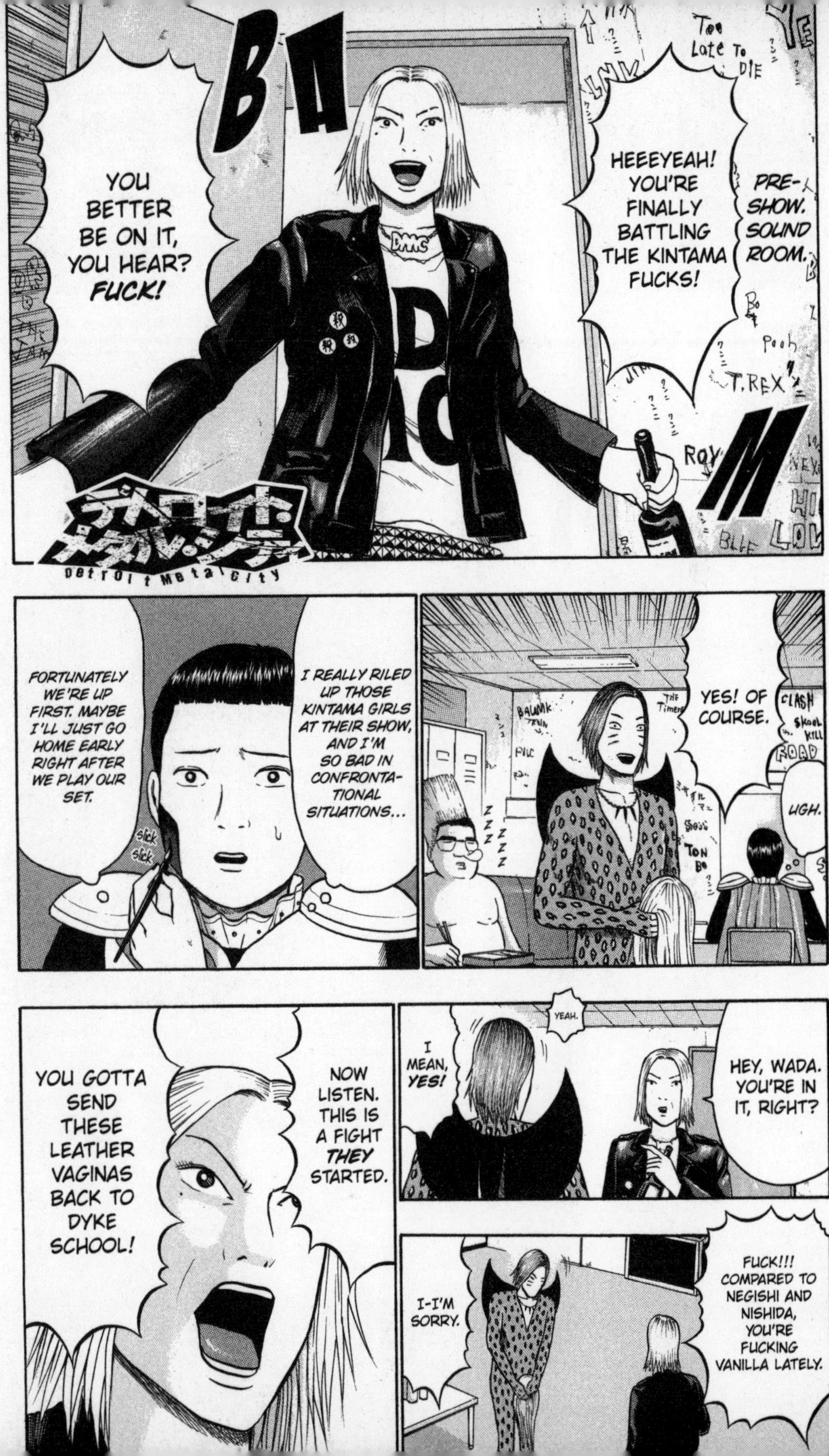
PRE-SHOW. SOUND ROOM.
HEEEYEAH! YOU'RE FINALLY BATTLING THE KINTAMA FUCKS!
BAM
YOU BETTER BE ON IT, YOU HEAR? FUCK!
Too Late To DIE
T.REX
Pooh
Detroit Metal City
YES! OF COURSE.
UGH.
I REALLY RILED UP THOSE KINTAMA GIRLS AT THEIR SHOW, AND I'M SO BAD IN CONFRONTATIONAL SITUATIONS...
FORTUNATELY WE'RE UP FIRST. MAYBE I'LL JUST GO HOME EARLY RIGHT AFTER WE PLAY OUR SET.
slick slick
HEY, WADA. YOU'RE IN IT, RIGHT?
YEAH.
I MEAN, YES!
FUCK!!! COMPARED TO NEGISHI AND NISHIDA, YOU'RE FUCKING VANILLA LATELY.
I-I'M SORRY.
NOW LISTEN. THIS IS A FIGHT THEY STARTED.
YOU GOTTA SEND THESE LEATHER VAGINAS BACK TO DYKE SCHOOL!

Detroit Metal City

TRACK 15 Punk, Part 2

GOLDEN BOWL ITINERARY
KINTAMA GIRLS
MOMO, DRUMS
NINA, VOCALS
REI, GUITAR
SAE, BASS
PUNK vs. METAL BATTLE of THE GENRES
DOORS OPEN 18:30 SHOW AT 19:00 SHIBUYA RUTAFA
VS
DMC
CHAKI
KRESYER II
CAMEO
SEND OUT THE CLOWNS!!
WANTED

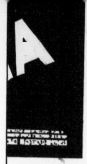

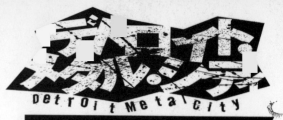

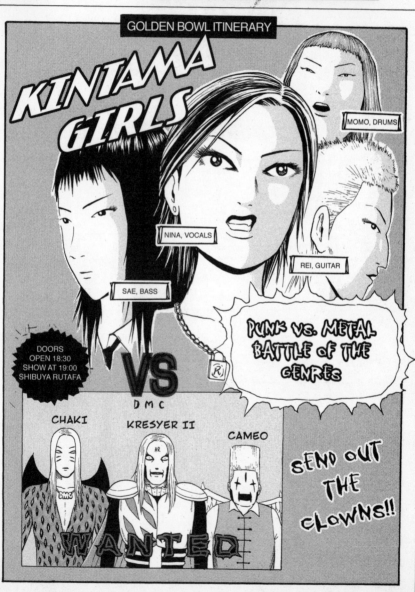

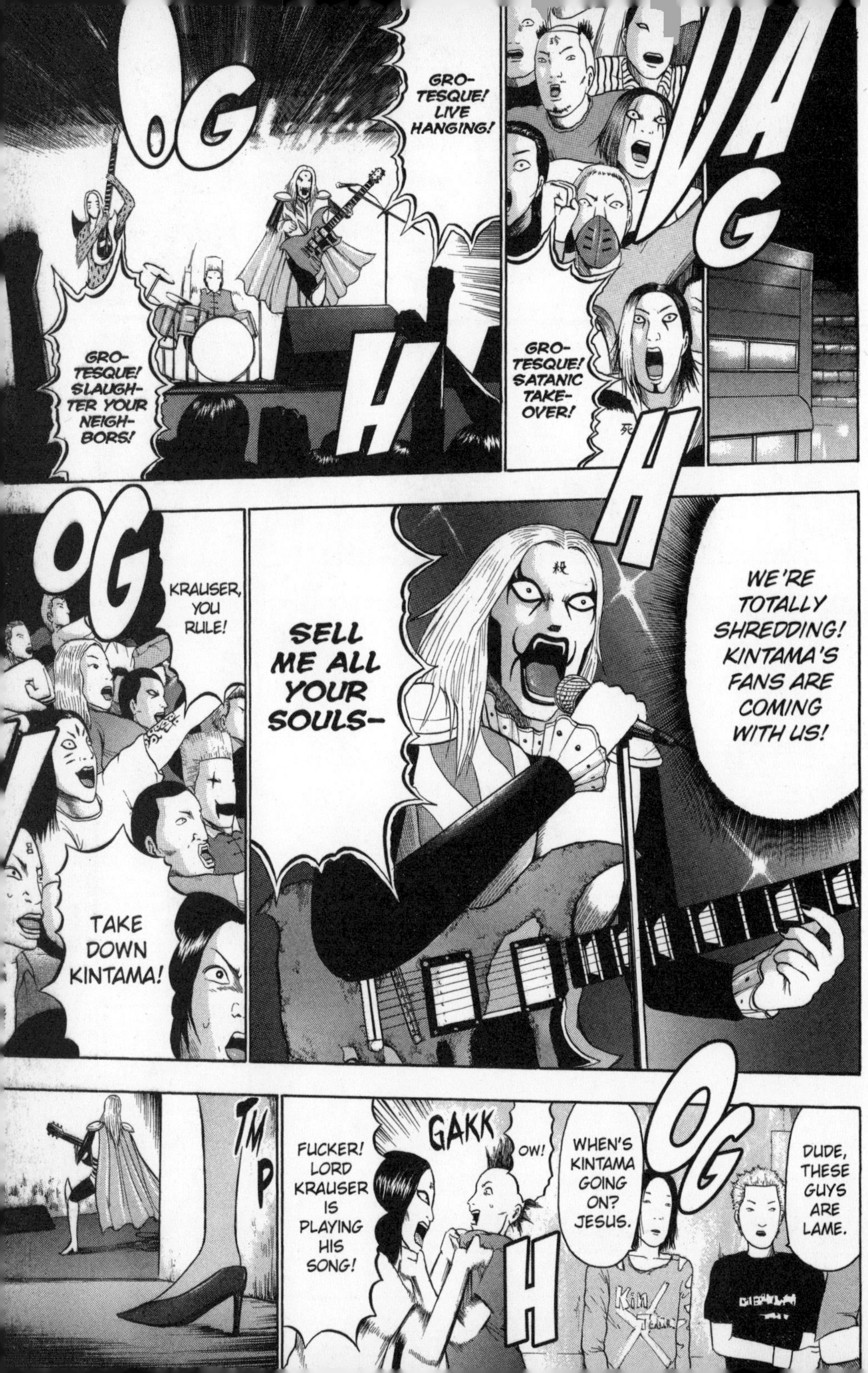
VA
G
GRO-TESQUE! SATANIC TAKE-OVER!
GRO-TESQUE! LIVE HANGING!
OG
H
GRO-TESQUE! SLAUGHTER YOUR NEIGHBORS!
H
WE'RE TOTALLY SHREDDING! KINTAMA'S FANS ARE COMING WITH US!
SELL ME ALL YOUR SOULS-
OG
KRAUSER, YOU RULE!
TAKE DOWN KINTAMA!
DUDE, THESE GUYS ARE LAME.
OG
WHEN'S KINTAMA GOING ON? JESUS.
OW!
GAKK
FUCKER! LORD KRAUSER IS PLAYING HIS SONG!
H
TMP

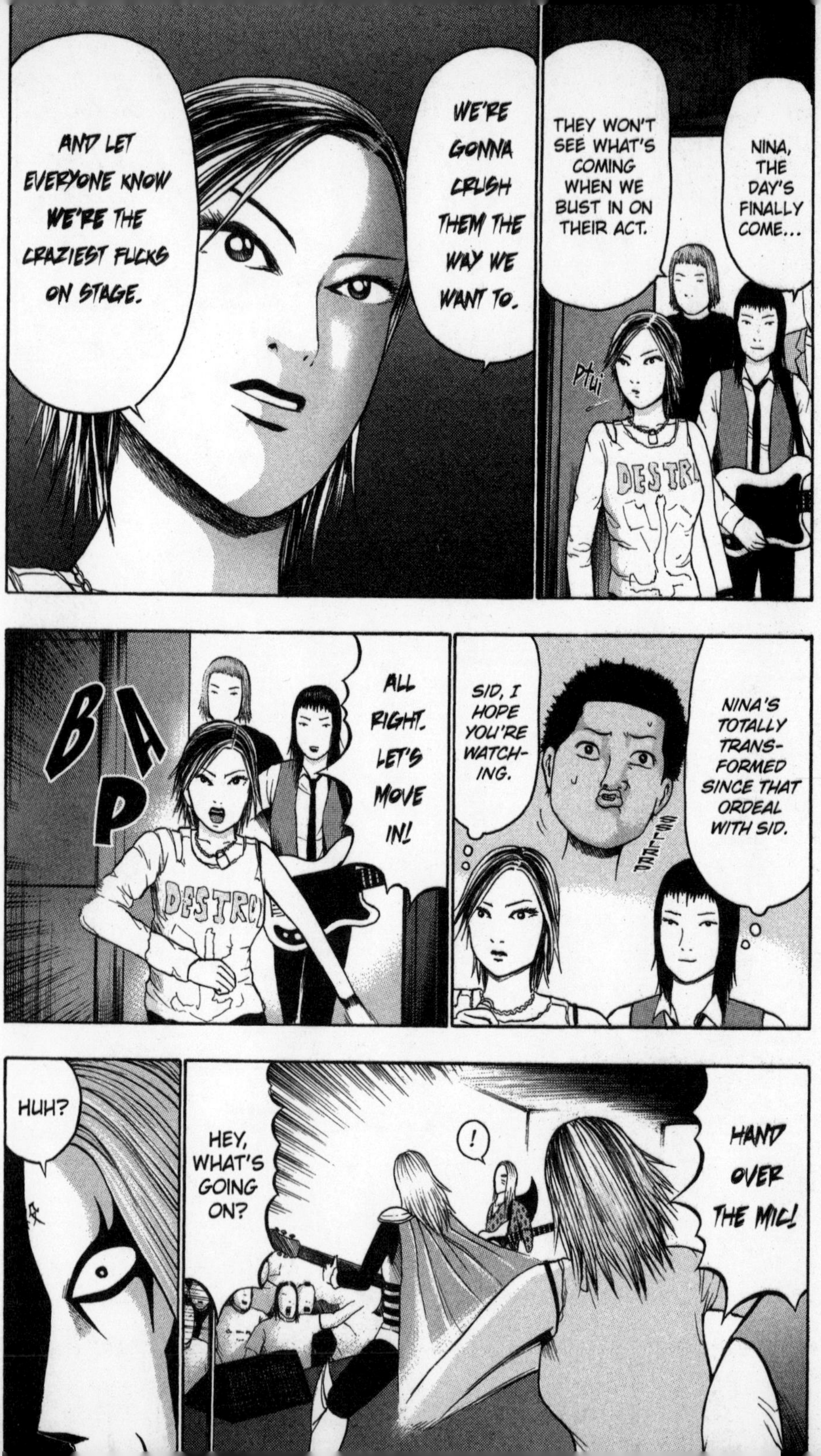
NINA, THE DAY'S FINALLY COME...
THEY WON'T SEE WHAT'S COMING WHEN WE BUST IN ON THEIR ACT.
PTUI
WE'RE GONNA CRUSH THEM THE WAY WE WANT TO.
AND LET EVERYONE KNOW WE'RE THE CRAZIEST FUCKS ON STAGE.
NINA'S TOTALLY TRANS-FORMED SINCE THAT ORDEAL WITH SID.
SSLERP
SID, I HOPE YOU'RE WATCHING.
ALL RIGHT. LET'S MOVE IN!
BAP
HAND OVER THE MIC!
!
HEY, WHAT'S GOING ON?
HUH?

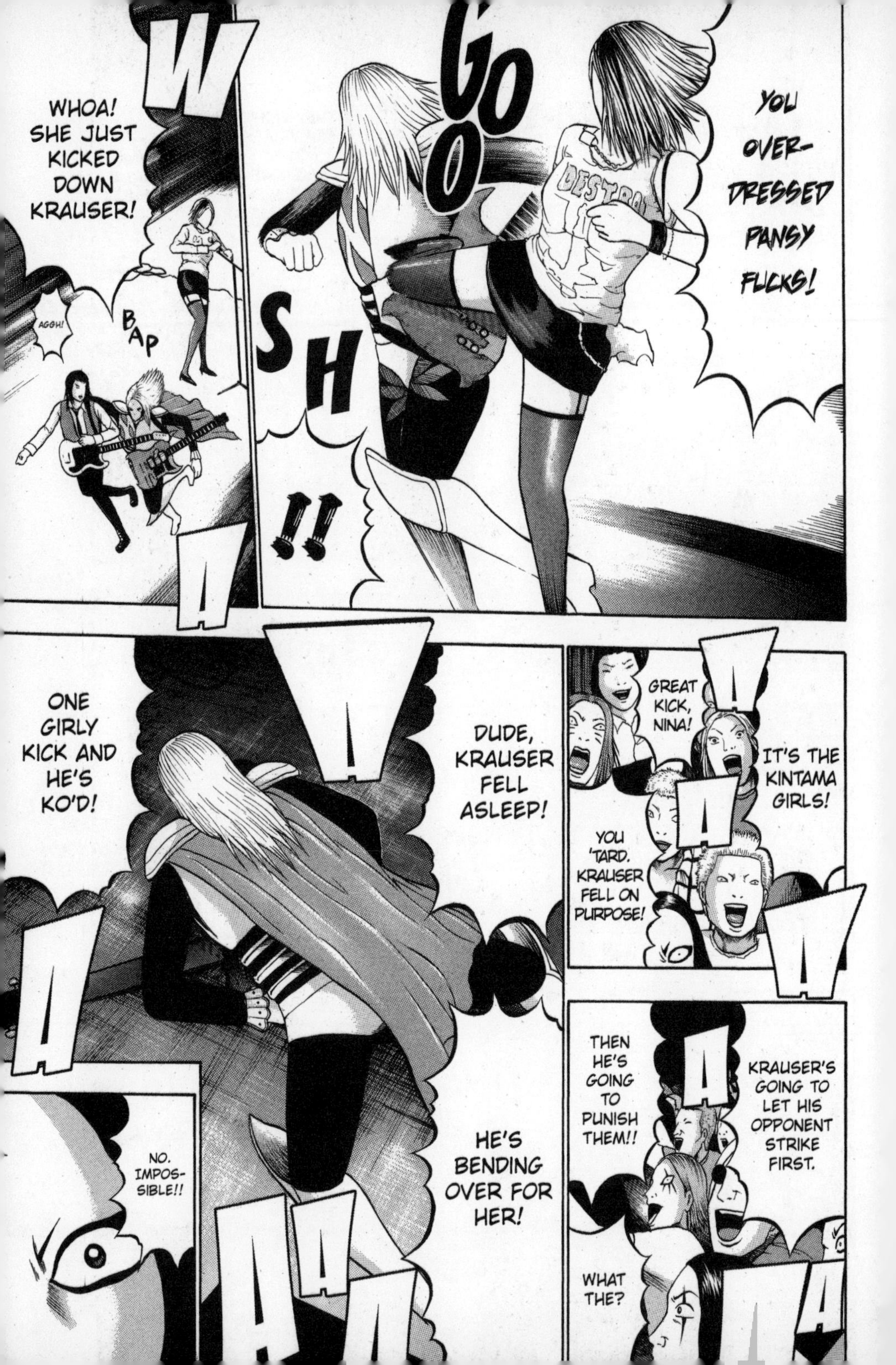
GOOO
SH
!!
YOU OVER-DRESSED PANSY FUCKS!
W
WHOA! SHE JUST KICKED DOWN KRAUSER!
AGGH!
BAP
GREAT KICK, NINA!
IT'S THE KINTAMA GIRLS!
YOU 'TARD. KRAUSER FELL ON PURPOSE!
KRAUSER'S GOING TO LET HIS OPPONENT STRIKE FIRST.
THEN HE'S GOING TO PUNISH THEM!!
WHAT THE?
DUDE, KRAUSER FELL ASLEEP!
ONE GIRLY KICK AND HE'S KO'D!
HE'S BENDING OVER FOR HER!
NO. IMPOSSIBLE!!

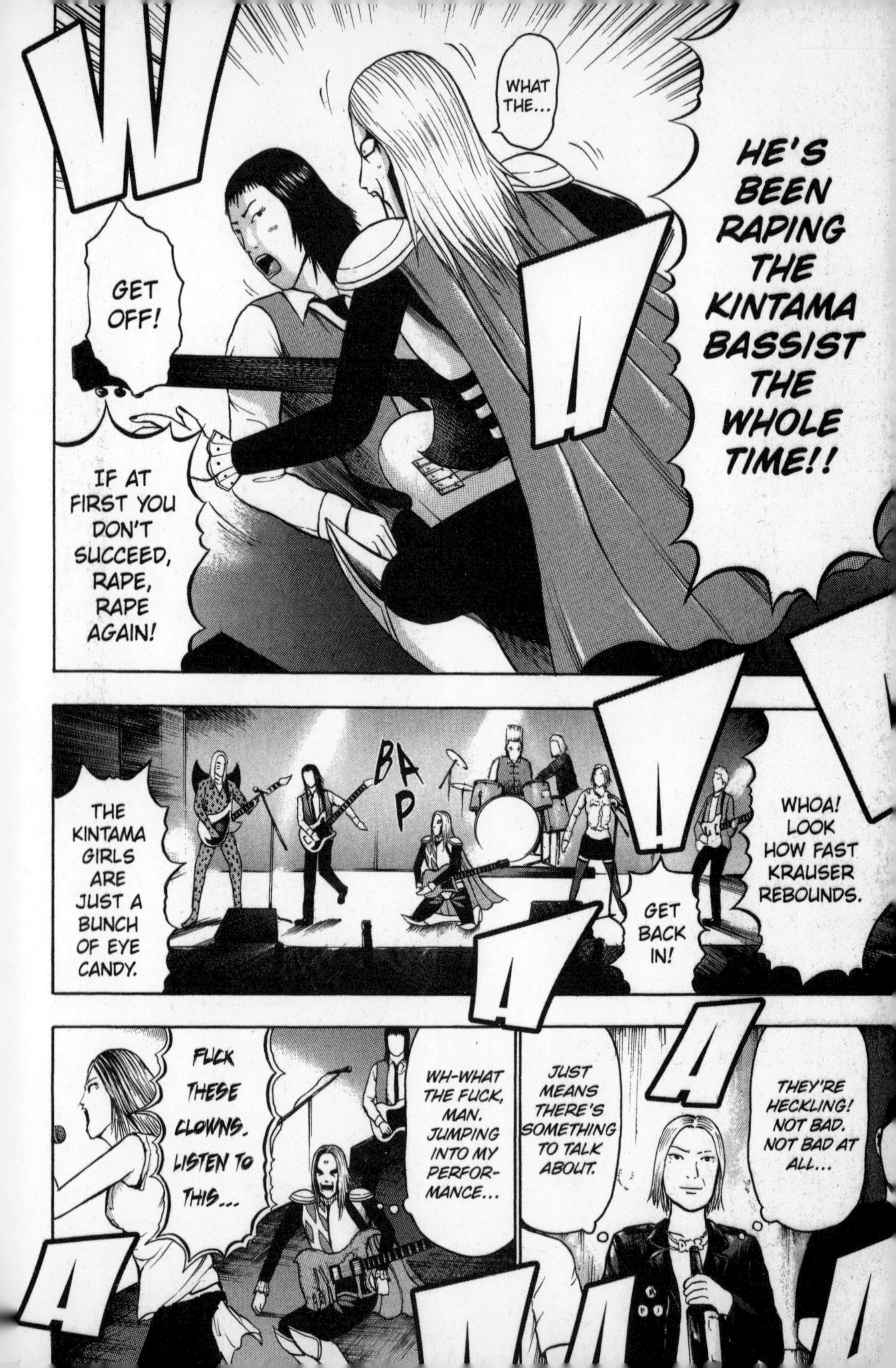
WHAT THE...
HE'S BEEN RAPING THE KINTAMA BASSIST THE WHOLE TIME!!
GET OFF!
IF AT FIRST YOU DON'T SUCCEED, RAPE, RAPE AGAIN!
WHOA! LOOK HOW FAST KRAUSER REBOUNDS.
GET BACK IN!
BAP
THE KINTAMA GIRLS ARE JUST A BUNCH OF EYE CANDY.
THEY'RE HECKLING! NOT BAD. NOT BAD AT ALL...
JUST MEANS THERE'S SOMETHING TO TALK ABOUT.
WH-WHAT THE FUCK, MAN. JUMPING INTO MY PERFORMANCE...
FUCK THESE CLOWNS. LISTEN TO THIS...

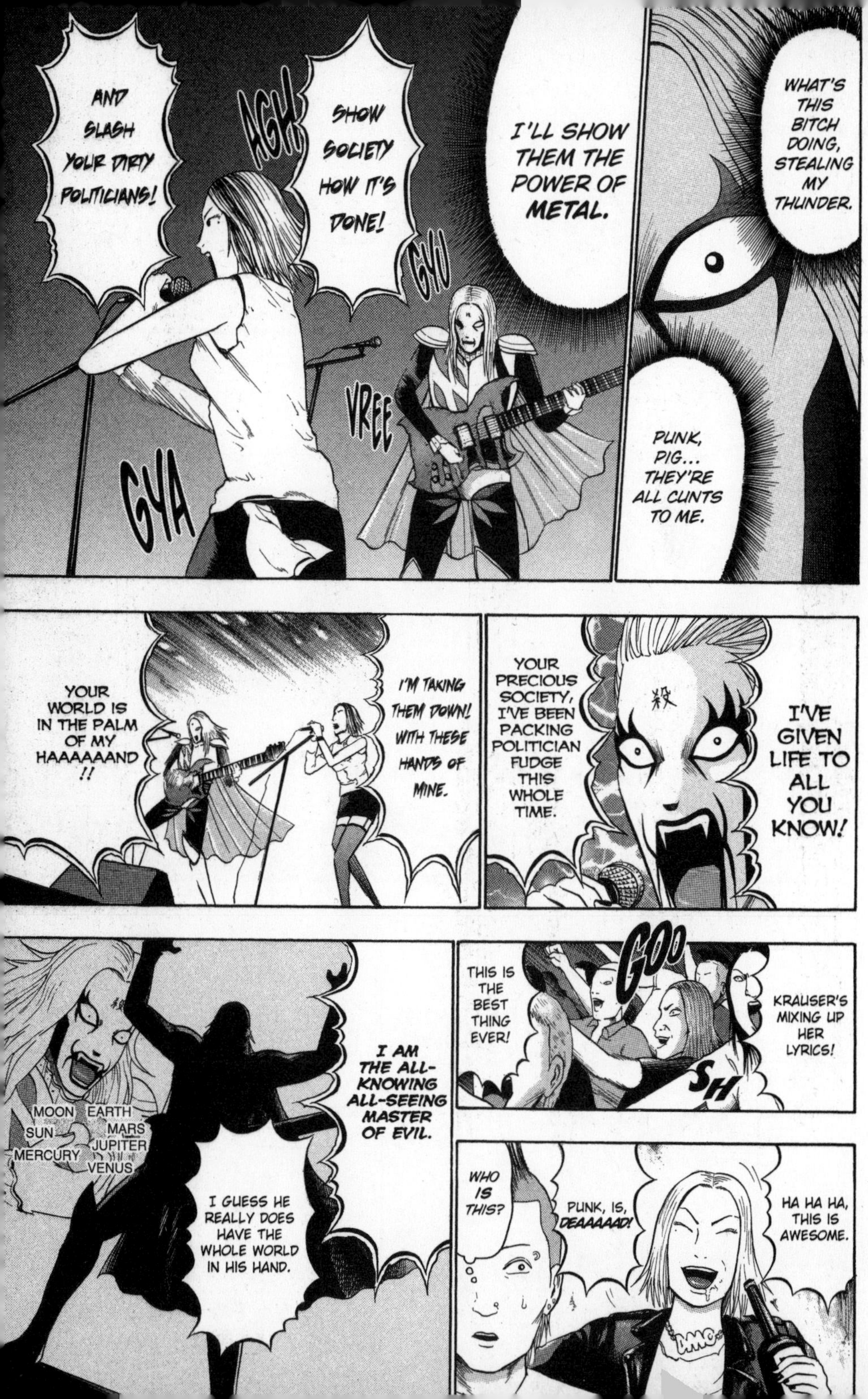
WHAT'S THIS BITCH DOING, STEALING MY THUNDER.
I'LL SHOW THEM THE POWER OF METAL.
PUNK, PIG... THEY'RE ALL CUNTS TO ME.
SHOW SOCIETY HOW IT'S DONE!
AGH
AND SLASH YOUR DIRTY POLITICIANS!
GYU
VREE
GYA
I'VE GIVEN LIFE TO ALL YOU KNOW!
YOUR PRECIOUS SOCIETY, I'VE BEEN PACKING POLITICIAN FUDGE THIS WHOLE TIME.
I'M TAKING THEM DOWN! WITH THESE HANDS OF MINE.
YOUR WORLD IS IN THE PALM OF MY HAAAAAAND !!
KRAUSER'S MIXING UP HER LYRICS!
GOO
THIS IS THE BEST THING EVER!
SH
HA HA HA, THIS IS AWESOME.
PUNK, IS, DEAAAAAD!
WHO IS THIS?
I AM THE ALL-KNOWING ALL-SEEING MASTER OF EVIL.
MOON
EARTH
SUN
MARS
MERCURY
JUPITER
VENUS
I GUESS HE REALLY DOES HAVE THE WHOLE WORLD IN HIS HAND.

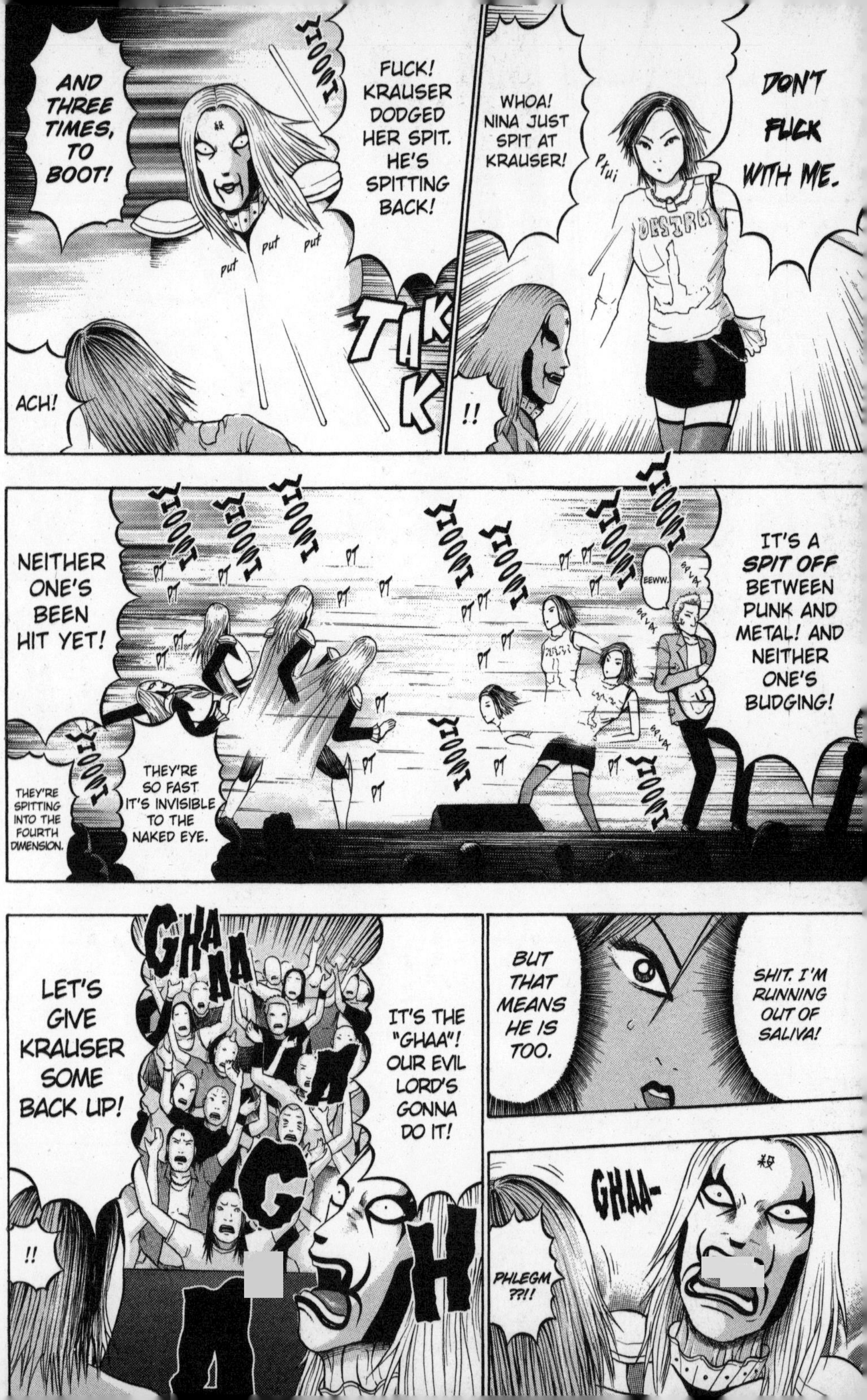
DON'T FUCK WITH ME.
Ptui
WHOA! NINA JUST SPIT AT KRAUSER!
!!
FUCK! KRAUSER DODGED HER SPIT. HE'S SPITTING BACK!
AND THREE TIMES, TO BOOT!
put put put
TAKK
ACH!
IT'S A SPIT OFF BETWEEN PUNK AND METAL! AND NEITHER ONE'S BUDGING!
EEWW.
NEITHER ONE'S BEEN HIT YET!
THEY'RE SO FAST IT'S INVISIBLE TO THE NAKED EYE.
THEY'RE SPITTING INTO THE FOURTH DIMENSION.
SHIT. I'M RUNNING OUT OF SALIVA!
BUT THAT MEANS HE IS TOO.
GHAA-
PHLEGM ??!!
IT'S THE "GHAA"! OUR EVIL LORD'S GONNA DO IT!
GHAA
LET'S GIVE KRAUSER SOME BACK UP!
!!

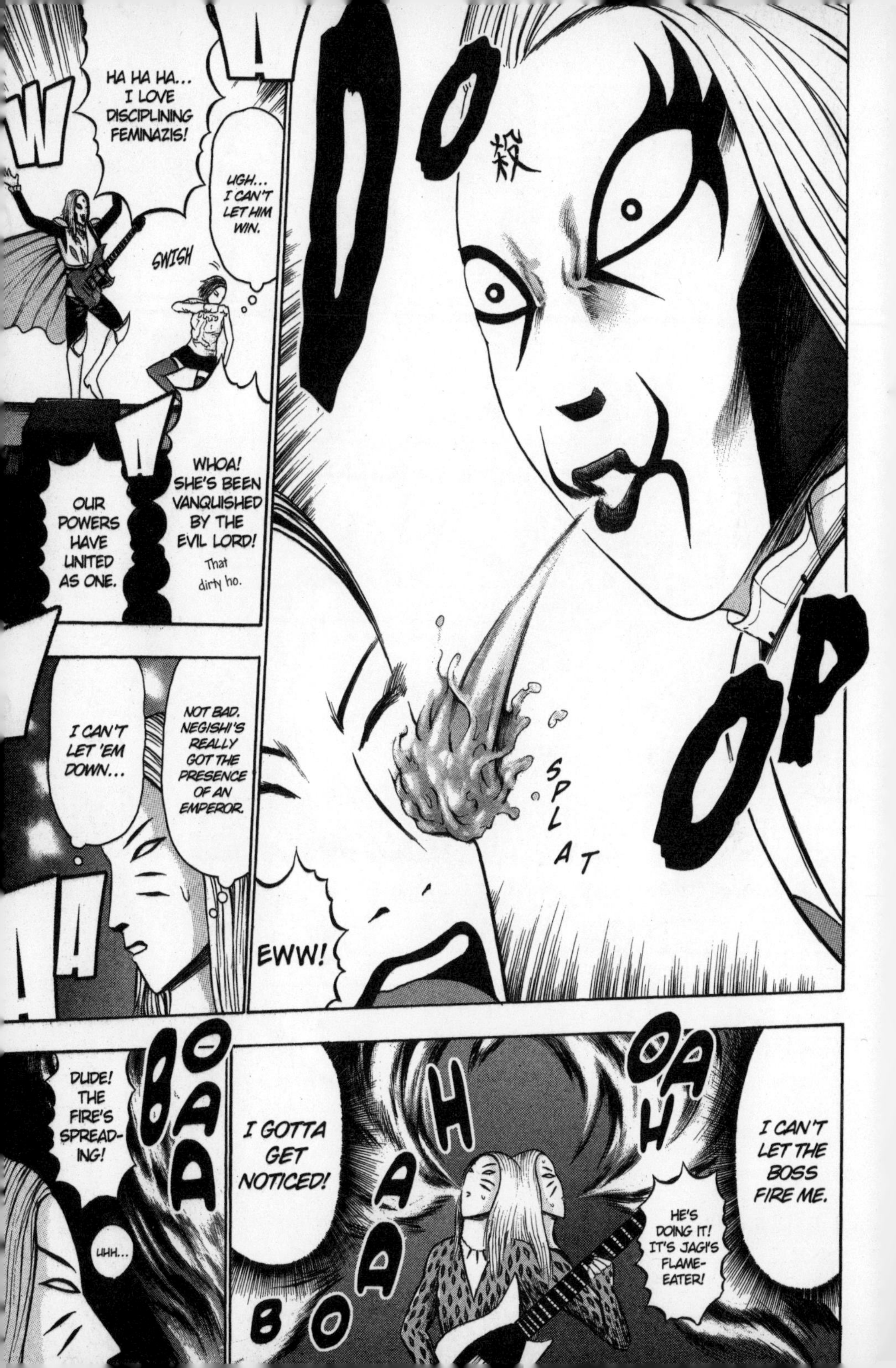
DOOOOP
SPLAT
EWW!
WAAAA
UGH... I CAN'T LET HIM WIN.
HA HA HA... I LOVE DISCIPLINING FEMINAZIS!
SWISH
WHOA! SHE'S BEEN VANQUISHED BY THE EVIL LORD!
That dirty ho.
OUR POWERS HAVE UNITED AS ONE.
NOT BAD. NEGISHI'S REALLY GOT THE PRESENCE OF AN EMPEROR.
I CAN'T LET 'EM DOWN...
I CAN'T LET THE BOSS FIRE ME.
HE'S DOING IT! IT'S JAGI'S FLAME-EATER!
I GOTTA GET NOTICED!
BOAAH
DUDE! THE FIRE'S SPREAD-ING!
UHH...
BOAA

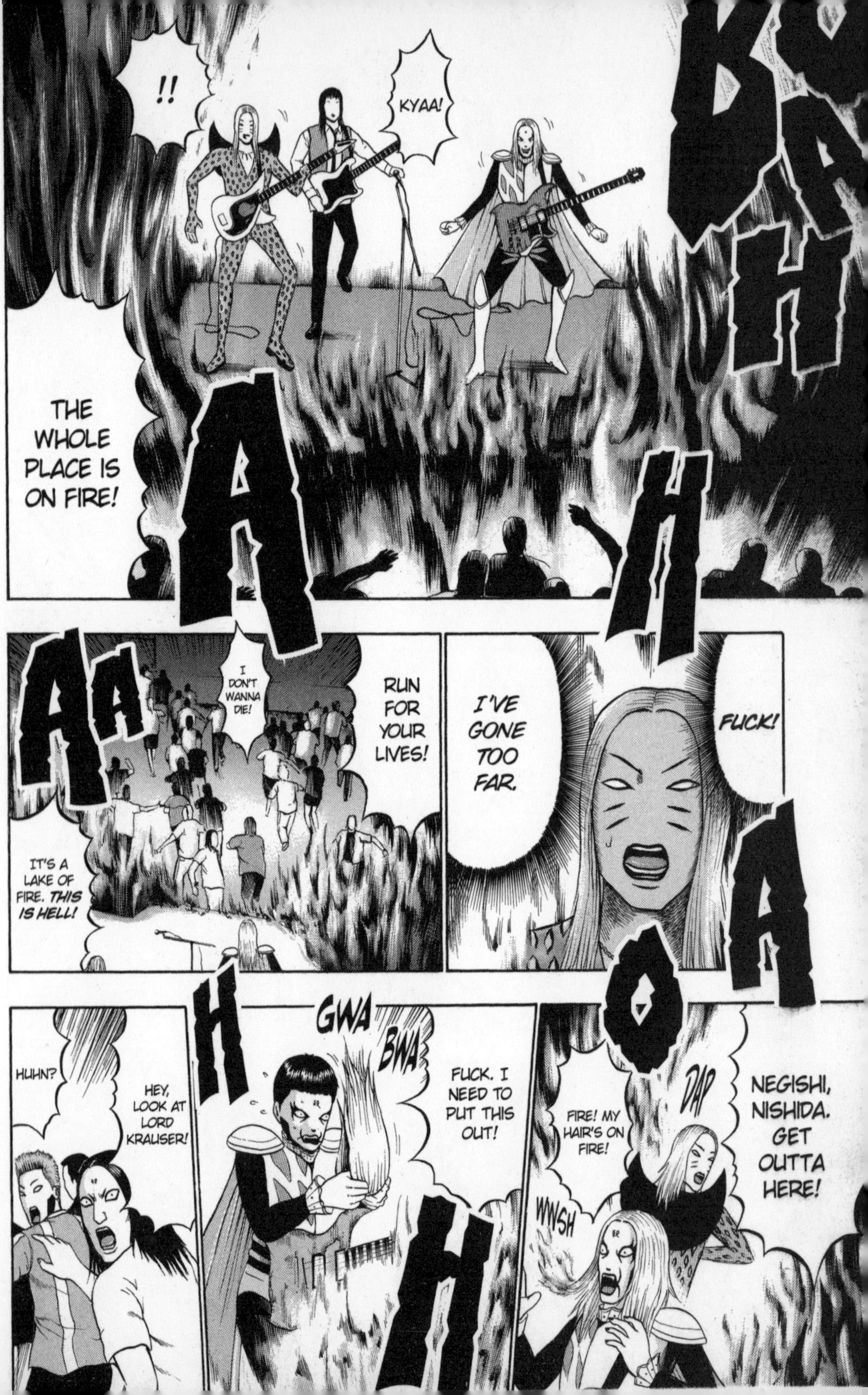
KYAA!
!!
THE WHOLE PLACE IS ON FIRE!
FUCK!
I'VE GONE TOO FAR.
RUN FOR YOUR LIVES!
I DON'T WANNA DIE!
IT'S A LAKE OF FIRE. *THIS IS HELL!*
NEGISHI, NISHIDA. GET OUTTA HERE!
DAP
FIRE! MY HAIR'S ON FIRE!
WWSH
FUCK. I NEED TO PUT THIS OUT!
GWA
BWA
HEY, LOOK AT LORD KRAUSER!
HUHN?

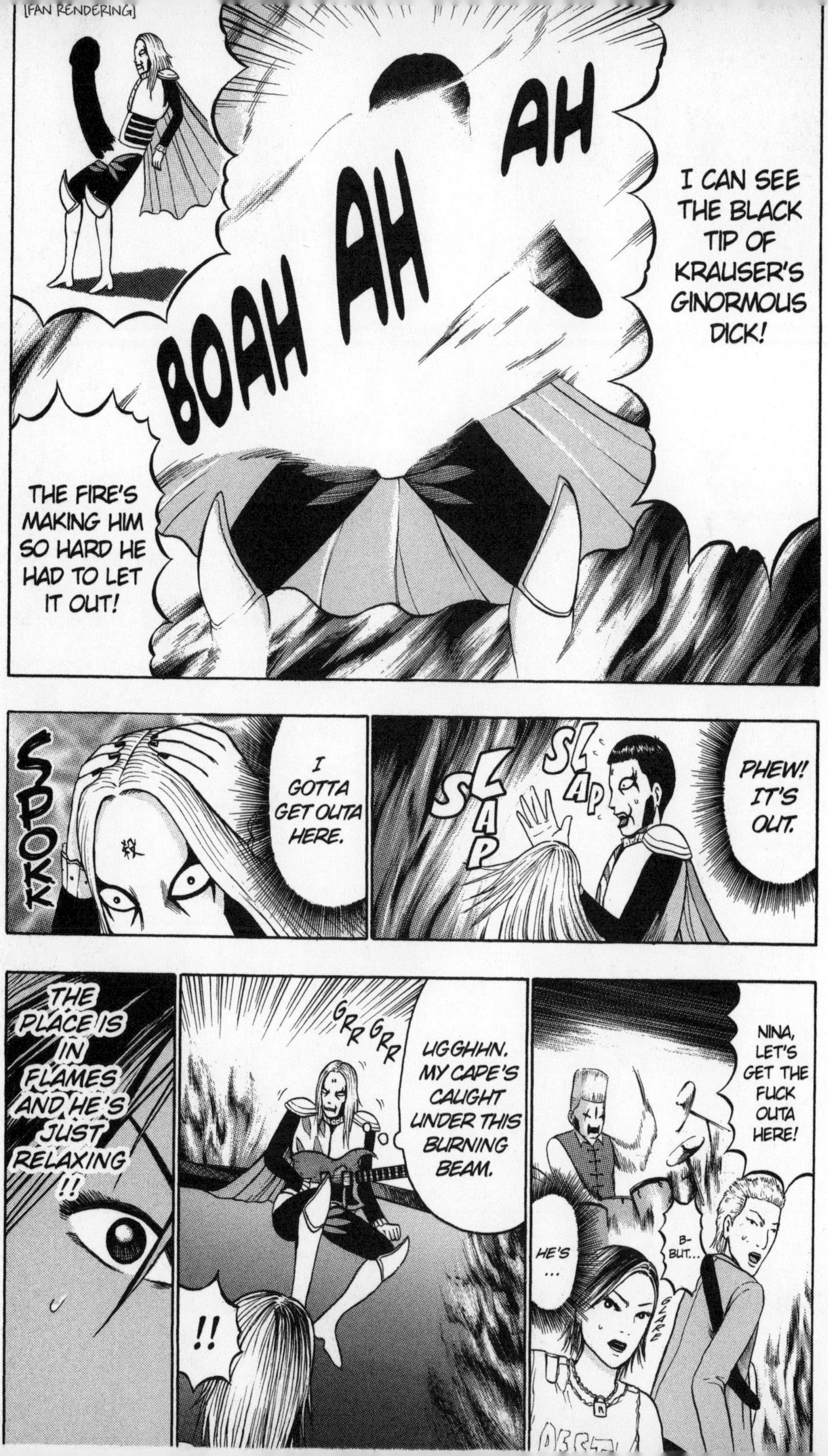
I CAN SEE THE BLACK TIP OF KRAUSER'S GINORMOUS DICK!
BOAH AH AH
[FAN RENDERING]
THE FIRE'S MAKING HIM SO HARD HE HAD TO LET IT OUT!
PHEW! IT'S OUT.
SLAP SLAP
I GOTTA GET OUTA HERE.
SPOKK
NINA, LET'S GET THE FUCK OUTA HERE!
B- BUT...
HE'S ...
GLARE
GRR GRR
UGGHHN. MY CAPE'S CAUGHT UNDER THIS BURNING BEAM.
!!
THE PLACE IS IN FLAMES AND HE'S JUST RELAXING!!

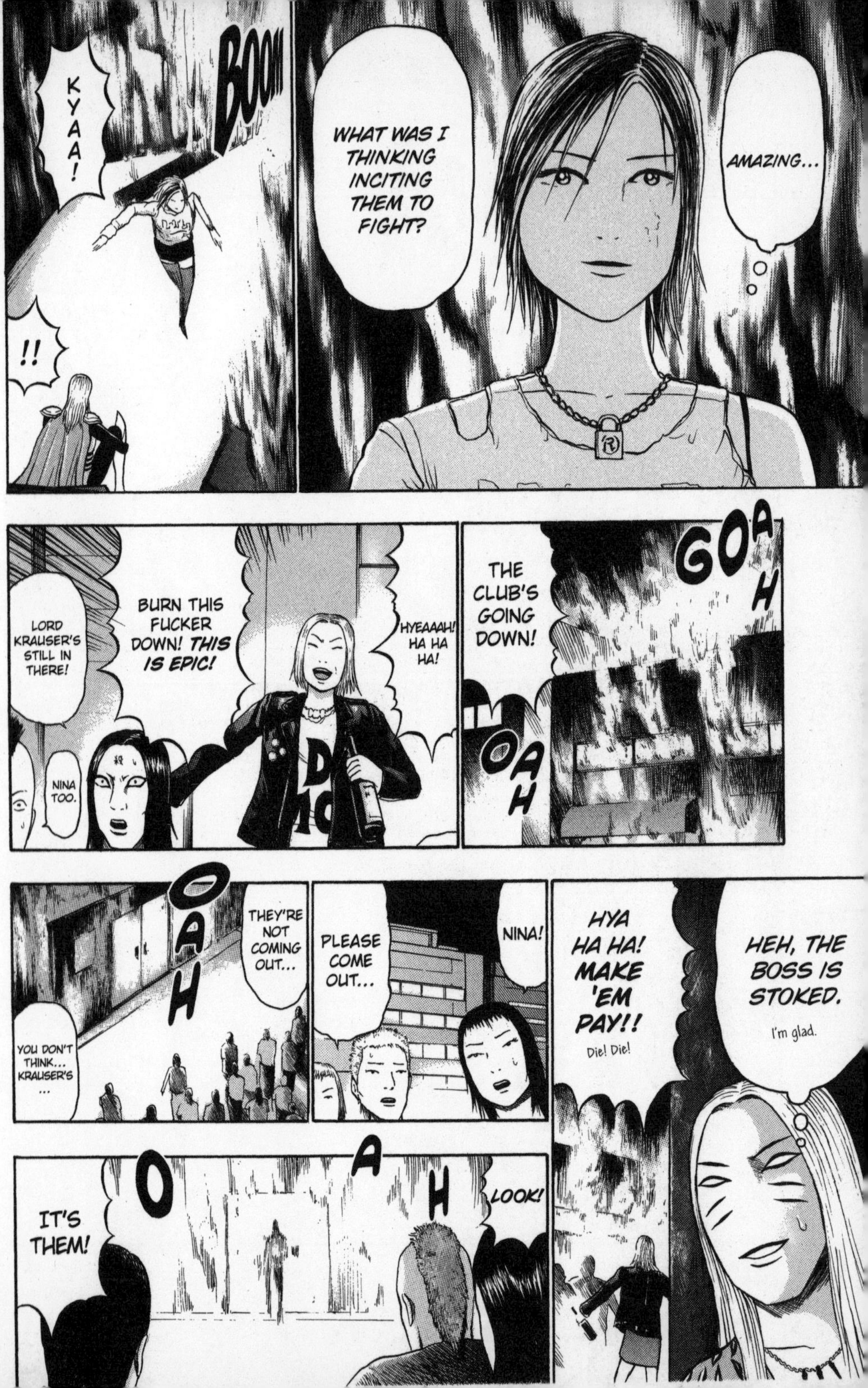

AMAZING...
WHAT WAS I THINKING INCITING THEM TO FIGHT?
BOOM
KYAA!
!!
GOAH
THE CLUB'S GOING DOWN!
OAH
HYEAAAH! HA HA HA!
BURN THIS FUCKER DOWN! THIS IS EPIC!
LORD KRAUSER'S STILL IN THERE!
NINA TOO.
HEH, THE BOSS IS STOKED.
I'm glad.
HYA HA HA! MAKE 'EM PAY!!
Die! Die!
NINA!
PLEASE COME OUT...
OAH
THEY'RE NOT COMING OUT...
YOU DON'T THINK... KRAUSER'S ...
LOOK!
OAH
IT'S THEM!

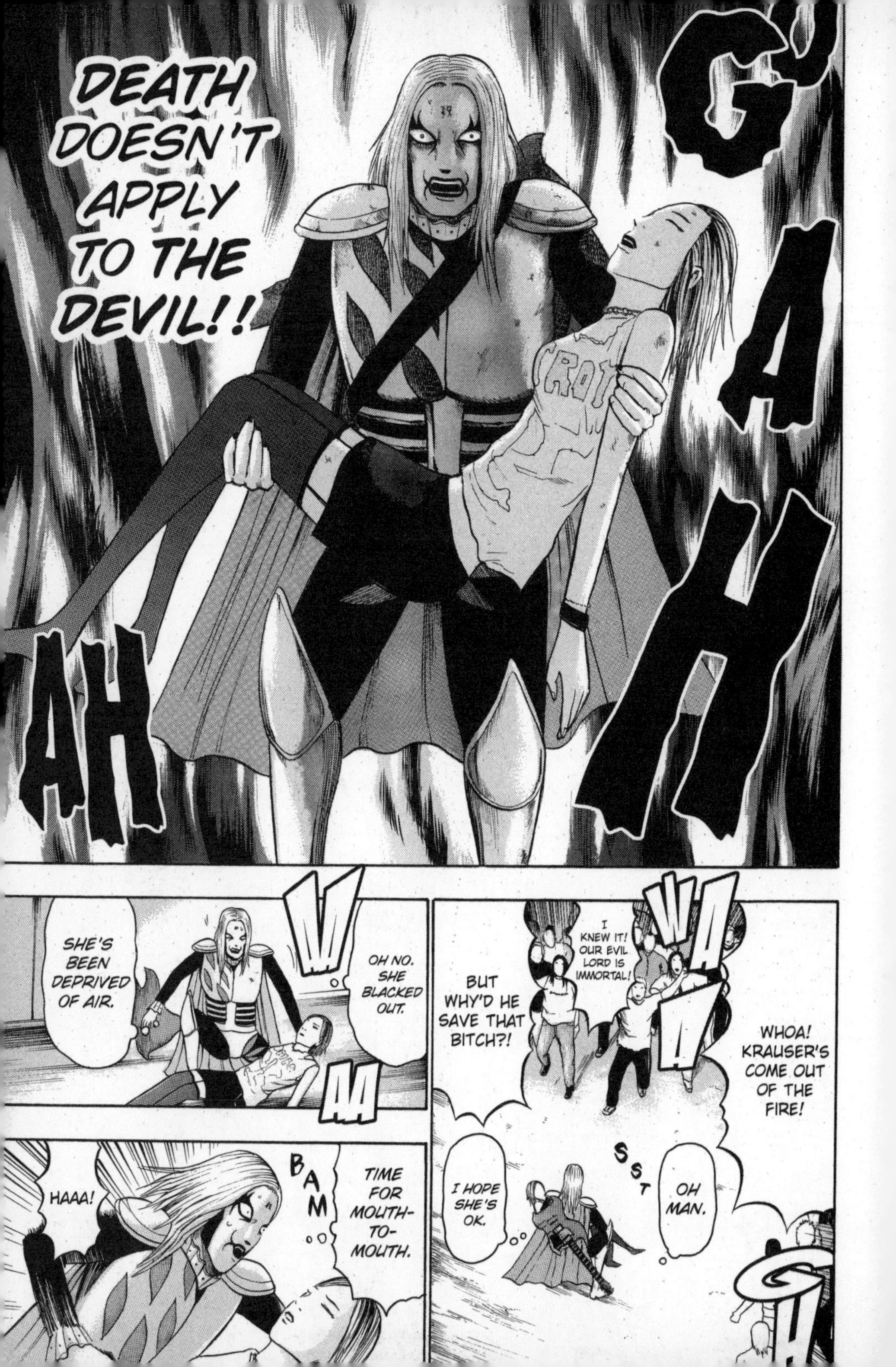
DEATH DOESN'T APPLY TO THE DEVIL!!
AH
WHOA! KRAUSER'S COME OUT OF THE FIRE!
I KNEW IT! OUR EVIL LORD IS IMMORTAL!
BUT WHY'D HE SAVE THAT BITCH?!
OH NO. SHE BLACKED OUT.
SHE'S BEEN DEPRIVED OF AIR.
OH MAN.
SSST
I HOPE SHE'S OK.
TIME FOR MOUTH-TO-MOUTH.
BAM
HAAA!

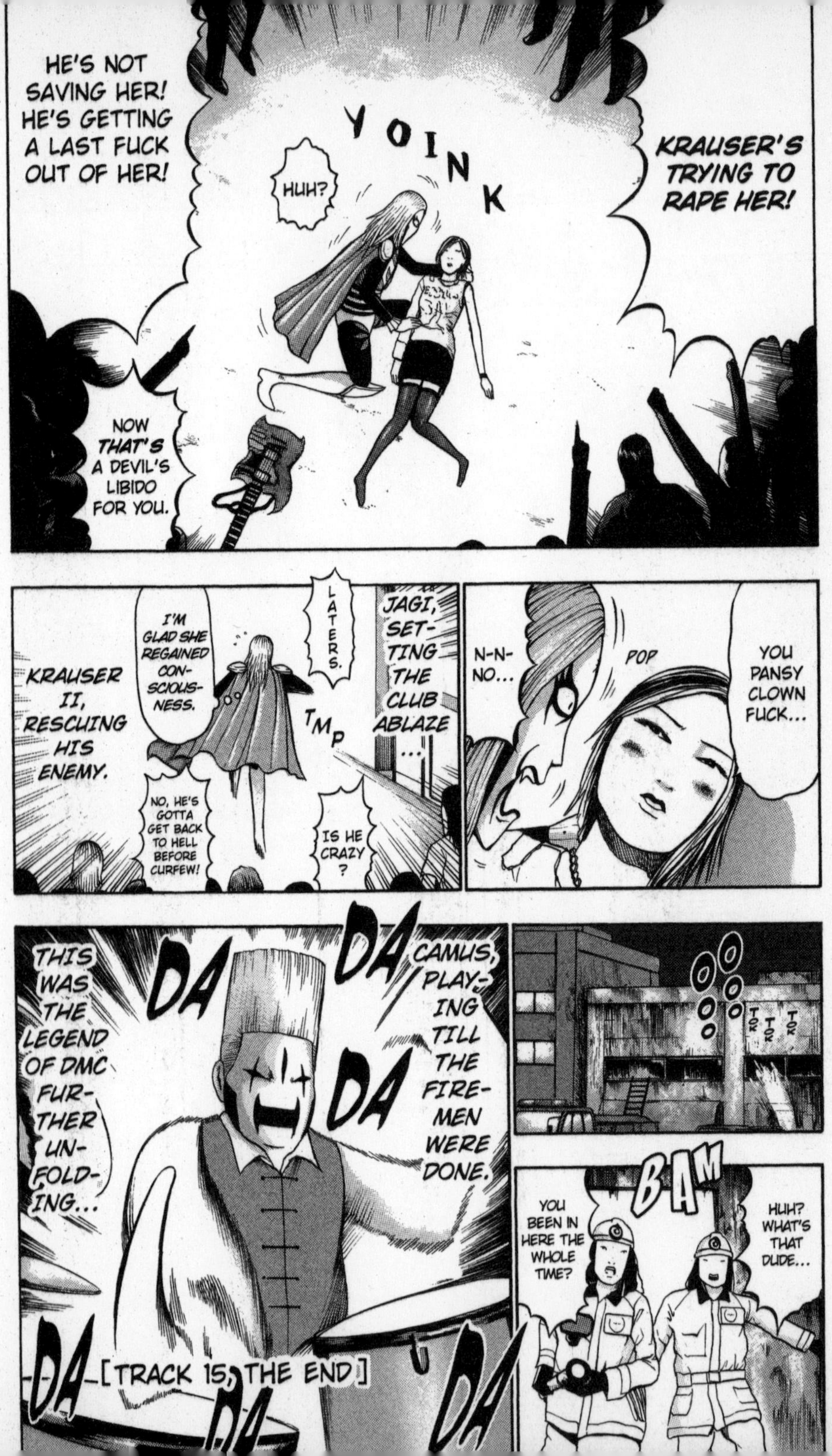
KRAUSER'S TRYING TO RAPE HER!
YOINK
HUH?
HE'S NOT SAVING HER! HE'S GETTING A LAST FUCK OUT OF HER!
NOW THAT'S A DEVIL'S LIBIDO FOR YOU.
YOU PANSY CLOWN FUCK...
POP
N-N-NO...
JAGI, SETTING THE CLUB ABLAZE...
LATERS.
I'M GLAD SHE REGAINED CONSCIOUSNESS.
KRAUSER II, RESCUING HIS ENEMY.
TMP
IS HE CRAZY?
NO, HE'S GOTTA GET BACK TO HELL BEFORE CURFEW!
TOK TOK TOK
BAM
HUH? WHAT'S THAT DUDE...
YOU BEEN IN HERE THE WHOLE TIME?
DA
CAMUS, PLAYING TILL THE FIREMEN WERE DONE.
DA
THIS WAS THE LEGEND OF DMC FURTHER UNFOLDING...
DA
DA
DA
[TRACK 15, THE END]

DMC LEXICON

 ## MOUTH-TO-MOUTH

A rescue method used to resuscitate breathing in someone who has passed out. Accomplished by forcing breath into the victim's body from your mouth into the theirs. When performing on a female, be careful not to confuse the mouth-on-their-face with the mouth-between-their-legs.

Usage: Hey Mom, are you ok? I noticed Dad was doing mouth-to-mouth on your butt all last night.

デトロイト・メタル・シティ

Detroit Metal City

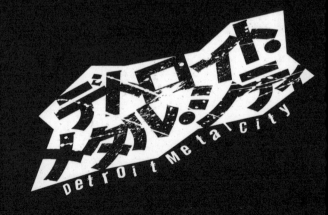

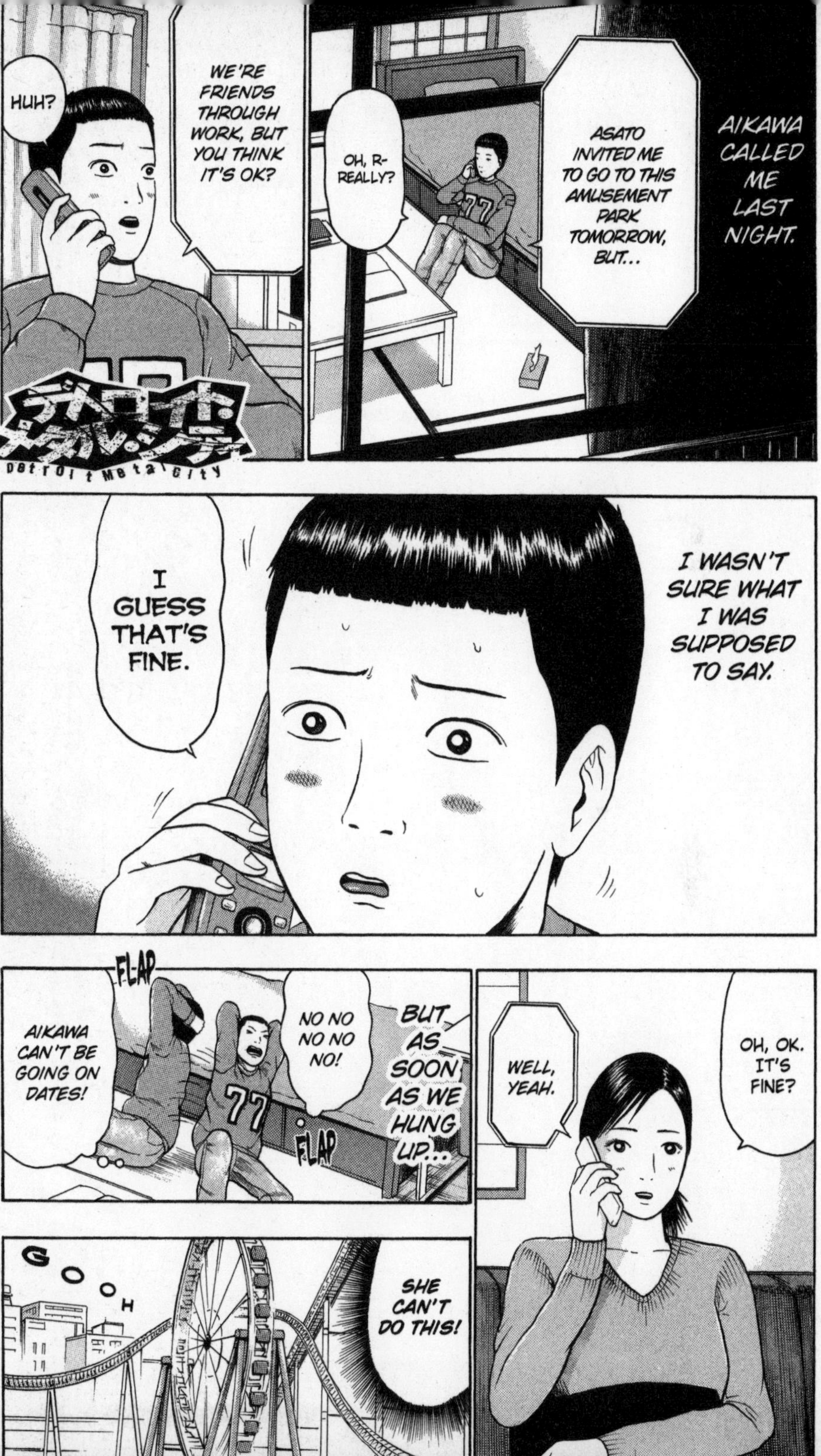

AIKAWA CALLED ME LAST NIGHT.
ASATO INVITED ME TO GO TO THIS AMUSEMENT PARK TOMORROW, BUT...
OH, R-REALLY?
WE'RE FRIENDS THROUGH WORK, BUT YOU THINK IT'S OK?
HUH?
I WASN'T SURE WHAT I WAS SUPPOSED TO SAY.
I GUESS THAT'S FINE.
OH, OK. IT'S FINE?
WELL, YEAH.
BUT AS SOON AS WE HUNG UP...
NO NO NO NO NO!
FLAP
FL-AP
AIKAWA CAN'T BE GOING ON DATES!
SHE CAN'T DO THIS!
GOOH

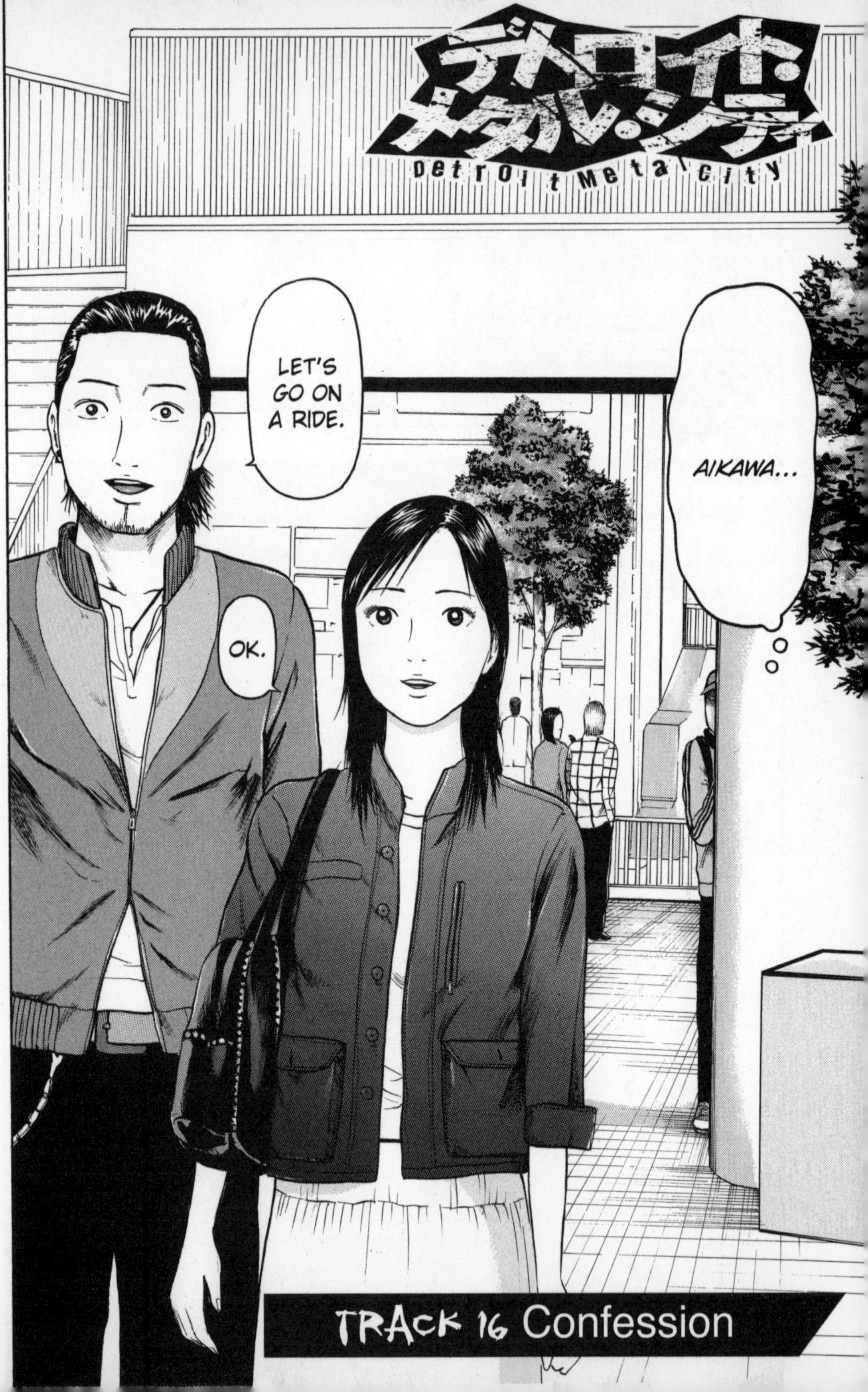
Detroit Metal City
AIKAWA...
LET'S GO ON A RIDE.
OK.
TRACK 16 Confession

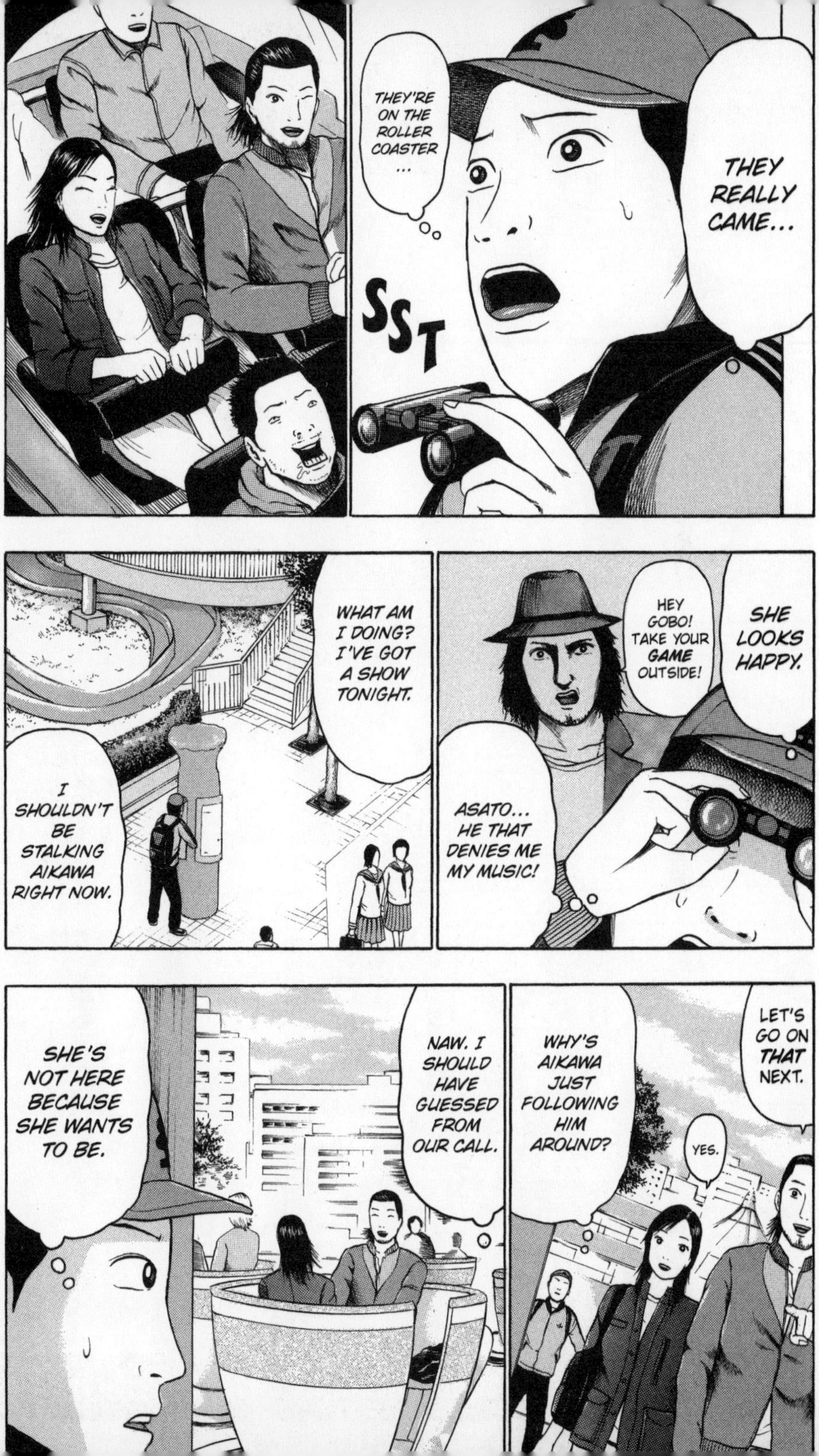
THEY REALLY CAME...
THEY'RE ON THE ROLLER COASTER ...
SST
SHE LOOKS HAPPY.
HEY GOBO! TAKE YOUR GAME OUTSIDE!
ASATO... HE THAT DENIES ME MY MUSIC!
WHAT AM I DOING? I'VE GOT A SHOW TONIGHT.
I SHOULDN'T BE STALKING AIKAWA RIGHT NOW.
LET'S GO ON THAT NEXT.
YES.
WHY'S AIKAWA JUST FOLLOWING HIM AROUND?
NAW. I SHOULD HAVE GUESSED FROM OUR CALL.
SHE'S NOT HERE BECAUSE SHE WANTS TO BE.

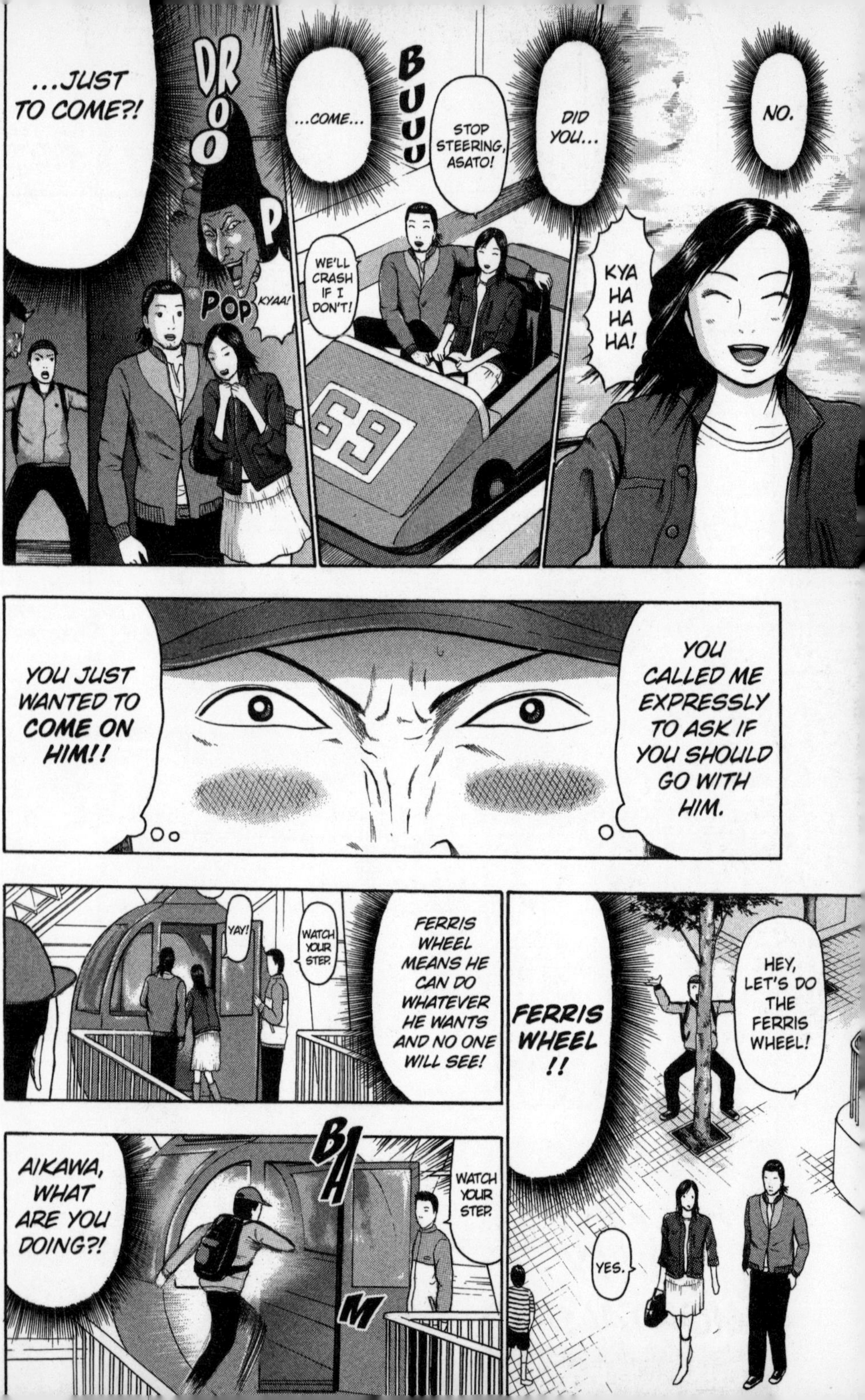
NO.
KYA HA HA HA!
DID YOU...
BUUU
STOP STEERING, ASATO!
WE'LL CRASH IF I DON'T!
...COME...
...JUST TO COME?!
DROOP
POP
KYAA!
YOU CALLED ME EXPRESSLY TO ASK IF YOU SHOULD GO WITH HIM.
YOU JUST WANTED TO COME ON HIM!!
HEY, LET'S DO THE FERRIS WHEEL!
YES.
FERRIS WHEEL!!
FERRIS WHEEL MEANS HE CAN DO WHATEVER HE WANTS AND NO ONE WILL SEE!
WATCH YOUR STEP.
YAY!
BAM
WATCH YOUR STEP.
AIKAWA, WHAT ARE YOU DOING?!

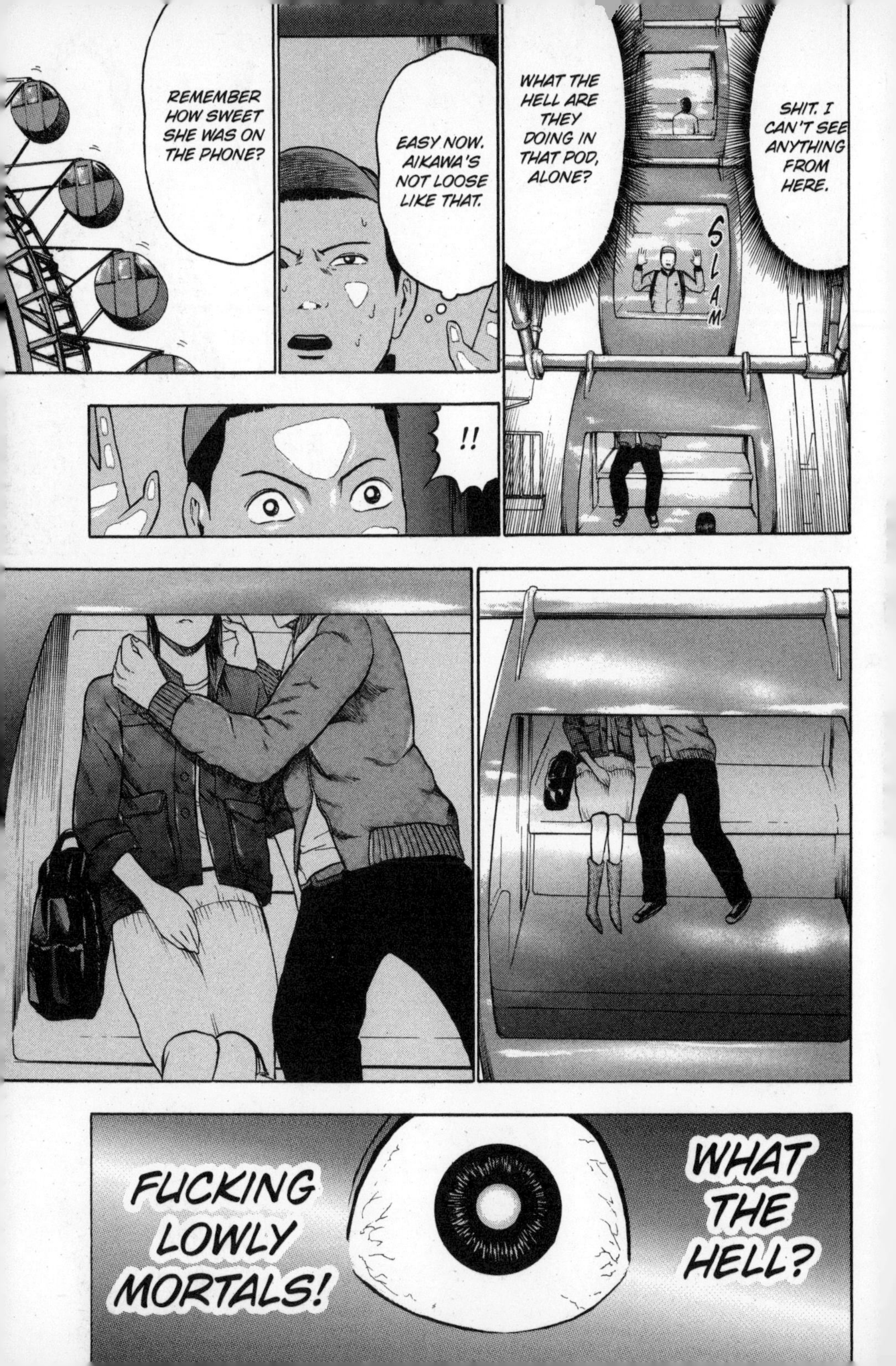
SHIT. I CAN'T SEE ANYTHING FROM HERE.
WHAT THE HELL ARE THEY DOING IN THAT POD, ALONE?
SLAM
EASY NOW. AIKAWA'S NOT LOOSE LIKE THAT.
REMEMBER HOW SWEET SHE WAS ON THE PHONE?
!!
WHAT THE HELL?
FUCKING LOWLY MORTALS!

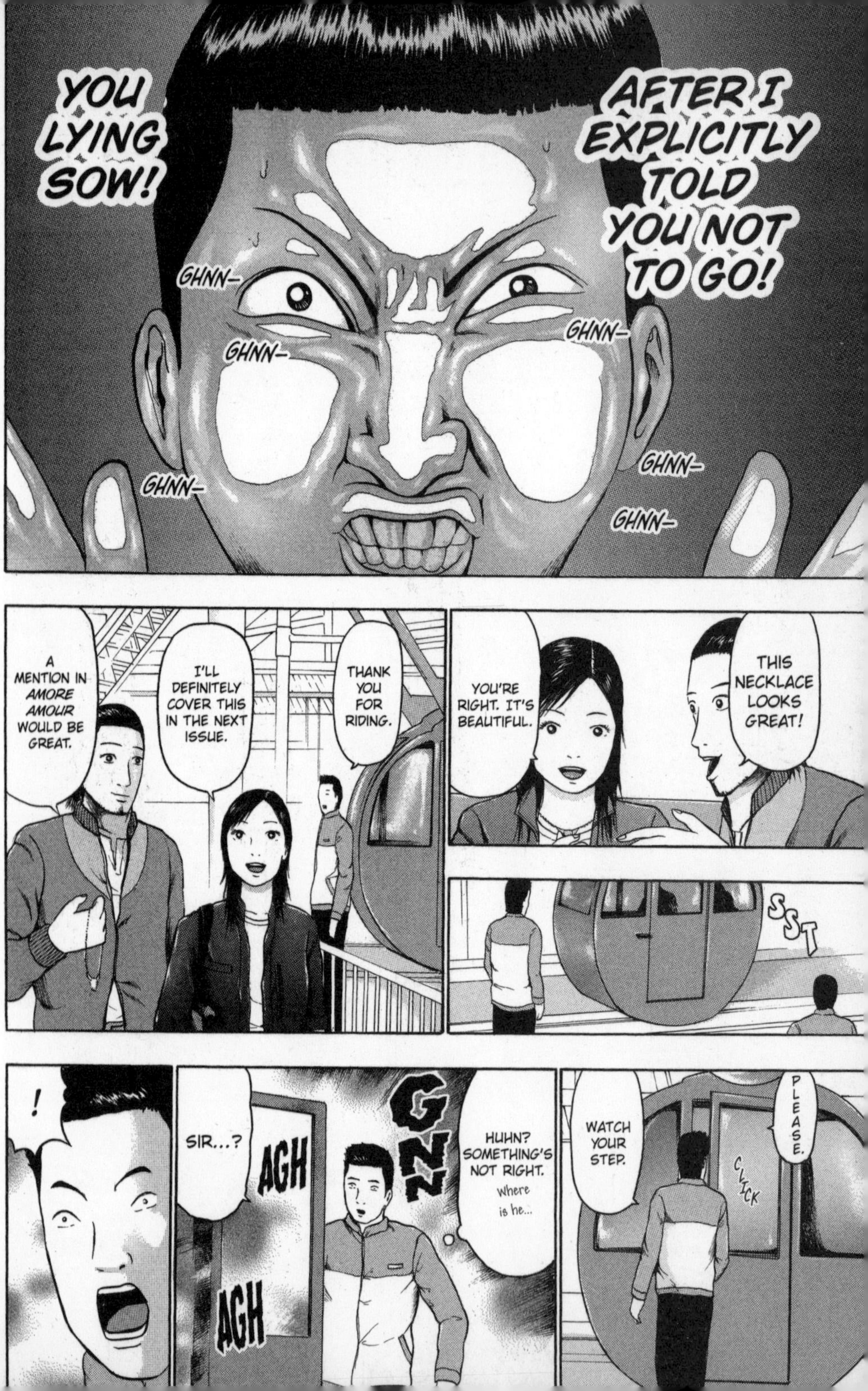
AFTER I EXPLICITLY TOLD YOU NOT TO GO!
YOU LYING SOW!
GHNN-
GHNN-
GHNN-
GHNN-
GHNN-
GHNN-
THIS NECKLACE LOOKS GREAT!
YOU'RE RIGHT. IT'S BEAUTIFUL.
SST
THANK YOU FOR RIDING.
I'LL DEFINITELY COVER THIS IN THE NEXT ISSUE.
A MENTION IN AMORE AMOUR WOULD BE GREAT.
PLEASE.
WATCH YOUR STEP.
CLICK
GNN
HUHN? SOMETHING'S NOT RIGHT.
Where is he...
SIR...?
AGH
AGH
!

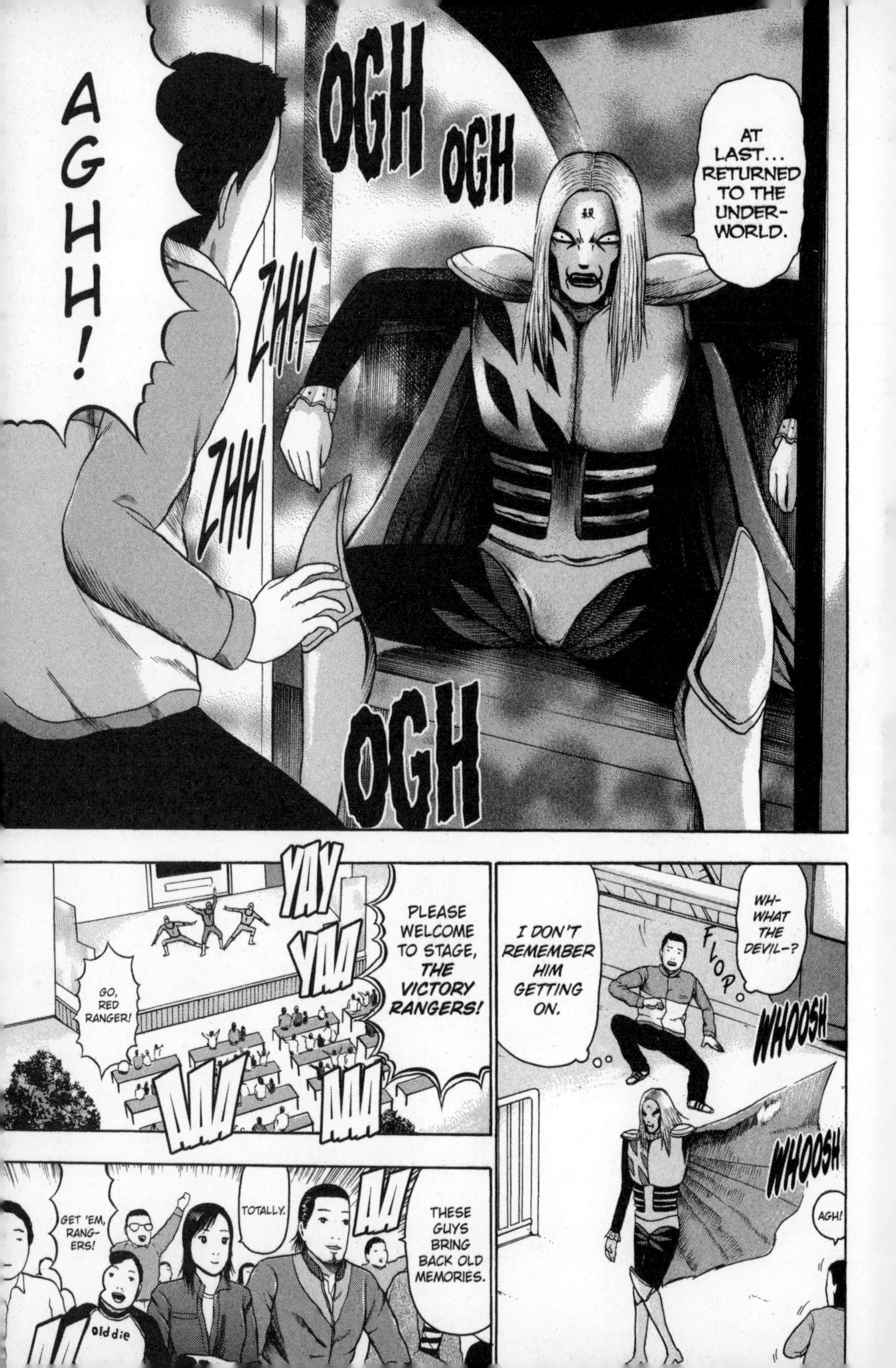
AT LAST... RETURNED TO THE UNDER-WORLD.
OGH OGH
ZHH ZHH
AGHH!
OGH
WH- WHAT THE DEVIL-?
FLOP
I DON'T REMEMBER HIM GETTING ON.
WHOOSH
WHOOSH
AGH!
YAY YAY
PLEASE WELCOME TO STAGE, THE VICTORY RANGERS!
GO, RED RANGER!
THESE GUYS BRING BACK OLD MEMORIES.
TOTALLY.
GET 'EM, RANGERS!

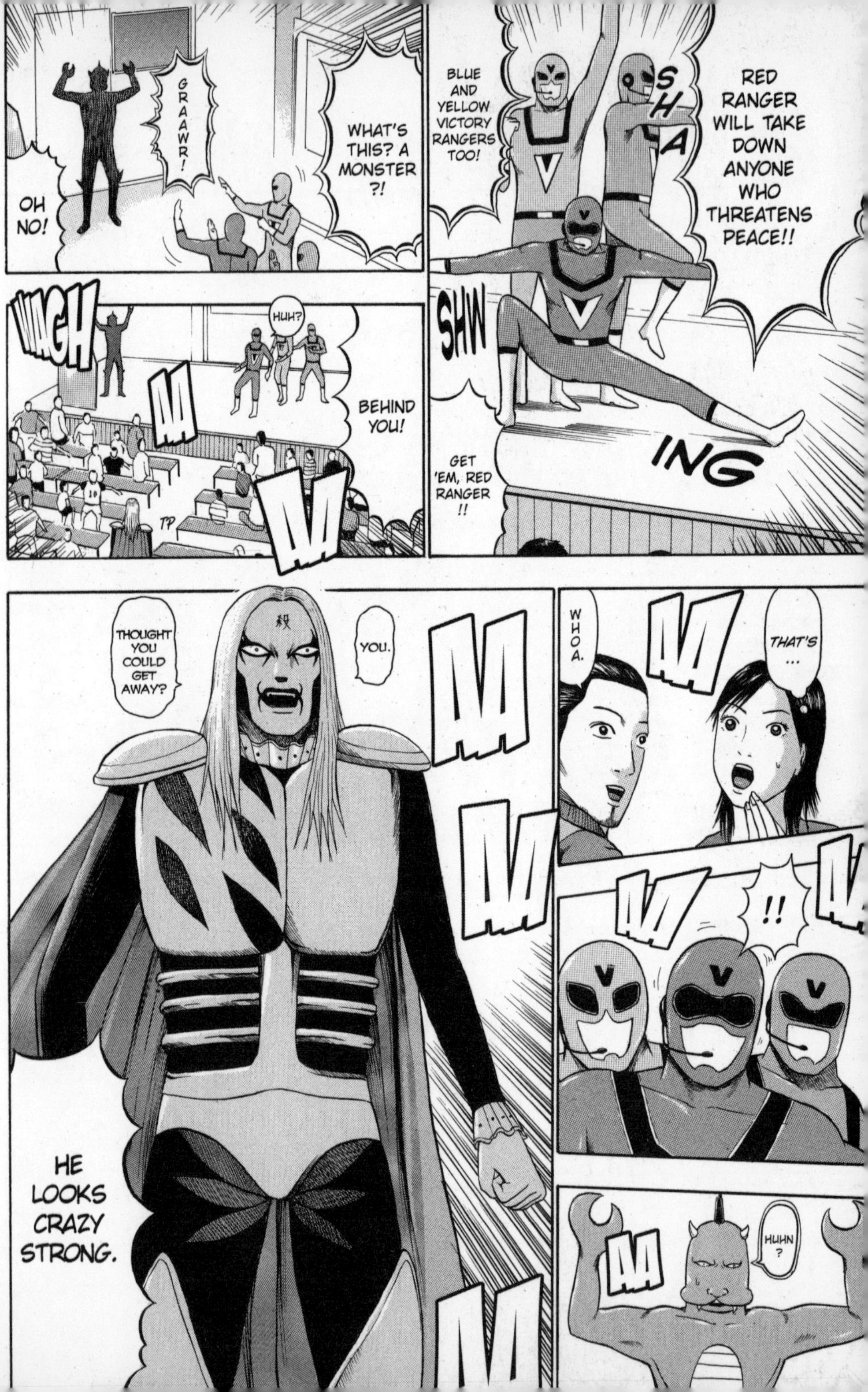
RED RANGER WILL TAKE DOWN ANYONE WHO THREATENS PEACE!!
SHA
BLUE AND YELLOW VICTORY RANGERS TOO!
SHW
ING
GET 'EM, RED RANGER!!
WHAT'S THIS? A MONSTER?!
GRAAWR!
OH NO!
HUH?
BEHIND YOU!
WAGH
AA
AA
TP
THAT'S ...
AA
WHOA.
!!
AA
AA
HUHN?
AA
AA
YOU.
THOUGHT YOU COULD GET AWAY?
AA
HE LOOKS CRAZY STRONG.

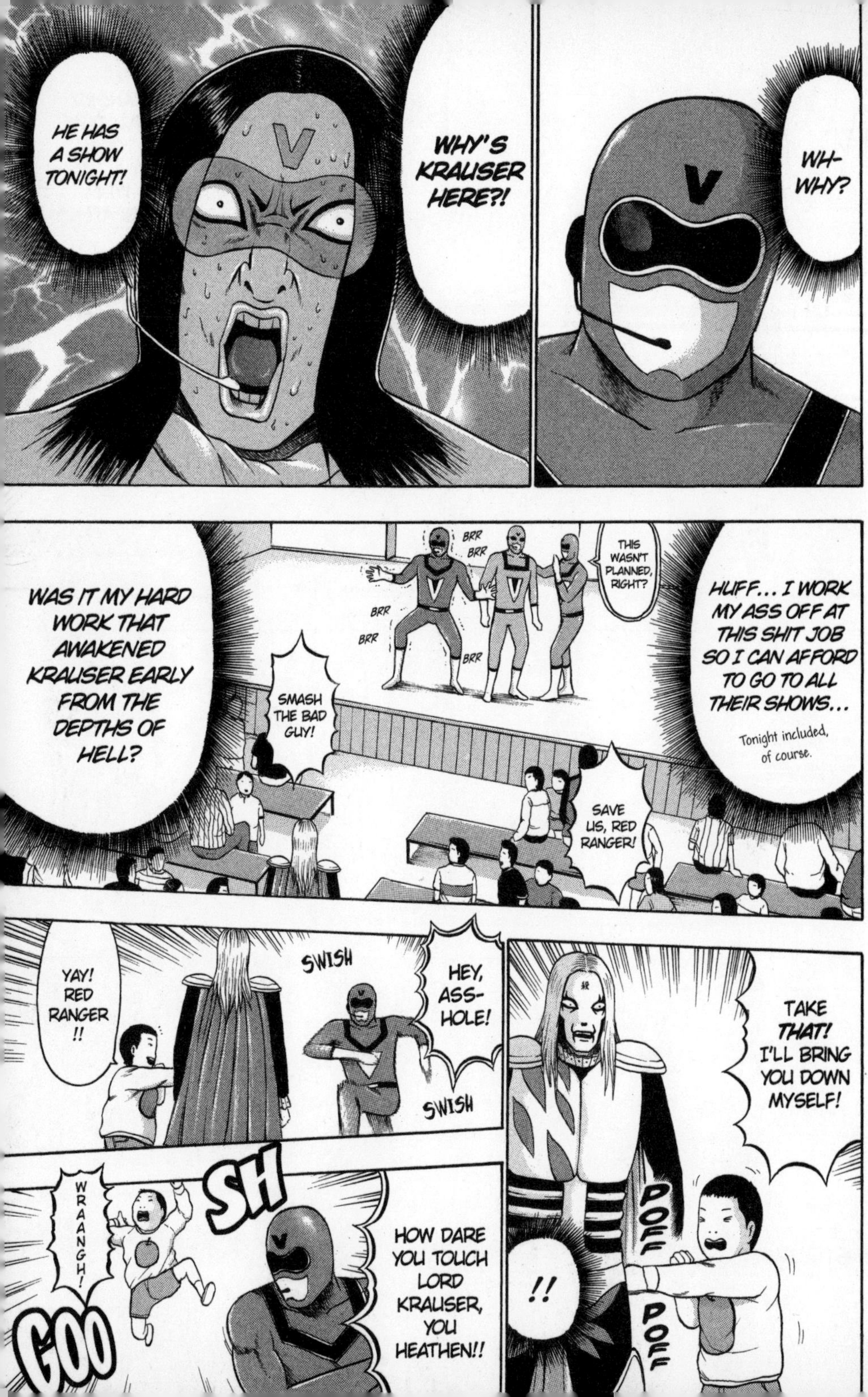
WH- WHY?
WHY'S KRAUSER HERE?!
HE HAS A SHOW TONIGHT!
HUFF… I WORK MY ASS OFF AT THIS SHIT JOB SO I CAN AFFORD TO GO TO ALL THEIR SHOWS…
Tonight included, of course.
THIS WASN'T PLANNED, RIGHT?
BRR
BRR
BRR
BRR
BRR
SAVE US, RED RANGER!
SMASH THE BAD GUY!
WAS IT MY HARD WORK THAT AWAKENED KRAUSER EARLY FROM THE DEPTHS OF HELL?
TAKE THAT! I'LL BRING YOU DOWN MYSELF!
POFF
POFF
POFF
!!
HEY, ASS-HOLE!
SWISH
SWISH
YAY! RED RANGER !!
SH
GOO
HOW DARE YOU TOUCH LORD KRAUSER, YOU HEATHEN!!
WRAAANGH!

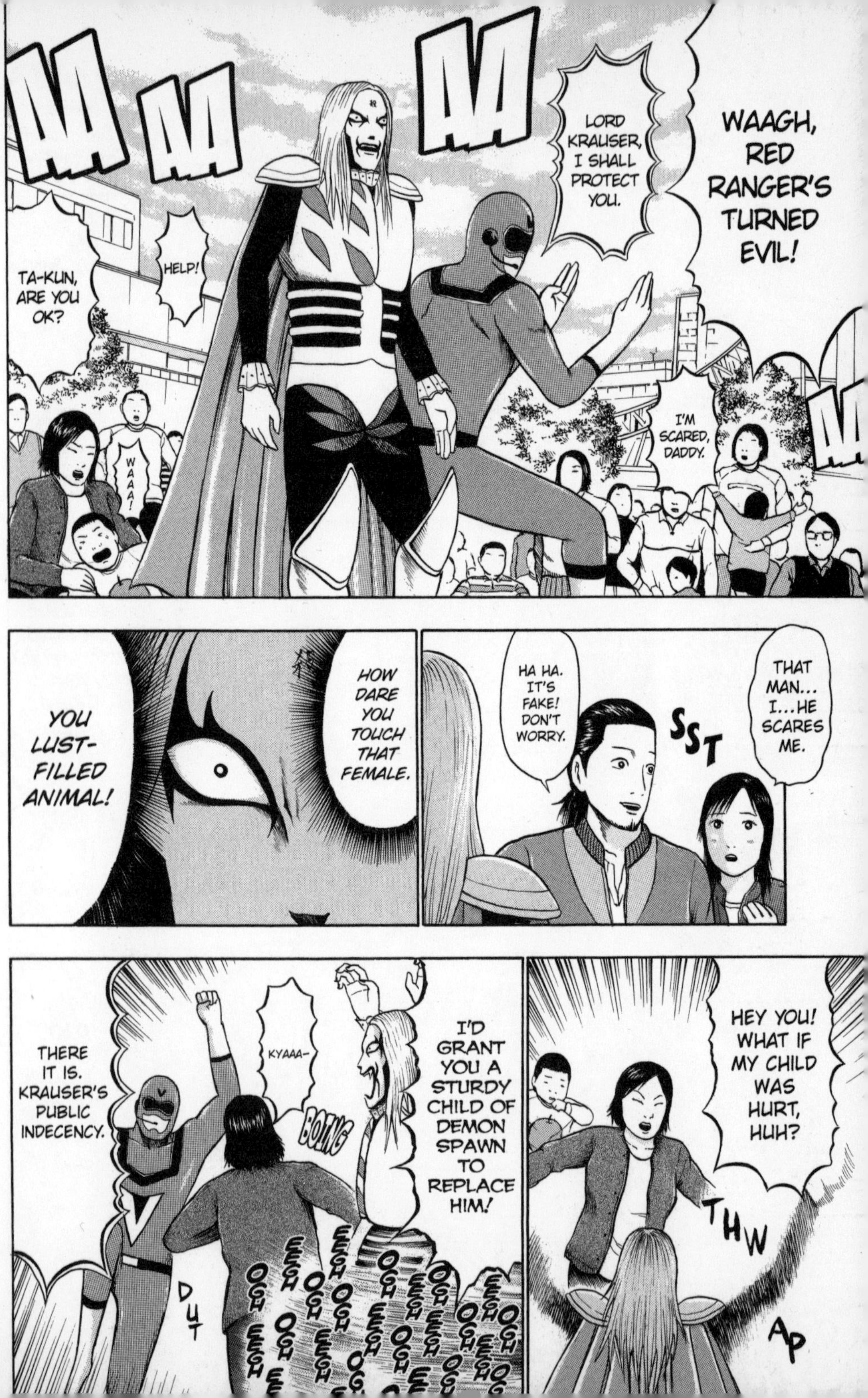
WAAGH, RED RANGER'S TURNED EVIL!
LORD KRAUSER, I SHALL PROTECT YOU.
AA
AA
AA
I'M SCARED, DADDY.
HELP!
TA-KUN, ARE YOU OK?
WAAA!
THAT MAN... I...HE SCARES ME.
SST
HA HA. IT'S FAKE! DON'T WORRY.
HOW DARE YOU TOUCH THAT FEMALE.
YOU LUST-FILLED ANIMAL!
HEY YOU! WHAT IF MY CHILD WAS HURT, HUH?
THW
AP
I'D GRANT YOU A STURDY CHILD OF DEMON SPAWN TO REPLACE HIM!
KYAAA-
BOING
THERE IT IS. KRAUSER'S PUBLIC INDECENCY.
DUT
EEGH OGH EEGH OGH

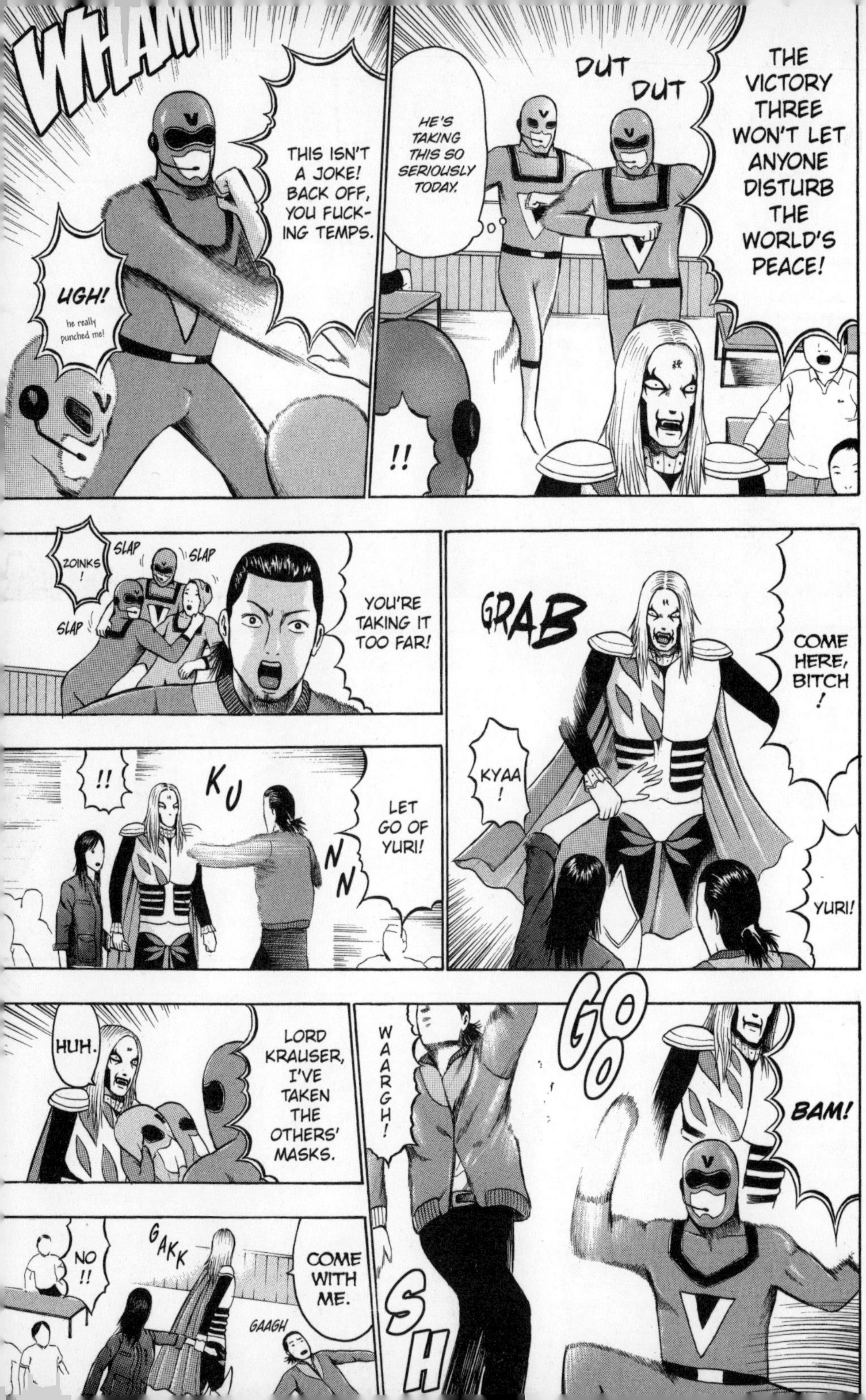
THE VICTORY THREE WON'T LET ANYONE DISTURB THE WORLD'S PEACE!
DUT DUT
HE'S TAKING THIS SO SERIOUSLY TODAY.
!!
WHAM
THIS ISN'T A JOKE! BACK OFF, YOU FUCKING TEMPS.
UGH!
he really punched me!
GRAB
COME HERE, BITCH!
KYAA!
YURI!
YOU'RE TAKING IT TOO FAR!
SLAP
SLAP
ZOINKS!
SLAP
LET GO OF YURI!
KUNN
!!
GOGO
BAM!
WAAARGH!
SHH
LORD KRAUSER, I'VE TAKEN THE OTHERS' MASKS.
HUH.
COME WITH ME.
GAKK
NO!!
GAAGH

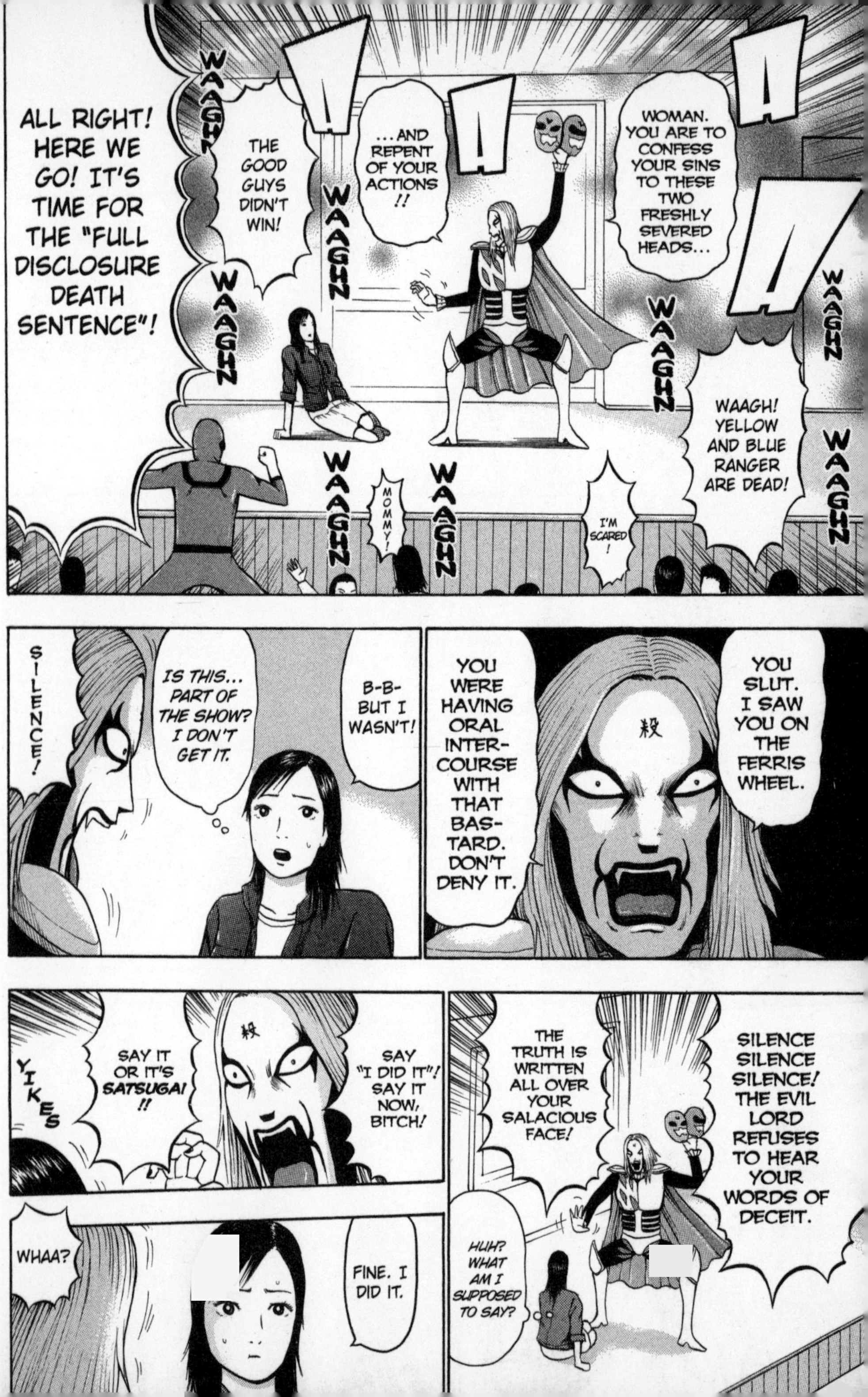
WOMAN. YOU ARE TO CONFESS YOUR SINS TO THESE TWO FRESHLY SEVERED HEADS...
...AND REPENT OF YOUR ACTIONS!!
WAAGHN
WAAGH! YELLOW AND BLUE RANGER ARE DEAD!
WAAGHN
WAAGHN
I'M SCARED!
WAAGHN
MOMMY!
WAAGHN
WAAGHN
THE GOOD GUYS DIDN'T WIN!
WAAGHN
WAAGHN
ALL RIGHT! HERE WE GO! IT'S TIME FOR THE "FULL DISCLOSURE DEATH SENTENCE"!
YOU SLUT. I SAW YOU ON THE FERRIS WHEEL.
殺
YOU WERE HAVING ORAL INTER-COURSE WITH THAT BAS-TARD. DON'T DENY IT.
B-B-BUT I WASN'T!
IS THIS... PART OF THE SHOW? I DON'T GET IT.
SILENCE!
SILENCE SILENCE SILENCE! THE EVIL LORD REFUSES TO HEAR YOUR WORDS OF DECEIT.
THE TRUTH IS WRITTEN ALL OVER YOUR SALACIOUS FACE!
HUH? WHAT AM I SUPPOSED TO SAY?
殺
SAY "I DID IT"! SAY IT NOW, BITCH!
SAY IT OR IT'S SATSUGAI!!
YIKES
FINE. I DID IT.
WHAA?

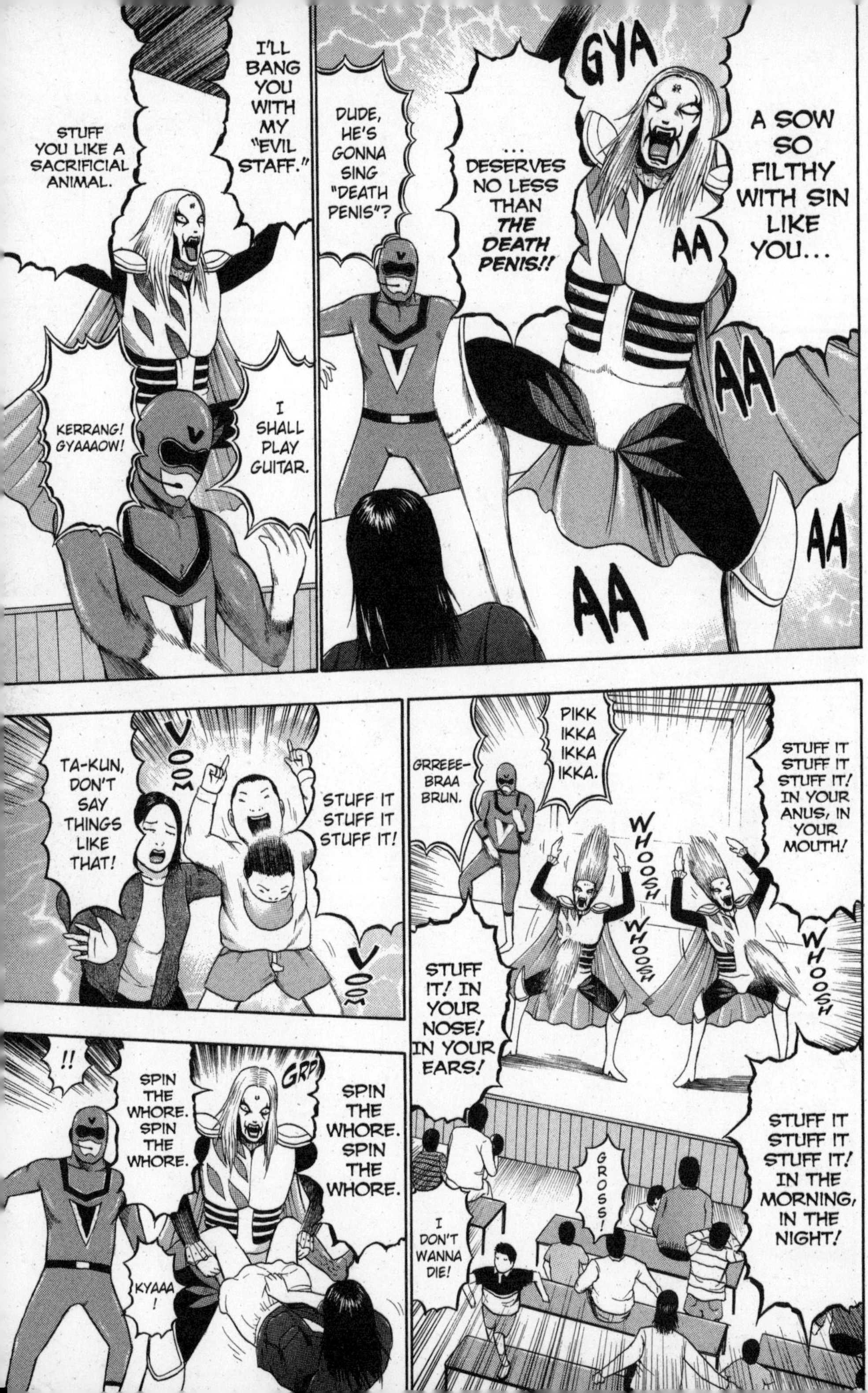
A SOW SO FILTHY WITH SIN LIKE YOU...
GYA
AA
AA
AA
AA
...DESERVES NO LESS THAN ***THE DEATH PENIS!!***
DUDE, HE'S GONNA SING "DEATH PENIS"?
I'LL BANG YOU WITH MY "EVIL STAFF."
STUFF YOU LIKE A SACRIFICIAL ANIMAL.
I SHALL PLAY GUITAR.
KERRANG! GYAAAOW!
STUFF IT STUFF IT STUFF IT! IN YOUR ANUS, IN YOUR MOUTH!
PIKK IKKA IKKA IKKA.
GRREEE-BRAA BRUN.
WHOOSH
WHOOSH
WHOOSH
WHOOSH
STUFF IT! IN YOUR NOSE! IN YOUR EARS!
STUFF IT STUFF IT STUFF IT! IN THE MORNING, IN THE NIGHT!
GROSS!
I DON'T WANNA DIE!
VOOM
STUFF IT STUFF IT STUFF IT!
TA-KUN, DON'T SAY THINGS LIKE THAT!
VOOM
GRP
SPIN THE WHORE. SPIN THE WHORE.
SPIN THE WHORE. SPIN THE WHORE.
!!
KYAAA!

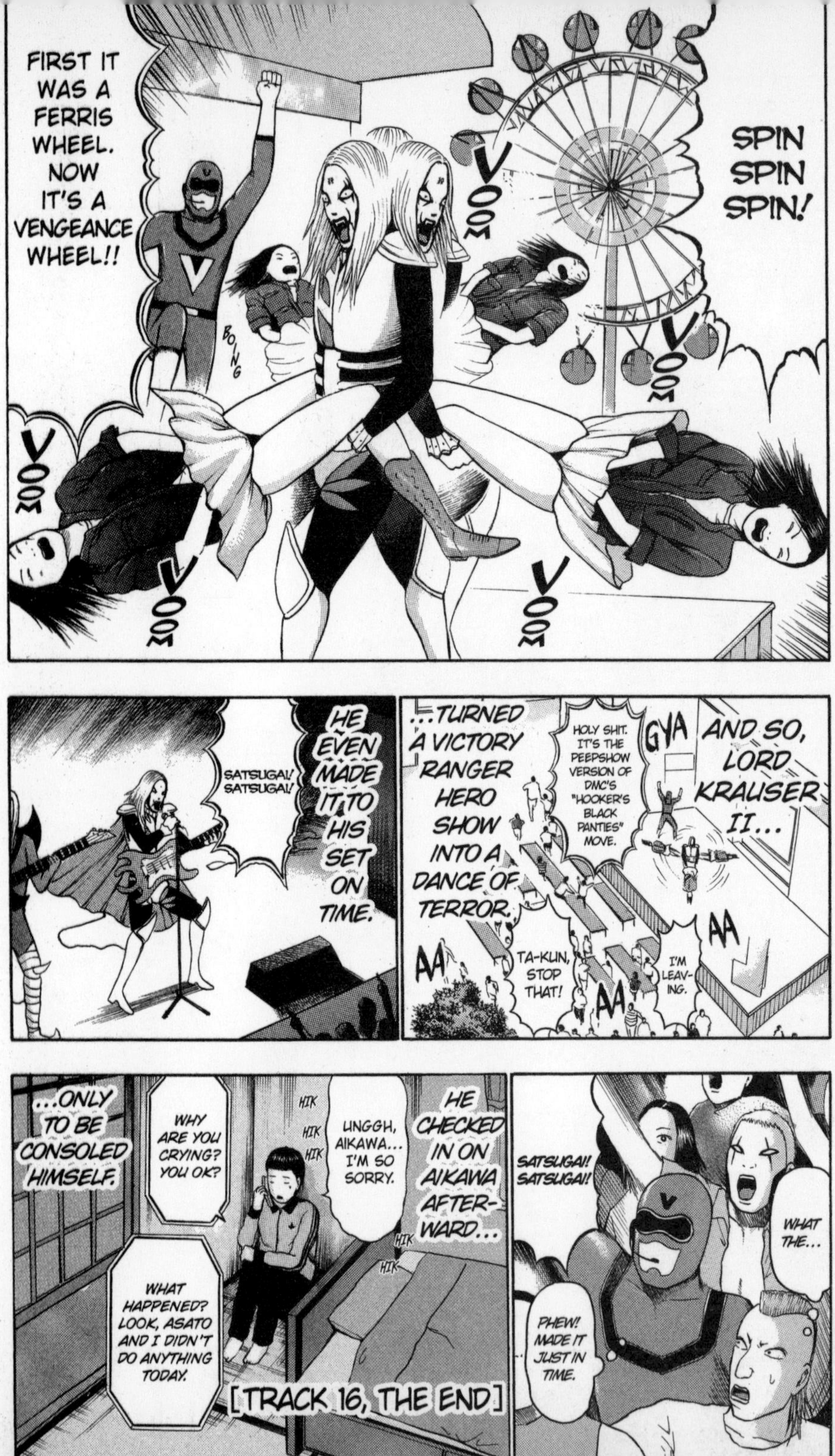

SPIN SPIN SPIN!
VOOM
VOOM
FIRST IT WAS A FERRIS WHEEL. NOW IT'S A VENGEANCE WHEEL!!
BOING
VOOM
VOOM
VOOM
AND SO, LORD KRAUSER II...
GYA
...TURNED A VICTORY RANGER HERO SHOW INTO A DANCE OF TERROR.
HOLY SHIT. IT'S THE PEEPSHOW VERSION OF DMC'S "HOOKER'S BLACK PANTIES" MOVE.
AA
I'M LEAVING.
TA-KUN, STOP THAT!
AA
AA
HE EVEN MADE IT TO HIS SET ON TIME.
SATSUGAI! SATSUGAI!
WHAT THE...
SATSUGAI! SATSUGAI!
PHEW! MADE IT JUST IN TIME.
HE CHECKED IN ON AIKAWA AFTERWARD...
HIK
HIK
UNGGH, AIKAWA... I'M SO SORRY.
HIK
HIK
HIK
WHY ARE YOU CRYING? YOU OK?
...ONLY TO BE CONSOLED HIMSELF.
WHAT HAPPENED? LOOK, ASATO AND I DIDN'T DO ANYTHING TODAY.
[TRACK 16, THE END]

DMC LEXICON

♥ HERO SHOW

A martial arts hero show put on at amusement
parks. For a long time, the shows featured "good
vanquishing evil." However, since Krauser's first
appearance on stage, the balance in power
between good and evil has undergone a radical
shift favoring evil.

Usage: Oi, Blue! If you don't kick that monster's ass in the hero
show tomorrow, we're transferring you straight to the wardrobe
department.

デトロイト・メタル・シティ
Detroit Metal City

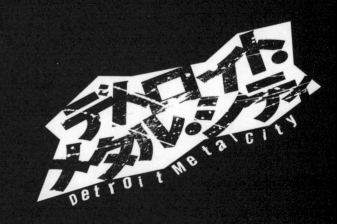

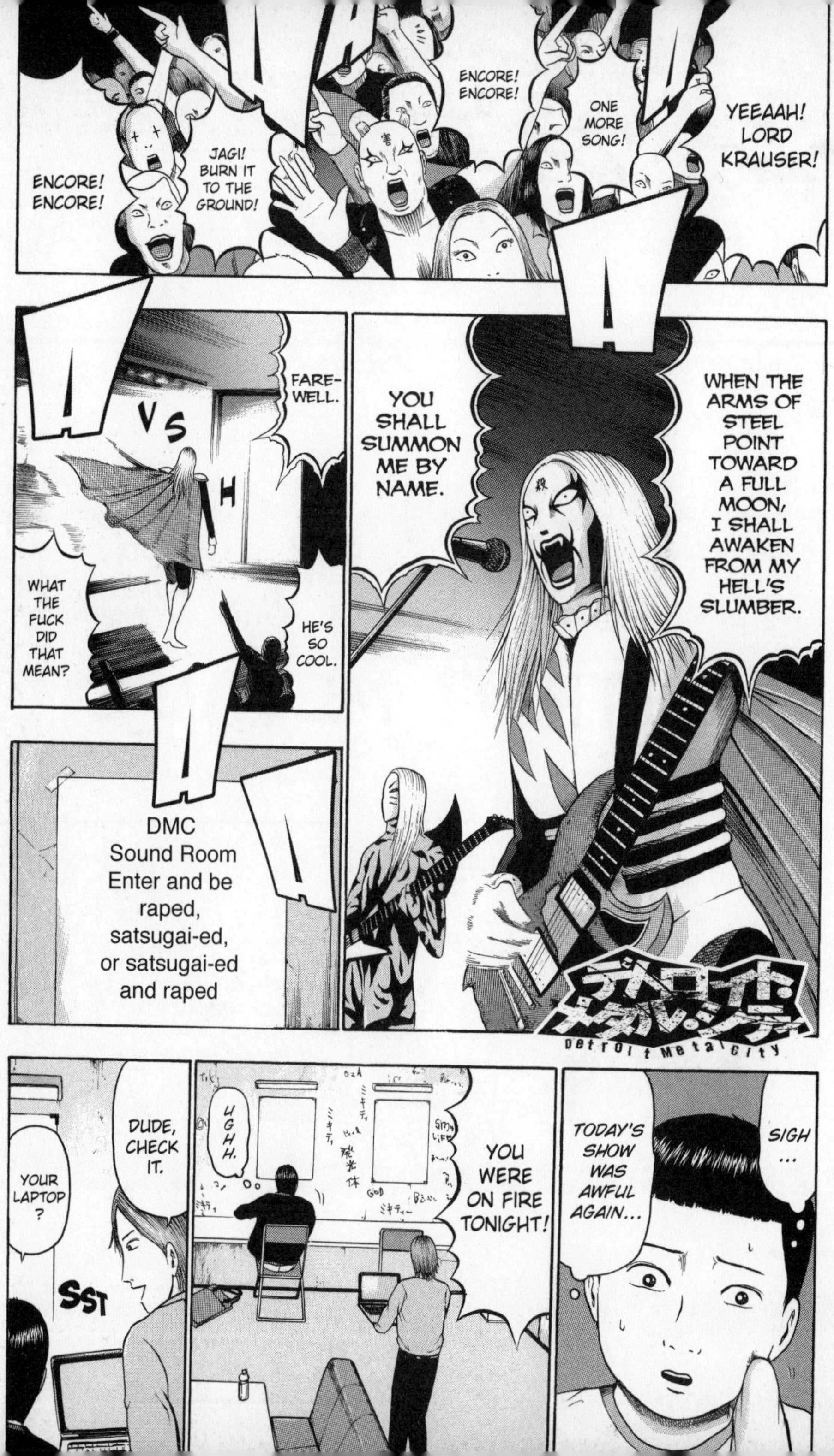
YEEAAH! LORD KRAUSER!
ONE MORE SONG!
ENCORE! ENCORE!
JAGI! BURN IT TO THE GROUND!
ENCORE! ENCORE!
WHEN THE ARMS OF STEEL POINT TOWARD A FULL MOON, I SHALL AWAKEN FROM MY HELL'S SLUMBER.
YOU SHALL SUMMON ME BY NAME.
FARE-WELL.
HE'S SO COOL.
WHAT THE FUCK DID THAT MEAN?
DMC Sound Room Enter and be raped, satsugai-ed, or satsugai-ed and raped
Detroit Metal City
SIGH...
TODAY'S SHOW WAS AWFUL AGAIN...
YOU WERE ON FIRE TONIGHT!
UGHH.
DUDE, CHECK IT.
YOUR LAPTOP?
SST

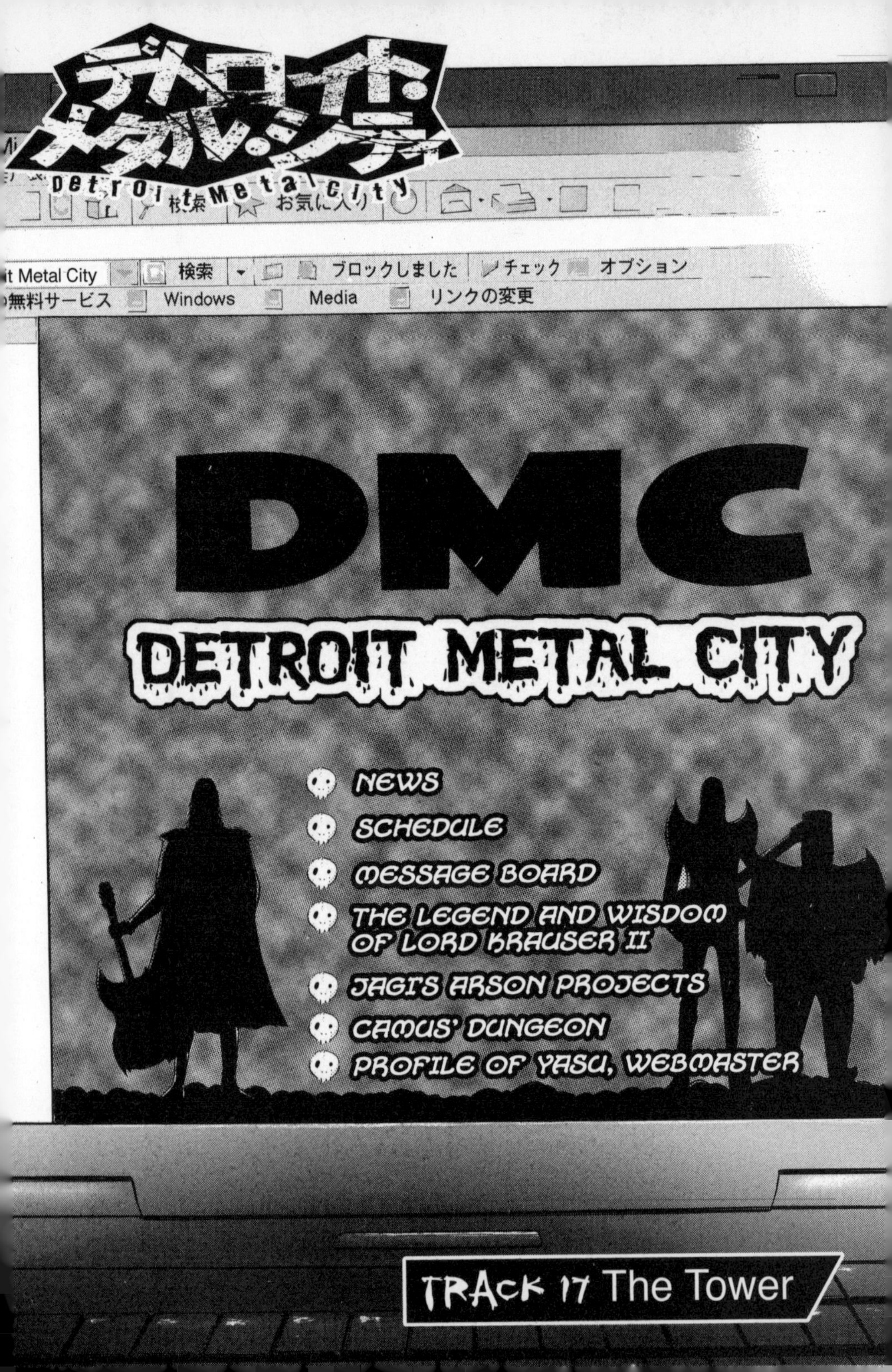
デトロイト・メタル・シティ
Detroit Metal City
お気に入り
it Metal City
検索
ブロックしました
チェック
オプション
無料サービス
Windows
Media
リンクの変更
DMC
DETROIT METAL CITY
NEWS
SCHEDULE
MESSAGE BOARD
THE LEGEND AND WISDOM OF LORD KRAUSER II
JAGI'S ARSON PROJECTS
CAMUS' DUNGEON
PROFILE OF YASU, WEBMASTER
TRACK 17 The Tower

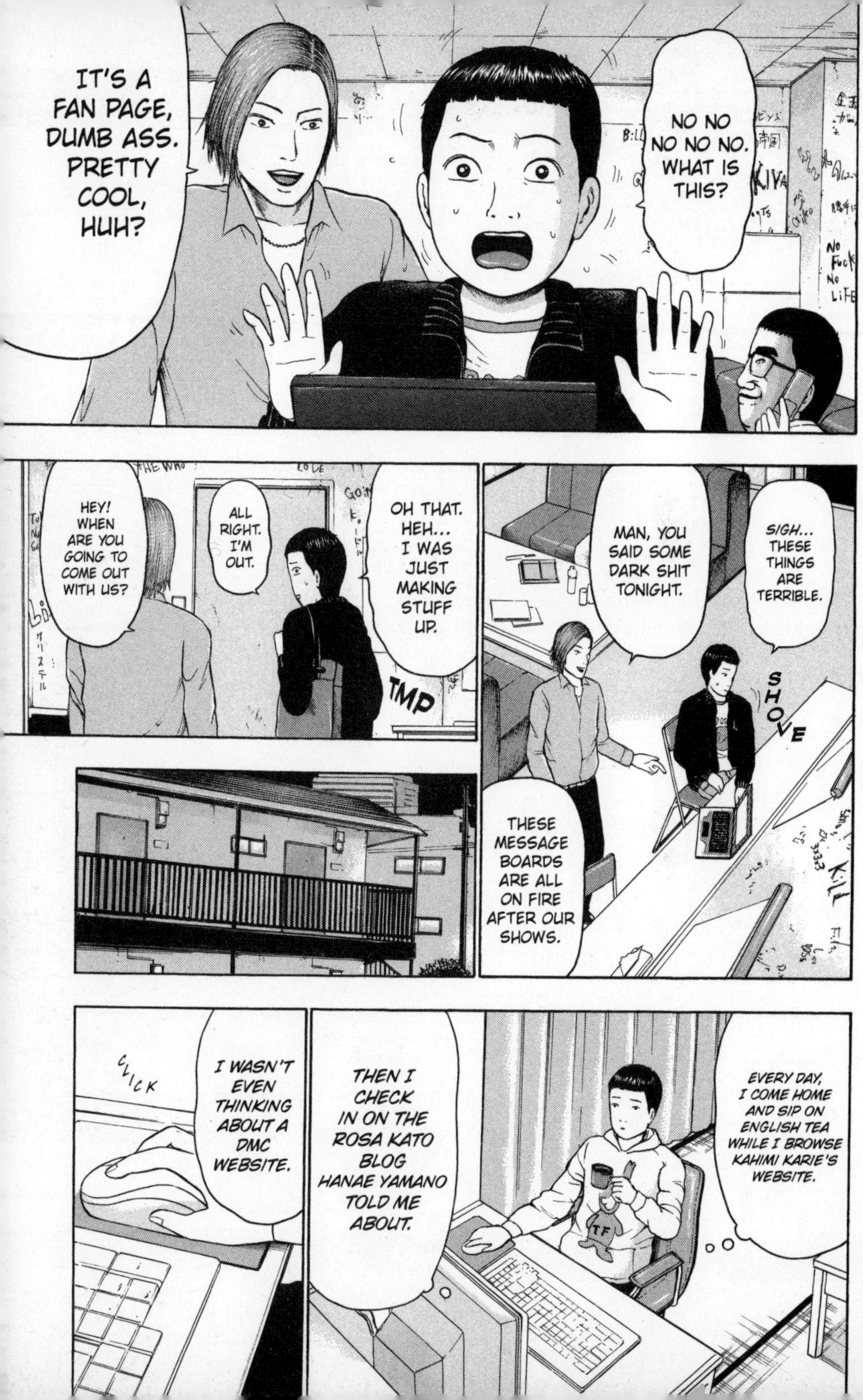

NO NO NO NO NO. WHAT IS THIS?
IT'S A FAN PAGE, DUMB ASS. PRETTY COOL, HUH?
SIGH... THESE THINGS ARE TERRIBLE.
MAN, YOU SAID SOME DARK SHIT TONIGHT.
SHOVE
THESE MESSAGE BOARDS ARE ALL ON FIRE AFTER OUR SHOWS.
OH THAT. HEH... I WAS JUST MAKING STUFF UP.
TMP
ALL RIGHT. I'M OUT.
HEY! WHEN ARE YOU GOING TO COME OUT WITH US?
EVERY DAY, I COME HOME AND SIP ON ENGLISH TEA WHILE I BROWSE KAHIMI KARIE'S WEBSITE.
THEN I CHECK IN ON THE ROSA KATO BLOG HANAE YAMANO TOLD ME ABOUT.
I WASN'T EVEN THINKING ABOUT A DMC WEBSITE.
CLICK

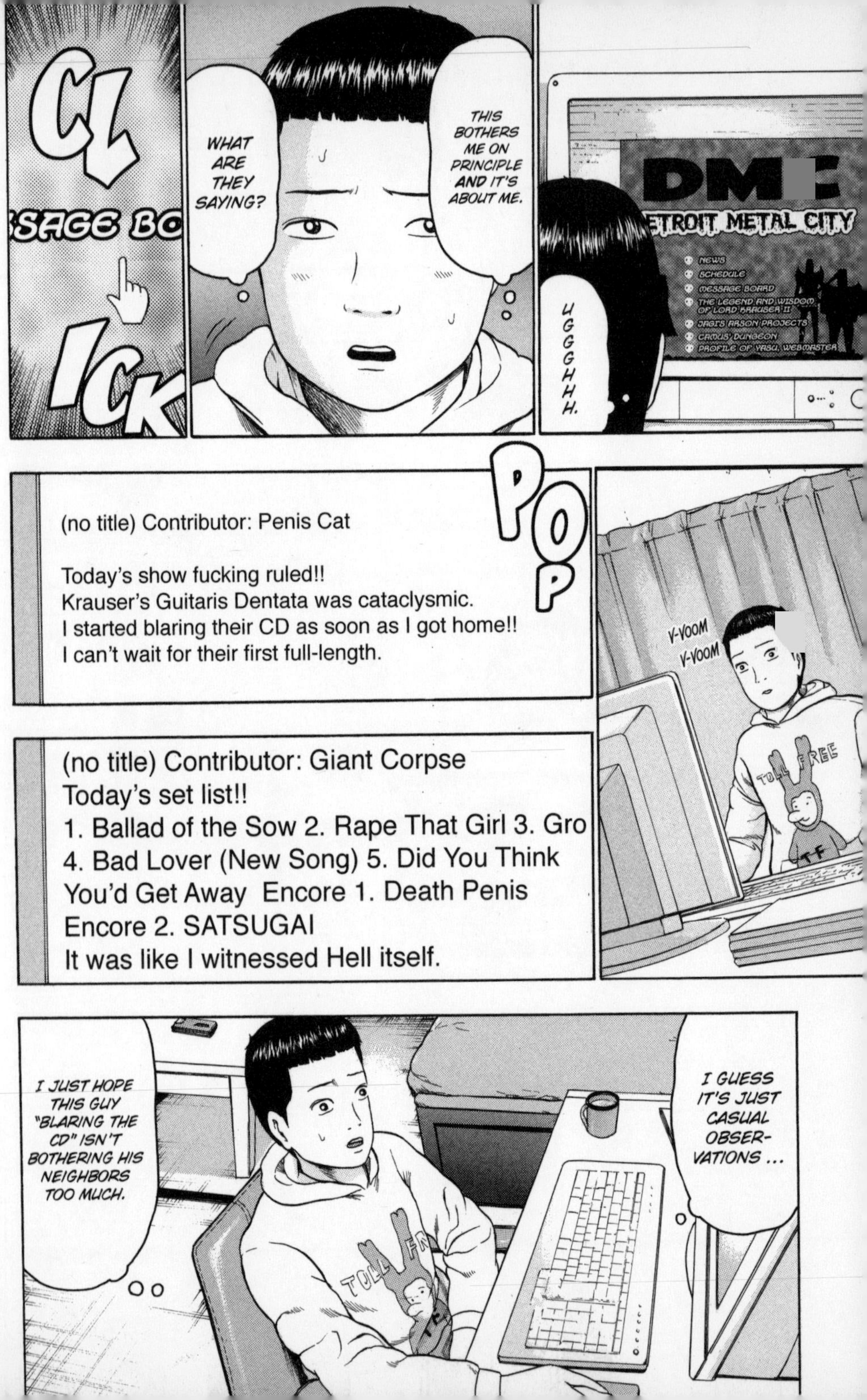
DMC
ETROIT METAL CITY
NEWS
SCHEDULE
MESSAGE BOARD
THE LEGEND AND WISDOM OF LORD KRAUSER II
JAGI'S ARSON PROJECTS
CAMUS' DUNGEON
PROFILE OF YASU, WEBMASTER
UGGGHHH.
THIS BOTHERS ME ON PRINCIPLE AND IT'S ABOUT ME.
WHAT ARE THEY SAYING?
CLICK
SAGE BO
V-VOOM
V-VOOM
TOLL FREE
POP
(no title) Contributor: Penis Cat
Today's show fucking ruled!!
Krauser's Guitaris Dentata was cataclysmic.
I started blaring their CD as soon as I got home!!
I can't wait for their first full-length.
(no title) Contributor: Giant Corpse
Today's set list!!
1. Ballad of the Sow 2. Rape That Girl 3. Gro
4. Bad Lover (New Song) 5. Did You Think
You'd Get Away Encore 1. Death Penis
Encore 2. SATSUGAI
It was like I witnessed Hell itself.
I GUESS IT'S JUST CASUAL OBSERVATIONS ...
I JUST HOPE THIS GUY "BLARING THE CD" ISN'T BOTHERING HIS NEIGHBORS TOO MUCH.

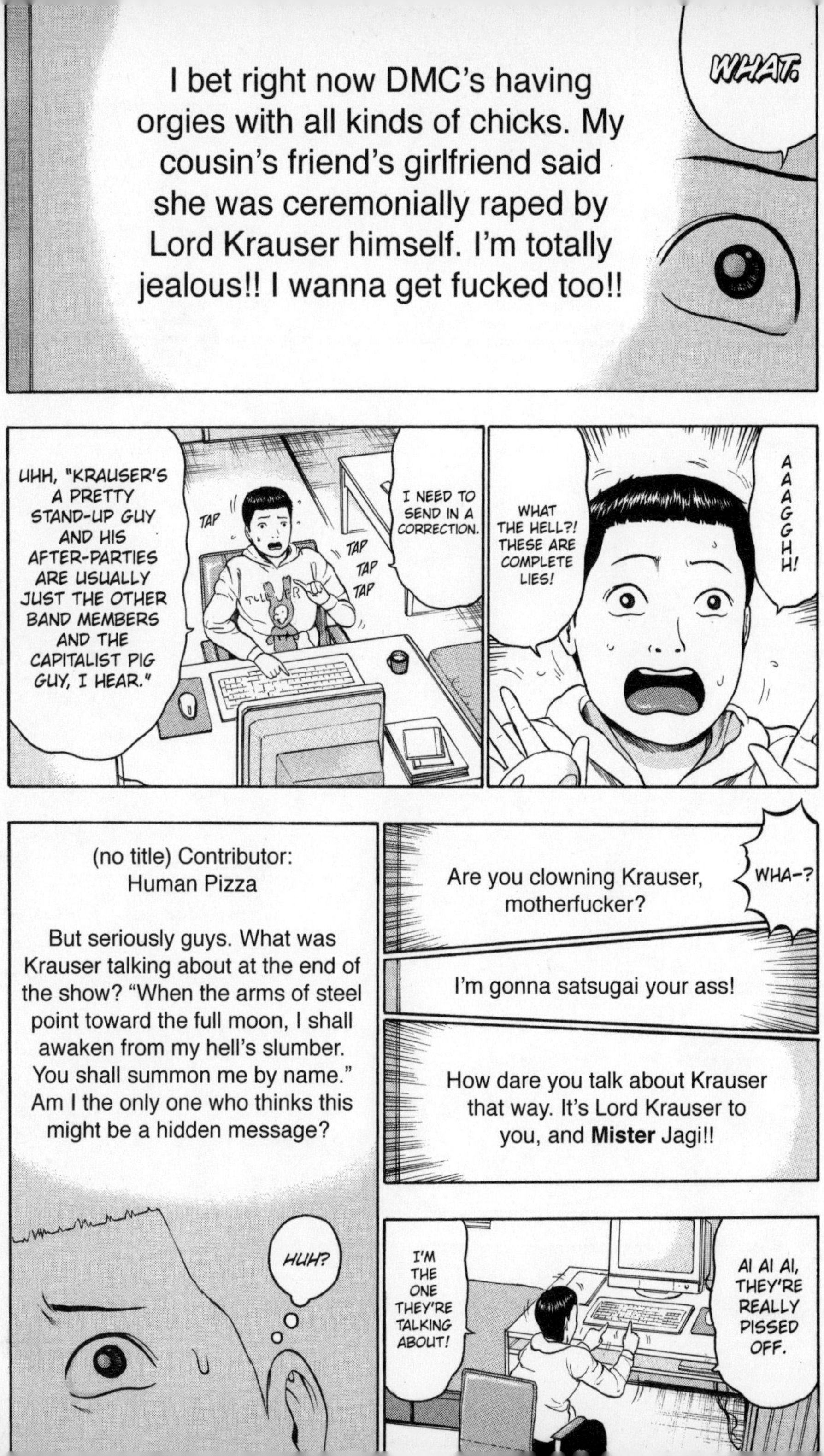
WHAT.
I bet right now DMC's having orgies with all kinds of chicks. My cousin's friend's girlfriend said she was ceremonially raped by Lord Krauser himself. I'm totally jealous!! I wanna get fucked too!!
AAAGGHH!
WHAT THE HELL?! THESE ARE COMPLETE LIES!
I NEED TO SEND IN A CORRECTION.
TAP
TAP TAP TAP
UHH, "KRAUSER'S A PRETTY STAND-UP GUY AND HIS AFTER-PARTIES ARE USUALLY JUST THE OTHER BAND MEMBERS AND THE CAPITALIST PIG GUY, I HEAR."
WHA-?
Are you clowning Krauser, motherfucker?
I'm gonna satsugai your ass!
How dare you talk about Krauser that way. It's Lord Krauser to you, and **Mister** Jagi!!
AI AI AI, THEY'RE REALLY PISSED OFF.
I'M THE ONE THEY'RE TALKING ABOUT!
(no title) Contributor: Human Pizza
But seriously guys. What was Krauser talking about at the end of the show? "When the arms of steel point toward the full moon, I shall awaken from my hell's slumber. You shall summon me by name." Am I the only one who thinks this might be a hidden message?
HUH?

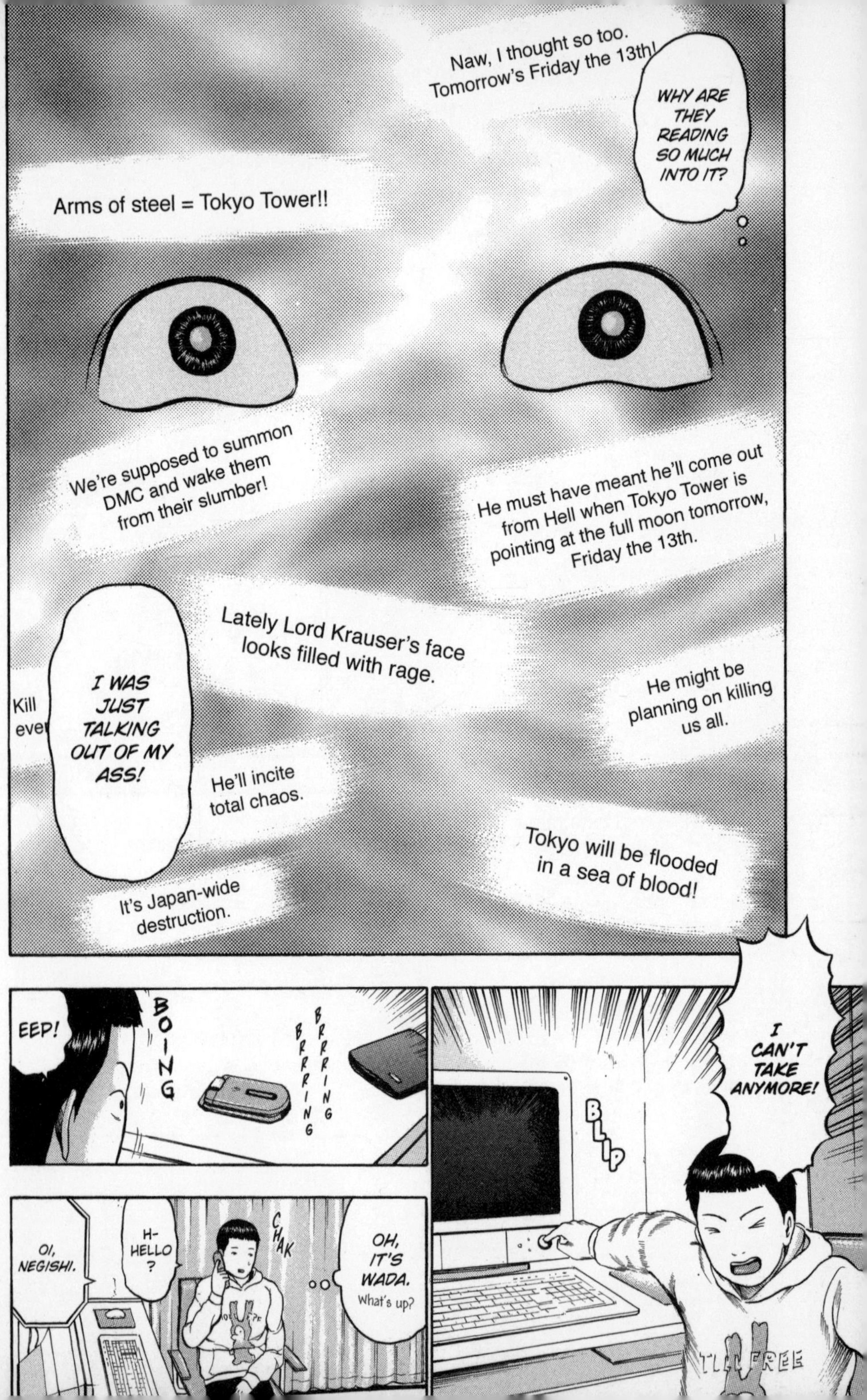
Naw, I thought so too. Tomorrow's Friday the 13th!
WHY ARE THEY READING SO MUCH INTO IT?
Arms of steel = Tokyo Tower!!
He must have meant he'll come out from Hell when Tokyo Tower is pointing at the full moon tomorrow, Friday the 13th.
We're supposed to summon DMC and wake them from their slumber!
Lately Lord Krauser's face looks filled with rage.
He might be planning on killing us all.
I WAS JUST TALKING OUT OF MY ASS!
He'll incite total chaos.
Tokyo will be flooded in a sea of blood!
It's Japan-wide destruction.
I CAN'T TAKE ANYMORE!
BLIP
BOING
BRRRING BRRRING
EEP!
OH, IT'S WADA. What's up?
CHAK
H- HELLO?
OI, NEGISHI.

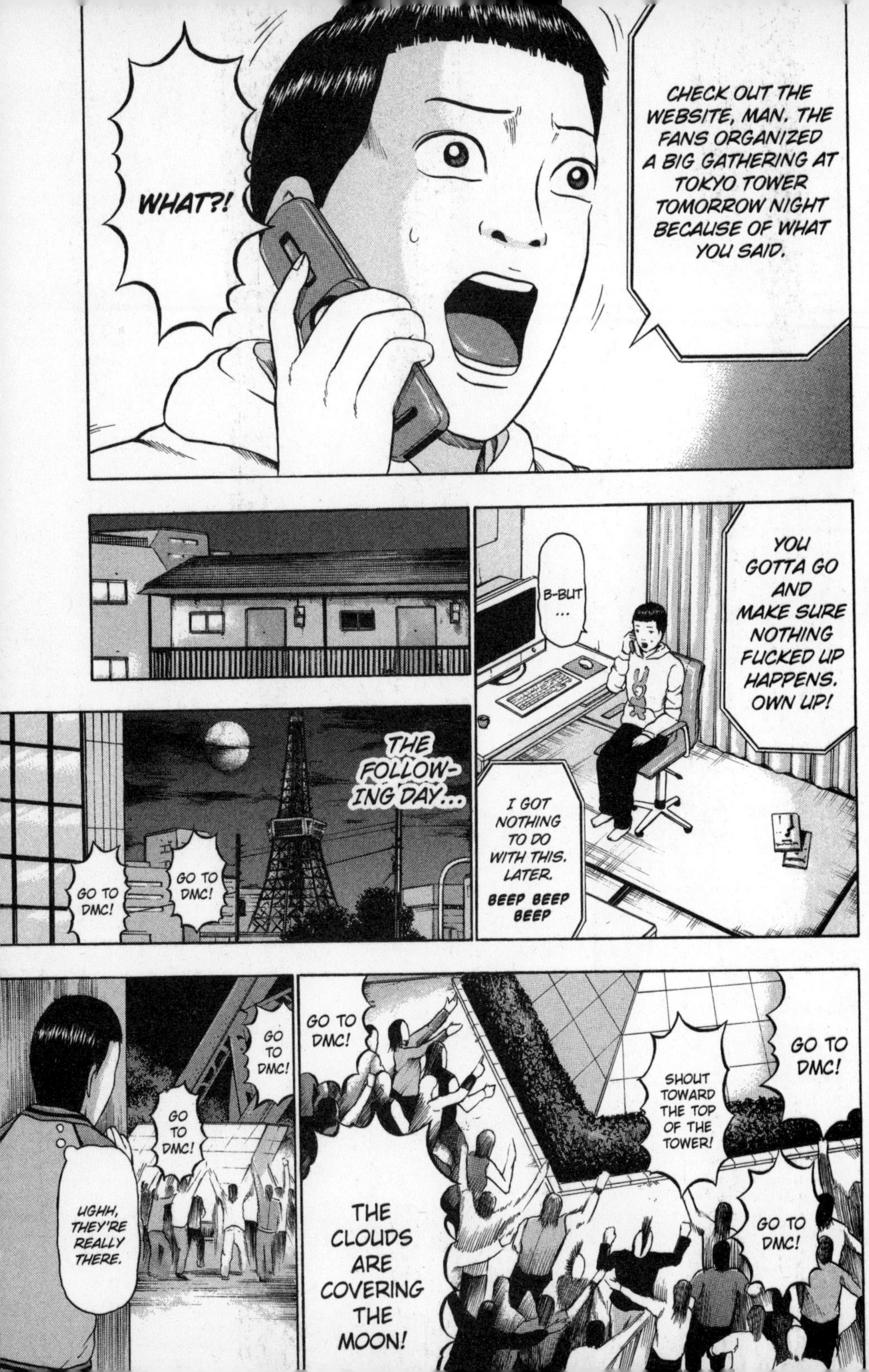
CHECK OUT THE WEBSITE, MAN. THE FANS ORGANIZED A BIG GATHERING AT TOKYO TOWER TOMORROW NIGHT BECAUSE OF WHAT YOU SAID.
WHAT?!
YOU GOTTA GO AND MAKE SURE NOTHING FUCKED UP HAPPENS. OWN UP!
B-BUT ...
I GOT NOTHING TO DO WITH THIS. LATER.
BEEP BEEP BEEP
THE FOLLOWING DAY...
GO TO DMC!
GO TO DMC!
GO TO DMC!
GO TO DMC!
SHOUT TOWARD THE TOP OF THE TOWER!
GO TO DMC!
THE CLOUDS ARE COVERING THE MOON!
GO TO DMC!
GO TO DMC!
UGHH, THEY'RE REALLY THERE.

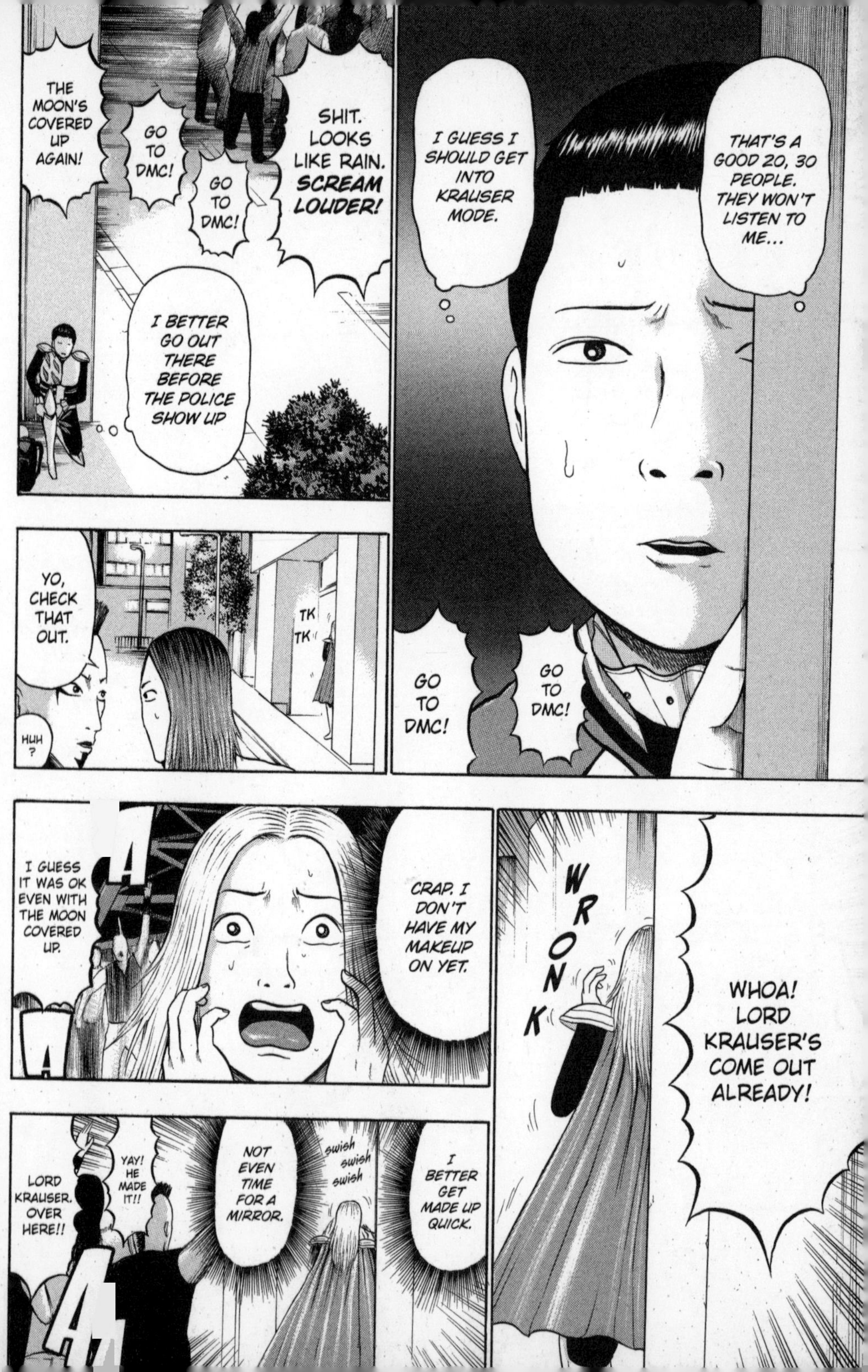
THAT'S A GOOD 20, 30 PEOPLE. THEY WON'T LISTEN TO ME...
I GUESS I SHOULD GET INTO KRAUSER MODE.
GO TO DMC!
GO TO DMC!
SHIT. LOOKS LIKE RAIN. SCREAM LOUDER!
GO TO DMC!
GO TO DMC!
THE MOON'S COVERED UP AGAIN!
I BETTER GO OUT THERE BEFORE THE POLICE SHOW UP
TK TK
YO, CHECK THAT OUT.
HUH?
WHOA! LORD KRAUSER'S COME OUT ALREADY!
WRONK
CRAP. I DON'T HAVE MY MAKEUP ON YET.
I GUESS IT WAS OK EVEN WITH THE MOON COVERED UP.
I BETTER GET MADE UP QUICK.
swish swish swish
NOT EVEN TIME FOR A MIRROR.
YAY! HE MADE IT!!
LORD KRAUSER. OVER HERE!!

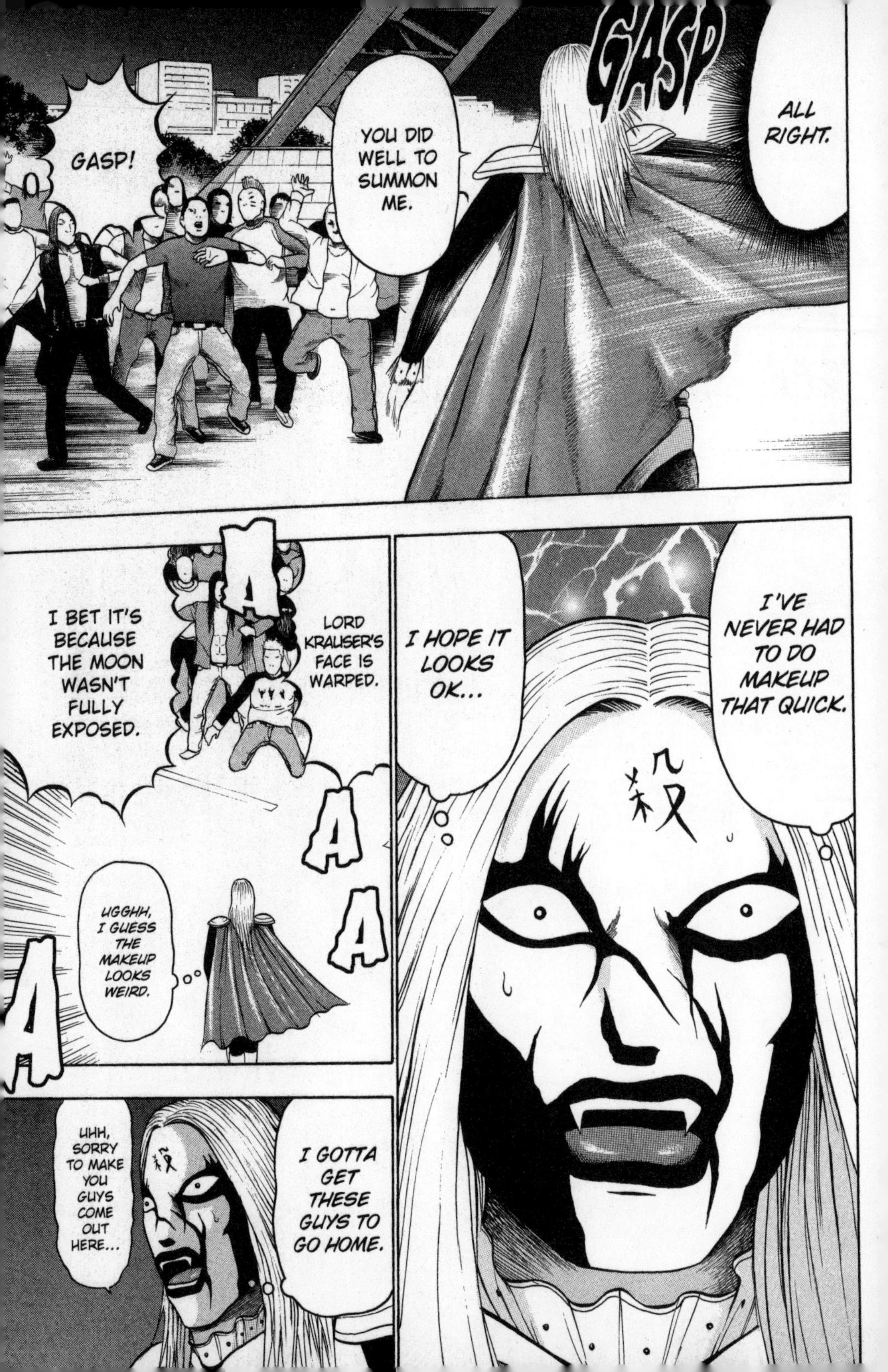
GASP
ALL RIGHT.
YOU DID WELL TO SUMMON ME.
GASP!
I'VE NEVER HAD TO DO MAKEUP THAT QUICK.
I HOPE IT LOOKS OK...
LORD KRAUSER'S FACE IS WARPED.
I BET IT'S BECAUSE THE MOON WASN'T FULLY EXPOSED.
A A A A
UGGHH, I GUESS THE MAKEUP LOOKS WEIRD.
I GOTTA GET THESE GUYS TO GO HOME.
UHH, SORRY TO MAKE YOU GUYS COME OUT HERE...

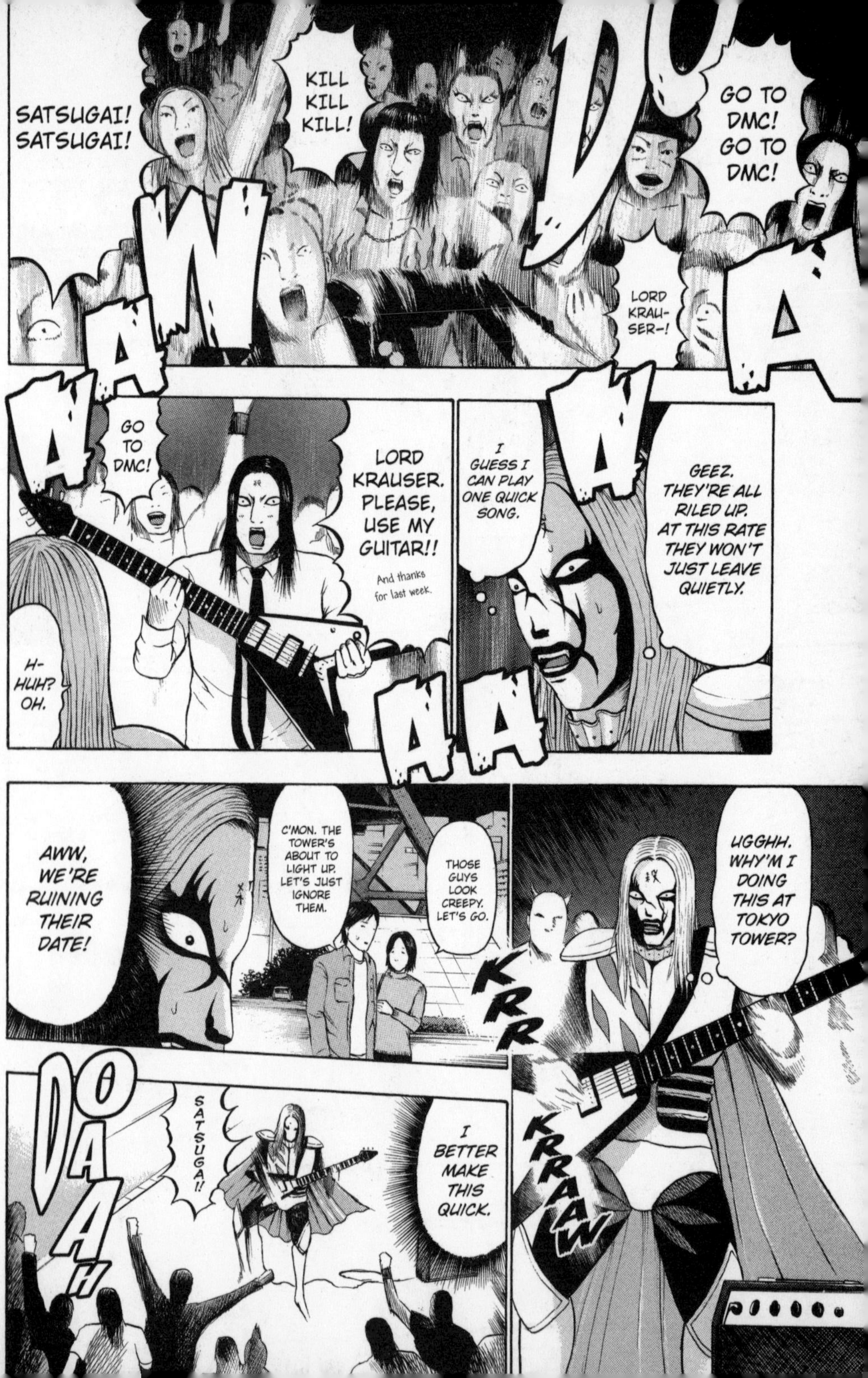
GO TO DMC! GO TO DMC!
LORD KRAU-SER-!
KILL KILL KILL!
SATSUGAI! SATSUGAI!
GEEZ. THEY'RE ALL RILED UP. AT THIS RATE THEY WON'T JUST LEAVE QUIETLY.
I GUESS I CAN PLAY ONE QUICK SONG.
LORD KRAUSER. PLEASE, USE MY GUITAR!!
And thanks for last week.
GO TO DMC!
H-HUH? OH.
UGGHH. WHY'M I DOING THIS AT TOKYO TOWER?
KRR
THOSE GUYS LOOK CREEPY. LET'S GO.
C'MON. THE TOWER'S ABOUT TO LIGHT UP. LET'S JUST IGNORE THEM.
AWW, WE'RE RUINING THEIR DATE!
KRRAAW
I BETTER MAKE THIS QUICK.
SATSUGAI!!
DOAAAH

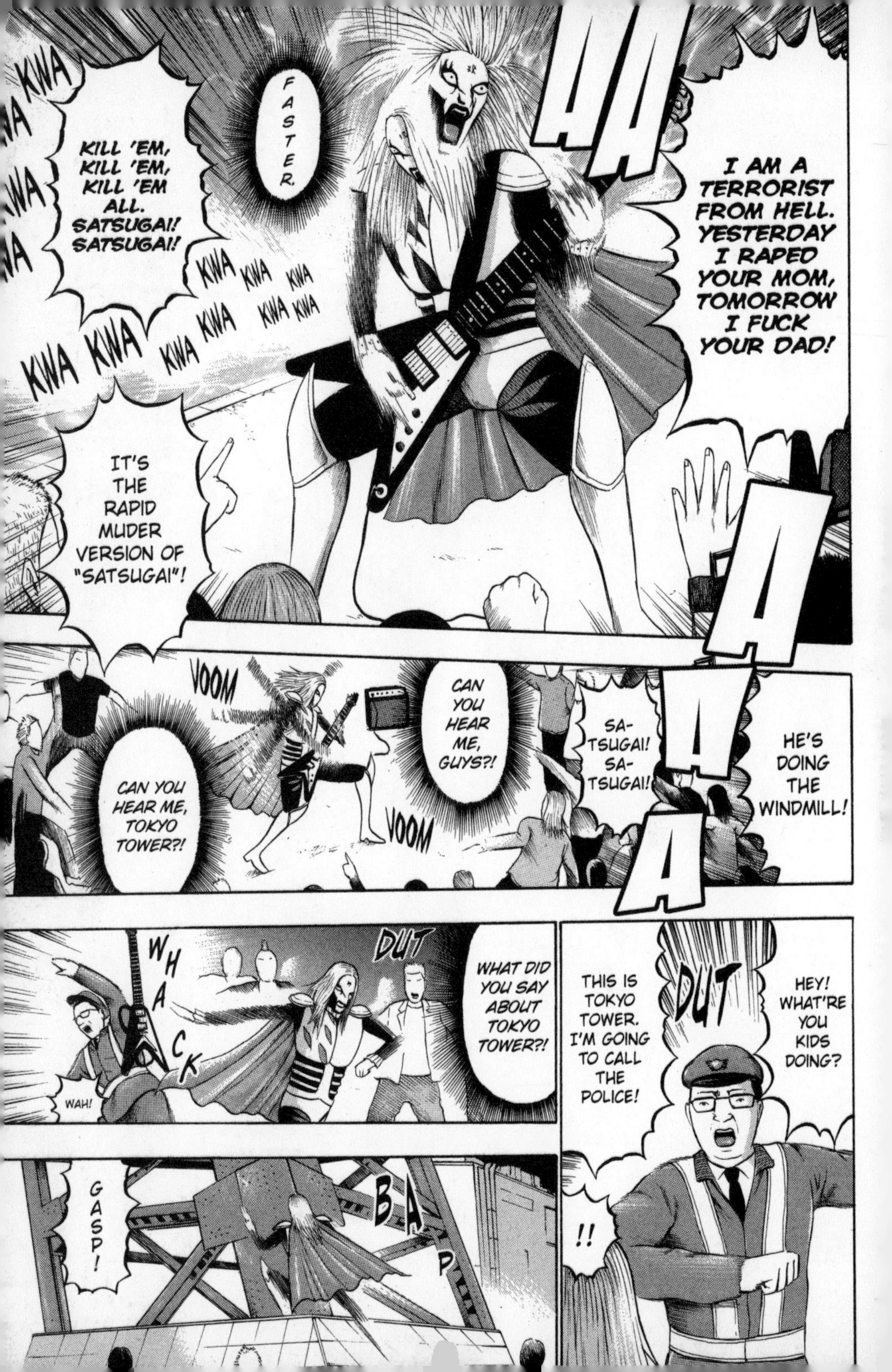

AA
I AM A TERRORIST FROM HELL. YESTERDAY I RAPED YOUR MOM, TOMORROW I FUCK YOUR DAD!
FASTER.
KILL 'EM, KILL 'EM, KILL 'EM ALL. SATSUGAI! SATSUGAI!
KWA KWA KWA KWA
KWA KWA KWA KWA KWA KWA KWA KWA KWA
IT'S THE RAPID MUDER VERSION OF "SATSUGAI"!
A
HE'S DOING THE WINDMILL!
SA-TSUGAI! SA-TSUGAI!
A
A
CAN YOU HEAR ME, GUYS?!
VOOM
VOOM
CAN YOU HEAR ME, TOKYO TOWER?!
HEY! WHAT'RE YOU KIDS DOING?
DUT
THIS IS TOKYO TOWER. I'M GOING TO CALL THE POLICE!
!!
WHAT DID YOU SAY ABOUT TOKYO TOWER?!
DUT
WHACK
WAH!
BAP
GASP!

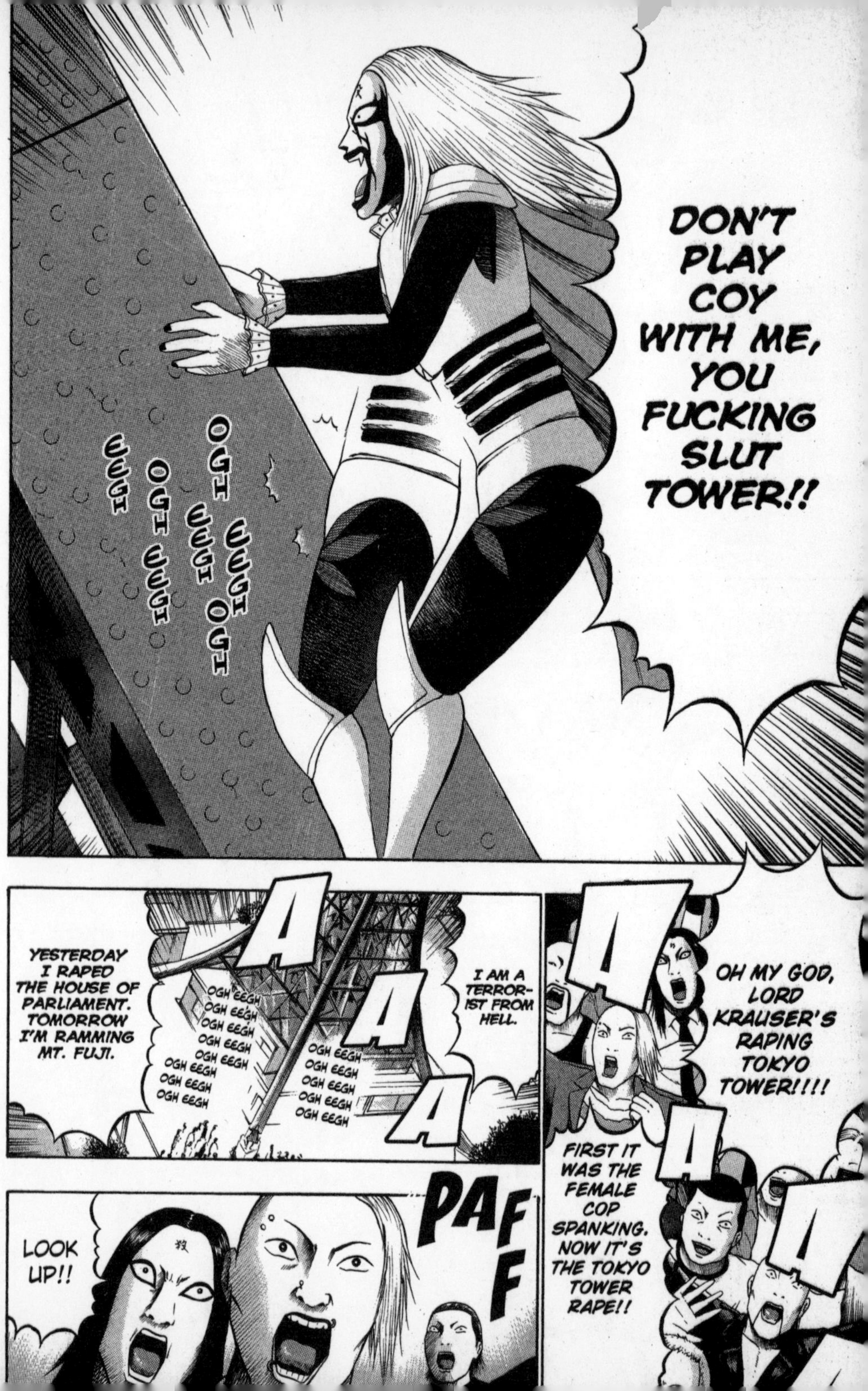
DON'T PLAY COY WITH ME, YOU FUCKING SLUT TOWER!!
OGH EEGH OGH EEGH OGH EEGH
OGH EEGH OGH EEGH
A A A A
OH MY GOD, LORD KRAUSER'S RAPING TOKYO TOWER!!!!
FIRST IT WAS THE FEMALE COP SPANKING. NOW IT'S THE TOKYO TOWER RAPE!!
A A A
I AM A TERRORIST FROM HELL.
OGH EEGH OGH EEGH OGH EEGH OGH EEGH OGH EEGH
YESTERDAY I RAPED THE HOUSE OF PARLIAMENT. TOMORROW I'M RAMMING MT. FUJI.
OGH EEGH OGH EEGH OGH EEGH OGH EEGH OGH EEGH OGH EEGH OGH EEGH OGH EEGH
PAFF
LOOK UP!!

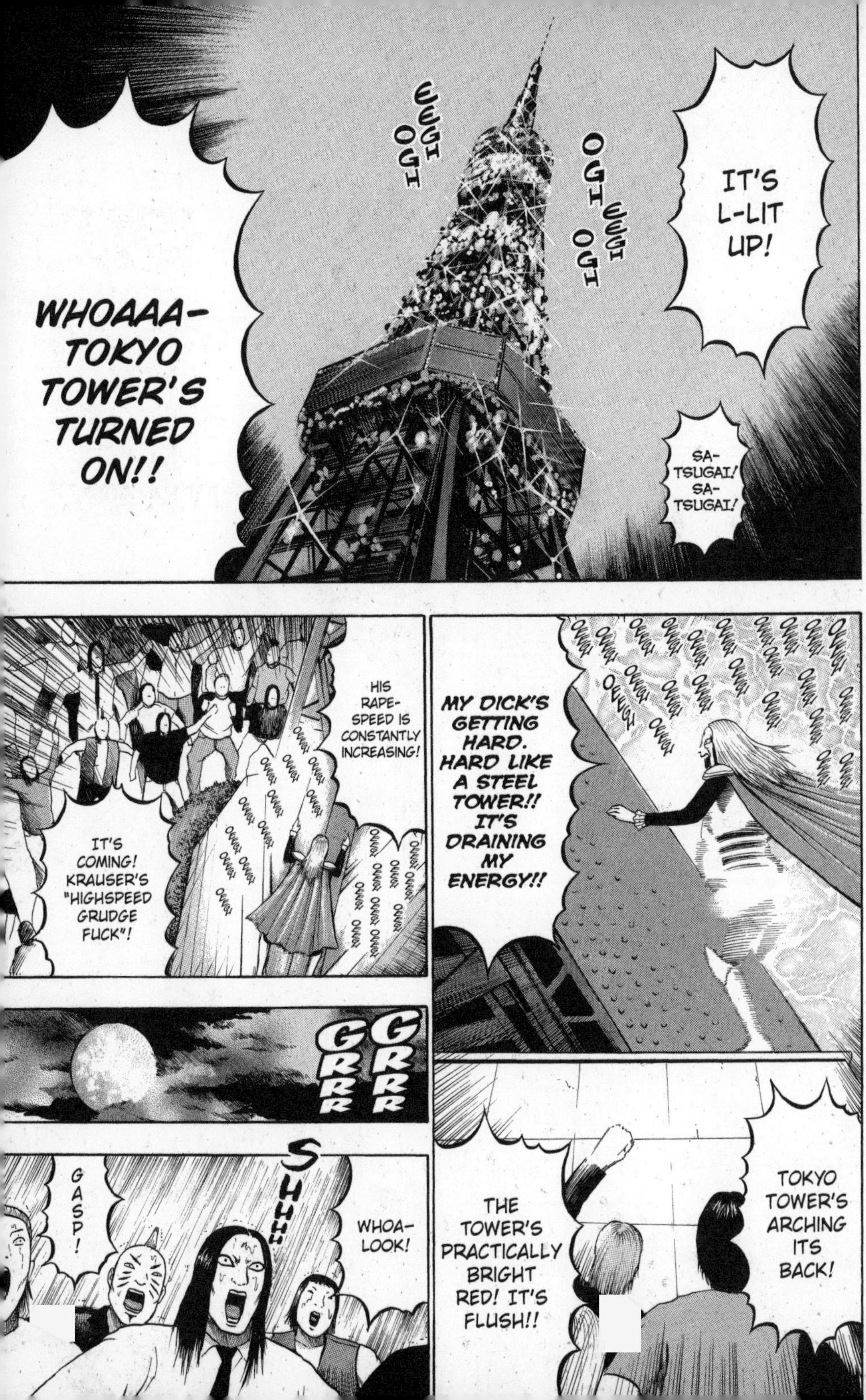
IT'S L-LIT UP!
OGH EEGH OGH
SA-TSUGAI! SA-TSUGAI!
OGH EEGH OGH
WHOAAA-TOKYO TOWER'S TURNED ON!!
MY DICK'S GETTING HARD. HARD LIKE A STEEL TOWER!! IT'S DRAINING MY ENERGY!!
HIS RAPE-SPEED IS CONSTANTLY INCREASING!
IT'S COMING! KRAUSER'S "HIGHSPEED GRUDGE FUCK"!
TOKYO TOWER'S ARCHING ITS BACK!
THE TOWER'S PRACTICALLY BRIGHT RED! IT'S FLUSH!!
GGRRR GRRR
SHHHH
WHOA-LOOK!
GASP!

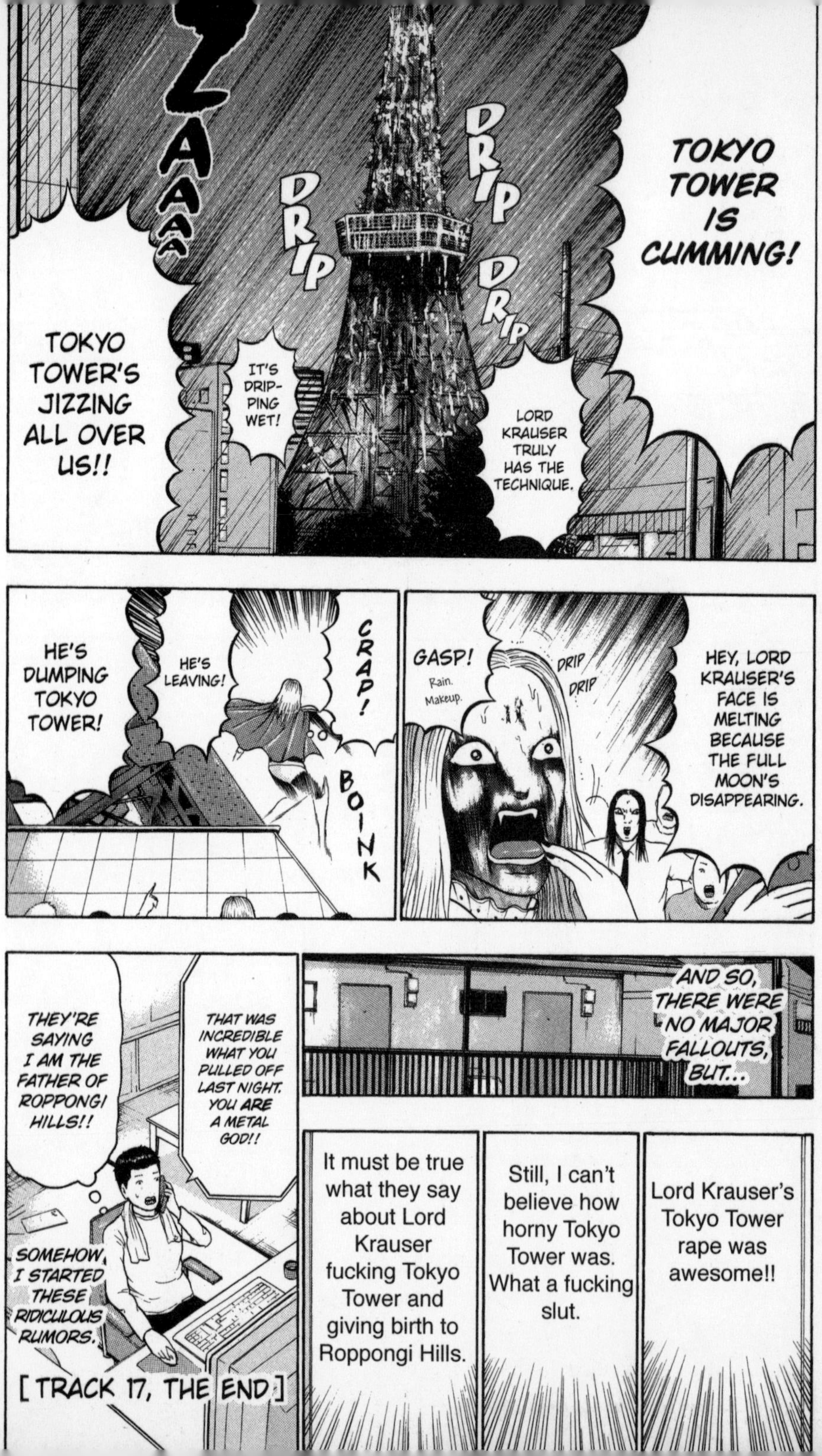
TOKYO TOWER IS CUMMING!
DRIP DRIP
DRIP DRIP
LORD KRAUSER TRULY HAS THE TECHNIQUE.
IT'S DRIP-PING WET!
TOKYO TOWER'S JIZZING ALL OVER US!!
ZAAAA
HEY, LORD KRAUSER'S FACE IS MELTING BECAUSE THE FULL MOON'S DISAPPEARING.
DRIP DRIP
GASP!
Rain.
Makeup.
CRAP!
BOINK
HE'S LEAVING!
HE'S DUMPING TOKYO TOWER!
AND SO, THERE WERE NO MAJOR FALLOUTS, BUT...
Lord Krauser's Tokyo Tower rape was awesome!!
Still, I can't believe how horny Tokyo Tower was. What a fucking slut.
It must be true what they say about Lord Krauser fucking Tokyo Tower and giving birth to Roppongi Hills.
THAT WAS INCREDIBLE WHAT YOU PULLED OFF LAST NIGHT. YOU ARE A METAL GOD!!
THEY'RE SAYING I AM THE FATHER OF ROPPONGI HILLS!!
SOMEHOW I STARTED THESE RIDICULOUS RUMORS.
[TRACK 17, THE END]

DMC LEXICON

🐱 TOKYO TOWER

A 333-meter radio tower capable of sending all kinds of television and radio transmissions. Its proper name is Japan Radio Tower. It is a popular tourist landmark. It looks down on men every day because it's such a popular site, but it's easy to turn on and is always pulsing red.

Usage: Aw baby, sorry. I met another tower. We can't go out anymore.

デトロイト・メタル・シティ
Detroit Metal City

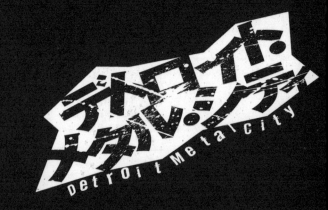

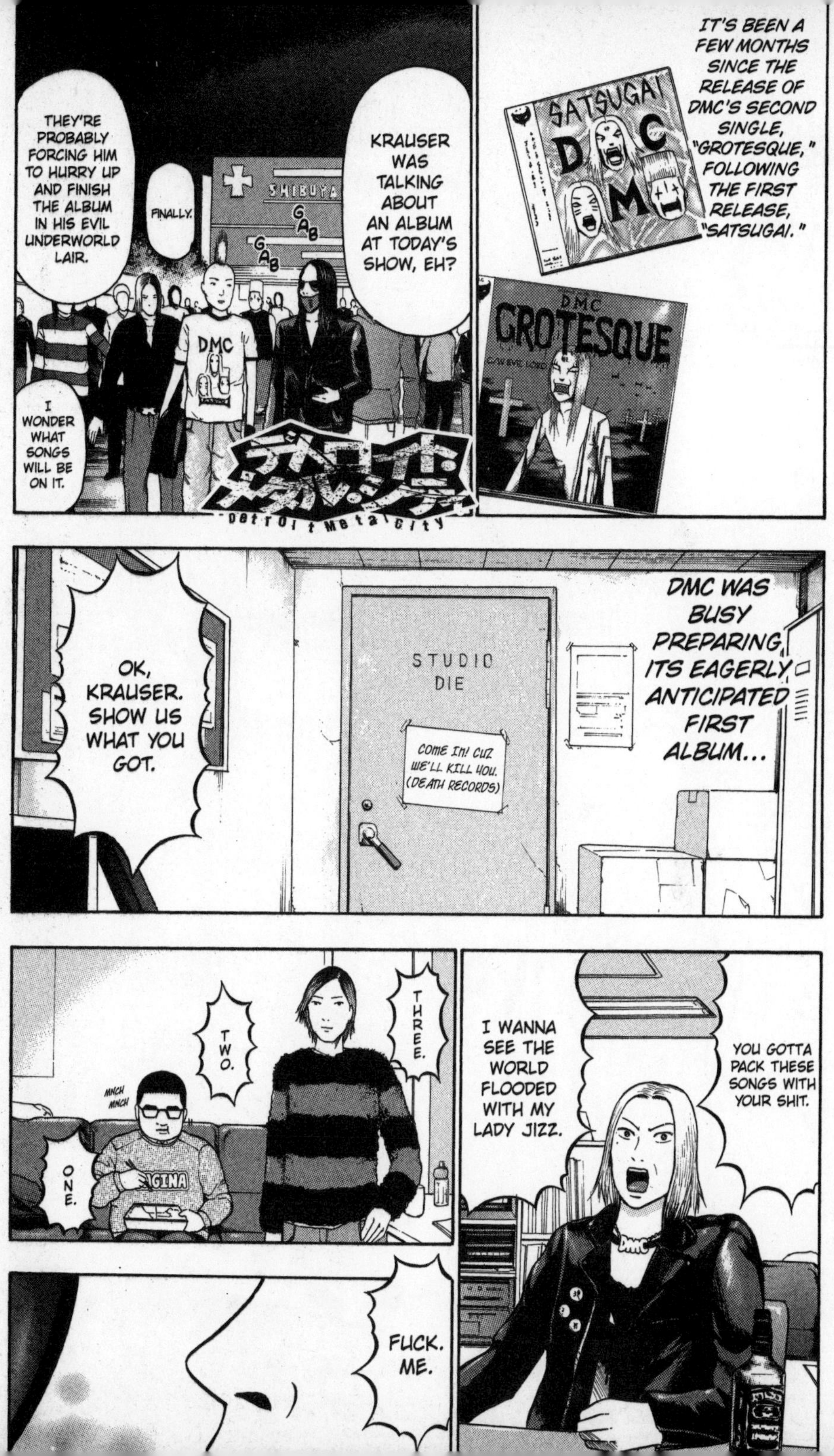
IT'S BEEN A FEW MONTHS SINCE THE RELEASE OF DMC'S SECOND SINGLE, "GROTESQUE," FOLLOWING THE FIRST RELEASE, "SATSUGAI."
SATSUGAI
DMC
DMC
GROTESQUE
C/W EVIL LORD
KRAUSER WAS TALKING ABOUT AN ALBUM AT TODAY'S SHOW, EH?
FINALLY.
THEY'RE PROBABLY FORCING HIM TO HURRY UP AND FINISH THE ALBUM IN HIS EVIL UNDERWORLD LAIR.
SHIBUYA
GAB
GAB
DMC
I WONDER WHAT SONGS WILL BE ON IT.
Detroit Metal City
DMC WAS BUSY PREPARING ITS EAGERLY ANTICIPATED FIRST ALBUM...
STUDIO DIE
COME IN! CUZ WE'LL KILL YOU. (DEATH RECORDS)
OK, KRAUSER. SHOW US WHAT YOU GOT.
YOU GOTTA PACK THESE SONGS WITH YOUR SHIT.
I WANNA SEE THE WORLD FLOODED WITH MY LADY JIZZ.
DMC
THREE.
TWO.
MNCH MNCH
ONE.
FUCK. ME.

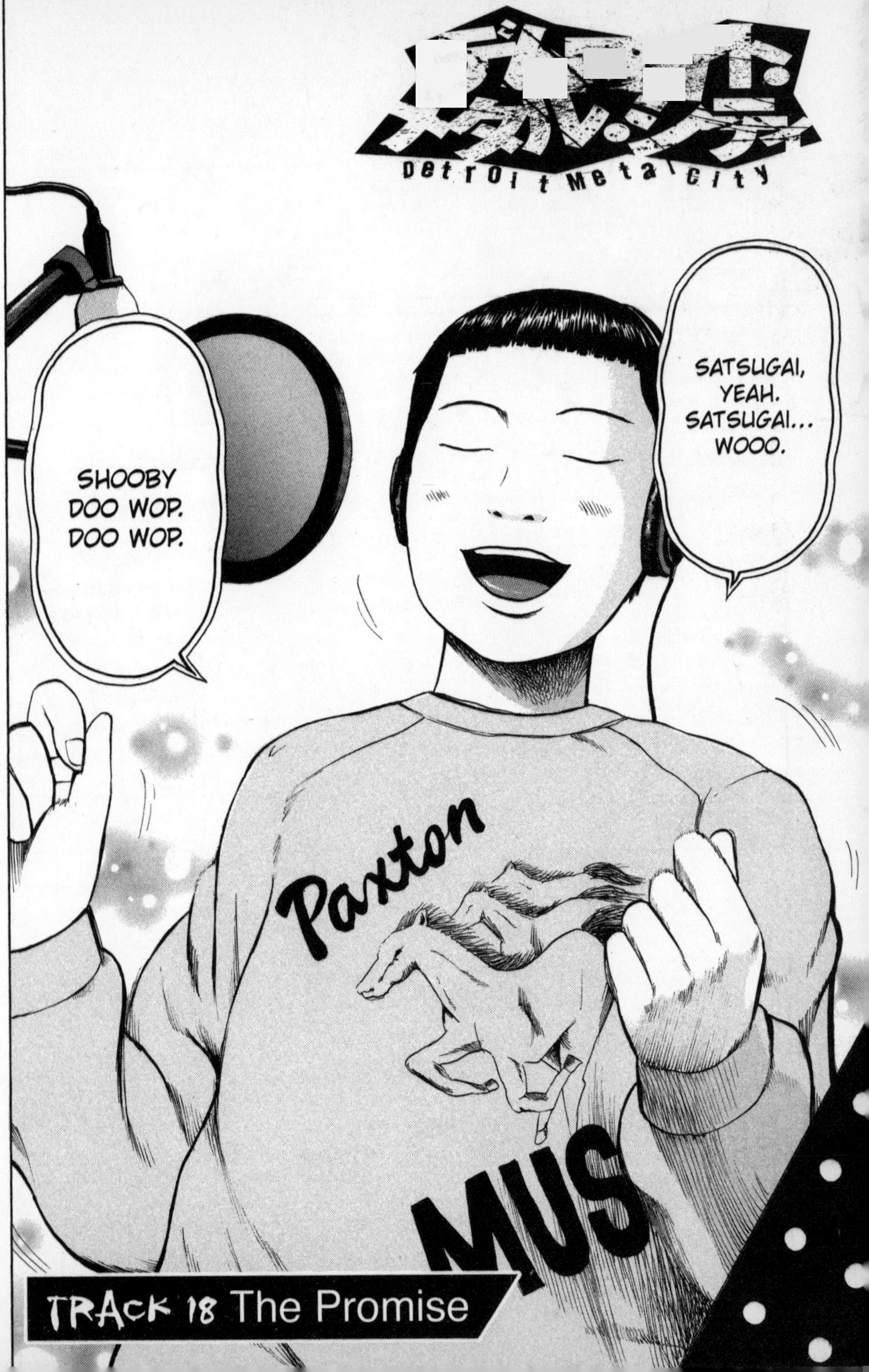
Detroit Metal City
SATSUGAI, YEAH. SATSUGAI... WOOO.
SHOOBY DOO WOP. DOO WOP.
Paxton
MUS
TRACK 18 The Promise

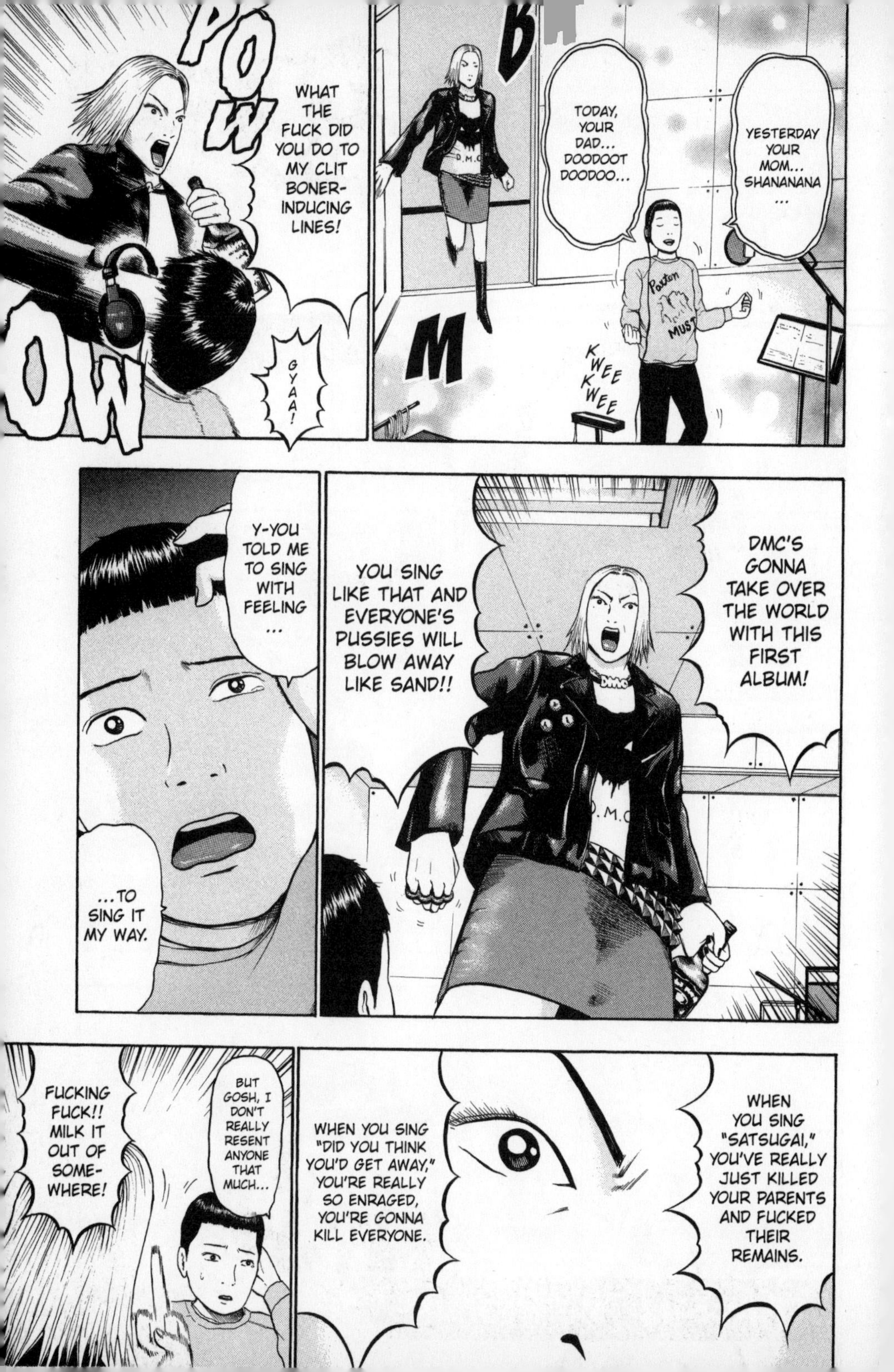
YESTERDAY YOUR MOM... SHANANANA ...
TODAY, YOUR DAD... DOODOOT DOODOO...
B
M
KWEE KWEE
POW
WHAT THE FUCK DID YOU DO TO MY CLIT BONER-INDUCING LINES!
GYAA!
OW
DMC'S GONNA TAKE OVER THE WORLD WITH THIS FIRST ALBUM!
YOU SING LIKE THAT AND EVERYONE'S PUSSIES WILL BLOW AWAY LIKE SAND!!
Y-YOU TOLD ME TO SING WITH FEELING ...
...TO SING IT MY WAY.
WHEN YOU SING "SATSUGAI," YOU'VE REALLY JUST KILLED YOUR PARENTS AND FUCKED THEIR REMAINS.
WHEN YOU SING "DID YOU THINK YOU'D GET AWAY," YOU'RE REALLY SO ENRAGED, YOU'RE GONNA KILL EVERYONE.
BUT GOSH, I DON'T REALLY RESENT ANYONE THAT MUCH...
FUCKING FUCK!! MILK IT OUT OF SOME-WHERE!

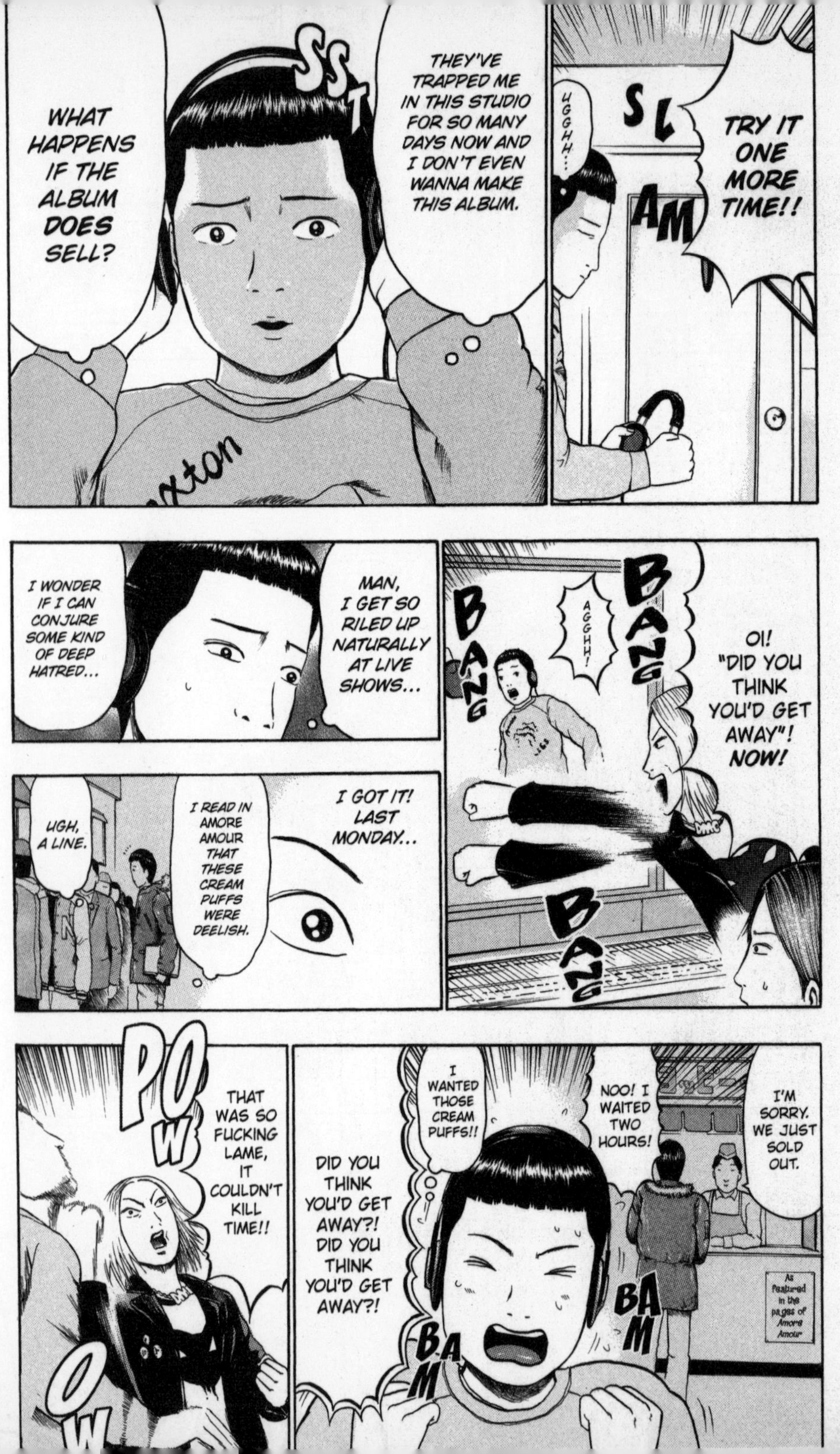
TRY IT ONE MORE TIME!!
SLAM
UGGHH...
THEY'VE TRAPPED ME IN THIS STUDIO FOR SO MANY DAYS NOW AND I DON'T EVEN WANNA MAKE THIS ALBUM.
SST
WHAT HAPPENS IF THE ALBUM DOES SELL?
OI! "DID YOU THINK YOU'D GET AWAY"! NOW!
BANG
AGGHH!
BANG
BANG
MAN, I GET SO RILED UP NATURALLY AT LIVE SHOWS...
I WONDER IF I CAN CONJURE SOME KIND OF DEEP HATRED...
I GOT IT! LAST MONDAY...
I READ IN AMORE AMOUR THAT THESE CREAM PUFFS WERE DEELISH.
UGH, A LINE.
I'M SORRY. WE JUST SOLD OUT.
NOO! I WAITED TWO HOURS!
I WANTED THOSE CREAM PUFFS!!
As Featured in the pages of Amore Amour
BAM
DID YOU THINK YOU'D GET AWAY?! DID YOU THINK YOU'D GET AWAY?!
BAM
POW
THAT WAS SO FUCKING LAME, IT COULDN'T KILL TIME!!
OOW

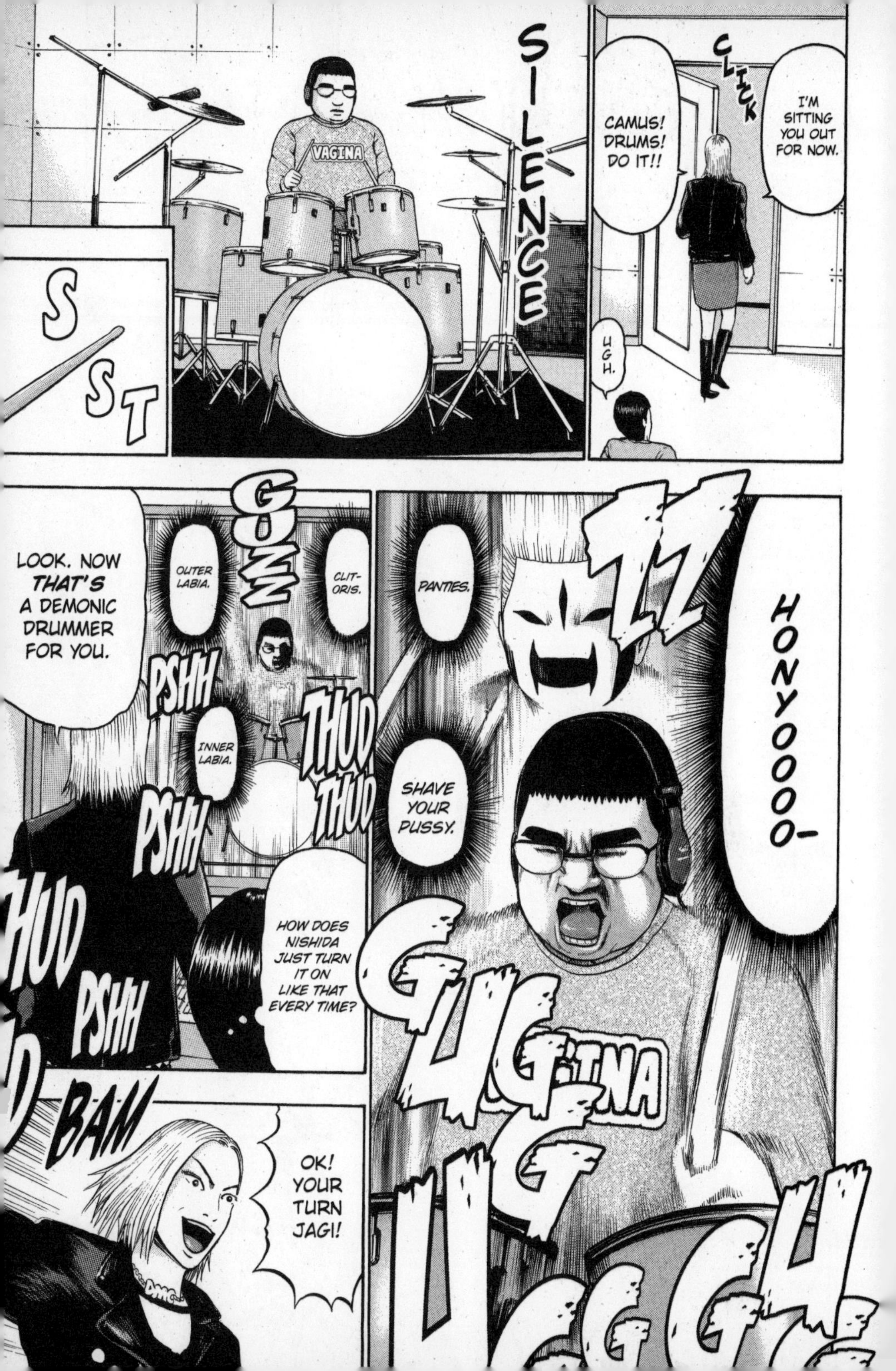
CLICK
I'M SITTING YOU OUT FOR NOW.
CAMUS! DRUMS! DO IT!!
UGH.
SILENCE
SST
HONYOOOOO-
PANTIES.
CLIT-ORIS.
OUTER LABIA.
LOOK. NOW *THAT'S* A DEMONIC DRUMMER FOR YOU.
SHAVE YOUR PUSSY.
INNER LABIA.
THUD
THUD THUD
PSHH
PSHH
THUD
PSHH
HOW DOES NISHIDA JUST TURN IT ON LIKE THAT EVERY TIME?
BAM
OK! YOUR TURN JAGI!

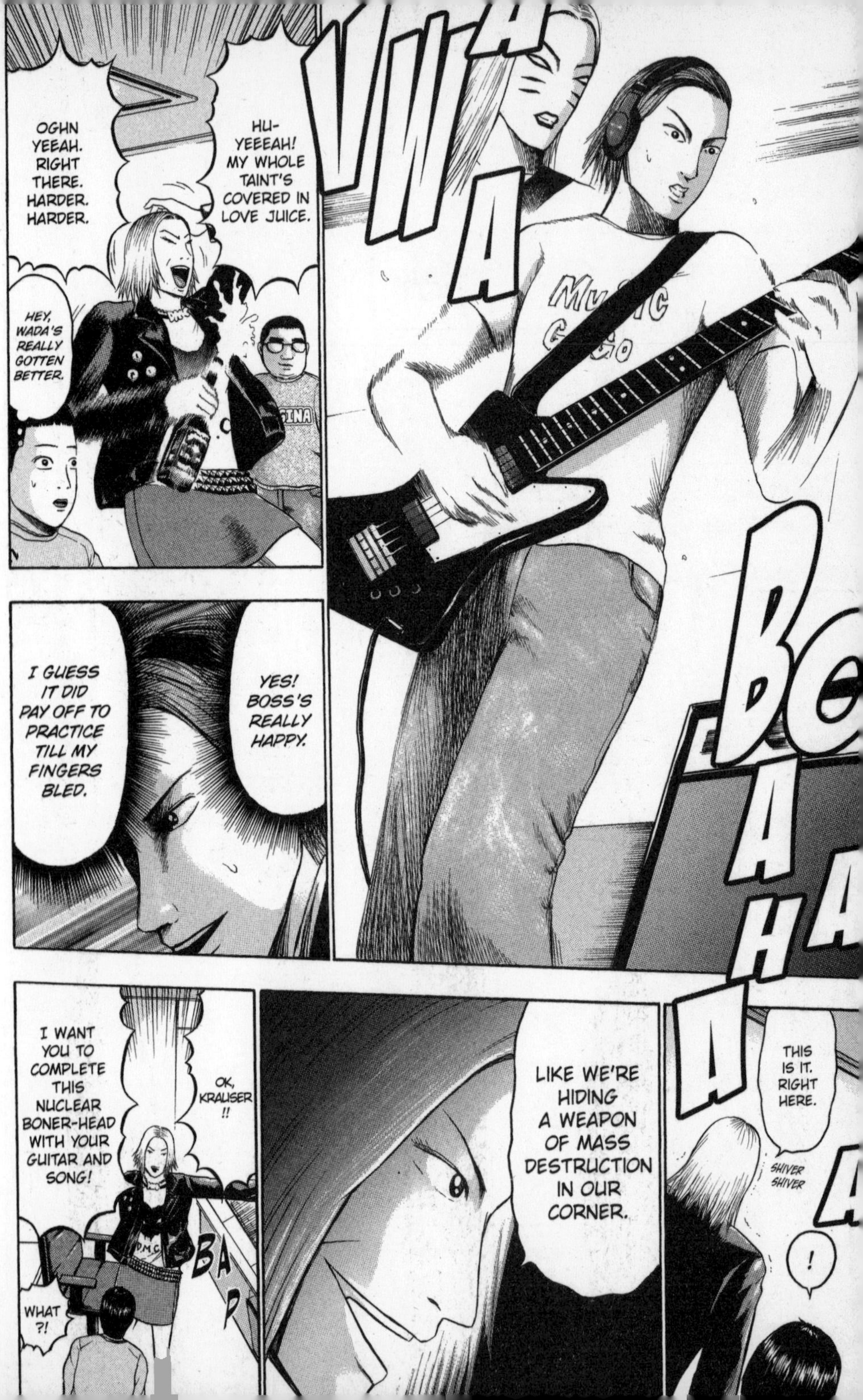
VWAA
BOAAHAHA
HU-YEEEAH! MY WHOLE TAINT'S COVERED IN LOVE JUICE.
OGHN YEEAH. RIGHT THERE. HARDER. HARDER.
HEY, WADA'S REALLY GOTTEN BETTER.
YES! BOSS'S REALLY HAPPY.
I GUESS IT DID PAY OFF TO PRACTICE TILL MY FINGERS BLED.
THIS IS IT. RIGHT HERE.
SHIVER SHIVER
!
LIKE WE'RE HIDING A WEAPON OF MASS DESTRUCTION IN OUR CORNER.
OK, KRAUSER!!
I WANT YOU TO COMPLETE THIS NUCLEAR BONER-HEAD WITH YOUR GUITAR AND SONG!
BAP
WHAT?!

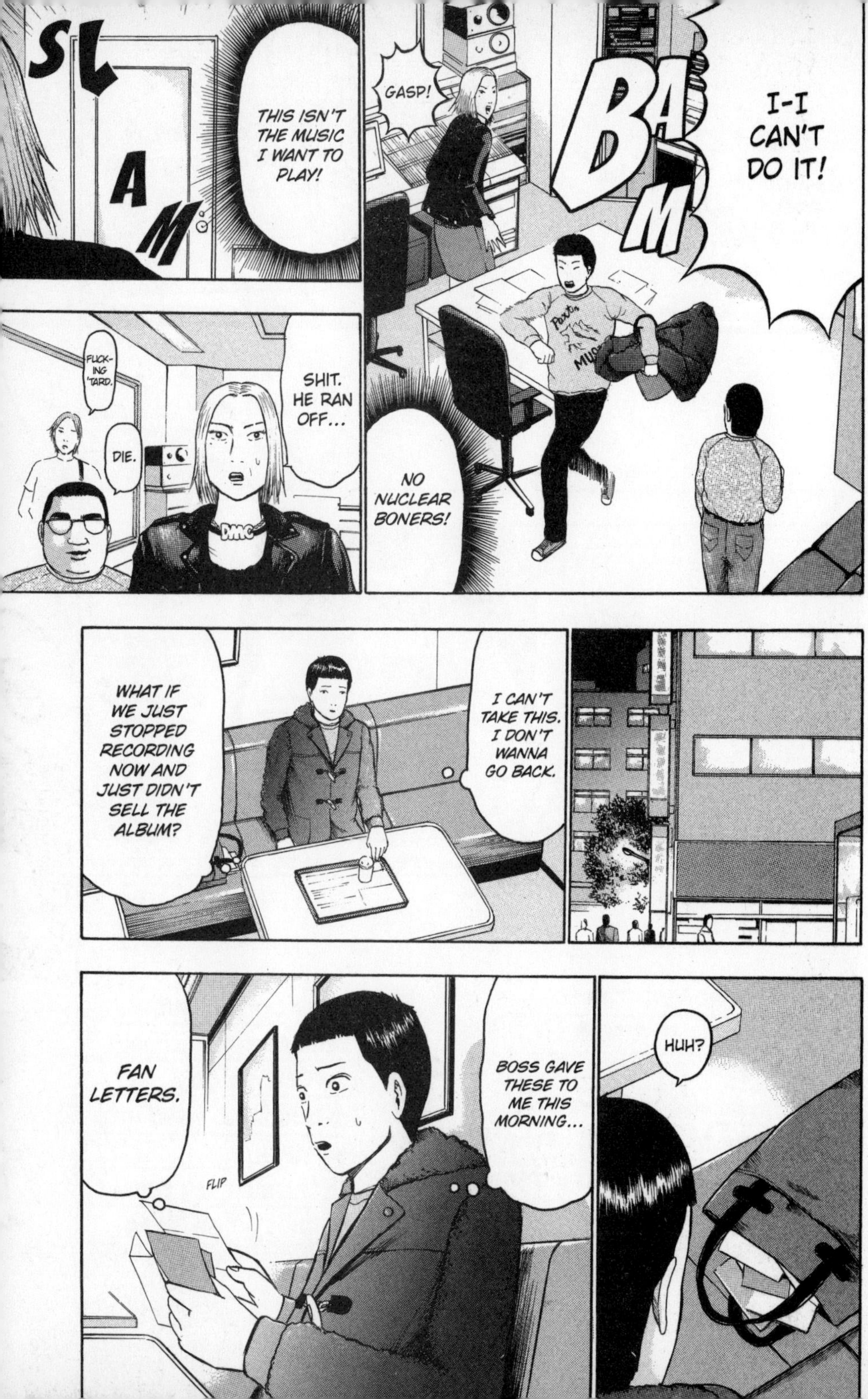
I-I CAN'T DO IT!
BAM
GASP!
NO NUCLEAR BONERS!
SLAM
THIS ISN'T THE MUSIC I WANT TO PLAY!
SHIT. HE RAN OFF...
FUCKING 'TARD.
DIE.
I CAN'T TAKE THIS. I DON'T WANNA GO BACK.
WHAT IF WE JUST STOPPED RECORDING NOW AND JUST DIDN'T SELL THE ALBUM?
HUH?
BOSS GAVE THESE TO ME THIS MORNING...
FAN LETTERS.
FLIP

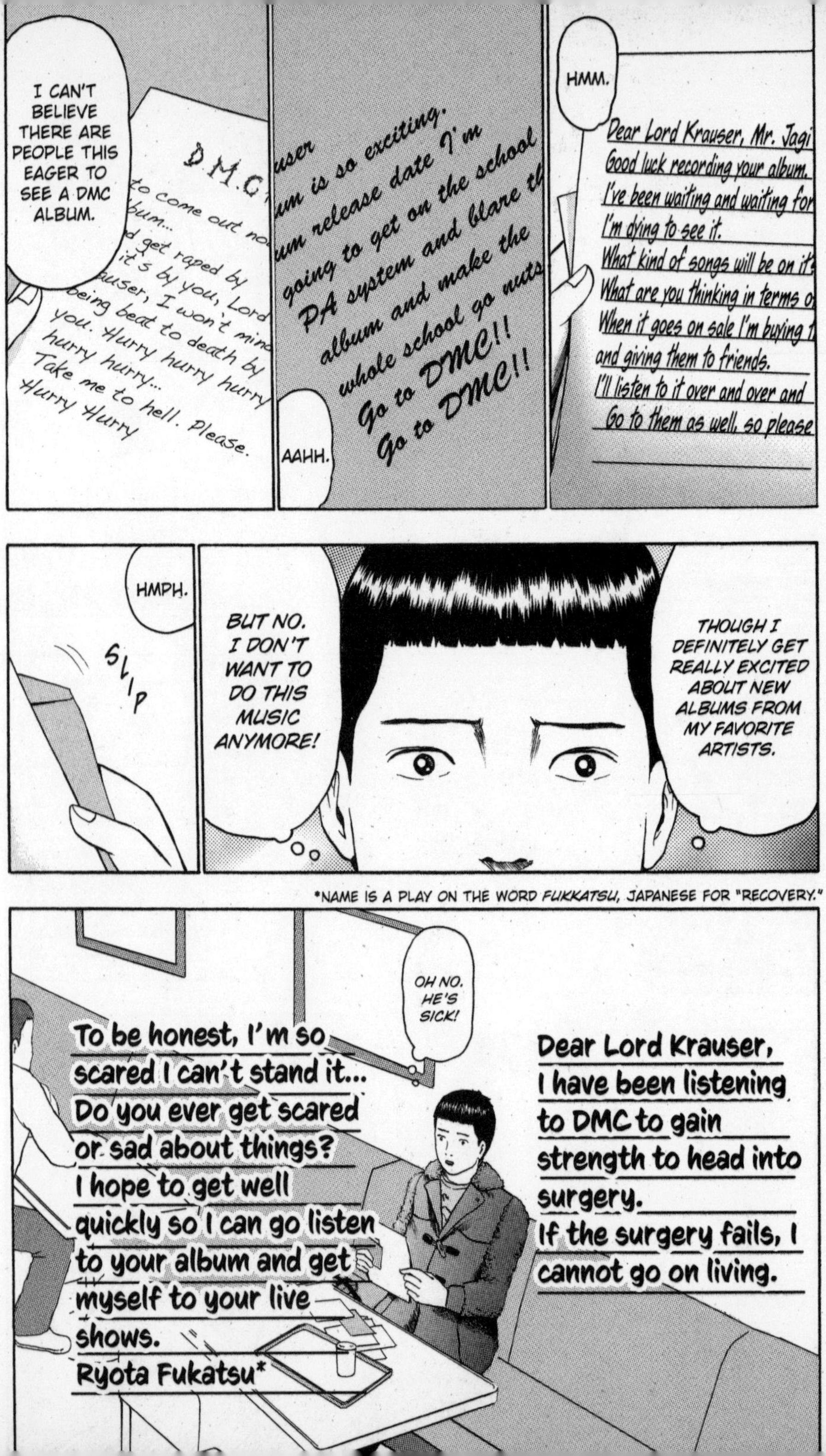
HMM.
Dear Lord Krauser, Mr. Jagi
Good luck recording your album.
I've been waiting and waiting for
I'm dying to see it.
What kind of songs will be on it
What are you thinking in terms o
When it goes on sale I'm buying
and giving them to friends.
I'll listen to it over and over and
Go to them as well, so please
user
um is so exciting.
um release date I'm
going to get on the school
PA system and blare th
album and make the
whole school go nuts
Go to DMC!!
Go to DMC!!
AAHH.
I CAN'T BELIEVE THERE ARE PEOPLE THIS EAGER TO SEE A DMC ALBUM.
D.M.C.
to come out no
bum...
d get raped by
it's by you, Lord
rauser, I won't mind
being beat to death by
you. Hurry hurry hurry
hurry hurry...
Take me to hell. Please.
Hurry Hurry
THOUGH I DEFINITELY GET REALLY EXCITED ABOUT NEW ALBUMS FROM MY FAVORITE ARTISTS.
BUT NO. I DON'T WANT TO DO THIS MUSIC ANYMORE!
HMPH.
SLIP
OH NO. HE'S SICK!
Dear Lord Krauser,
I have been listening
to DMC to gain
strength to head into
surgery.
If the surgery fails, I
cannot go on living.
To be honest, I'm so
scared I can't stand it...
Do you ever get scared
or sad about things?
I hope to get well
quickly so I can go listen
to your album and get
myself to your live
shows.
Ryota Fukatsu*

*NAME IS A PLAY ON THE WORD *FUKKATSU*, JAPANESE FOR "RECOVERY."

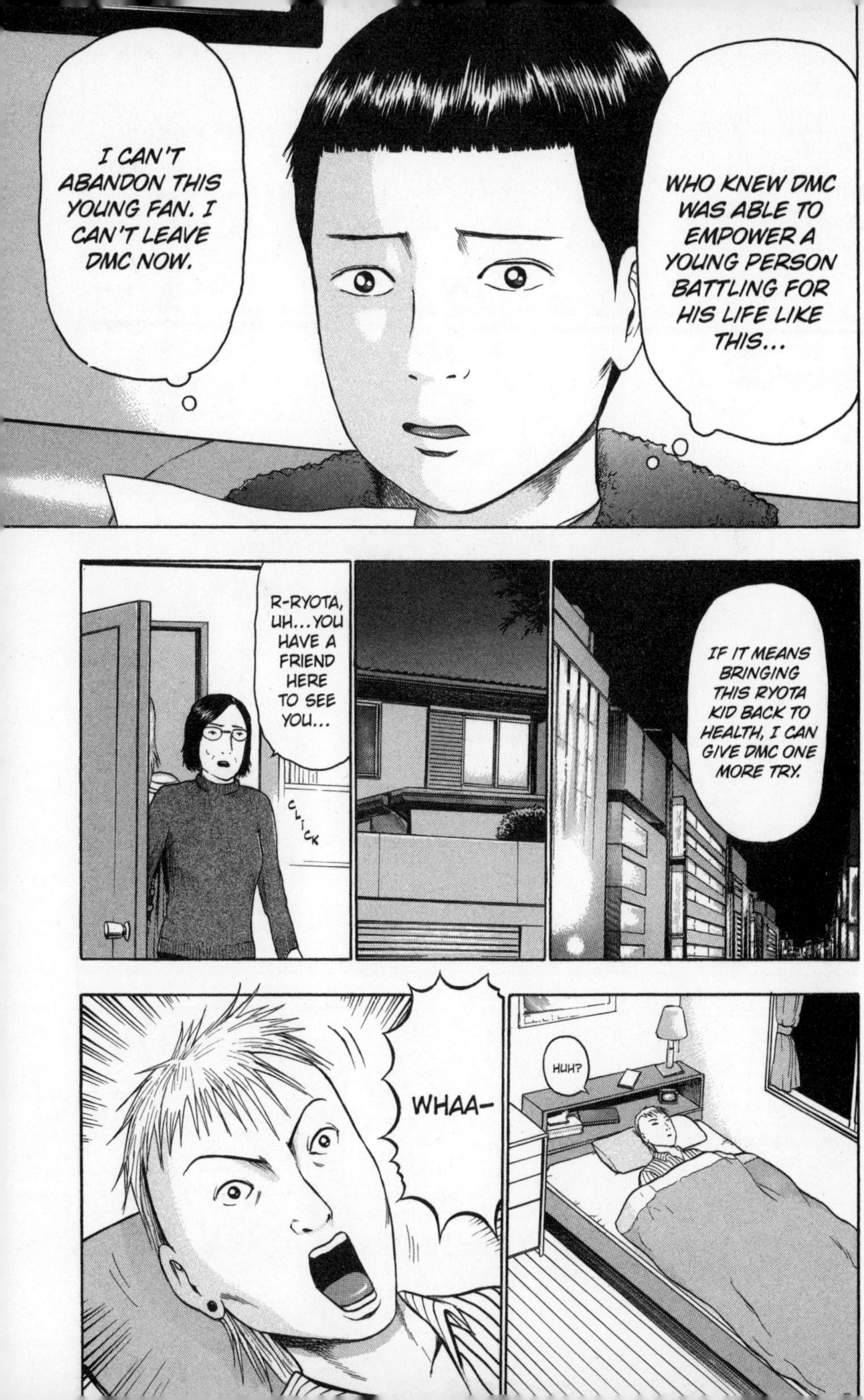
WHO KNEW DMC WAS ABLE TO EMPOWER A YOUNG PERSON BATTLING FOR HIS LIFE LIKE THIS...
I CAN'T ABANDON THIS YOUNG FAN. I CAN'T LEAVE DMC NOW.
IF IT MEANS BRINGING THIS RYOTA KID BACK TO HEALTH, I CAN GIVE DMC ONE MORE TRY.
R-RYOTA, UH...YOU HAVE A FRIEND HERE TO SEE YOU...
CLICK
HUH?
WHAA-

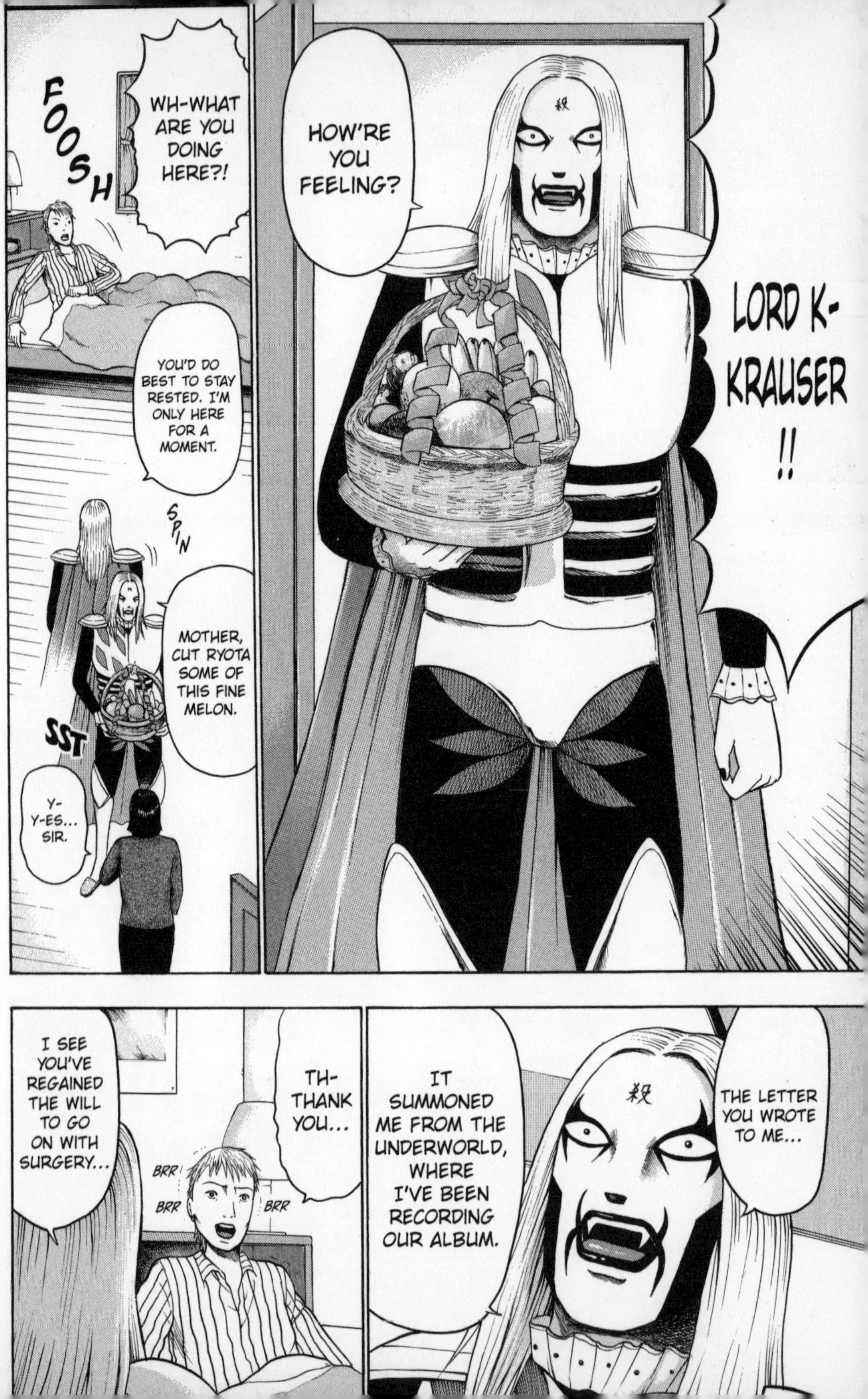
LORD K-KRAUSER!!
HOW'RE YOU FEELING?
WH-WHAT ARE YOU DOING HERE?!
FOOSH
YOU'D DO BEST TO STAY RESTED. I'M ONLY HERE FOR A MOMENT.
SPIN
MOTHER, CUT RYOTA SOME OF THIS FINE MELON.
SST
Y- Y-ES... SIR.
THE LETTER YOU WROTE TO ME...
IT SUMMONED ME FROM THE UNDERWORLD, WHERE I'VE BEEN RECORDING OUR ALBUM.
TH- THANK YOU...
I SEE YOU'VE REGAINED THE WILL TO GO ON WITH SURGERY...
BRR
BRR
BRR

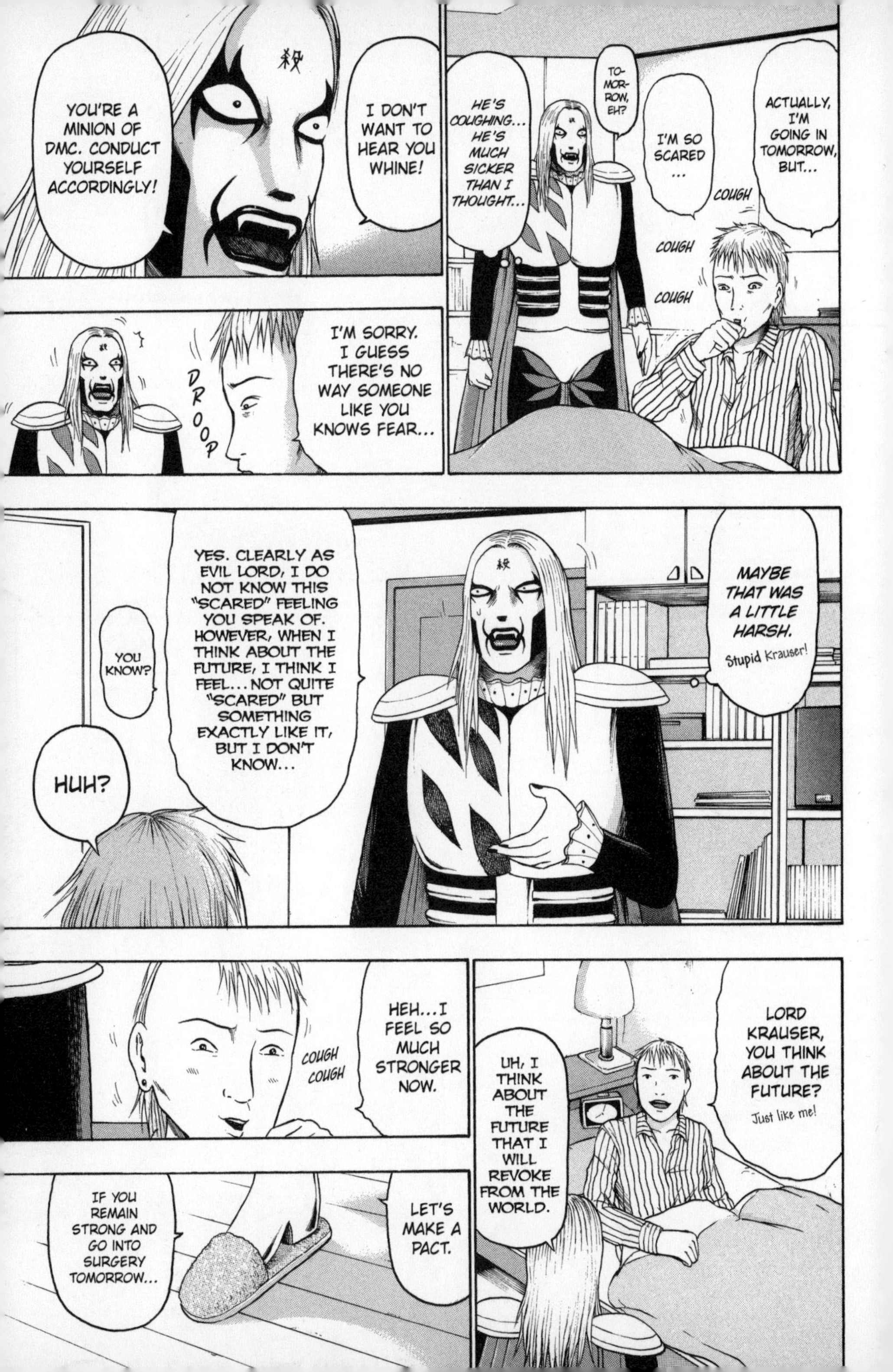
ACTUALLY, I'M GOING IN TOMORROW, BUT...
COUGH
COUGH
COUGH
I'M SO SCARED...
TO-MOR-ROW, EH?
HE'S COUGHING... HE'S MUCH SICKER THAN I THOUGHT...
I DON'T WANT TO HEAR YOU WHINE!
YOU'RE A MINION OF DMC. CONDUCT YOURSELF ACCORDINGLY!
I'M SORRY. I GUESS THERE'S NO WAY SOMEONE LIKE YOU KNOWS FEAR...
DROOP
MAYBE THAT WAS A LITTLE HARSH.
Stupid Krauser!
YES. CLEARLY AS EVIL LORD, I DO NOT KNOW THIS "SCARED" FEELING YOU SPEAK OF. HOWEVER, WHEN I THINK ABOUT THE FUTURE, I THINK I FEEL... NOT QUITE "SCARED" BUT SOMETHING EXACTLY LIKE IT, BUT I DON'T KNOW...
YOU KNOW?
HUH?
LORD KRAUSER, YOU THINK ABOUT THE FUTURE?
Just like me!
UH, I THINK ABOUT THE FUTURE THAT I WILL REVOKE FROM THE WORLD.
HEH...I FEEL SO MUCH STRONGER NOW.
COUGH COUGH
LET'S MAKE A PACT.
IF YOU REMAIN STRONG AND GO INTO SURGERY TOMORROW...

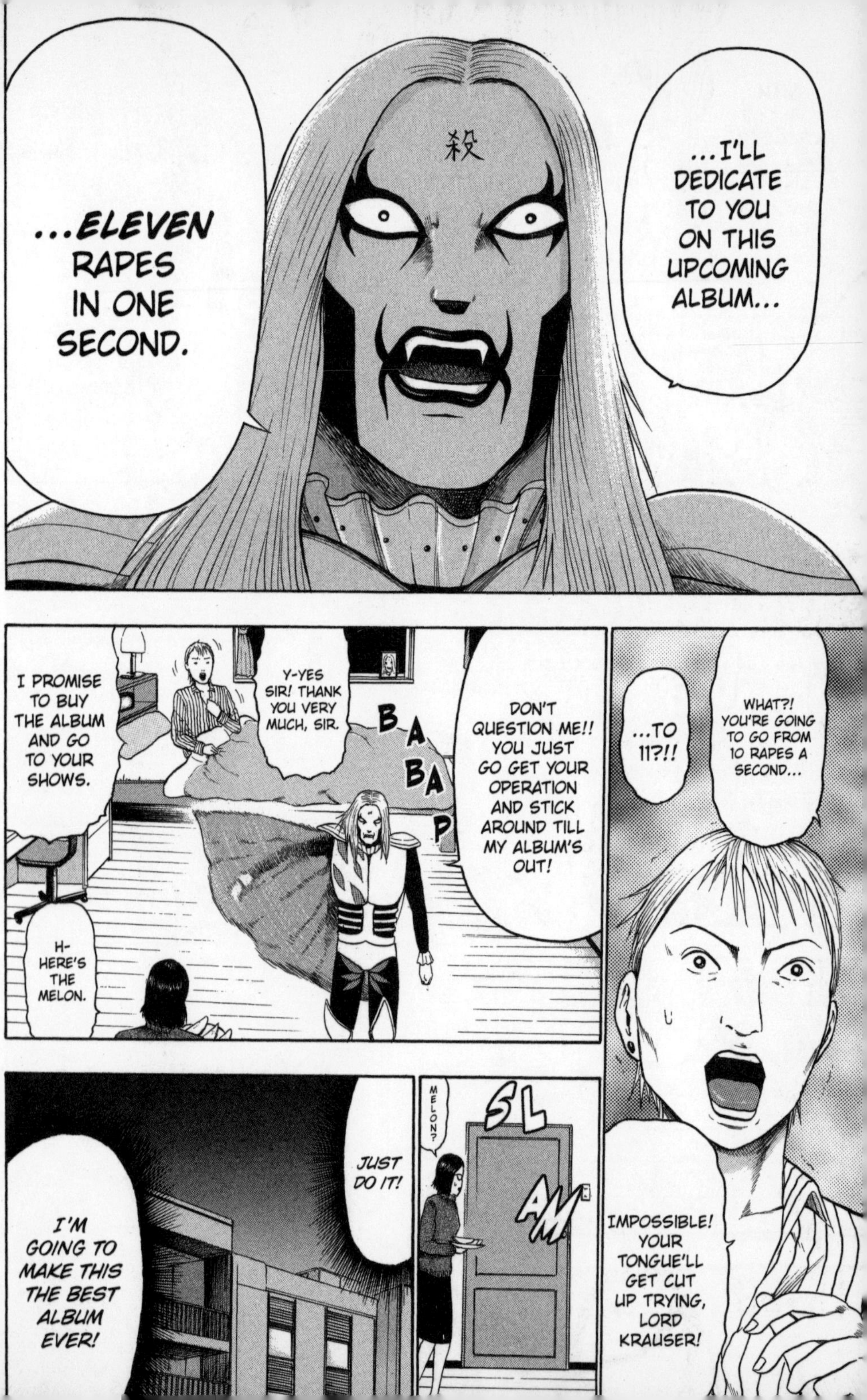
...I'LL DEDICATE TO YOU ON THIS UPCOMING ALBUM...
殺
...ELEVEN RAPES IN ONE SECOND.
WHAT?! YOU'RE GOING TO GO FROM 10 RAPES A SECOND...
...TO 11?!!
IMPOSSIBLE! YOUR TONGUE'LL GET CUT UP TRYING, LORD KRAUSER!
DON'T QUESTION ME!! YOU JUST GO GET YOUR OPERATION AND STICK AROUND TILL MY ALBUM'S OUT!
BABAP
Y-YES SIR! THANK YOU VERY MUCH, SIR.
I PROMISE TO BUY THE ALBUM AND GO TO YOUR SHOWS.
H-HERE'S THE MELON.
SLAM
MELON?
JUST DO IT!
I'M GOING TO MAKE THIS THE BEST ALBUM EVER!

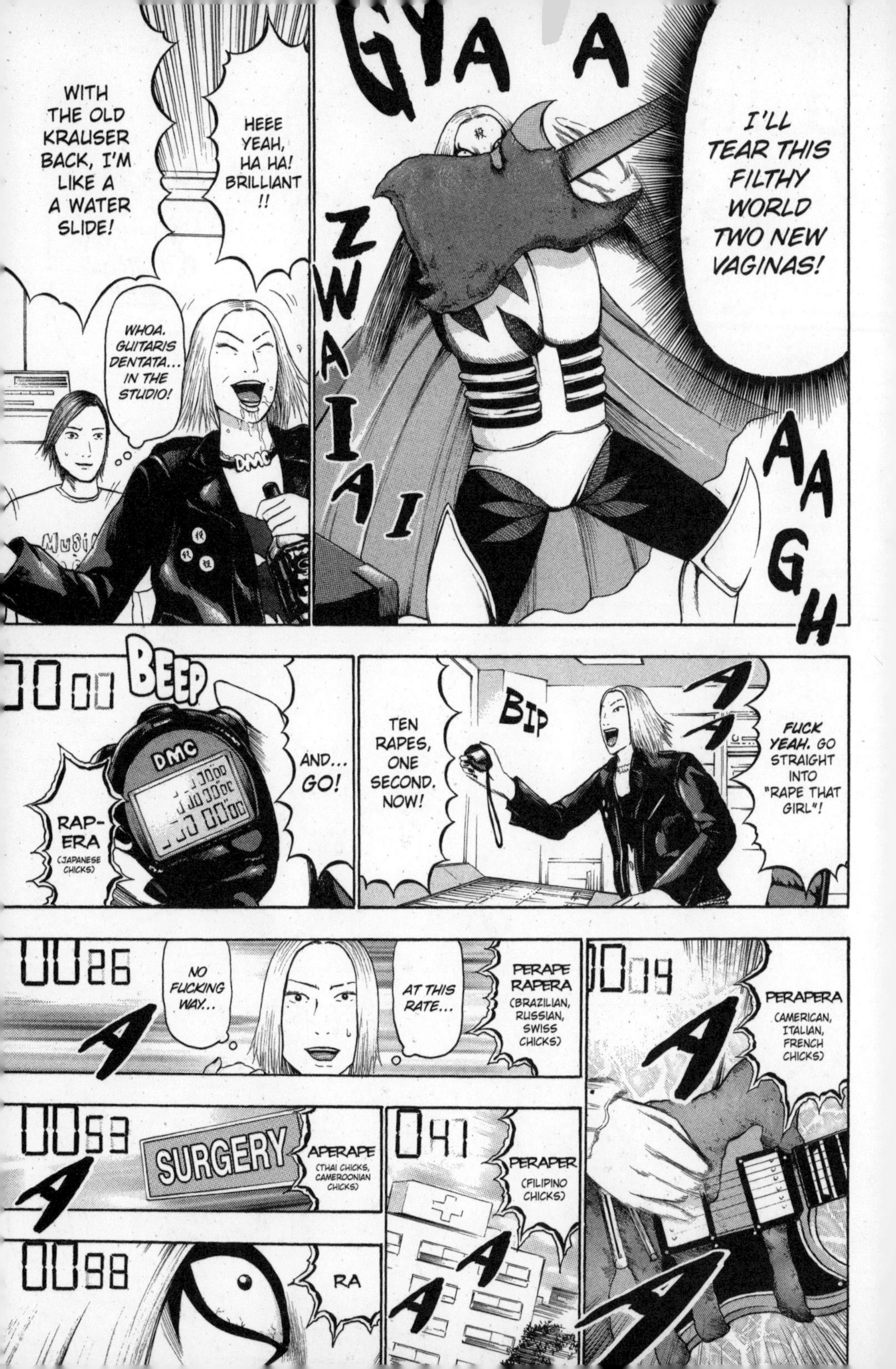
GYA A
A A A
G
H
I'LL TEAR THIS FILTHY WORLD TWO NEW VAGINAS!
ZWAI
AI
HEEE YEAH, HA HA! BRILLIANT !!
WITH THE OLD KRAUSER BACK, I'M LIKE A A WATER SLIDE!
WHOA. GUITARIS DENTATA... IN THE STUDIO!
BIP
A A
FUCK YEAH. GO STRAIGHT INTO "RAPE THAT GIRL"!
TEN RAPES, ONE SECOND. NOW!
AND... GO!
BEEP
DMC
RAP-ERA
(JAPANESE CHICKS)
PERAPERA
(AMERICAN, ITALIAN, FRENCH CHICKS)
A
PERAPE RAPERA
(BRAZILIAN, RUSSIAN, SWISS CHICKS)
AT THIS RATE...
NO FUCKING WAY...
A
PERAPER
(FILIPINO CHICKS)
APERAPE
(THAI CHICKS, CAMEROONIAN CHICKS)
SURGERY
A
A
A
RA
A

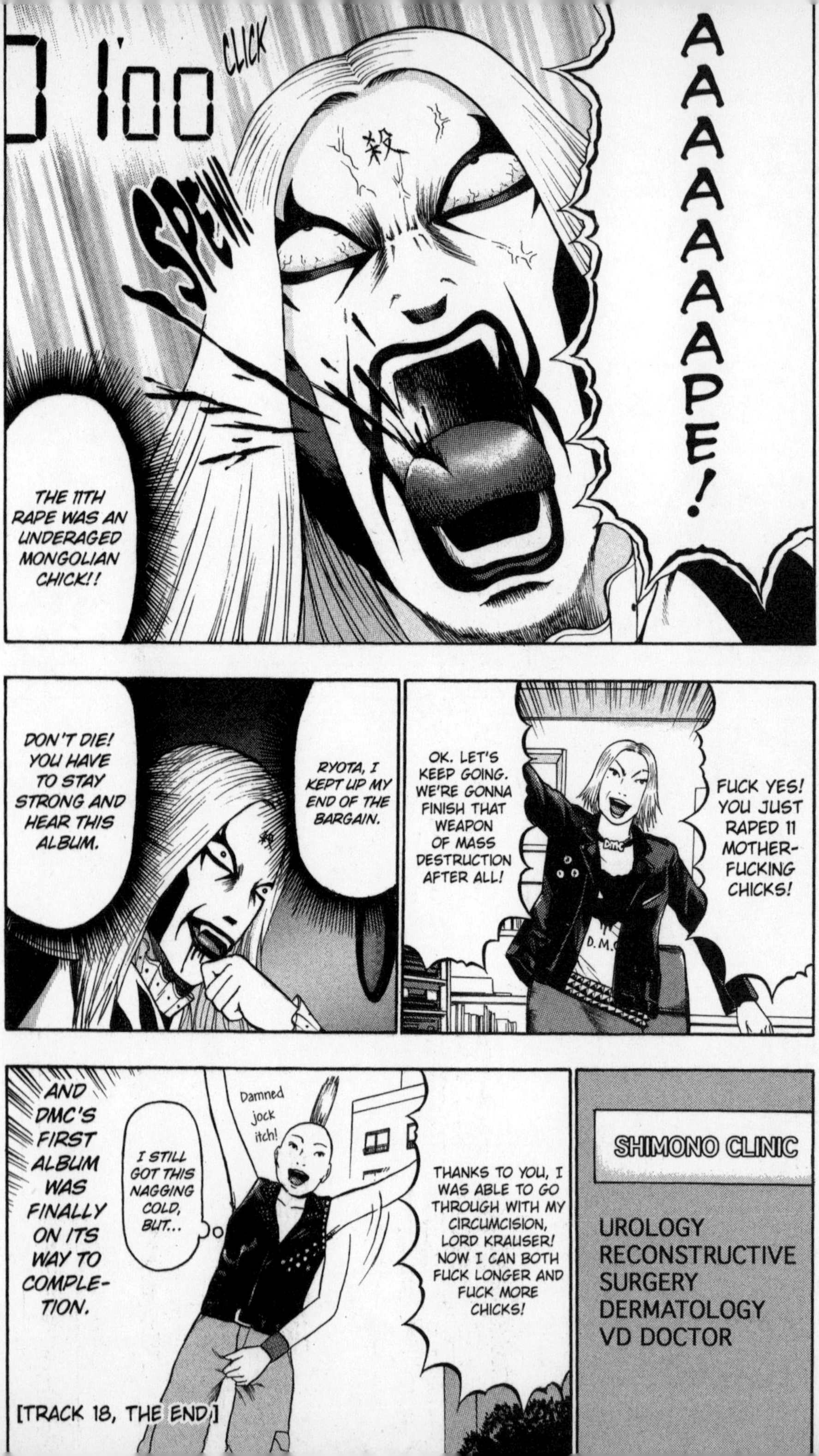
AAAAAAAPE!
CLICK
0 1'00
SPEW!
THE 11TH RAPE WAS AN UNDERAGED MONGOLIAN CHICK!!
FUCK YES! YOU JUST RAPED 11 MOTHER-FUCKING CHICKS!
OK. LET'S KEEP GOING. WE'RE GONNA FINISH THAT WEAPON OF MASS DESTRUCTION AFTER ALL!
D.M.C
RYOTA, I KEPT UP MY END OF THE BARGAIN.
DON'T DIE! YOU HAVE TO STAY STRONG AND HEAR THIS ALBUM.
SHIMONO CLINIC
UROLOGY
RECONSTRUCTIVE SURGERY
DERMATOLOGY
VD DOCTOR
THANKS TO YOU, I WAS ABLE TO GO THROUGH WITH MY CIRCUMCISION, LORD KRAUSER! NOW I CAN BOTH FUCK LONGER AND FUCK MORE CHICKS!
Damned jock itch!
I STILL GOT THIS NAGGING COLD, BUT...
AND DMC'S FIRST ALBUM WAS FINALLY ON ITS WAY TO COMPLE-TION.
[TRACK 18, THE END]

DMC LEXICON

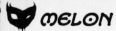 ## MELON

A very standard gift when visiting the sick. From the squash family. Easily considered a fruit but actually classified as a vegetable. If you drop this little snippet of trivia on a group of friends at a bar or some such, you're sure to enjoy admiration sweeter than any melon.

Usage: "Well hello hello. I see two honeydew melons here."
"No, Mr. President, I told you that's a 'no touch' zone."

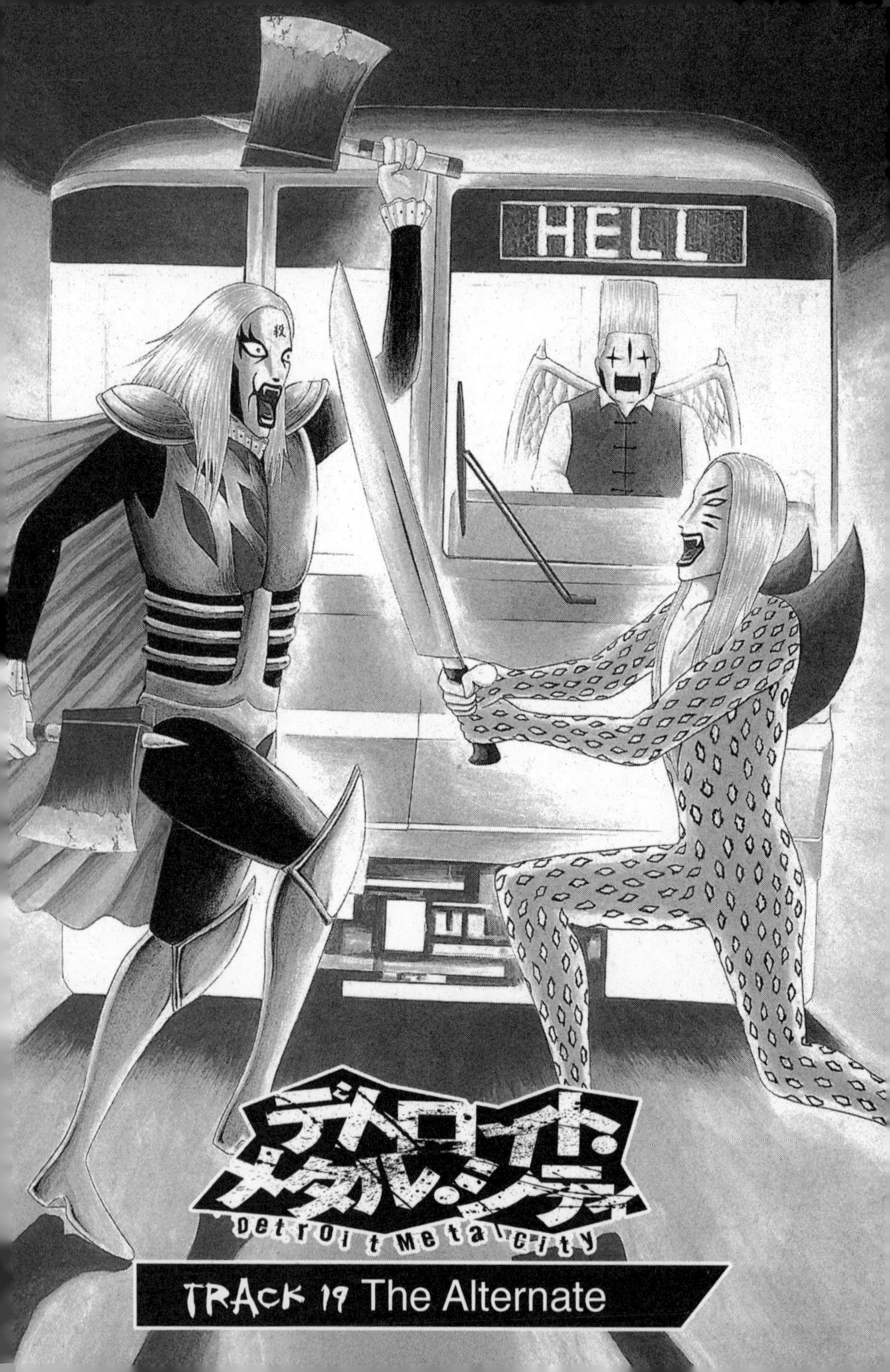
HELL
デトロイト・メタル・シティ
Detroit Metal City
TRACK 19 The Alternate

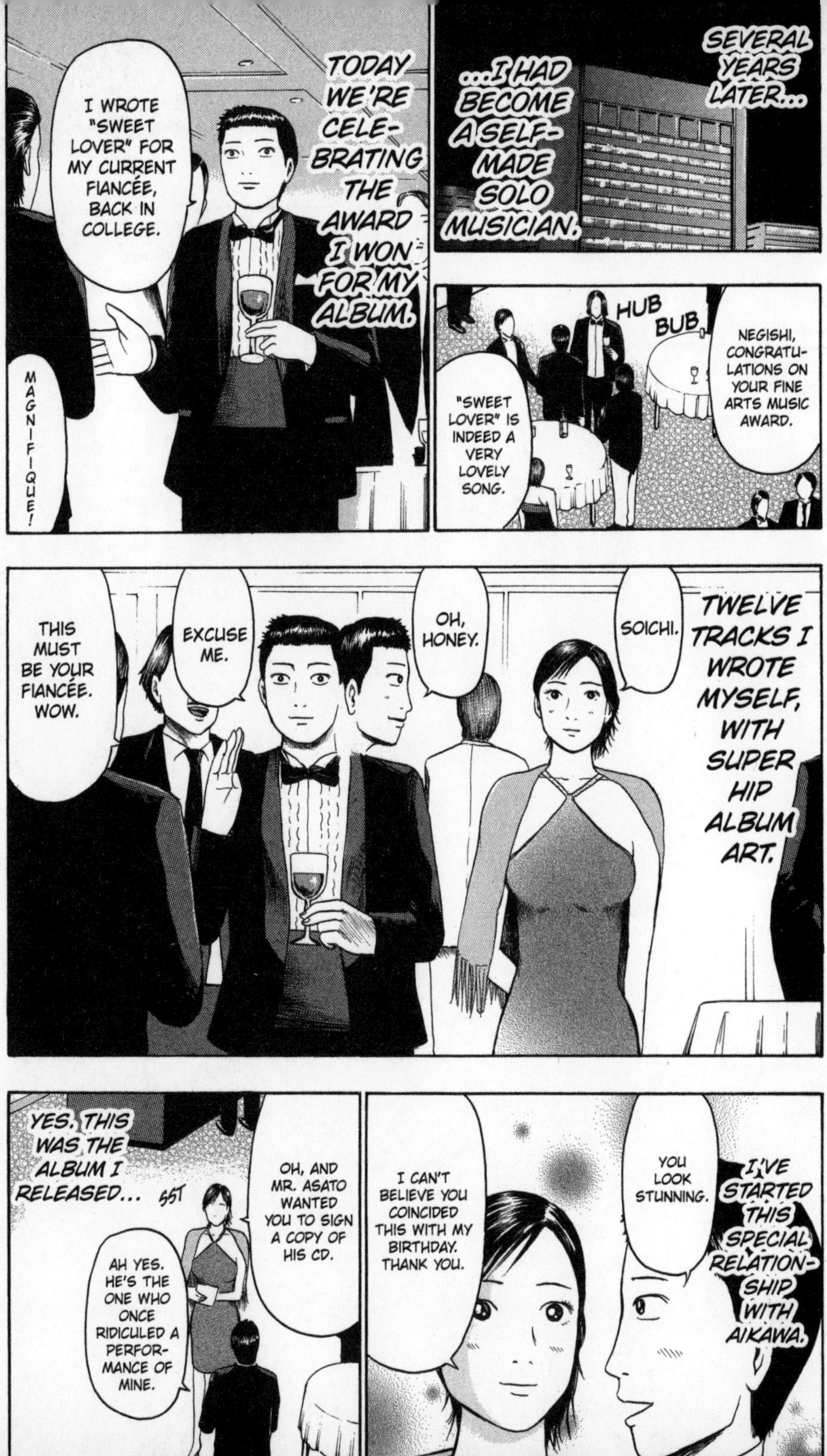
SEVERAL YEARS LATER...
...I HAD BECOME A SELF-MADE SOLO MUSICIAN.
HUB BUB
NEGISHI, CONGRATULATIONS ON YOUR FINE ARTS MUSIC AWARD.
"SWEET LOVER" IS INDEED A VERY LOVELY SONG.
TODAY WE'RE CELEBRATING THE AWARD I WON FOR MY ALBUM.
I WROTE "SWEET LOVER" FOR MY CURRENT FIANCÉE, BACK IN COLLEGE.
MAGNIFIQUE!
TWELVE TRACKS I WROTE MYSELF, WITH SUPER HIP ALBUM ART.
SOICHI.
OH, HONEY.
EXCUSE ME.
THIS MUST BE YOUR FIANCÉE. WOW.
I'VE STARTED THIS SPECIAL RELATIONSHIP WITH AIKAWA.
YOU LOOK STUNNING.
I CAN'T BELIEVE YOU COINCIDED THIS WITH MY BIRTHDAY. THANK YOU.
YES. THIS WAS THE ALBUM I RELEASED...
OH, AND MR. ASATO WANTED YOU TO SIGN A COPY OF HIS CD.
SST
AH YES. HE'S THE ONE WHO ONCE RIDICULED A PERFORMANCE OF MINE.

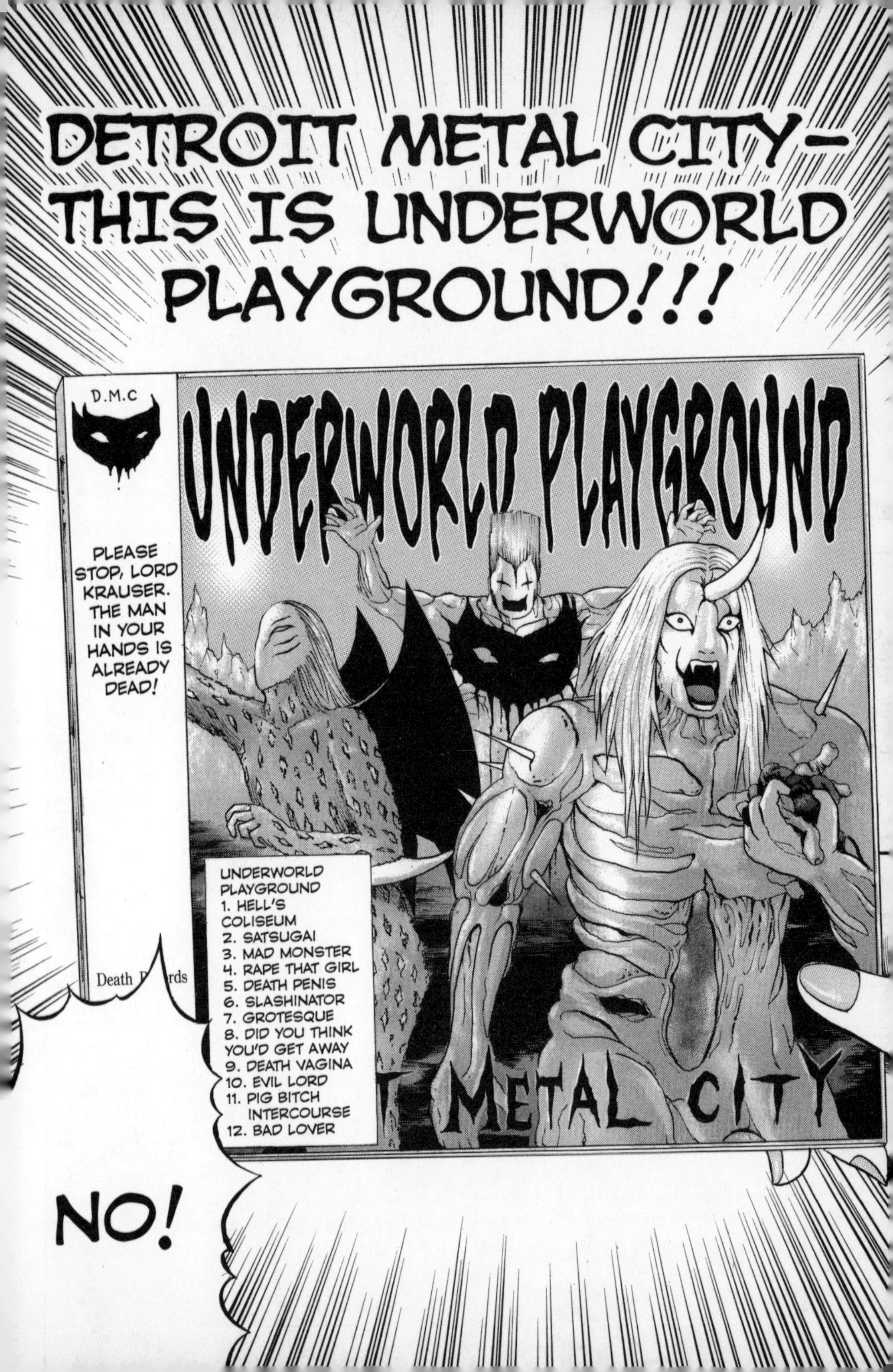
DETROIT METAL CITY—THIS IS UNDERWORLD PLAYGROUND!!!
D.M.C
UNDERWORLD PLAYGROUND
PLEASE STOP, LORD KRAUSER. THE MAN IN YOUR HANDS IS ALREADY DEAD!
UNDERWORLD PLAYGROUND
1. HELL'S COLISEUM
2. SATSUGAI
3. MAD MONSTER
4. RAPE THAT GIRL
5. DEATH PENIS
6. SLASHINATOR
7. GROTESQUE
8. DID YOU THINK YOU'D GET AWAY
9. DEATH VAGINA
10. EVIL LORD
11. PIG BITCH INTERCOURSE
12. BAD LOVER
METAL CITY
NO!

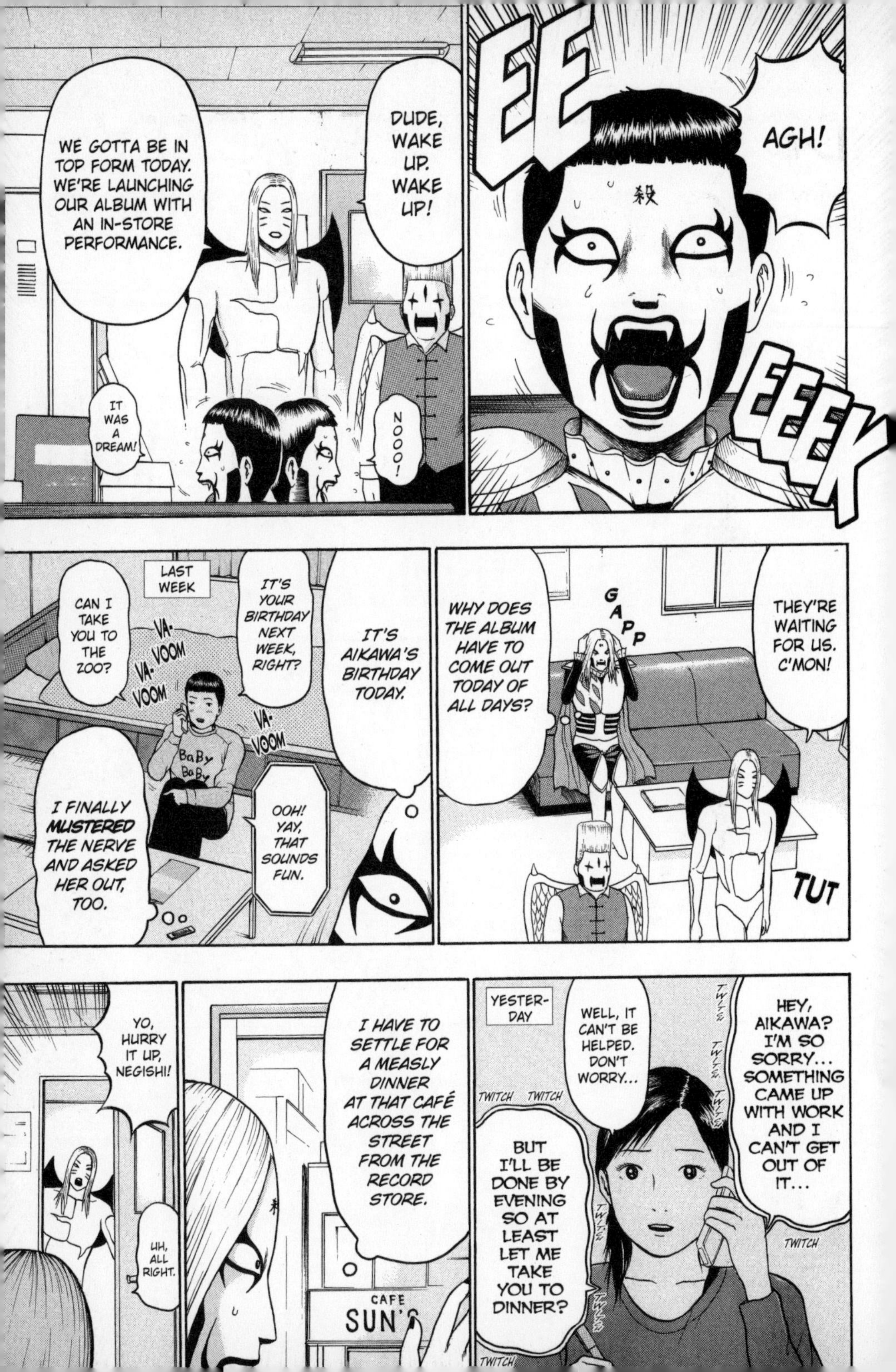
EE
AGH!
EEEK
DUDE, WAKE UP. WAKE UP!
WE GOTTA BE IN TOP FORM TODAY. WE'RE LAUNCHING OUR ALBUM WITH AN IN-STORE PERFORMANCE.
NOOOO!
IT WAS A DREAM!
THEY'RE WAITING FOR US. C'MON!
GAPP
WHY DOES THE ALBUM HAVE TO COME OUT TODAY OF ALL DAYS?
TUT
IT'S AIKAWA'S BIRTHDAY TODAY.
IT'S YOUR BIRTHDAY NEXT WEEK, RIGHT?
LAST WEEK
CAN I TAKE YOU TO THE ZOO?
VA-VOOM
VA-VOOM
VA-VOOM
OOH! YAY, THAT SOUNDS FUN.
I FINALLY **MUSTERED** THE NERVE AND ASKED HER OUT, TOO.
HEY, AIKAWA? I'M SO SORRY... SOMETHING CAME UP WITH WORK AND I CAN'T GET OUT OF IT...
WELL, IT CAN'T BE HELPED. DON'T WORRY...
YESTER-DAY
TWITCH TWITCH
BUT I'LL BE DONE BY EVENING SO AT LEAST LET ME TAKE YOU TO DINNER?
TWITCH
TWITCH
I HAVE TO SETTLE FOR A MEASLY DINNER AT THAT CAFÉ ACROSS THE STREET FROM THE RECORD STORE.
CAFE SUN'S
YO, HURRY IT UP, NEGISHI!
UH, ALL RIGHT.

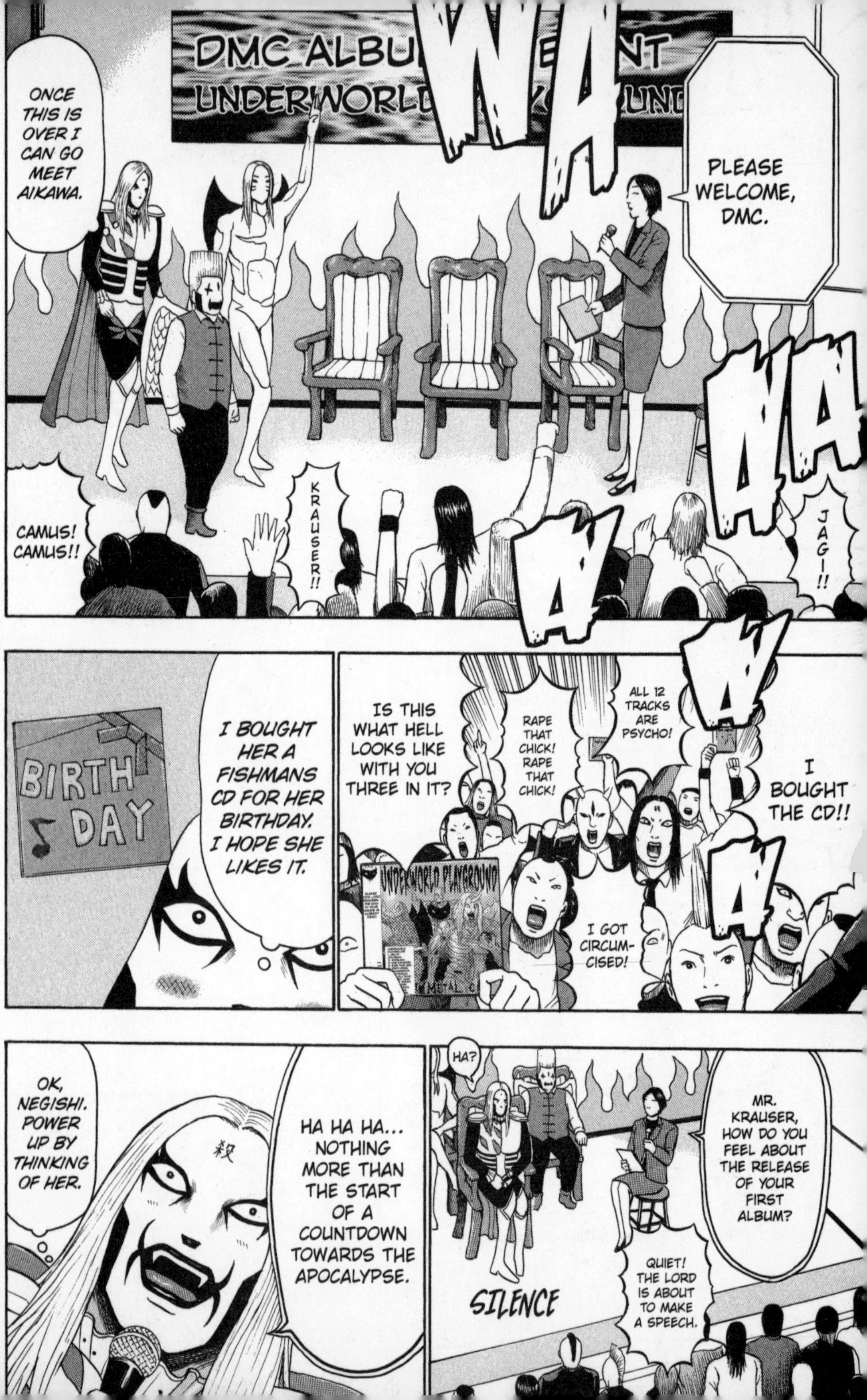
DMC ALBU
PLEASE WELCOME, DMC.
WA
ONCE THIS IS OVER I CAN GO MEET AIKAWA.
WA
JAGI!!
A
KRAUSER!!
CAMUS! CAMUS!!
WA
I BOUGHT THE CD!!
ALL 12 TRACKS ARE PSYCHO!
RAPE THAT CHICK! RAPE THAT CHICK!
IS THIS WHAT HELL LOOKS LIKE WITH YOU THREE IN IT?
A
I GOT CIRCUM-CISED!
UNDERWORLD PLAYGROUND
I BOUGHT HER A FISHMANS CD FOR HER BIRTHDAY. I HOPE SHE LIKES IT.
BIRTH DAY
MR. KRAUSER, HOW DO YOU FEEL ABOUT THE RELEASE OF YOUR FIRST ALBUM?
HA?
QUIET! THE LORD IS ABOUT TO MAKE A SPEECH.
SILENCE
HA HA HA... NOTHING MORE THAN THE START OF A COUNTDOWN TOWARDS THE APOCALYPSE.
殺
OK, NEGISHI. POWER UP BY THINKING OF HER.

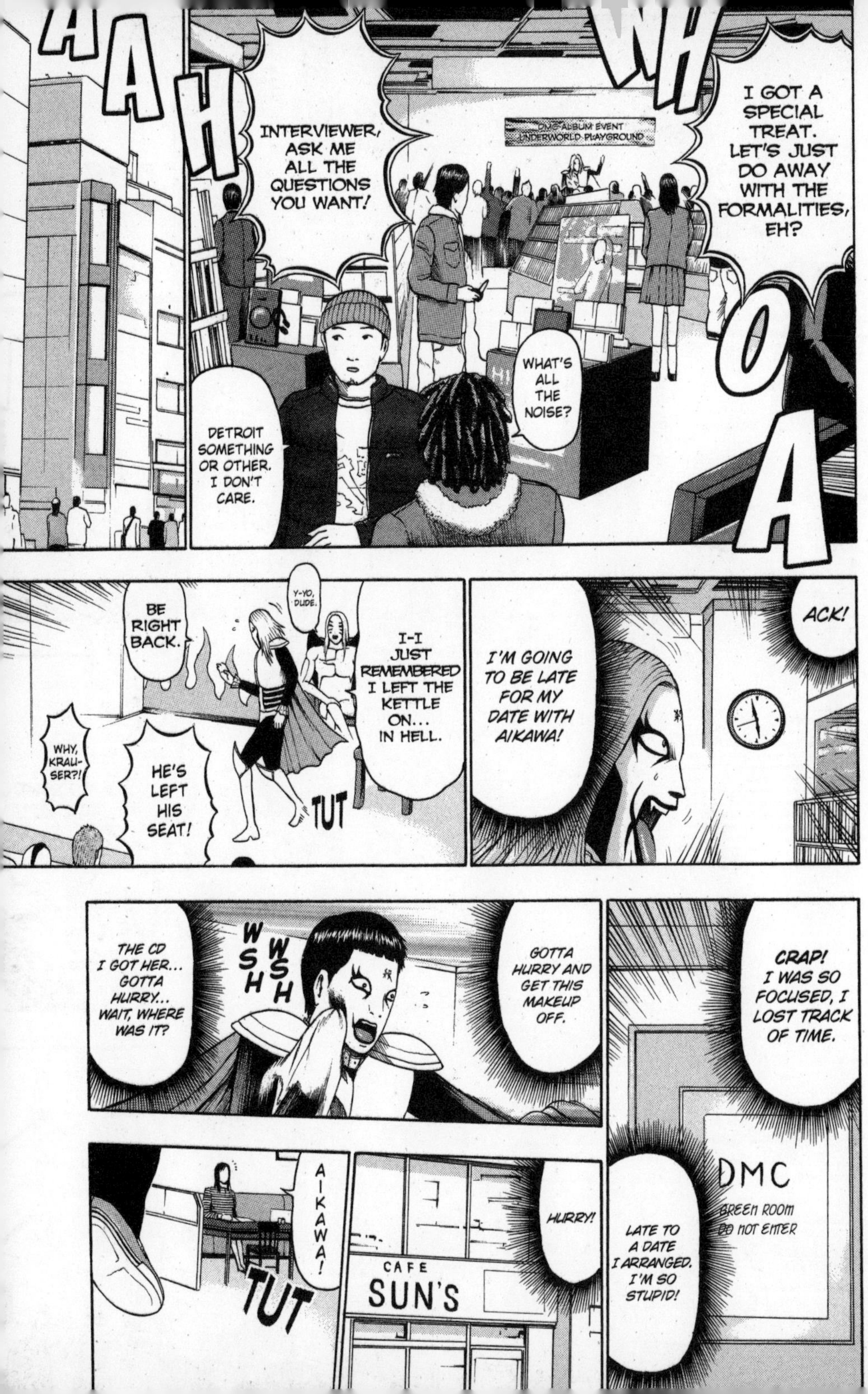
WH
O
A
A
A
H
I GOT A SPECIAL TREAT. LET'S JUST DO AWAY WITH THE FORMALITIES, EH?
DMC ALBUM EVENT
UNDERWORLD PLAYGROUND
INTERVIEWER, ASK ME ALL THE QUESTIONS YOU WANT!
WHAT'S ALL THE NOISE?
DETROIT SOMETHING OR OTHER. I DON'T CARE.
ACK!
I'M GOING TO BE LATE FOR MY DATE WITH AIKAWA!
I-I JUST REMEMBERED I LEFT THE KETTLE ON... IN HELL.
Y-YO, DUDE.
BE RIGHT BACK.
TUT
HE'S LEFT HIS SEAT!
WHY, KRAUSER?!
CRAP! I WAS SO FOCUSED, I LOST TRACK OF TIME.
DMC
GREEN ROOM
DO NOT ENTER
LATE TO A DATE I ARRANGED. I'M SO STUPID!
GOTTA HURRY AND GET THIS MAKEUP OFF.
WSH WSH
THE CD I GOT HER... GOTTA HURRY... WAIT, WHERE WAS IT?
HURRY!
CAFE
SUN'S
AIKAWA!
TUT

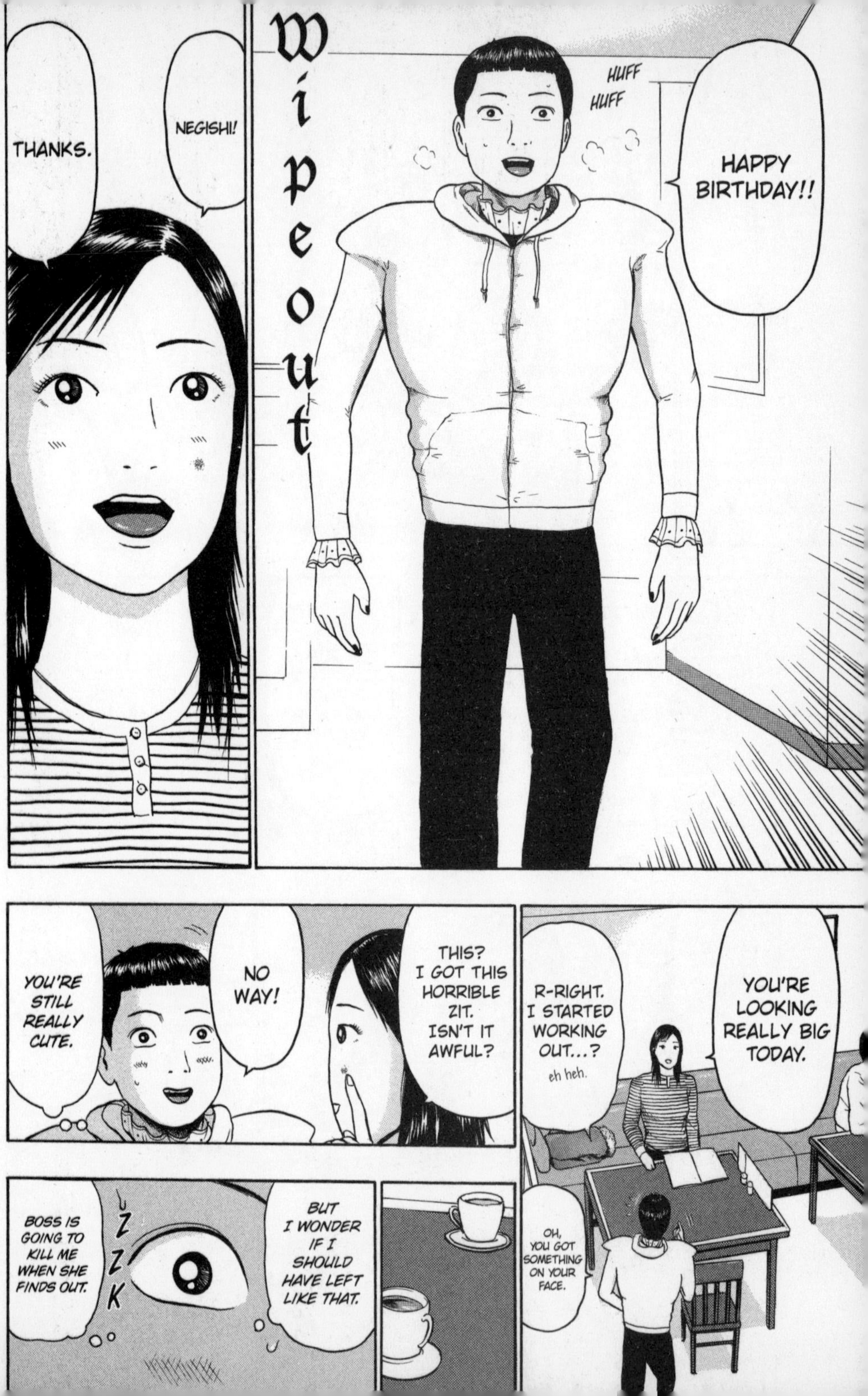
HAPPY BIRTHDAY!!
HUFF HUFF
Wipeout
NEGISHI!
THANKS.
YOU'RE LOOKING REALLY BIG TODAY.
R-RIGHT. I STARTED WORKING OUT...?
eh heh.
OH, YOU GOT SOMETHING ON YOUR FACE.
THIS? I GOT THIS HORRIBLE ZIT. ISN'T IT AWFUL?
NO WAY!
YOU'RE STILL REALLY CUTE.
BUT I WONDER IF I SHOULD HAVE LEFT LIKE THAT.
ZZK
BOSS IS GOING TO KILL ME WHEN SHE FINDS OUT.

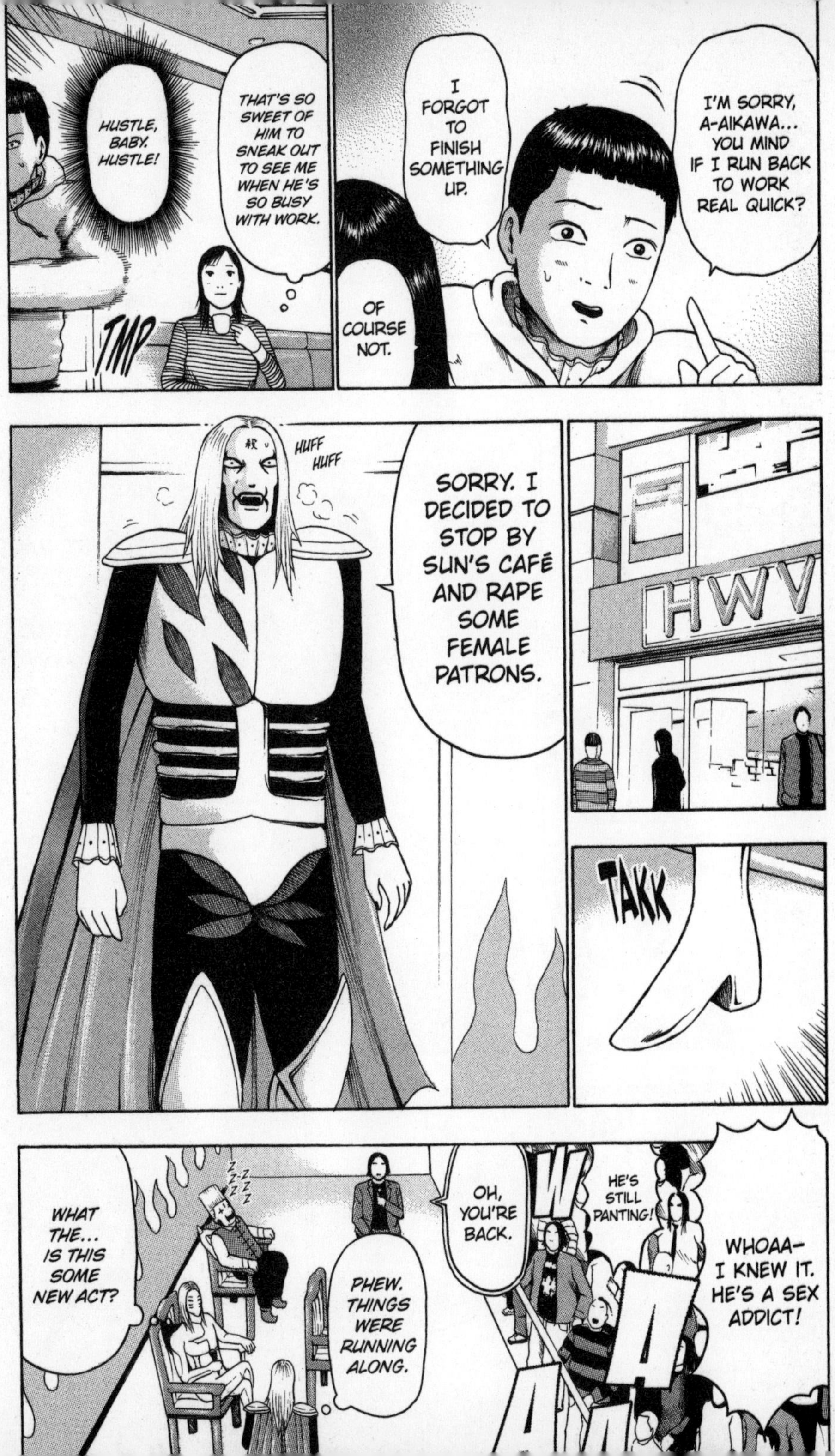
I'M SORRY, A-AIKAWA... YOU MIND IF I RUN BACK TO WORK REAL QUICK?
I FORGOT TO FINISH SOMETHING UP.
OF COURSE NOT.
THAT'S SO SWEET OF HIM TO SNEAK OUT TO SEE ME WHEN HE'S SO BUSY WITH WORK.
HUSTLE, BABY. HUSTLE!
TMP
HWV
TAKK
HUFF HUFF
SORRY. I DECIDED TO STOP BY SUN'S CAFÉ AND RAPE SOME FEMALE PATRONS.
WHOAA- I KNEW IT. HE'S A SEX ADDICT!
HE'S STILL PANTING!
WAA
OH, YOU'RE BACK.
PHEW. THINGS WERE RUNNING ALONG.
WHAT THE... IS THIS SOME NEW ACT?

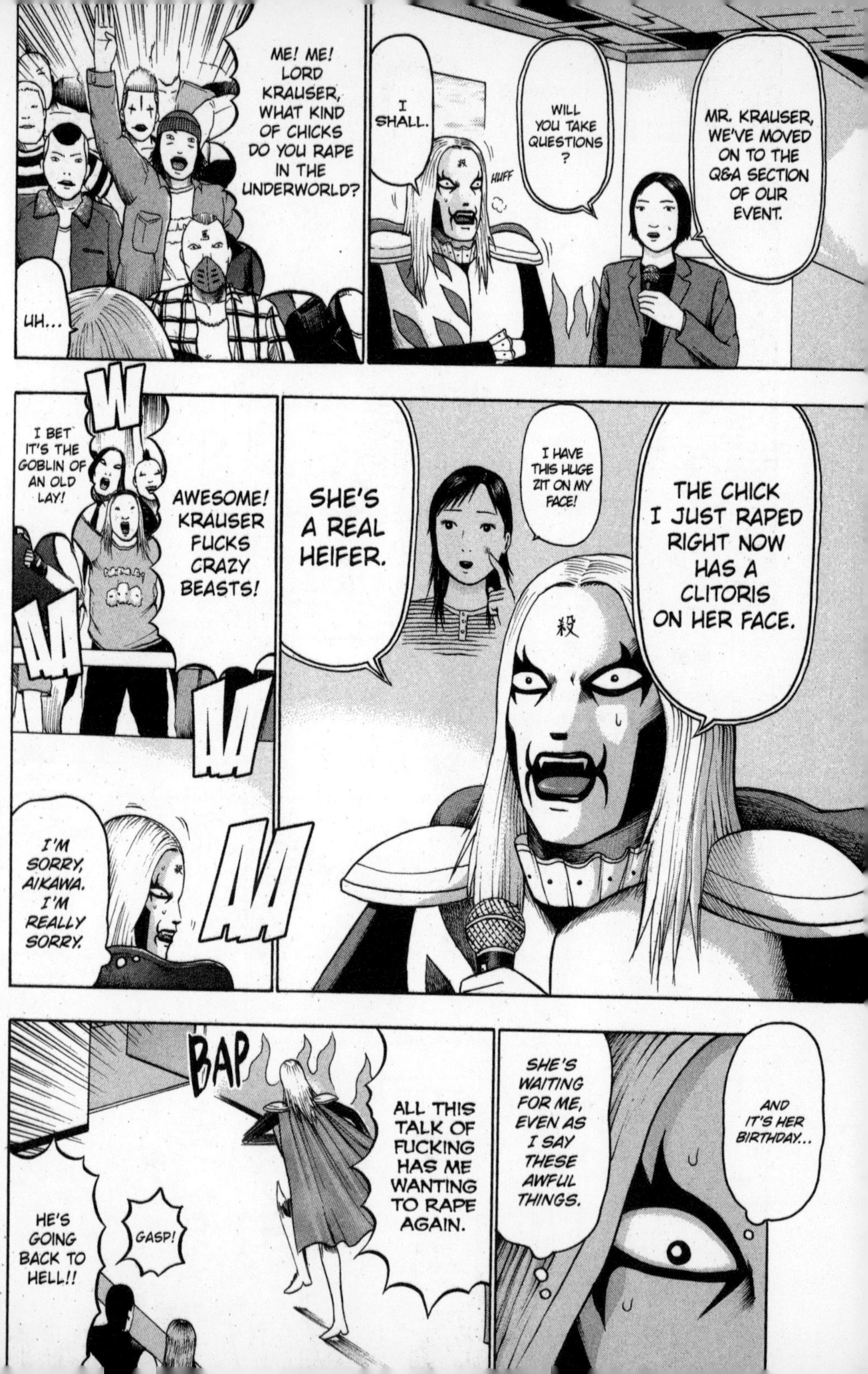
MR. KRAUSER, WE'VE MOVED ON TO THE Q&A SECTION OF OUR EVENT.
WILL YOU TAKE QUESTIONS?
HUFF
I SHALL.
ME! ME! LORD KRAUSER, WHAT KIND OF CHICKS DO YOU RAPE IN THE UNDERWORLD?
UH...
THE CHICK I JUST RAPED RIGHT NOW HAS A CLITORIS ON HER FACE.
I HAVE THIS HUGE ZIT ON MY FACE!
SHE'S A REAL HEIFER.
W
AWESOME! KRAUSER FUCKS CRAZY BEASTS!
I BET IT'S THE GOBLIN OF AN OLD LAY!
AA
AA
AA
I'M SORRY, AIKAWA. I'M REALLY SORRY.
AND IT'S HER BIRTHDAY...
SHE'S WAITING FOR ME, EVEN AS I SAY THESE AWFUL THINGS.
ALL THIS TALK OF FUCKING HAS ME WANTING TO RAPE AGAIN.
BAP
GASP!
HE'S GOING BACK TO HELL!!

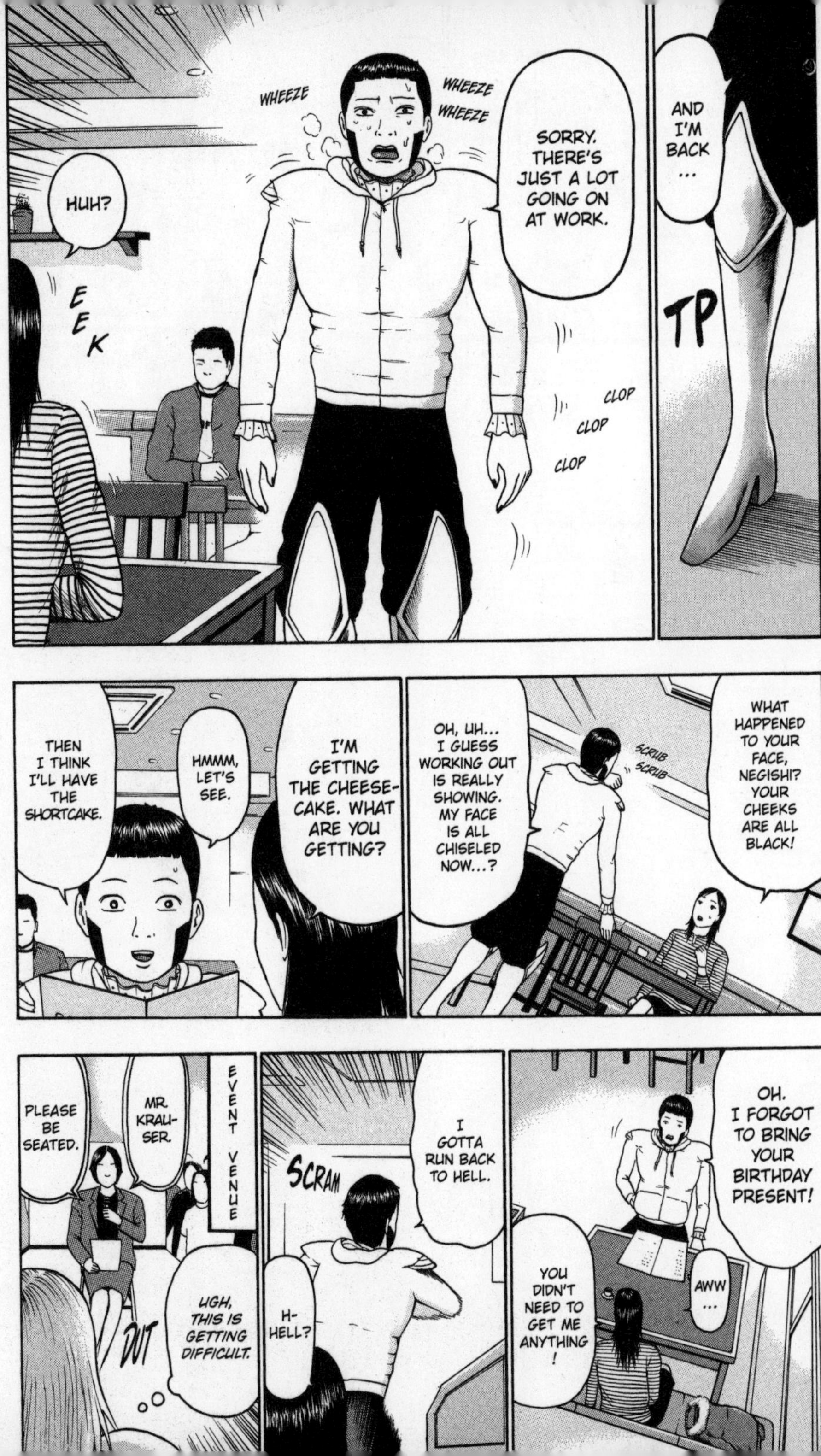
AND I'M BACK ...
TP
WHEEZE
WHEEZE
WHEEZE
SORRY. THERE'S JUST A LOT GOING ON AT WORK.
CLOP
CLOP
CLOP
HUH?
EEK
WHAT HAPPENED TO YOUR FACE, NEGISHI? YOUR CHEEKS ARE ALL BLACK!
SCRUB SCRUB
OH, UH... I GUESS WORKING OUT IS REALLY SHOWING. MY FACE IS ALL CHISELED NOW...?
I'M GETTING THE CHEESE-CAKE. WHAT ARE YOU GETTING?
HMMM, LET'S SEE.
THEN I THINK I'LL HAVE THE SHORTCAKE.
OH. I FORGOT TO BRING YOUR BIRTHDAY PRESENT!
AWW ...
YOU DIDN'T NEED TO GET ME ANYTHING !
I GOTTA RUN BACK TO HELL.
SCRAM
H-HELL?
EVENT VENUE
MR. KRAUSER.
PLEASE BE SEATED.
UGH, THIS IS GETTING DIFFICULT.
DUT

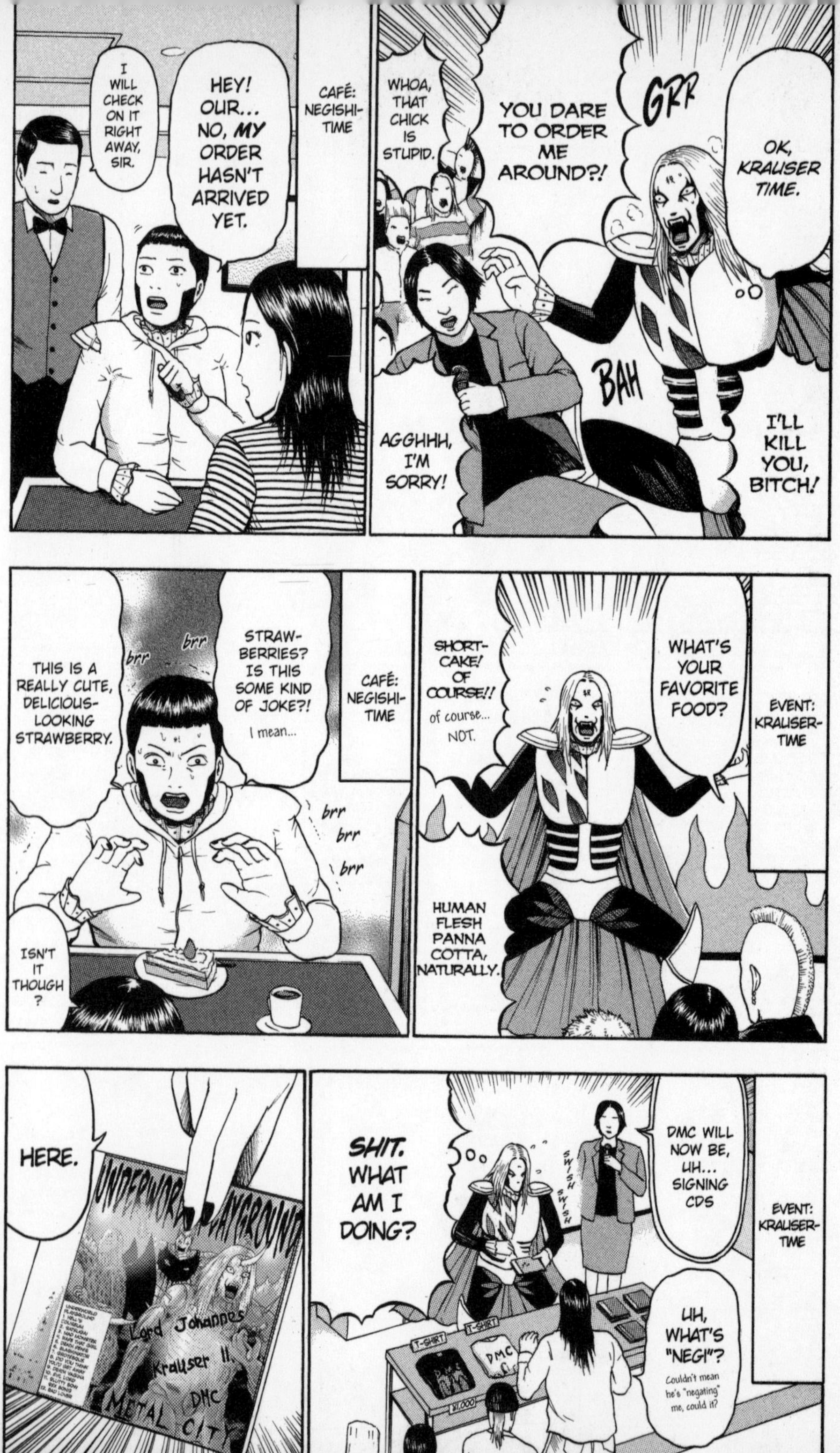
OK, KRAUSER TIME.
GRR
YOU DARE TO ORDER ME AROUND?!
WHOA, THAT CHICK IS STUPID.
BAH
I'LL KILL YOU, BITCH!
AGGHHH, I'M SORRY!
CAFÉ: NEGISHI-TIME
HEY! OUR... NO, MY ORDER HASN'T ARRIVED YET.
I WILL CHECK ON IT RIGHT AWAY, SIR.
EVENT: KRAUSER-TIME
WHAT'S YOUR FAVORITE FOOD?
SHORT-CAKE! OF COURSE!!
of course... NOT.
HUMAN FLESH PANNA COTTA, NATURALLY.
CAFÉ: NEGISHI-TIME
STRAW-BERRIES? IS THIS SOME KIND OF JOKE?!
I mean...
brr
brr
THIS IS A REALLY CUTE, DELICIOUS-LOOKING STRAWBERRY.
brr
brr
brr
ISN'T IT THOUGH?
EVENT: KRAUSER-TIME
DMC WILL NOW BE, UH... SIGNING CDS
SWISH SWISH
SHIT. WHAT AM I DOING?
UH, WHAT'S "NEGI"?
Couldn't mean he's "negating" me, could it?
T-SHIRT
T-SHIRT
DMC
HERE.
UNDERWORLD PLAYGROUND
Lord Johannes Krauser II
DMC METAL CITY

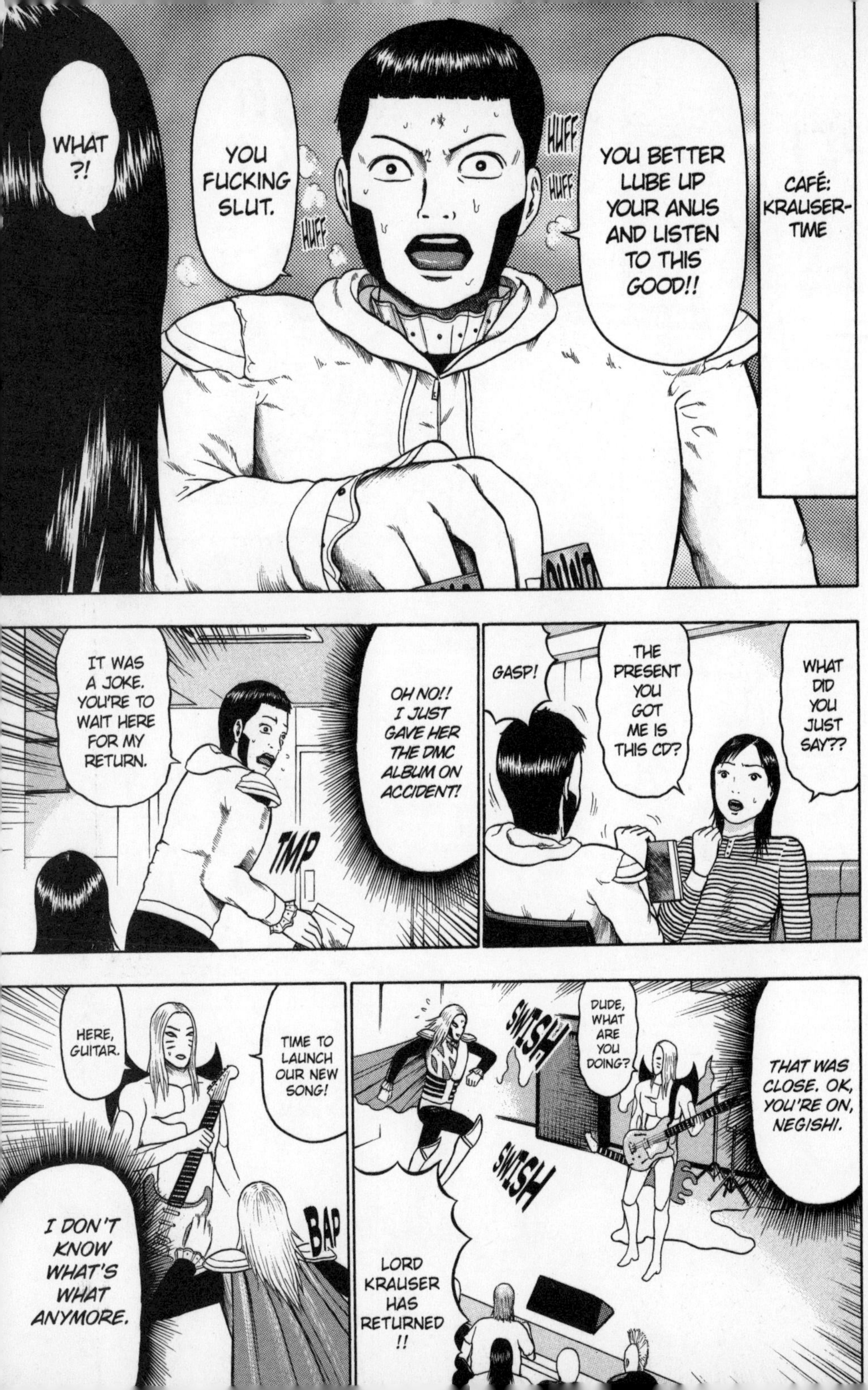
CAFÉ: KRAUSER-TIME
YOU BETTER LUBE UP YOUR ANUS AND LISTEN TO THIS GOOD!!
HUFF
HUFF
HUFF
YOU FUCKING SLUT.
WHAT ?!
WHAT DID YOU JUST SAY??
THE PRESENT YOU GOT ME IS THIS CD?
GASP!
OH NO!! I JUST GAVE HER THE DMC ALBUM ON ACCIDENT!
IT WAS A JOKE. YOU'RE TO WAIT HERE FOR MY RETURN.
TMP
THAT WAS CLOSE. OK, YOU'RE ON, NEGISHI.
DUDE, WHAT ARE YOU DOING?
SWISH
SWISH
LORD KRAUSER HAS RETURNED !!
TIME TO LAUNCH OUR NEW SONG!
HERE, GUITAR.
BAP
I DON'T KNOW WHAT'S WHAT ANYMORE.

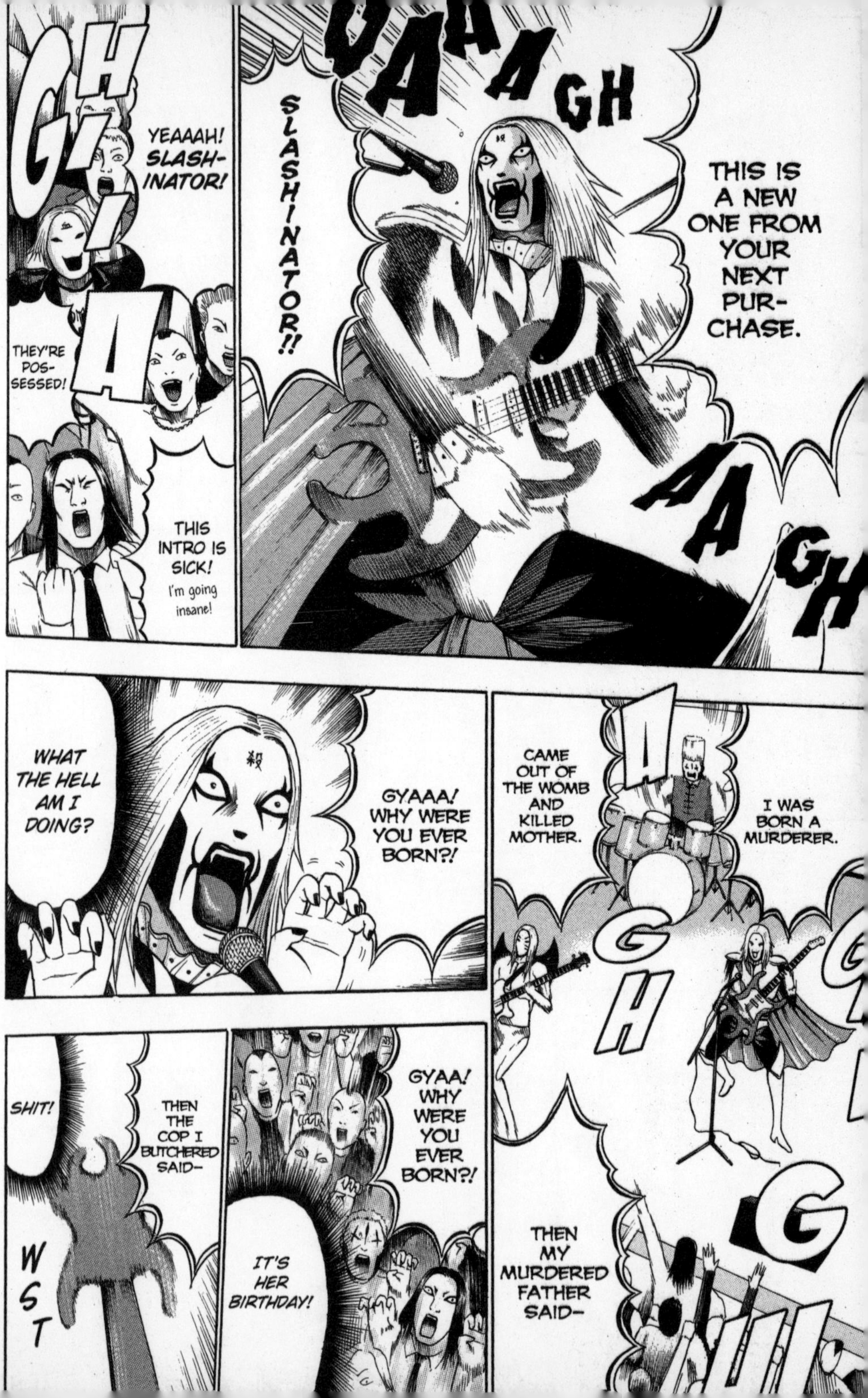
UAAAGH
SLASHINATOR?!
THIS IS A NEW ONE FROM YOUR NEXT PURCHASE.
AAGH
GHIIA
YEAAAH! SLASHINATOR!
THEY'RE POSSESSED!
THIS INTRO IS SICK!
I'm going insane!
A
I WAS BORN A MURDERER.
CAME OUT OF THE WOMB AND KILLED MOTHER.
GH
G
THEN MY MURDERED FATHER SAID-
GYAAA! WHY WERE YOU EVER BORN?!
WHAT THE HELL AM I DOING?
GYAA! WHY WERE YOU EVER BORN?!
IT'S HER BIRTHDAY!
THEN THE COP I BUTCHERED SAID-
SHIT!
WST

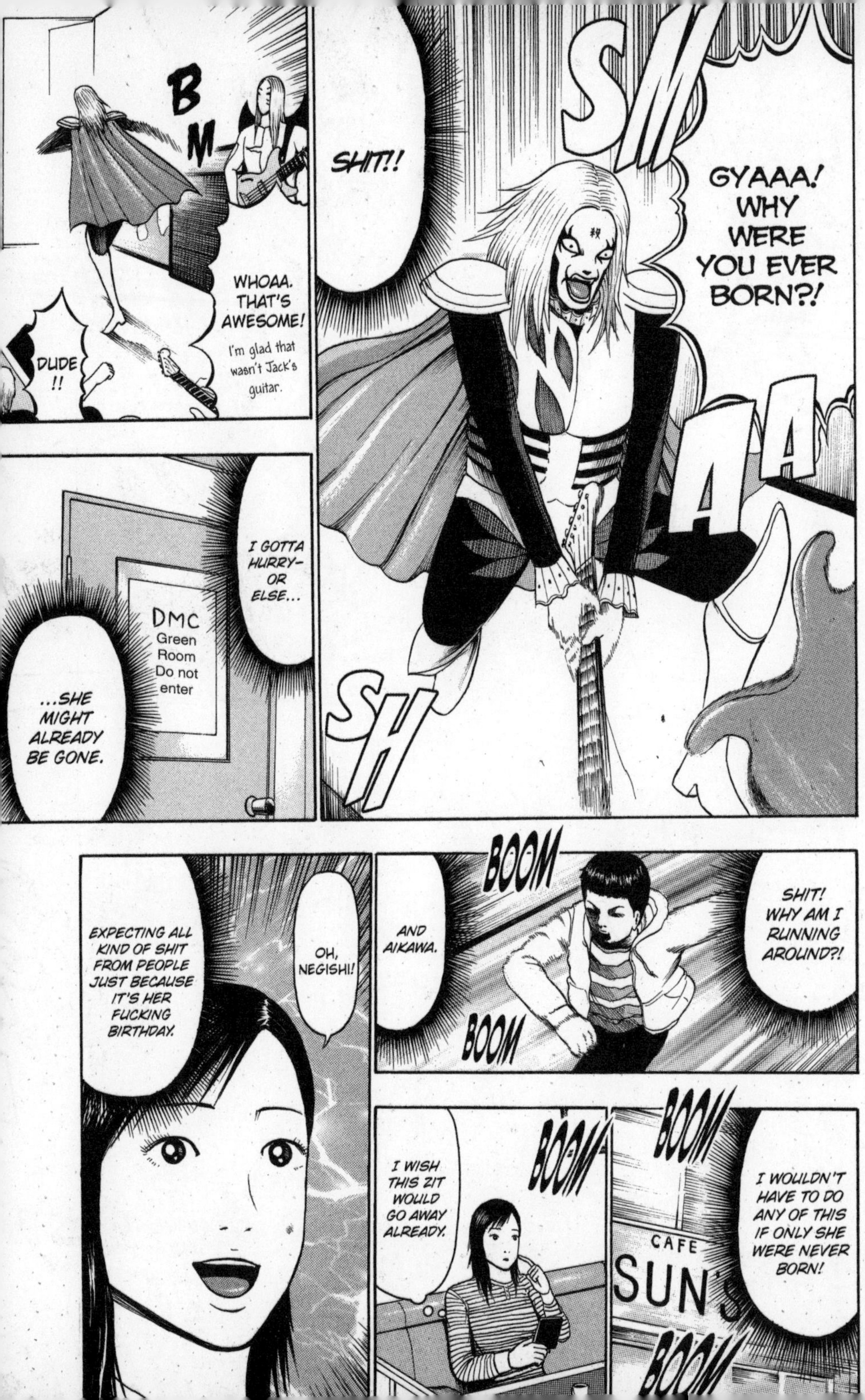
SM
GYAAA! WHY WERE YOU EVER BORN?!
SHIT!!
AA
A
SH
WHOAA. THAT'S AWESOME!
I'm glad that wasn't Jack's guitar.
DUDE!!
BM
I GOTTA HURRY— OR ELSE...
DMC Green Room Do not enter
...SHE MIGHT ALREADY BE GONE.
SHIT! WHY AM I RUNNING AROUND?!
BOOM
AND AIKAWA.
BOOM
I WOULDN'T HAVE TO DO ANY OF THIS IF ONLY SHE WERE NEVER BORN!
BOOM
BOOM
CAFE SUN'S
I WISH THIS ZIT WOULD GO AWAY ALREADY.
BOOM
OH, NEGISHI!
EXPECTING ALL KIND OF SHIT FROM PEOPLE JUST BECAUSE IT'S HER FUCKING BIRTHDAY.

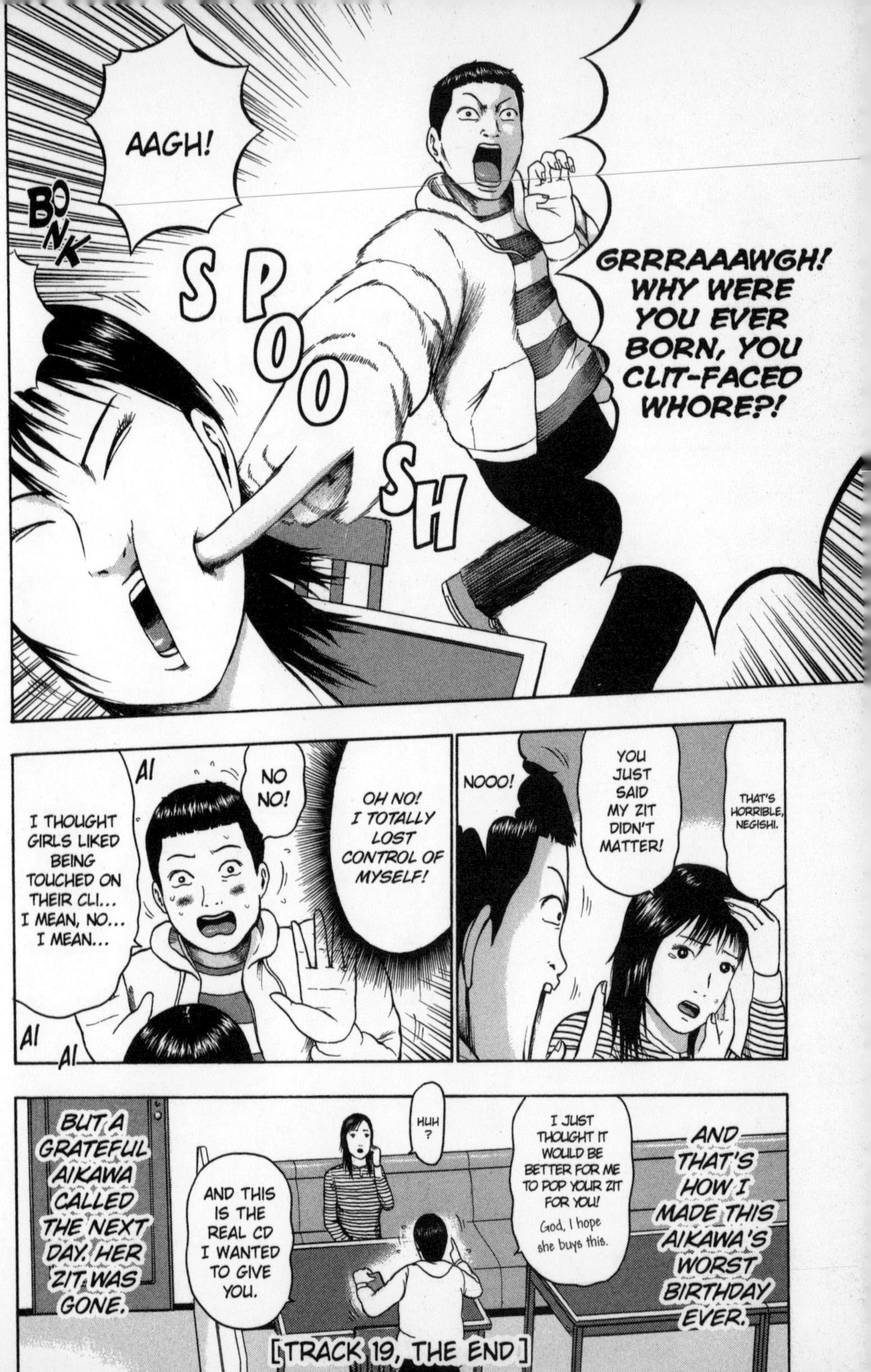
GRRRAAAWGH! WHY WERE YOU EVER BORN, YOU CLIT-FACED WHORE?!
AAGH!
BONK
SPOOSH
THAT'S HORRIBLE, NEGISHI.
YOU JUST SAID MY ZIT DIDN'T MATTER!
NOOO!
OH NO! I TOTALLY LOST CONTROL OF MYSELF!
NO NO!
AI
I THOUGHT GIRLS LIKED BEING TOUCHED ON THEIR CLI... I MEAN, NO... I MEAN...
AI
AI
AND THAT'S HOW I MADE THIS AIKAWA'S WORST BIRTHDAY EVER.
I JUST THOUGHT IT WOULD BE BETTER FOR ME TO POP YOUR ZIT FOR YOU!
God, I hope she buys this.
HUH?
AND THIS IS THE REAL CD I WANTED TO GIVE YOU.
BUT A GRATEFUL AIKAWA CALLED THE NEXT DAY. HER ZIT WAS GONE.
[TRACK 19, THE END]

DMC LEXICON

 ## DOING AWAY WITH FORMALITIES

Usually refers to when various ranks of people gather and drink without worrying about social mores or company protocol. One would say you've effectively **done away with formalities** if you've got your necktie wrapped on your forehead like Rambo, but you're also solid if you've simply started doing the cabbage patch as well.

Usage: Idiot! I don't care if we've done away with formalities. No one takes the boss's hairpiece and wears it on their face!

デトロイト・メタル・シティ
Detroit Metal City

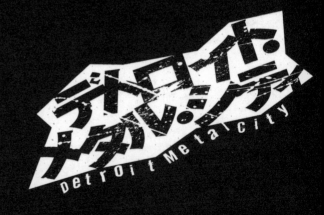

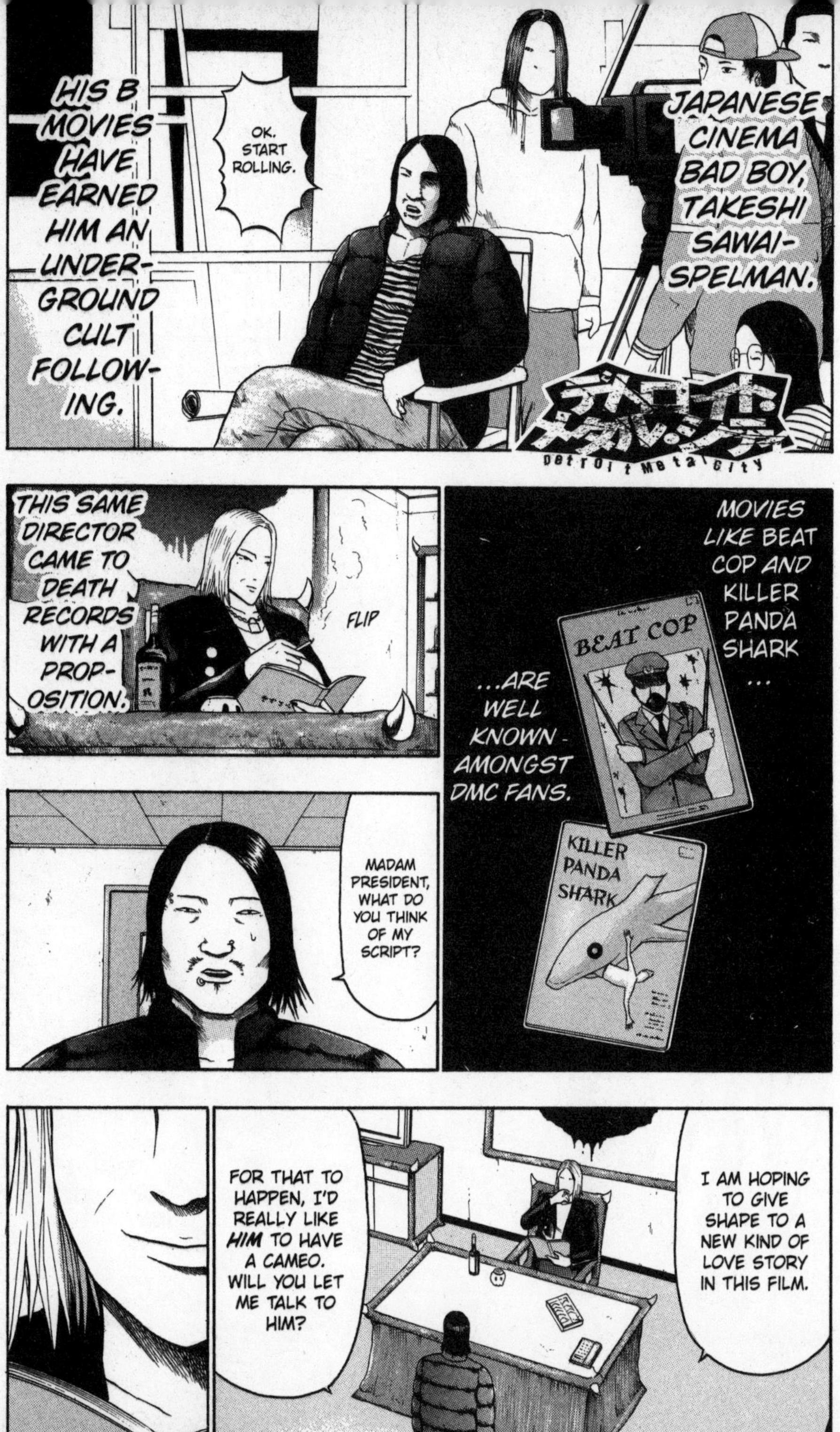
JAPANESE CINEMA BAD BOY, TAKESHI SAWAI-SPELMAN.
OK. START ROLLING.
HIS B MOVIES HAVE EARNED HIM AN UNDERGROUND CULT FOLLOWING.
Detroit Metal City
MOVIES LIKE BEAT COP AND KILLER PANDA SHARK...
BEAT COP
...ARE WELL KNOWN AMONGST DMC FANS.
KILLER PANDA SHARK
THIS SAME DIRECTOR CAME TO DEATH RECORDS WITH A PROPOSITION.
FLIP
MADAM PRESIDENT, WHAT DO YOU THINK OF MY SCRIPT?
I AM HOPING TO GIVE SHAPE TO A NEW KIND OF LOVE STORY IN THIS FILM.
FOR THAT TO HAPPEN, I'D REALLY LIKE *HIM* TO HAVE A CAMEO. WILL YOU LET ME TALK TO HIM?

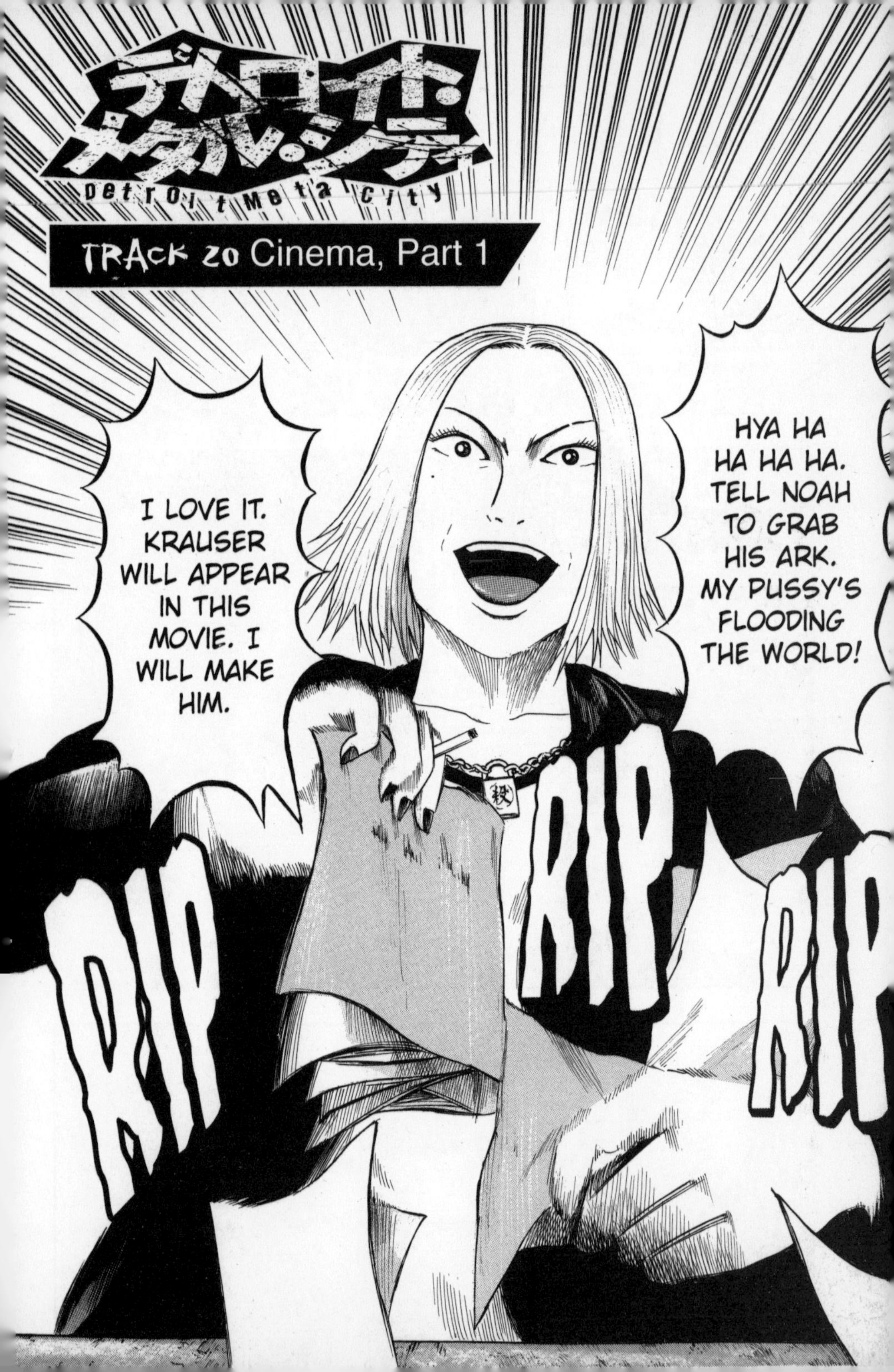
Detroit Metal City
TRACK 20 Cinema, Part 1
HYA HA HA HA HA. TELL NOAH TO GRAB HIS ARK. MY PUSSY'S FLOODING THE WORLD!
I LOVE IT. KRAUSER WILL APPEAR IN THIS MOVIE. I WILL MAKE HIM.
RIP
RIP
RIP

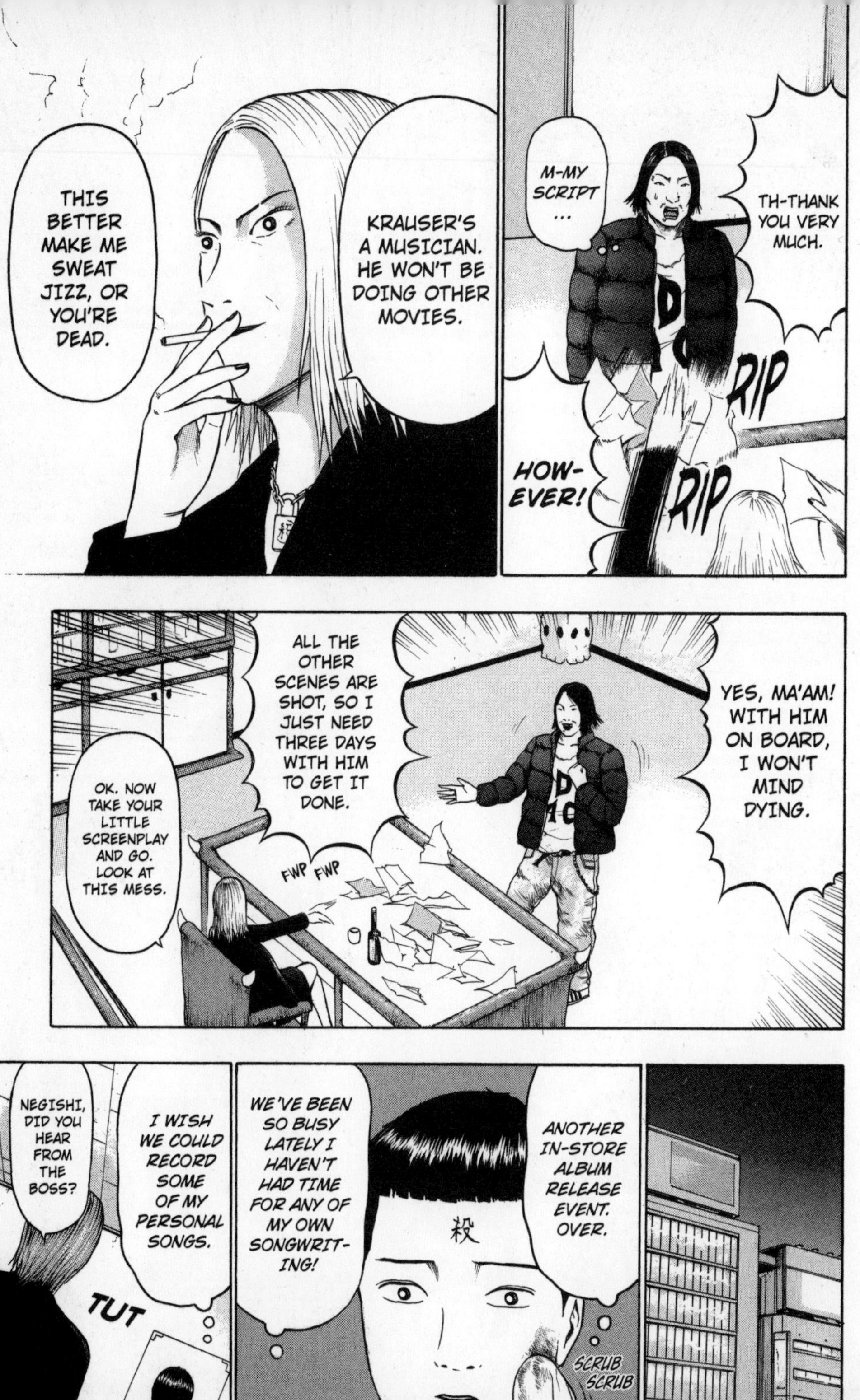
TH-THANK YOU VERY MUCH.
M-MY SCRIPT ...
RIP
RIP
HOW-EVER!
KRAUSER'S A MUSICIAN. HE WON'T BE DOING OTHER MOVIES.
THIS BETTER MAKE ME SWEAT JIZZ, OR YOU'RE DEAD.
YES, MA'AM! WITH HIM ON BOARD, I WON'T MIND DYING.
ALL THE OTHER SCENES ARE SHOT, SO I JUST NEED THREE DAYS WITH HIM TO GET IT DONE.
OK. NOW TAKE YOUR LITTLE SCREENPLAY AND GO. LOOK AT THIS MESS.
FWP FWP
ANOTHER IN-STORE ALBUM RELEASE EVENT. OVER.
WE'VE BEEN SO BUSY LATELY I HAVEN'T HAD TIME FOR ANY OF MY OWN SONGWRIT-ING!
SCRUB SCRUB
I WISH WE COULD RECORD SOME OF MY PERSONAL SONGS.
NEGISHI, DID YOU HEAR FROM THE BOSS?
TUT

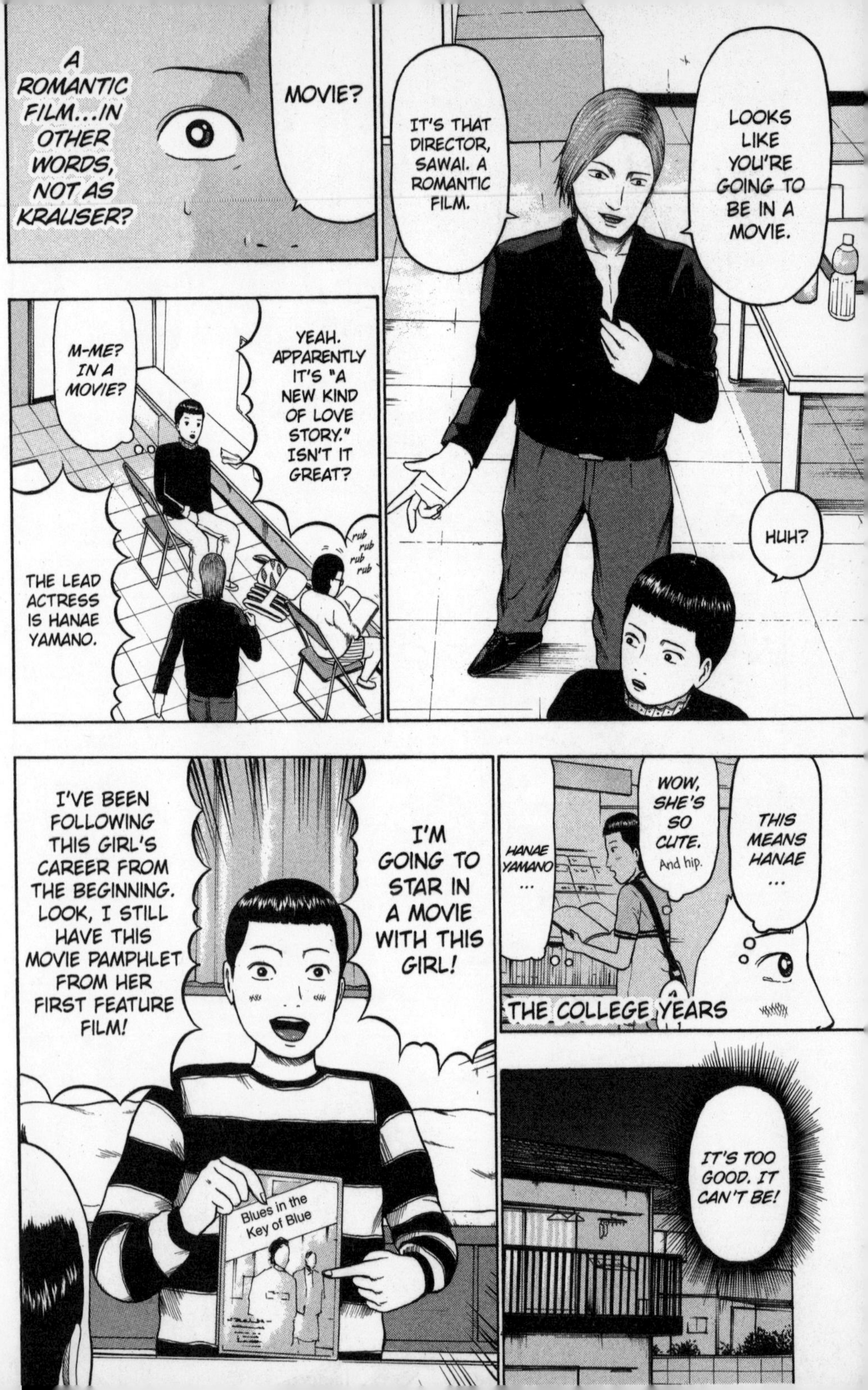
LOOKS LIKE YOU'RE GOING TO BE IN A MOVIE.
IT'S THAT DIRECTOR, SAWAI. A ROMANTIC FILM.
HUH?
MOVIE?
A ROMANTIC FILM...IN OTHER WORDS, NOT AS KRAUSER?
YEAH. APPARENTLY IT'S "A NEW KIND OF LOVE STORY." ISN'T IT GREAT?
M-ME? IN A MOVIE?
rub rub rub rub
THE LEAD ACTRESS IS HANAE YAMANO.
THIS MEANS HANAE ...
WOW, SHE'S SO CUTE. And hip.
HANAE YAMANO ...
THE COLLEGE YEARS
IT'S TOO GOOD. IT CAN'T BE!
I'M GOING TO STAR IN A MOVIE WITH THIS GIRL!
I'VE BEEN FOLLOWING THIS GIRL'S CAREER FROM THE BEGINNING. LOOK, I STILL HAVE THIS MOVIE PAMPHLET FROM HER FIRST FEATURE FILM!
Blues in the Key of Blue

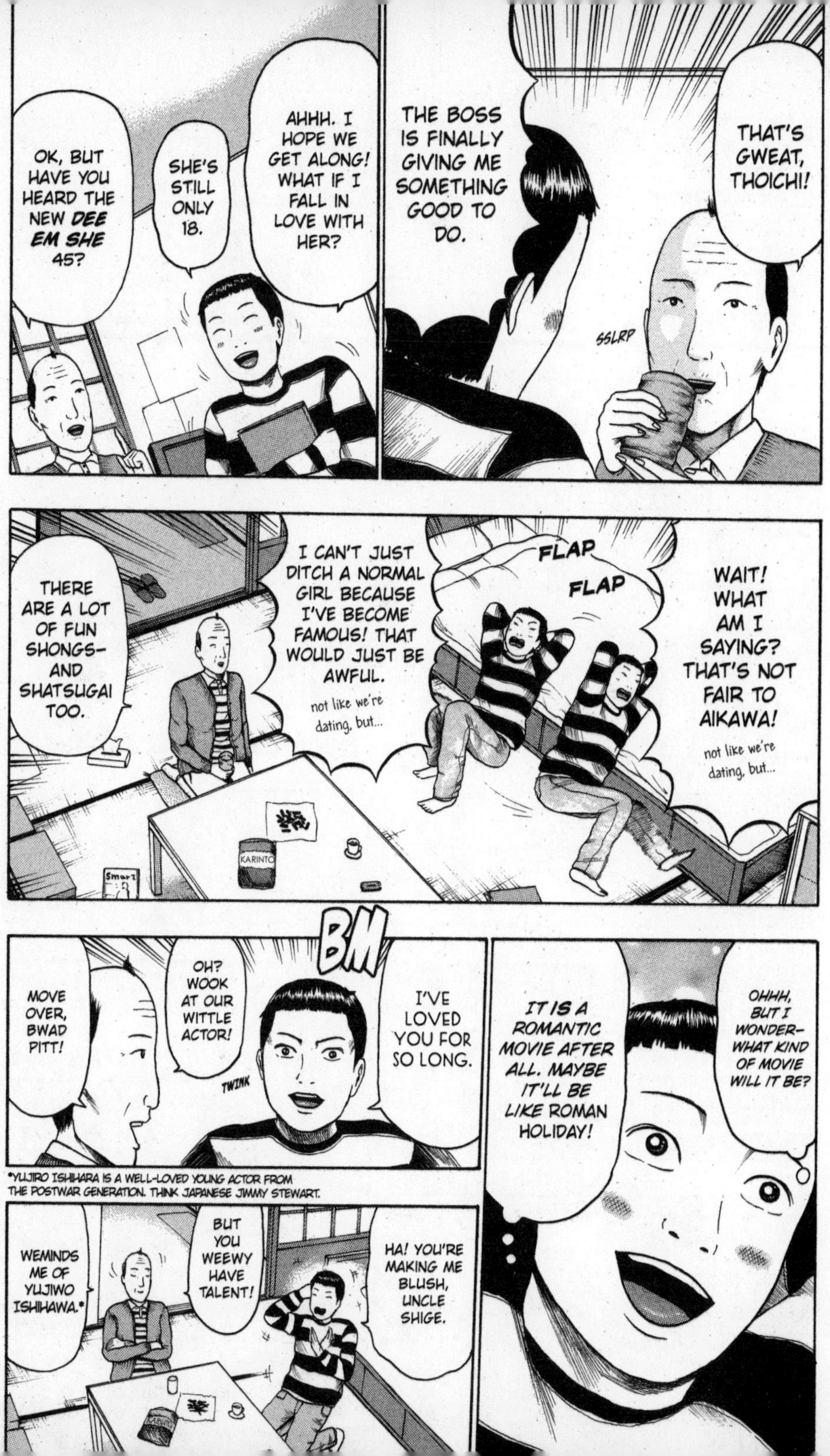
THAT'S GWEAT, THOICHI!
THE BOSS IS FINALLY GIVING ME SOMETHING GOOD TO DO.
SSLRP
AHHH. I HOPE WE GET ALONG! WHAT IF I FALL IN LOVE WITH HER?
SHE'S STILL ONLY 18.
OK, BUT HAVE YOU HEARD THE NEW DEE EM SHE 45?
WAIT! WHAT AM I SAYING? THAT'S NOT FAIR TO AIKAWA!
not like we're dating, but...
FLAP
FLAP
I CAN'T JUST DITCH A NORMAL GIRL BECAUSE I'VE BECOME FAMOUS! THAT WOULD JUST BE AWFUL.
not like we're dating, but...
THERE ARE A LOT OF FUN SHONGS- AND SHATSUGAI TOO.
KARINTO
OHHH, BUT I WONDER- WHAT KIND OF MOVIE WILL IT BE?
IT IS A ROMANTIC MOVIE AFTER ALL. MAYBE IT'LL BE LIKE ROMAN HOLIDAY!
BM
I'VE LOVED YOU FOR SO LONG.
OH? WOOK AT OUR WITTLE ACTOR!
TWINK
MOVE OVER, BWAD PITT!
*YUJIRO ISHIHARA IS A WELL-LOVED YOUNG ACTOR FROM THE POSTWAR GENERATION. THINK JAPANESE JIMMY STEWART.
HA! YOU'RE MAKING ME BLUSH, UNCLE SHIGE.
BUT YOU WEEWY HAVE TALENT!
WEMINDS ME OF YUJIWO ISHIHAWA.*

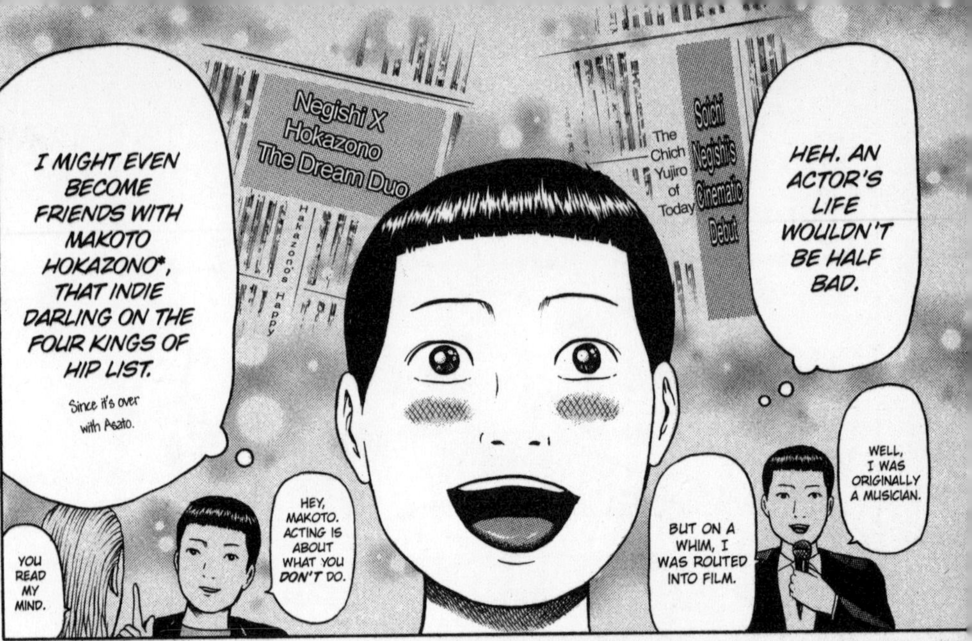
HEH. AN ACTOR'S LIFE WOULDN'T BE HALF BAD.
Soichi Negishi's Cinematic Debut
The Chich Yujiro of Today
Negishi X Hokazono The Dream Duo
I MIGHT EVEN BECOME FRIENDS WITH MAKOTO HOKAZONO*, THAT INDIE DARLING ON THE FOUR KINGS OF HIP LIST.
Since it's over with Asato.
WELL, I WAS ORIGINALLY A MUSICIAN.
BUT ON A WHIM, I WAS ROUTED INTO FILM.
HEY, MAKOTO. ACTING IS ABOUT WHAT YOU DON'T DO.
YOU READ MY MIND.

*MAKOTO HOKAZONO ALSO MEANS, "A REAL FOREIGNER."

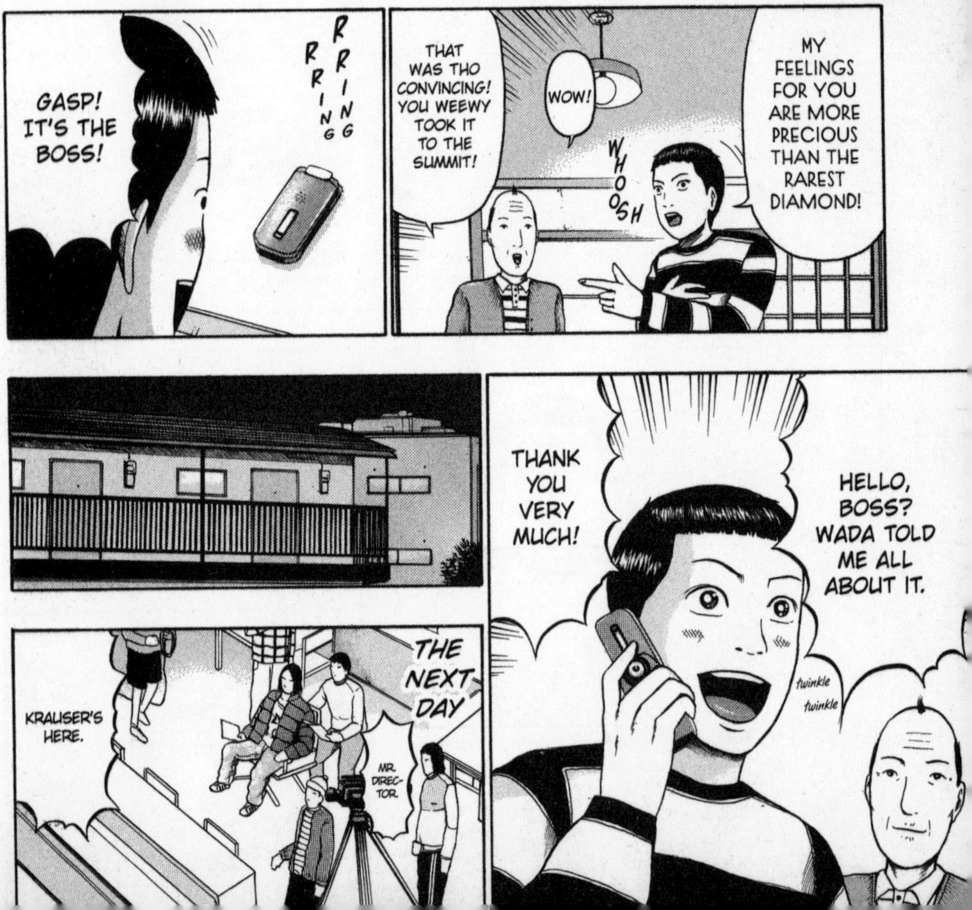
MY FEELINGS FOR YOU ARE MORE PRECIOUS THAN THE RAREST DIAMOND!
WHOOSH
WOW!
THAT WAS THO CONVINCING! YOU WEEWY TOOK IT TO THE SUMMIT!
RRING RRING
GASP! IT'S THE BOSS!
HELLO, BOSS? WADA TOLD ME ALL ABOUT IT.
THANK YOU VERY MUCH!
twinkle
twinkle
THE NEXT DAY
KRAUSER'S HERE.
MR. DIRECTOR.

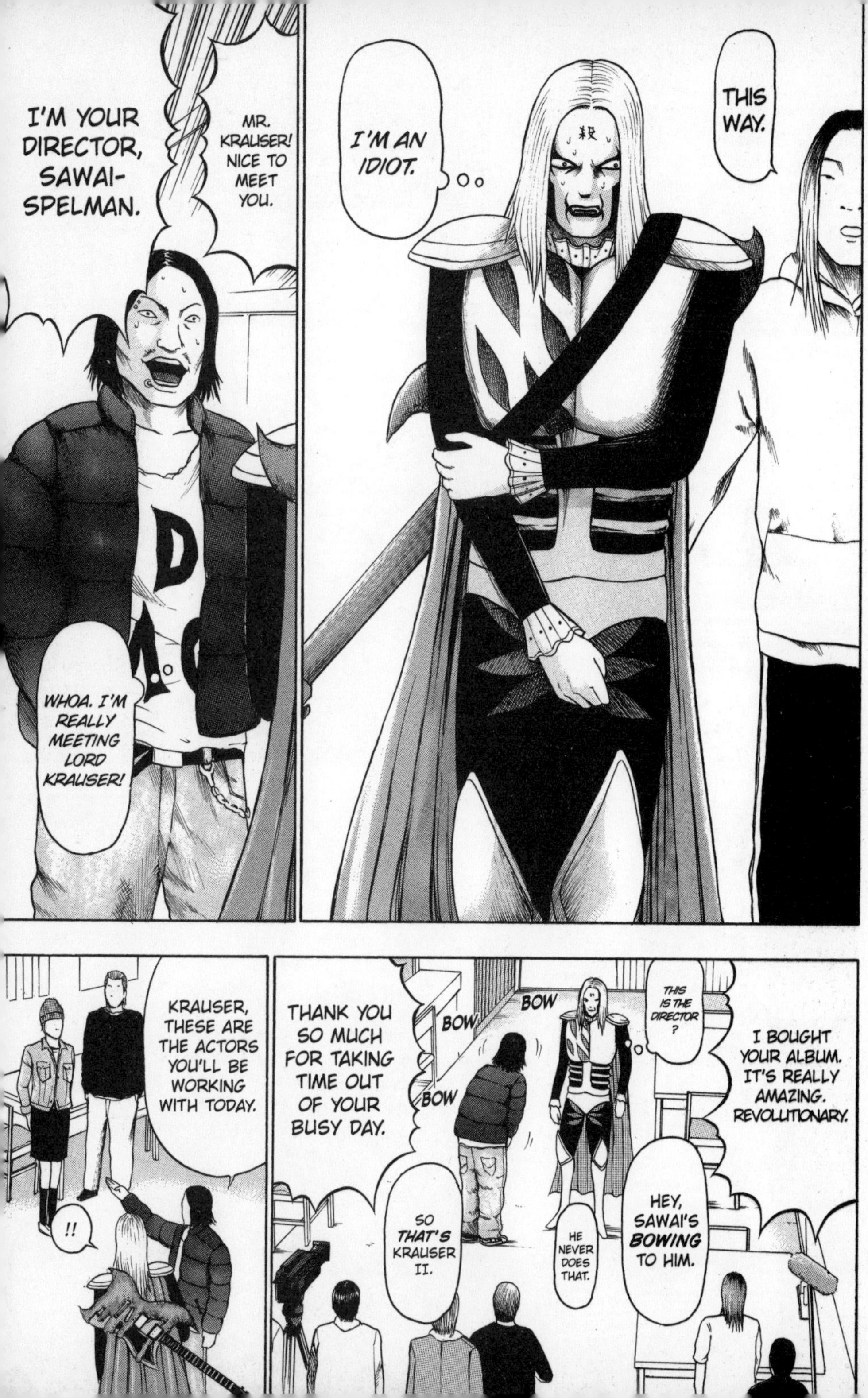
THIS WAY.
I'M AN IDIOT.
MR. KRAUSER! NICE TO MEET YOU.
I'M YOUR DIRECTOR, SAWAI-SPELMAN.
WHOA. I'M REALLY MEETING LORD KRAUSER!
THIS IS THE DIRECTOR?
I BOUGHT YOUR ALBUM. IT'S REALLY AMAZING. REVOLUTIONARY.
BOW
BOW
THANK YOU SO MUCH FOR TAKING TIME OUT OF YOUR BUSY DAY.
BOW
HEY, SAWAI'S BOWING TO HIM.
HE NEVER DOES THAT.
SO THAT'S KRAUSER II.
KRAUSER, THESE ARE THE ACTORS YOU'LL BE WORKING WITH TODAY.
!!

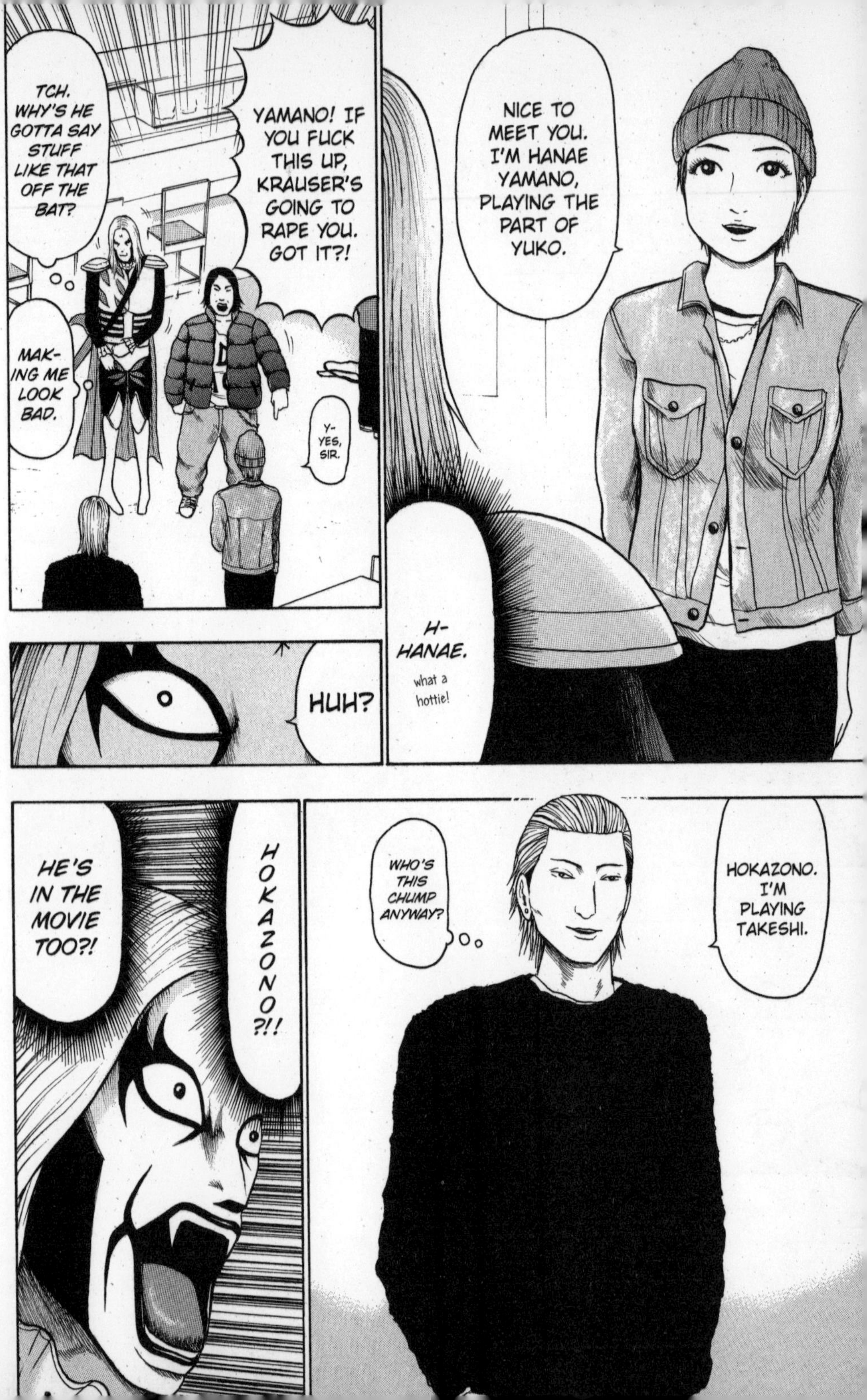
NICE TO MEET YOU. I'M HANAE YAMANO, PLAYING THE PART OF YUKO.
H-HANAE.
what a hottie!
YAMANO! IF YOU FUCK THIS UP, KRAUSER'S GOING TO RAPE YOU. GOT IT?!
Y-YES, SIR.
TCH. WHY'S HE GOTTA SAY STUFF LIKE THAT OFF THE BAT?
MAKING ME LOOK BAD.
HUH?
HOKAZONO. I'M PLAYING TAKESHI.
WHO'S THIS CHUMP ANYWAY?
HOKAZONO?!!
HE'S IN THE MOVIE TOO?!

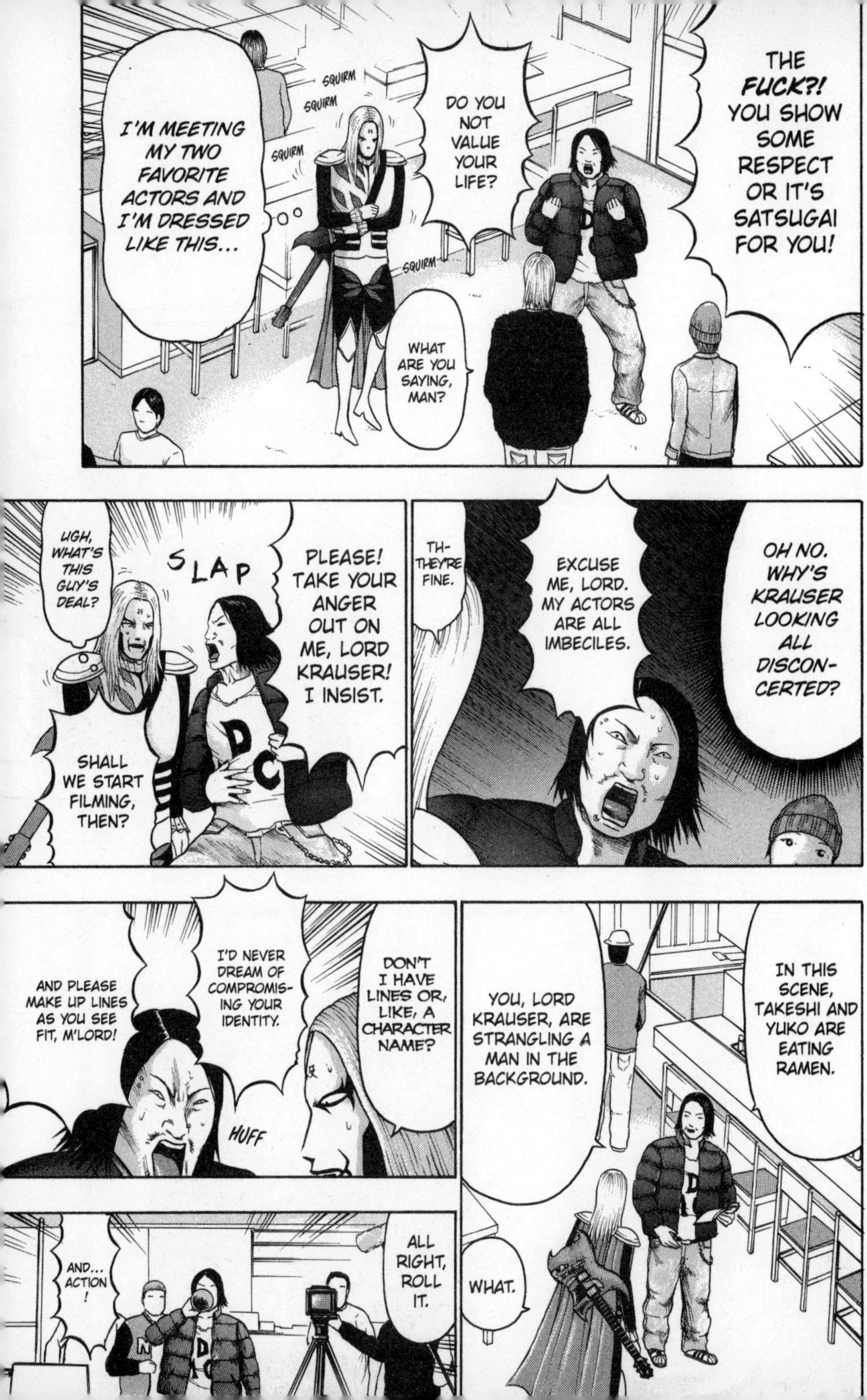
THE FUCK?! YOU SHOW SOME RESPECT OR IT'S SATSUGAI FOR YOU!
DO YOU NOT VALUE YOUR LIFE?
SQUIRM
SQUIRM
SQUIRM
SQUIRM
I'M MEETING MY TWO FAVORITE ACTORS AND I'M DRESSED LIKE THIS...
WHAT ARE YOU SAYING, MAN?
OH NO. WHY'S KRAUSER LOOKING ALL DISCONCERTED?
EXCUSE ME, LORD. MY ACTORS ARE ALL IMBECILES.
TH-THEY'RE FINE.
PLEASE! TAKE YOUR ANGER OUT ON ME, LORD KRAUSER! I INSIST.
SLAP
UGH, WHAT'S THIS GUY'S DEAL?
SHALL WE START FILMING, THEN?
IN THIS SCENE, TAKESHI AND YUKO ARE EATING RAMEN.
YOU, LORD KRAUSER, ARE STRANGLING A MAN IN THE BACKGROUND.
WHAT.
DON'T I HAVE LINES OR, LIKE, A CHARACTER NAME?
I'D NEVER DREAM OF COMPROMISING YOUR IDENTITY.
AND PLEASE MAKE UP LINES AS YOU SEE FIT, M'LORD!
HUFF
ALL RIGHT, ROLL IT.
AND... ACTION!

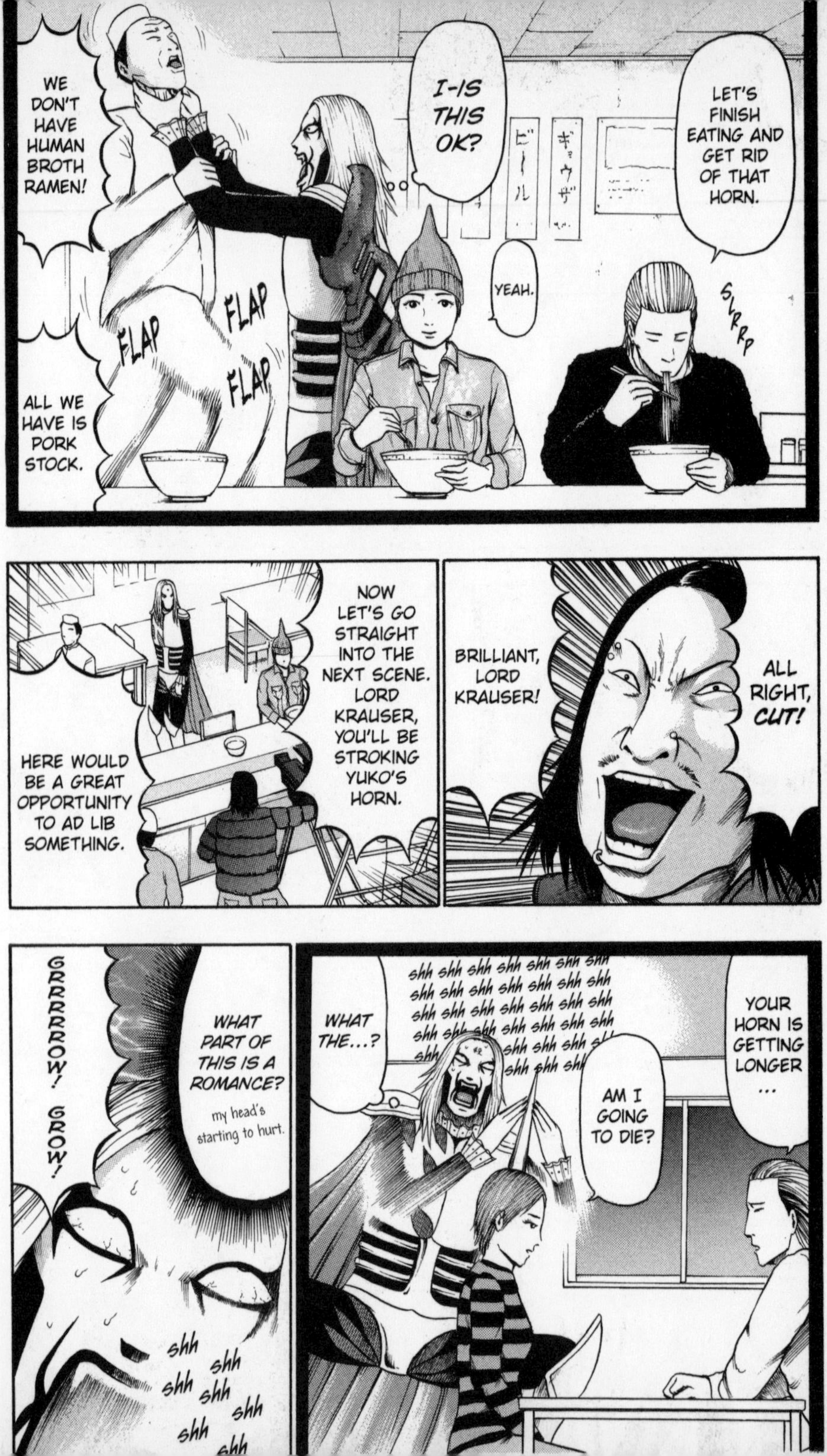
LET'S FINISH EATING AND GET RID OF THAT HORN.
SLRRP
I-IS THIS OK?
YEAH.
WE DON'T HAVE HUMAN BROTH RAMEN!
FLAP FLAP
FLAP
ALL WE HAVE IS PORK STOCK.
ALL RIGHT, CUT!
BRILLIANT, LORD KRAUSER!
NOW LET'S GO STRAIGHT INTO THE NEXT SCENE. LORD KRAUSER, YOU'LL BE STROKING YUKO'S HORN.
HERE WOULD BE A GREAT OPPORTUNITY TO AD LIB SOMETHING.
YOUR HORN IS GETTING LONGER...
shh shh shh shh shh shh shh
AM I GOING TO DIE?
WHAT THE...?
GRRRRROW! GROW!
WHAT PART OF THIS IS A ROMANCE?
my head's starting to hurt.
shh shh shh shh shh shh shh

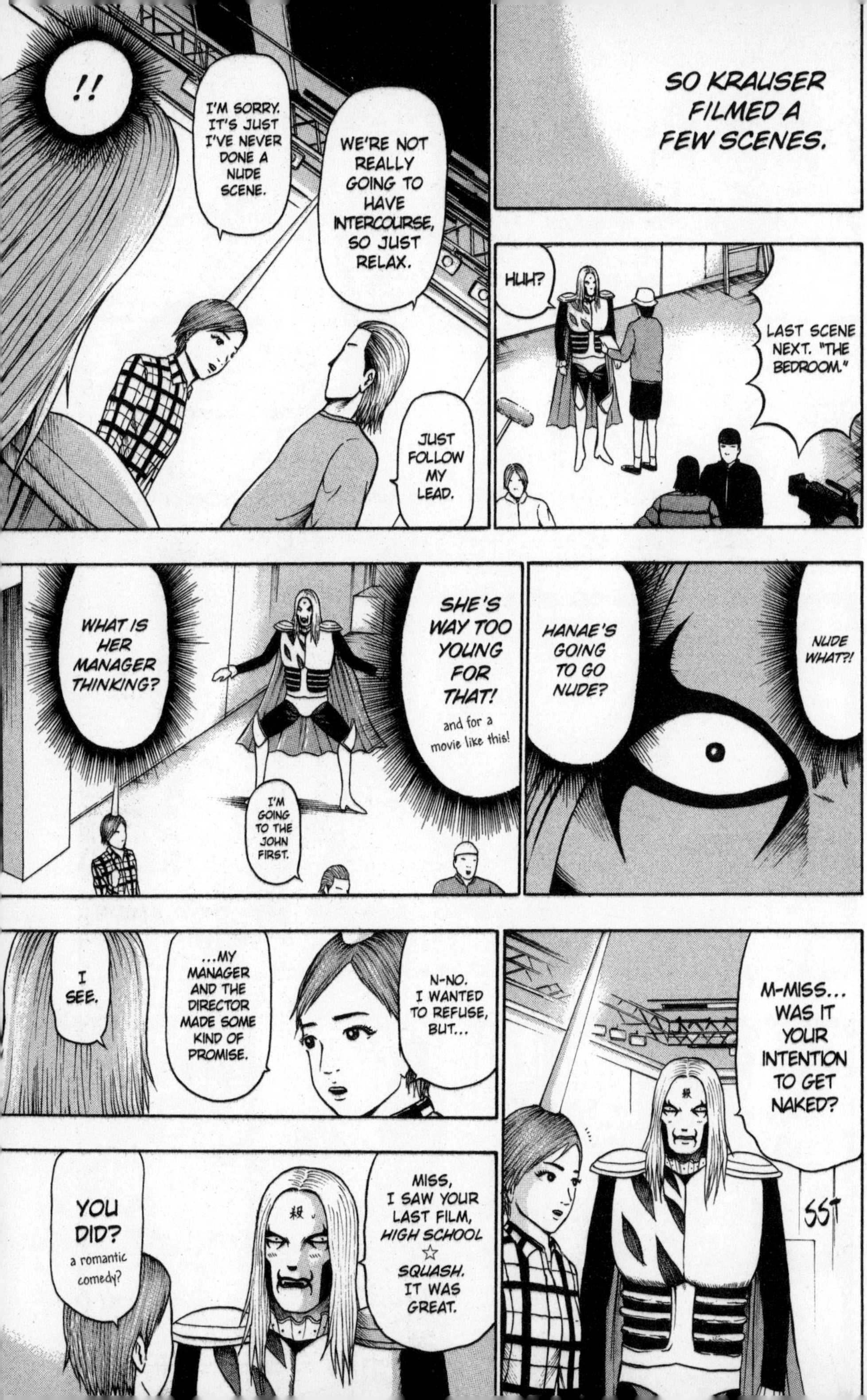
SO KRAUSER FILMED A FEW SCENES.
HUH?
LAST SCENE NEXT. "THE BEDROOM."
I'M SORRY. IT'S JUST I'VE NEVER DONE A NUDE SCENE.
WE'RE NOT REALLY GOING TO HAVE INTERCOURSE, SO JUST RELAX.
!!
JUST FOLLOW MY LEAD.
NUDE WHAT?!
HANAE'S GOING TO GO NUDE?
SHE'S WAY TOO YOUNG FOR THAT!
and for a movie like this!
WHAT IS HER MANAGER THINKING?
I'M GOING TO THE JOHN FIRST.
M-MISS... WAS IT YOUR INTENTION TO GET NAKED?
SST
N-NO. I WANTED TO REFUSE, BUT...
...MY MANAGER AND THE DIRECTOR MADE SOME KIND OF PROMISE.
I SEE.
MISS, I SAW YOUR LAST FILM, *HIGH SCHOOL ☆ SQUASH*. IT WAS GREAT.
YOU DID?
a romantic comedy?

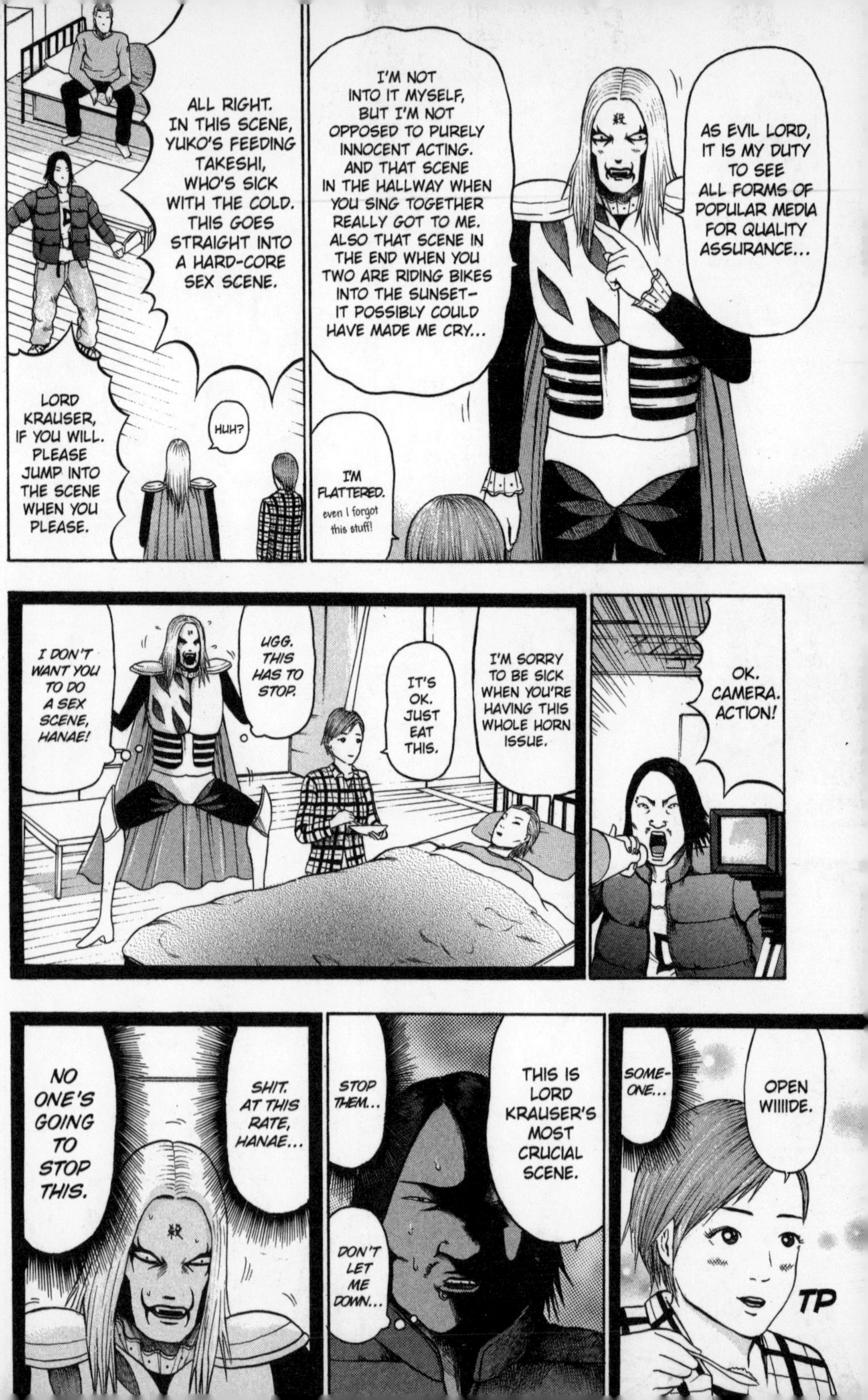
AS EVIL LORD, IT IS MY DUTY TO SEE ALL FORMS OF POPULAR MEDIA FOR QUALITY ASSURANCE...
I'M NOT INTO IT MYSELF, BUT I'M NOT OPPOSED TO PURELY INNOCENT ACTING. AND THAT SCENE IN THE HALLWAY WHEN YOU SING TOGETHER REALLY GOT TO ME. ALSO THAT SCENE IN THE END WHEN YOU TWO ARE RIDING BIKES INTO THE SUNSET- IT POSSIBLY COULD HAVE MADE ME CRY...
I'M FLATTERED.
even I forgot this stuff!
ALL RIGHT. IN THIS SCENE, YUKO'S FEEDING TAKESHI, WHO'S SICK WITH THE COLD. THIS GOES STRAIGHT INTO A HARD-CORE SEX SCENE.
HUH?
LORD KRAUSER, IF YOU WILL. PLEASE JUMP INTO THE SCENE WHEN YOU PLEASE.
OK. CAMERA. ACTION!
I'M SORRY TO BE SICK WHEN YOU'RE HAVING THIS WHOLE HORN ISSUE.
IT'S OK. JUST EAT THIS.
UGG. THIS HAS TO STOP.
I DON'T WANT YOU TO DO A SEX SCENE, HANAE!
OPEN WIIIDE.
SOME-ONE...
TP
THIS IS LORD KRAUSER'S MOST CRUCIAL SCENE.
STOP THEM...
DON'T LET ME DOWN...
SHIT. AT THIS RATE, HANAE...
NO ONE'S GOING TO STOP THIS.

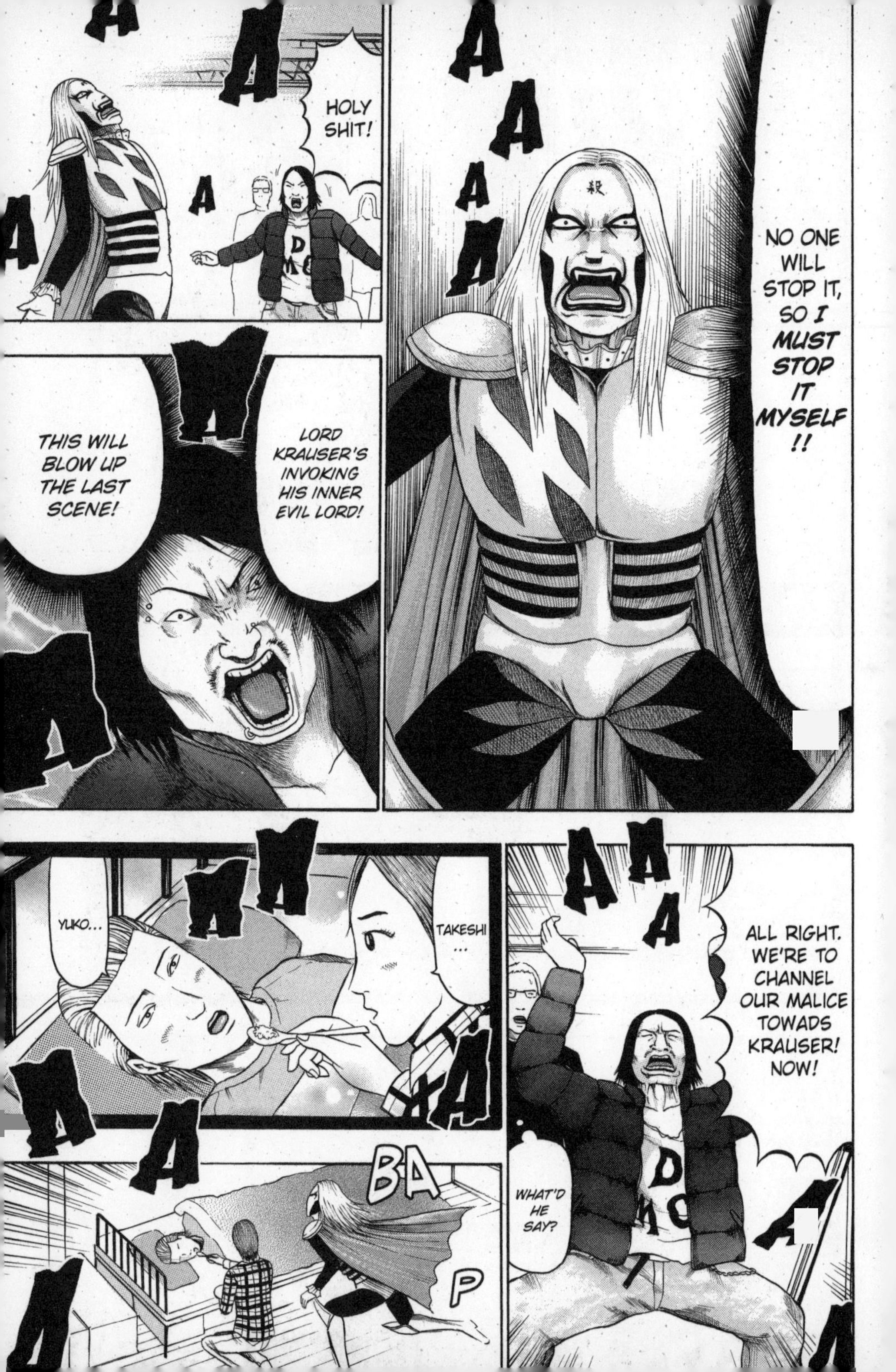
NO ONE WILL STOP IT, SO I MUST STOP IT MYSELF!!
HOLY SHIT!
LORD KRAUSER'S INVOKING HIS INNER EVIL LORD!
THIS WILL BLOW UP THE LAST SCENE!
ALL RIGHT. WE'RE TO CHANNEL OUR MALICE TOWADS KRAUSER! NOW!
WHAT'D HE SAY?
TAKESHI...
YUKO...
BA
P

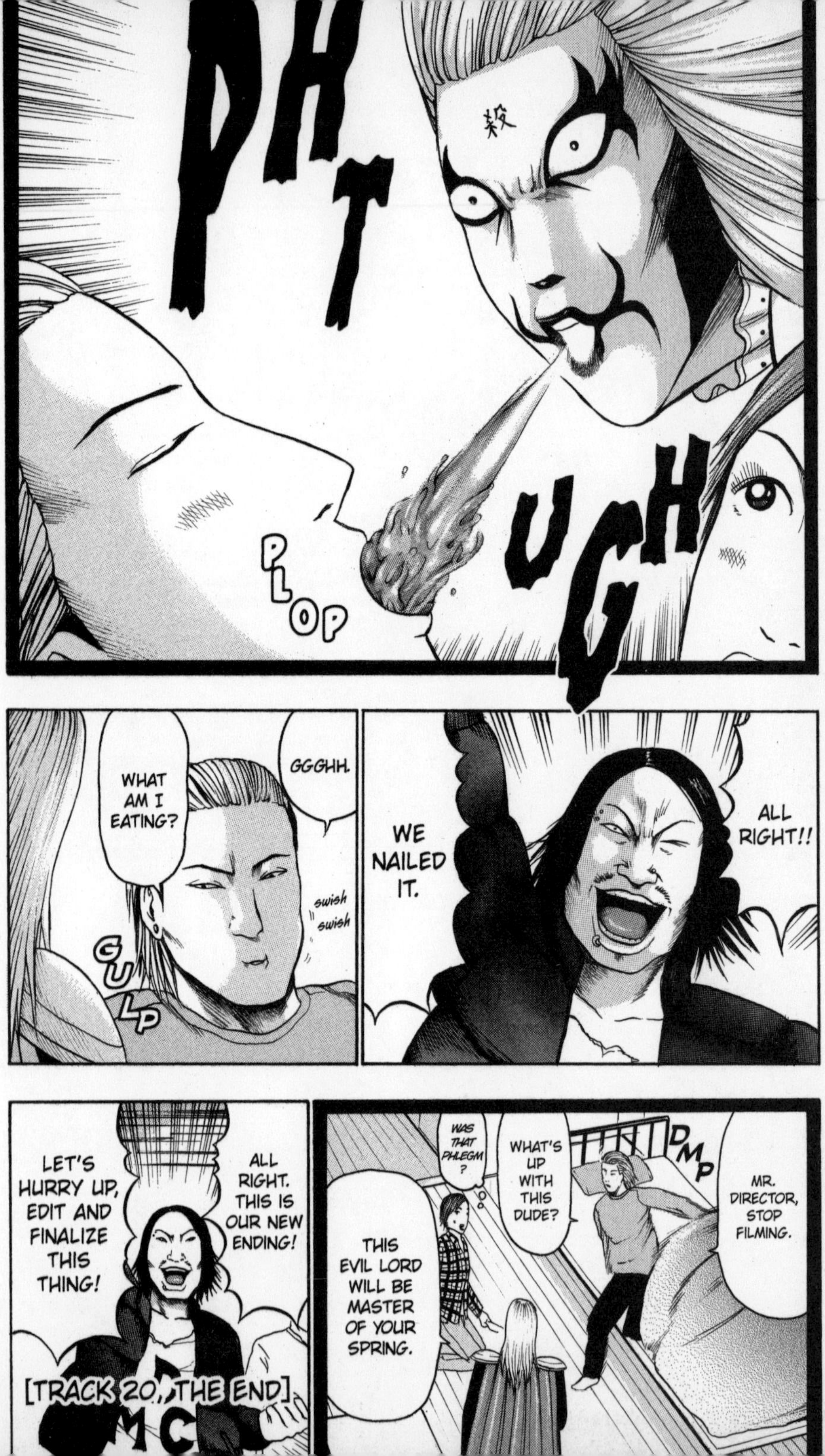
PHT
殺
UGH
PLOP
ALL RIGHT!!
WE NAILED IT.
GGGHH.
WHAT AM I EATING?
swish swish
GULP
MR. DIRECTOR, STOP FILMING.
DMP
WHAT'S UP WITH THIS DUDE?
WAS THAT PHLEGM?
THIS EVIL LORD WILL BE MASTER OF YOUR SPRING.
ALL RIGHT. THIS IS OUR NEW ENDING!
LET'S HURRY UP, EDIT AND FINALIZE THIS THING!
[TRACK 20, THE END]

DMC LEXICON

ROMAN HOLIDAY

Directed by William Wyler, starring Audrey Hepburn. A timeless classic loved by people still, teaching the beauty of love, romance and longing. Needless to say, the film has strongly influenced this manga.

Usage: Detroit Metal City? Oh, it's like the Japanese Roman Holiday!

デトロイト・メタル・シティ

Detroit Metal City

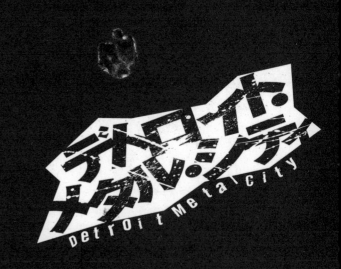

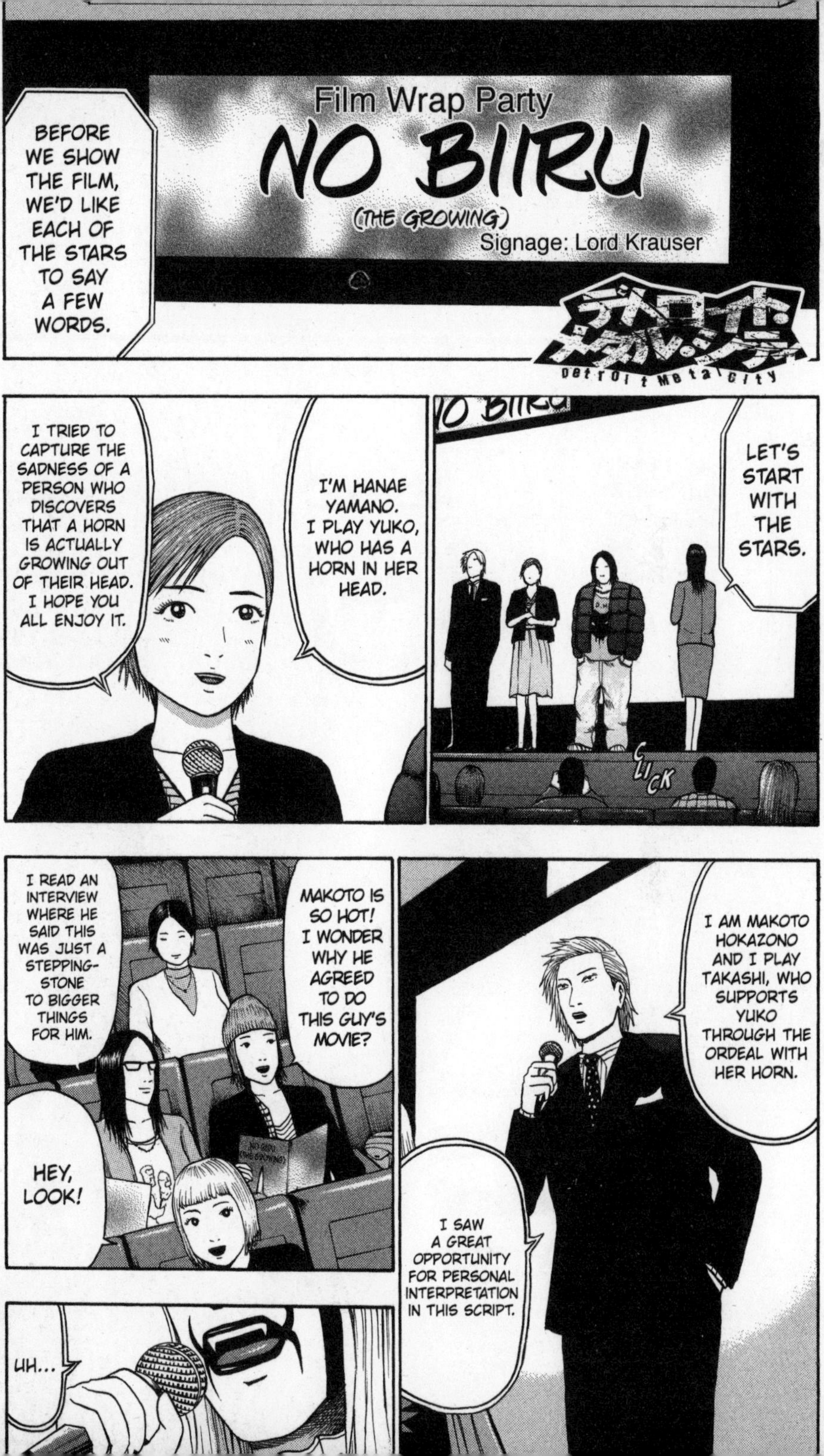
Film Wrap Party
NO BIIRU
(THE GROWING)
Signage: Lord Krauser
BEFORE WE SHOW THE FILM, WE'D LIKE EACH OF THE STARS TO SAY A FEW WORDS.
LET'S START WITH THE STARS.
CLICK
I'M HANAE YAMANO. I PLAY YUKO, WHO HAS A HORN IN HER HEAD.
I TRIED TO CAPTURE THE SADNESS OF A PERSON WHO DISCOVERS THAT A HORN IS ACTUALLY GROWING OUT OF THEIR HEAD. I HOPE YOU ALL ENJOY IT.
I AM MAKOTO HOKAZONO AND I PLAY TAKASHI, WHO SUPPORTS YUKO THROUGH THE ORDEAL WITH HER HORN.
I SAW A GREAT OPPORTUNITY FOR PERSONAL INTERPRETATION IN THIS SCRIPT.
MAKOTO IS SO HOT! I WONDER WHY HE AGREED TO DO THIS GUY'S MOVIE?
I READ AN INTERVIEW WHERE HE SAID THIS WAS JUST A STEPPING-STONE TO BIGGER THINGS FOR HIM.
HEY, LOOK!
UH...

デトロイト・メタル・シティ

Detroit Metal City

CHAPTER 21 Cinema, Part 2

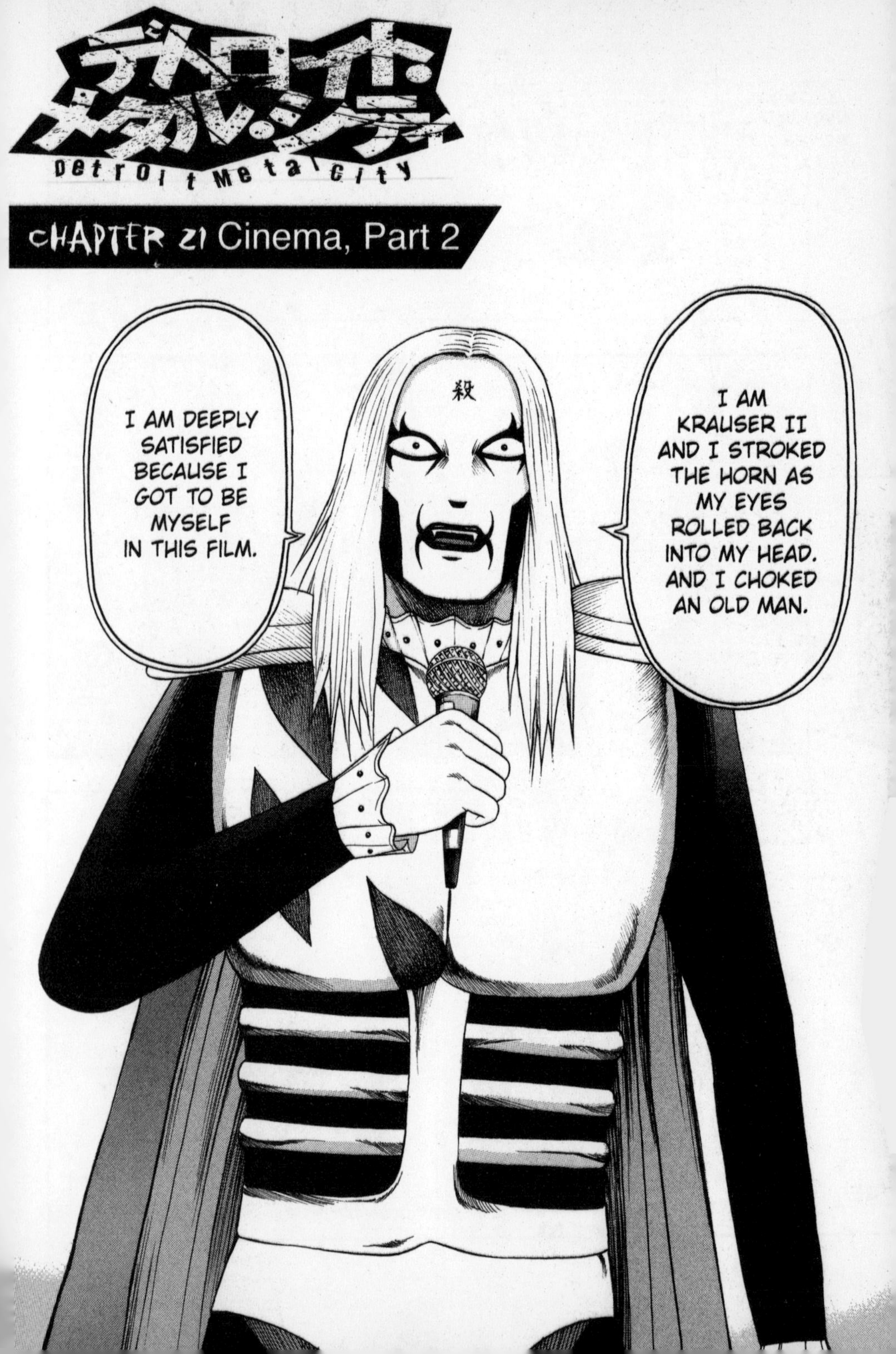
I AM KRAUSER II AND I STROKED THE HORN AS MY EYES ROLLED BACK INTO MY HEAD. AND I CHOKED AN OLD MAN.
殺
I AM DEEPLY SATISFIED BECAUSE I GOT TO BE MYSELF IN THIS FILM.

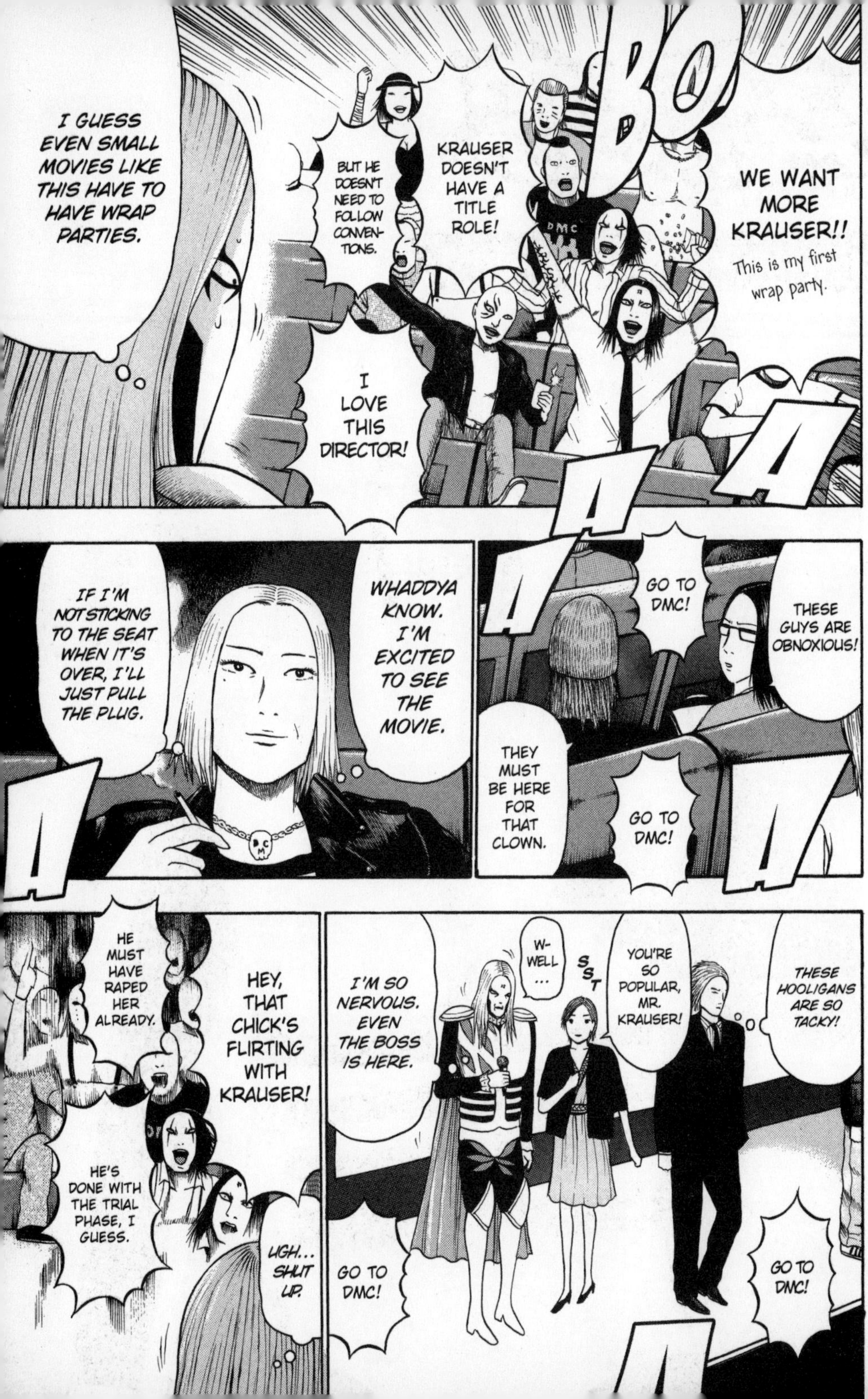
BO
WE WANT MORE KRAUSER!!
This is my first wrap party.
KRAUSER DOESN'T HAVE A TITLE ROLE!
BUT HE DOESN'T NEED TO FOLLOW CONVEN-TIONS.
I LOVE THIS DIRECTOR!
I GUESS EVEN SMALL MOVIES LIKE THIS HAVE TO HAVE WRAP PARTIES.
AAA
THESE GUYS ARE OBNOXIOUS!
GO TO DMC!
GO TO DMC!
THEY MUST BE HERE FOR THAT CLOWN.
AA
WHADDYA KNOW. I'M EXCITED TO SEE THE MOVIE.
IF I'M NOT STICKING TO THE SEAT WHEN IT'S OVER, I'LL JUST PULL THE PLUG.
A
THESE HOOLIGANS ARE SO TACKY!
GO TO DMC!
YOU'RE SO POPULAR, MR. KRAUSER!
SST
W-WELL...
I'M SO NERVOUS. EVEN THE BOSS IS HERE.
GO TO DMC!
HEY, THAT CHICK'S FLIRTING WITH KRAUSER!
HE MUST HAVE RAPED HER ALREADY.
HE'S DONE WITH THE TRIAL PHASE, I GUESS.
UGH... SHUT UP.

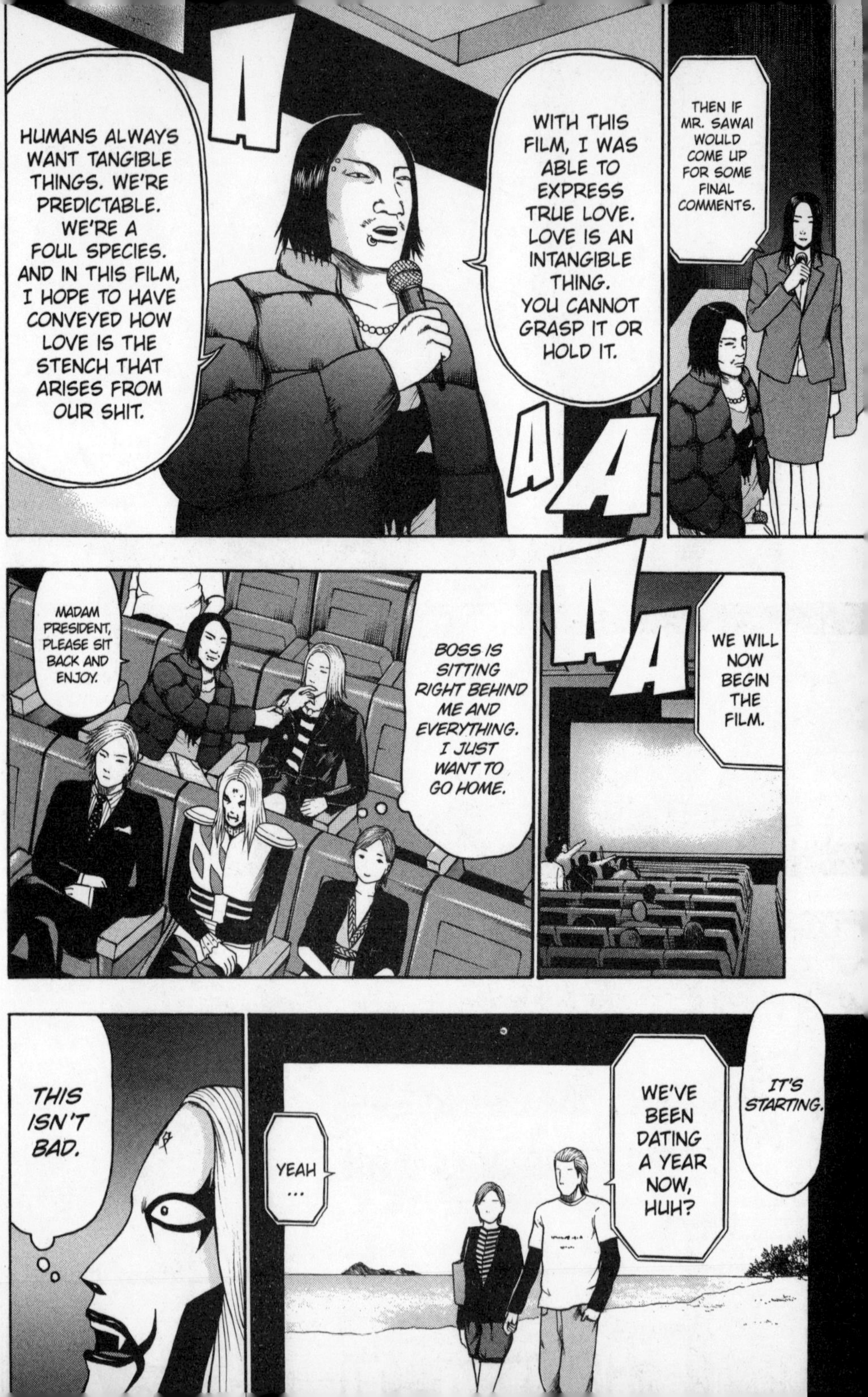
THEN IF MR. SAWAI WOULD COME UP FOR SOME FINAL COMMENTS.
WITH THIS FILM, I WAS ABLE TO EXPRESS TRUE LOVE. LOVE IS AN INTANGIBLE THING. YOU CANNOT GRASP IT OR HOLD IT.
A
HUMANS ALWAYS WANT TANGIBLE THINGS. WE'RE PREDICTABLE. WE'RE A FOUL SPECIES. AND IN THIS FILM, I HOPE TO HAVE CONVEYED HOW LOVE IS THE STENCH THAT ARISES FROM OUR SHIT.
A A
A A
WE WILL NOW BEGIN THE FILM.
BOSS IS SITTING RIGHT BEHIND ME AND EVERYTHING. I JUST WANT TO GO HOME.
MADAM PRESIDENT, PLEASE SIT BACK AND ENJOY.
IT'S STARTING.
WE'VE BEEN DATING A YEAR NOW, HUH?
YEAH...
THIS ISN'T BAD.

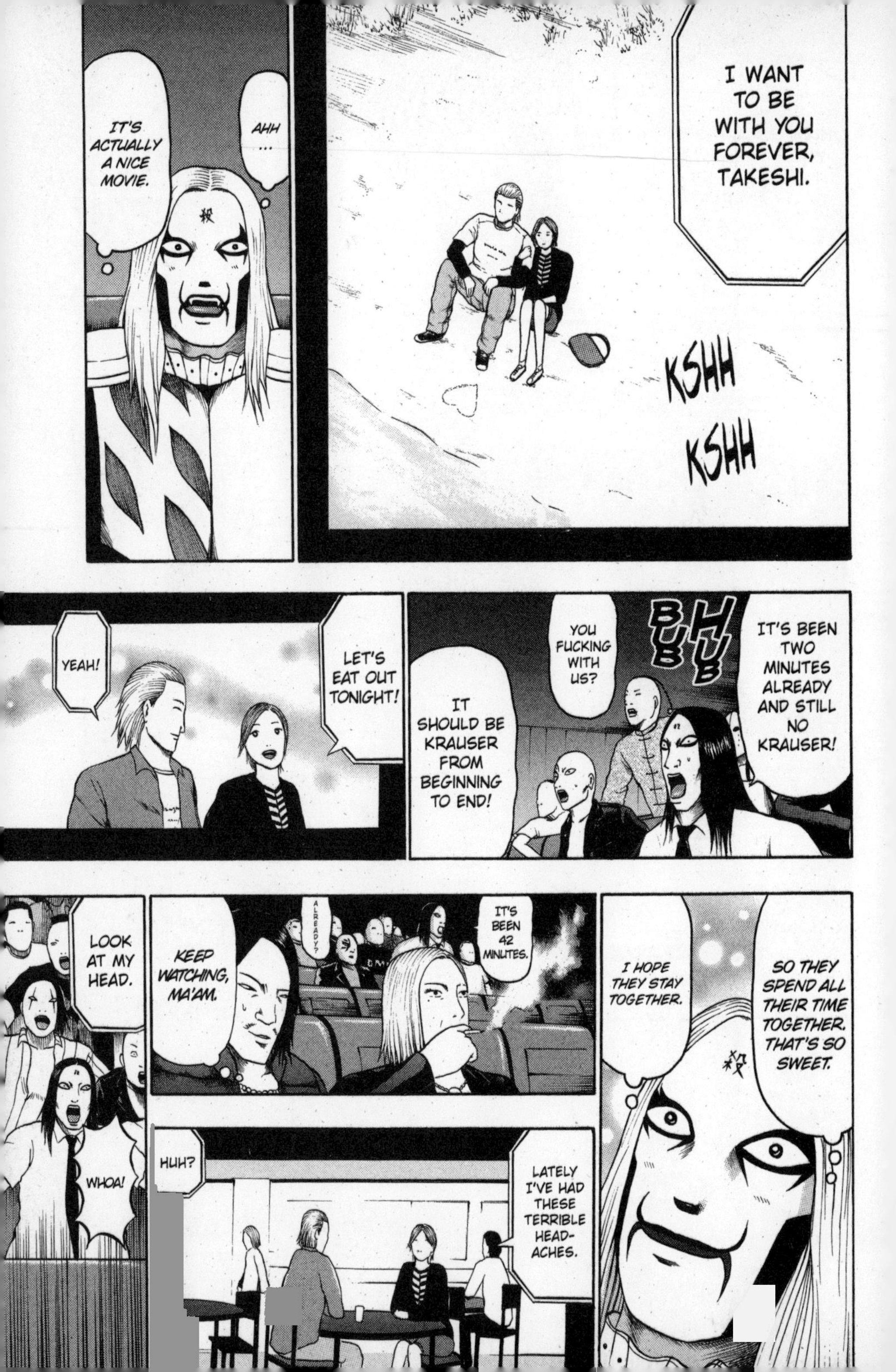
I WANT TO BE WITH YOU FOREVER, TAKESHI.
KSHH
KSHH
AHH ...
IT'S ACTUALLY A NICE MOVIE.
IT'S BEEN TWO MINUTES ALREADY AND STILL NO KRAUSER!
BUBHUB
YOU FUCKING WITH US?
IT SHOULD BE KRAUSER FROM BEGINNING TO END!
LET'S EAT OUT TONIGHT!
YEAH!
SO THEY SPEND ALL THEIR TIME TOGETHER. THAT'S SO SWEET.
I HOPE THEY STAY TOGETHER.
IT'S BEEN 42 MINUTES.
ALREADY?
KEEP WATCHING, MA'AM.
LATELY I'VE HAD THESE TERRIBLE HEAD-ACHES.
HUH?
LOOK AT MY HEAD.
WHOA!

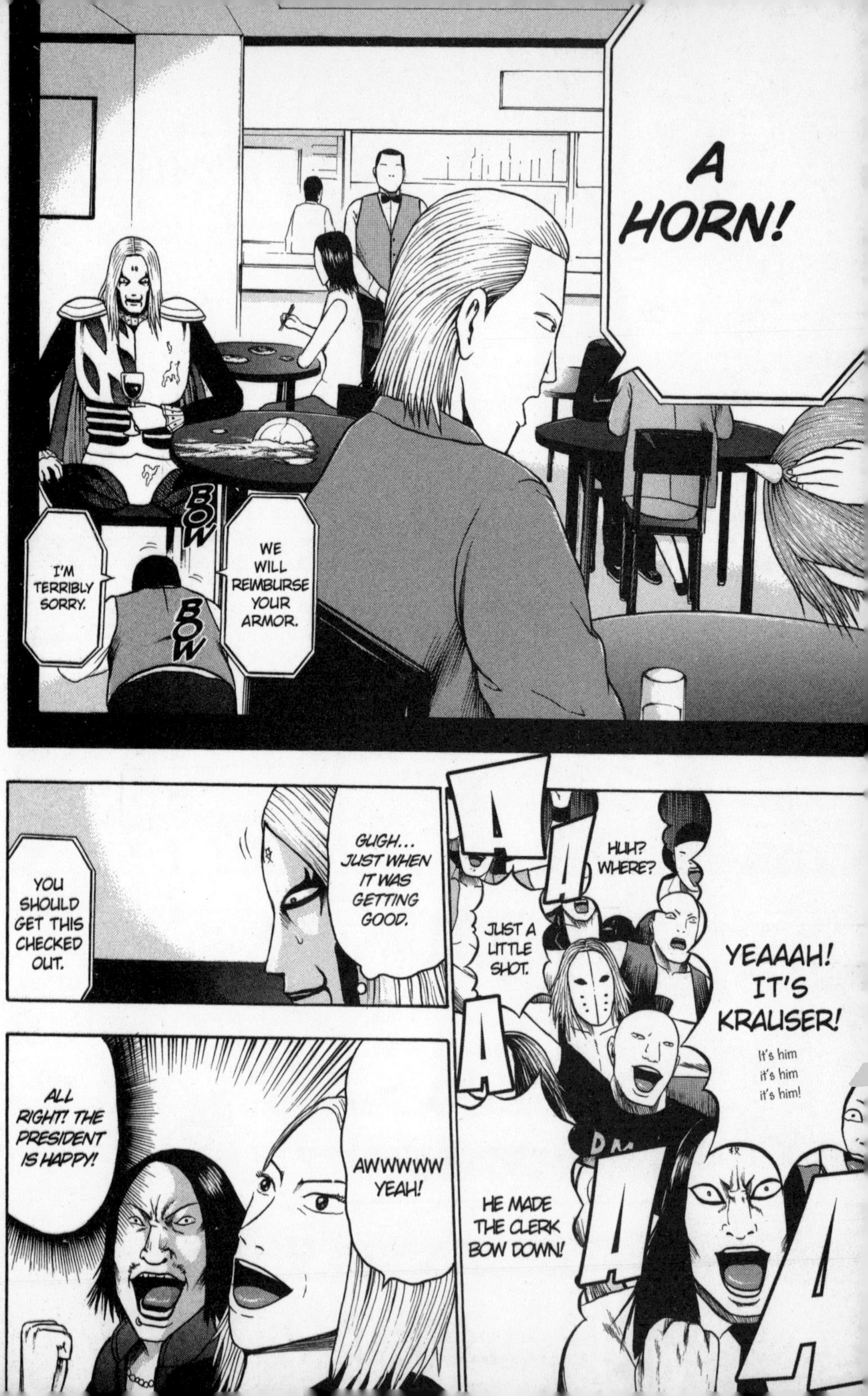
A HORN!
WE WILL REIMBURSE YOUR ARMOR.
BOW BOW
I'M TERRIBLY SORRY.
AAAA
HUH? WHERE?
YEAAAH! IT'S KRAUSER!
It's him it's him it's him!
JUST A LITTLE SHOT.
HE MADE THE CLERK BOW DOWN!
GUGH... JUST WHEN IT WAS GETTING GOOD.
YOU SHOULD GET THIS CHECKED OUT.
AWWWWW YEAH!
ALL RIGHT! THE PRESIDENT IS HAPPY!

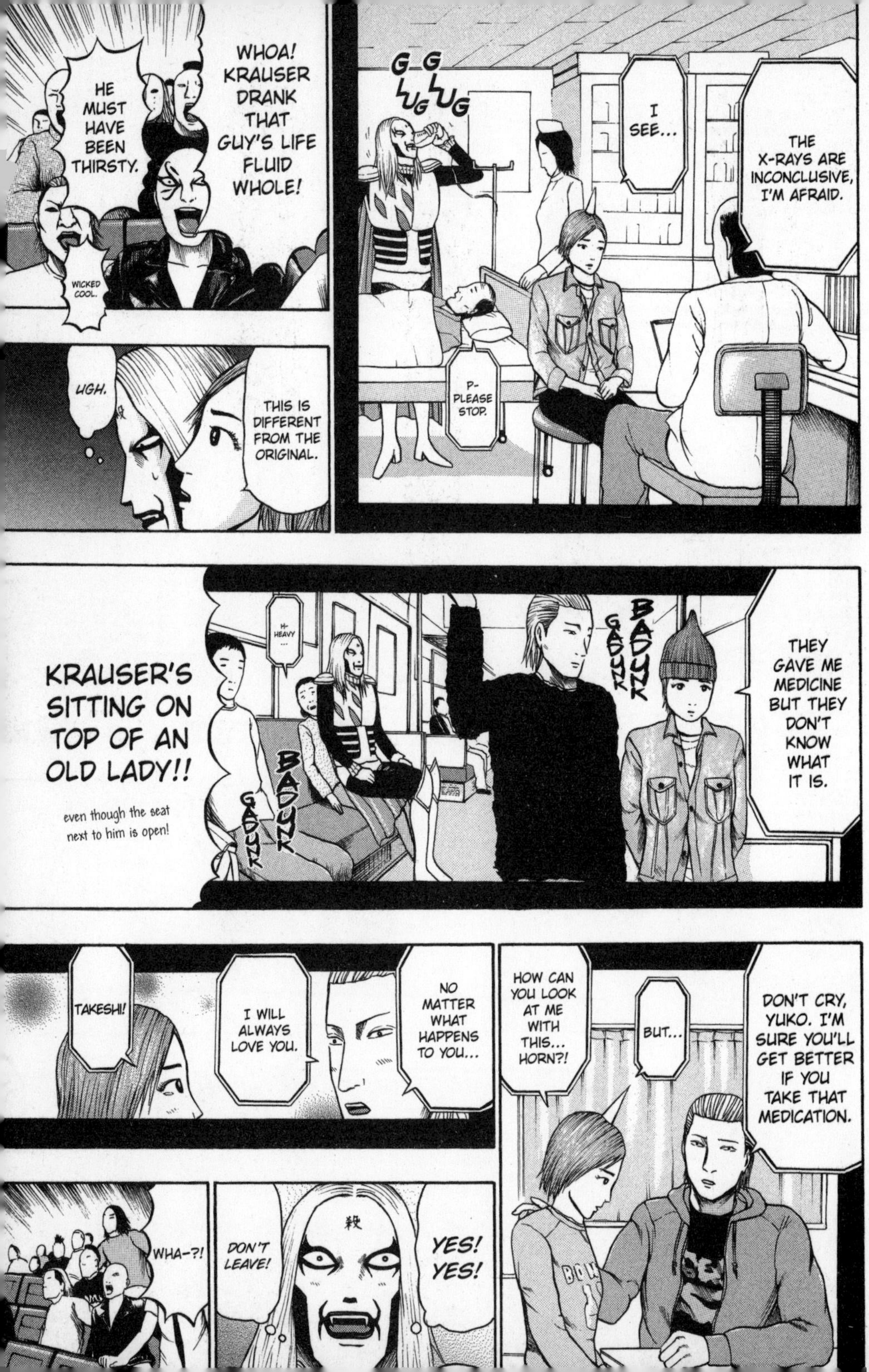
THE X-RAYS ARE INCONCLUSIVE, I'M AFRAID.
I SEE...
G G LUG LUG
P-PLEASE STOP.
WHOA! KRAUSER DRANK THAT GUY'S LIFE FLUID WHOLE!
HE MUST HAVE BEEN THIRSTY.
WICKED COOL.
THIS IS DIFFERENT FROM THE ORIGINAL.
UGH.
THEY GAVE ME MEDICINE BUT THEY DON'T KNOW WHAT IT IS.
BADUNK GADUNK
H-HEAVY...
BADUNK GADUNK
KRAUSER'S SITTING ON TOP OF AN OLD LADY!!
even though the seat next to him is open!
DON'T CRY, YUKO. I'M SURE YOU'LL GET BETTER IF YOU TAKE THAT MEDICATION.
BUT...
HOW CAN YOU LOOK AT ME WITH THIS... HORN?!
NO MATTER WHAT HAPPENS TO YOU...
I WILL ALWAYS LOVE YOU.
TAKESHI!
YES! YES!
DON'T LEAVE!
WHA-?!

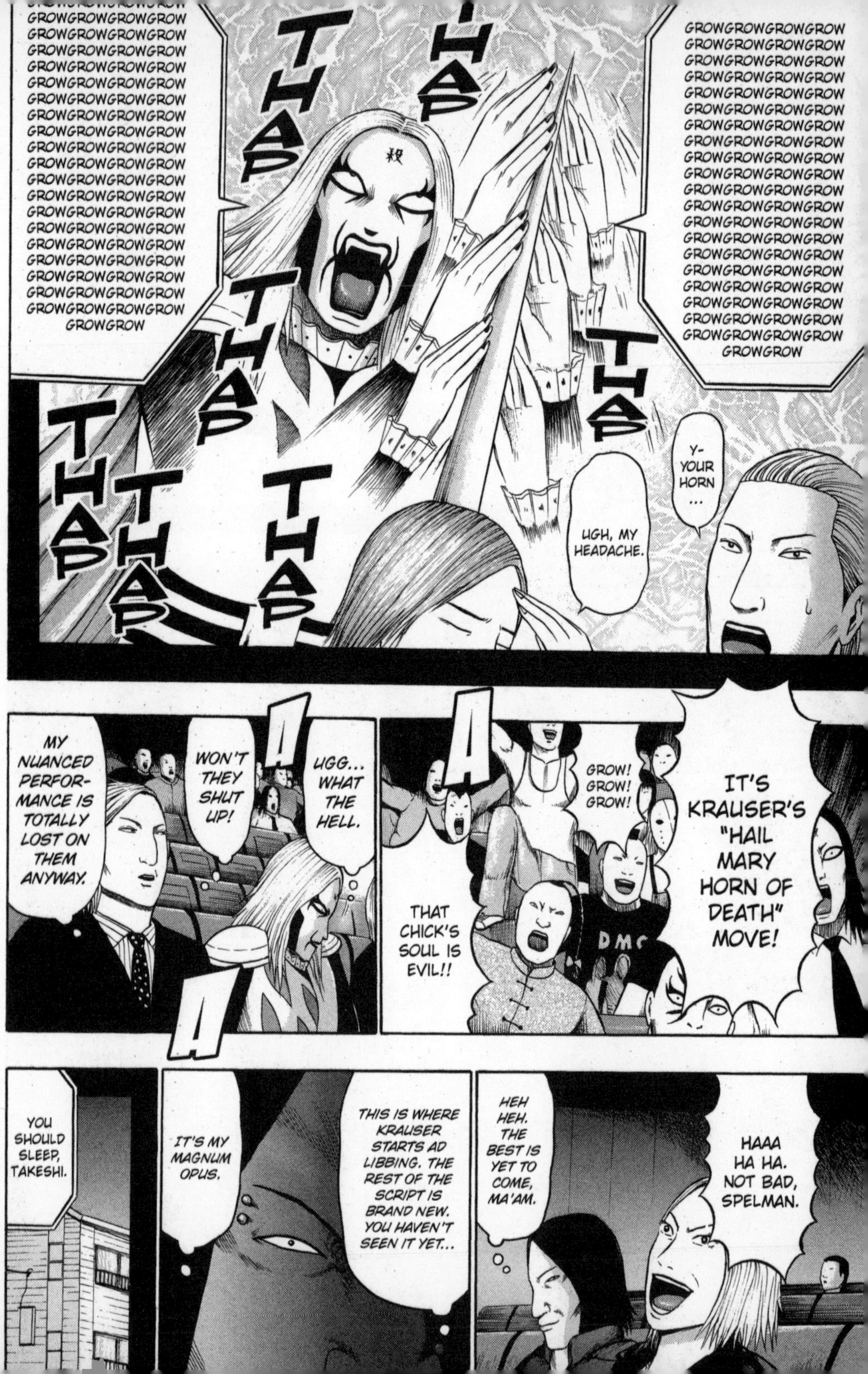
GROWGROWGROWGROW GROWGROWGROWGROW GROWGROWGROWGROW GROWGROWGROWGROW GROWGROWGROWGROW GROWGROWGROWGROW GROWGROWGROWGROW GROWGROWGROWGROW GROWGROWGROWGROW GROWGROWGROWGROW GROWGROWGROWGROW GROWGROWGROWGROW GROWGROWGROWGROW GROWGROWGROWGROW GROWGROWGROWGROW GROWGROWGROWGROW GROWGROWGROWGROW GROWGROWGROWGROW GROWGROWGROWGROW GROWGROW
GROWGROWGROWGROW GROWGROWGROWGROW GROWGROWGROWGROW GROWGROWGROWGROW GROWGROWGROWGROW GROWGROWGROWGROW GROWGROWGROWGROW GROWGROWGROWGROW GROWGROWGROWGROW GROWGROWGROWGROW GROWGROWGROWGROW GROWGROWGROWGROW GROWGROWGROWGROW GROWGROWGROWGROW GROWGROWGROWGROW GROWGROWGROWGROW GROWGROWGROWGROW GROWGROWGROWGROW GROWGROWGROWGROW GROWGROW
THAP
THAP
THAP
THAP
THAP
THAP
THAP
Y-YOUR HORN...
UGH, MY HEADACHE.
IT'S KRAUSER'S "HAIL MARY HORN OF DEATH" MOVE!
A
GROW! GROW! GROW!
THAT CHICK'S SOUL IS EVIL!!
A
UGG... WHAT THE HELL.
WON'T THEY SHUT UP!
MY NUANCED PERFORMANCE IS TOTALLY LOST ON THEM ANYWAY.
A
HAAA HA HA. NOT BAD, SPELMAN.
HEH HEH. THE BEST IS YET TO COME, MA'AM.
THIS IS WHERE KRAUSER STARTS AD LIBBING. THE REST OF THE SCRIPT IS BRAND NEW. YOU HAVEN'T SEEN IT YET...
IT'S MY MAGNUM OPUS.
YOU SHOULD SLEEP, TAKESHI.

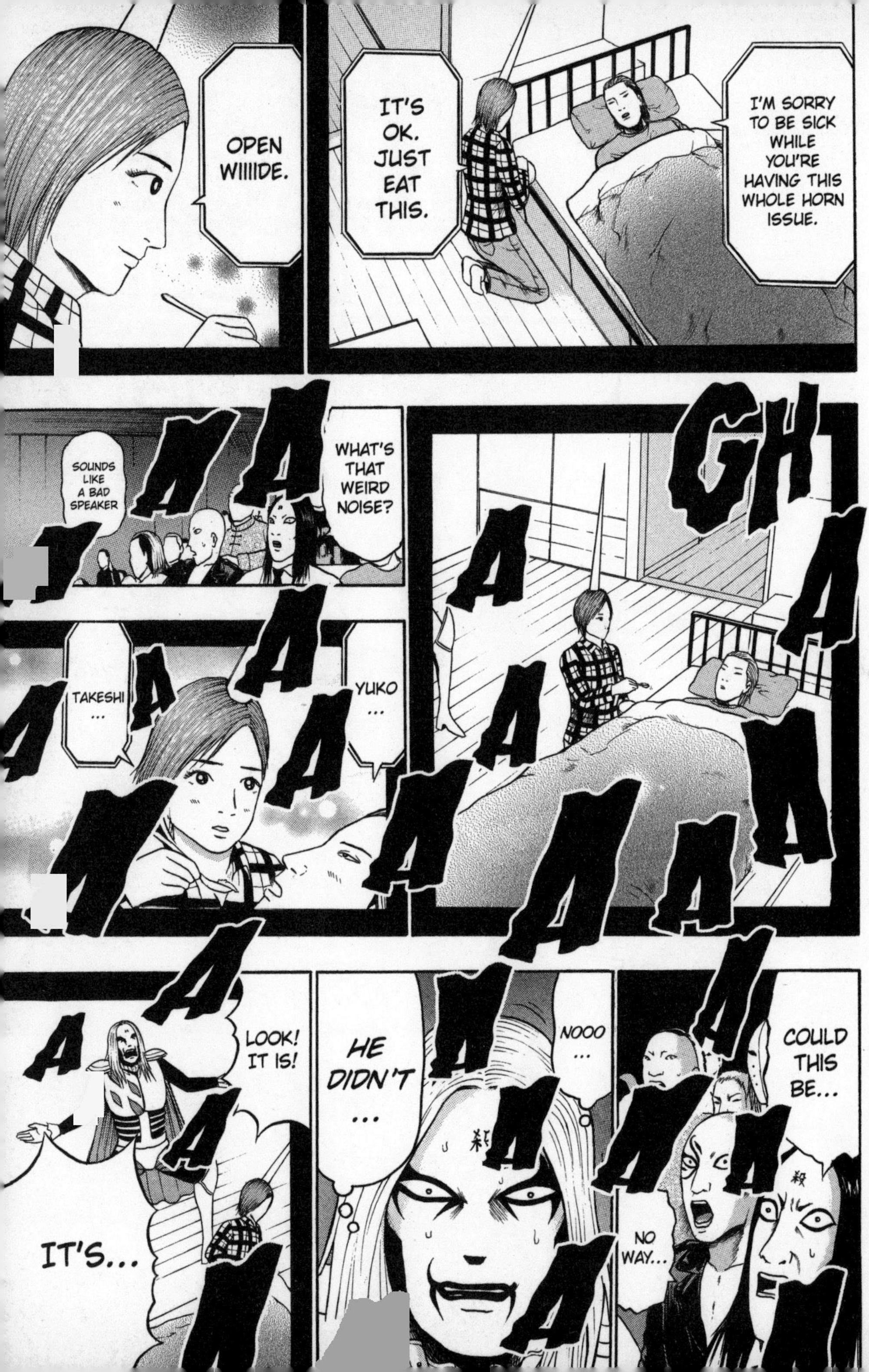

I'M SORRY TO BE SICK WHILE YOU'RE HAVING THIS WHOLE HORN ISSUE.
IT'S OK. JUST EAT THIS.
OPEN WIIIIDE.
GH
WHAT'S THAT WEIRD NOISE?
SOUNDS LIKE A BAD SPEAKER
YUKO ...
TAKESHI ...
COULD THIS BE...
NOOO ...
NO WAY...
HE DIDN'T ...
LOOK! IT IS!
IT'S...

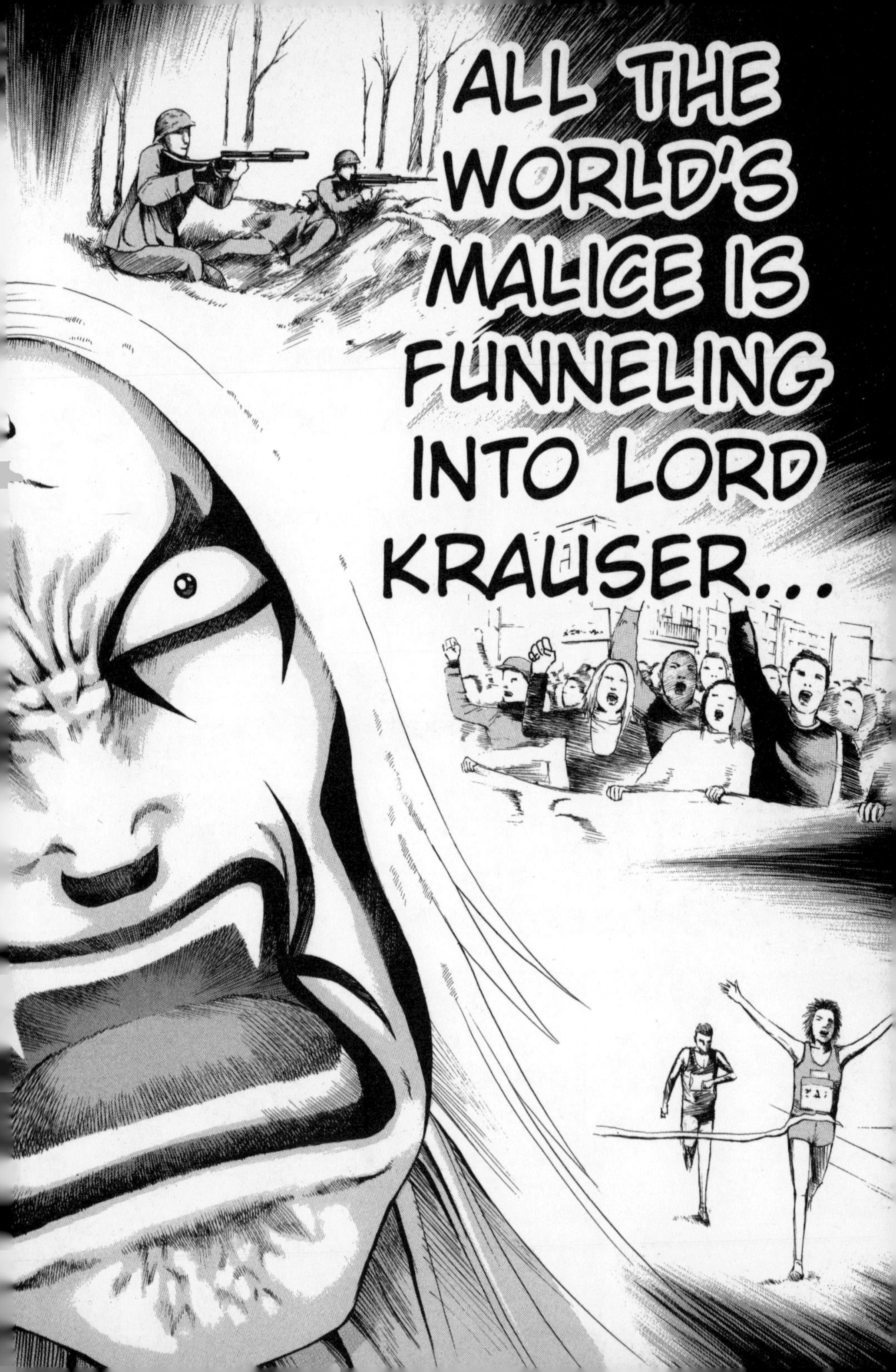
ALL THE WORLD'S MALICE IS FUNNELING INTO LORD KRAUSER...

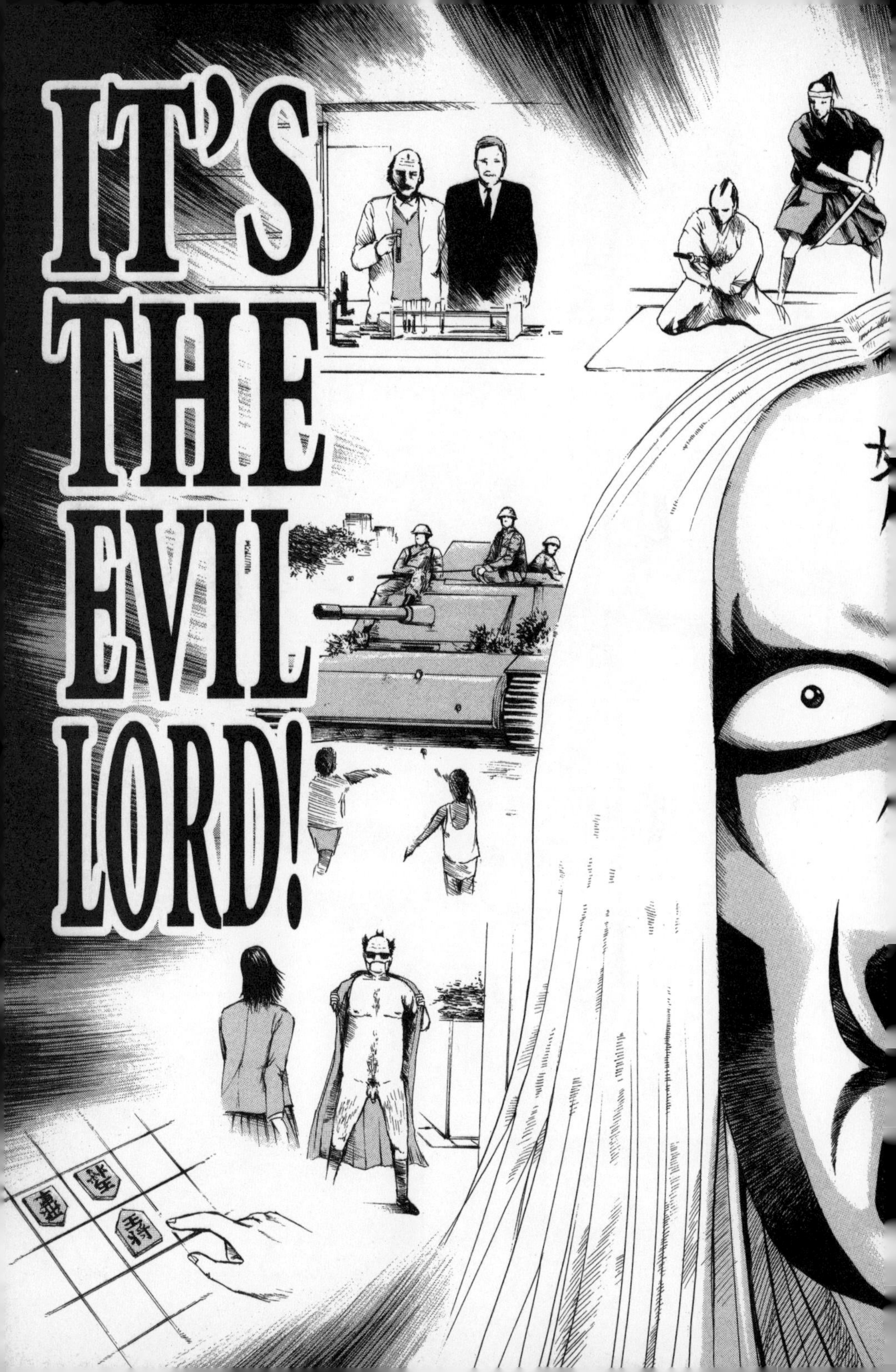
IT'S THE EVIL LORD!

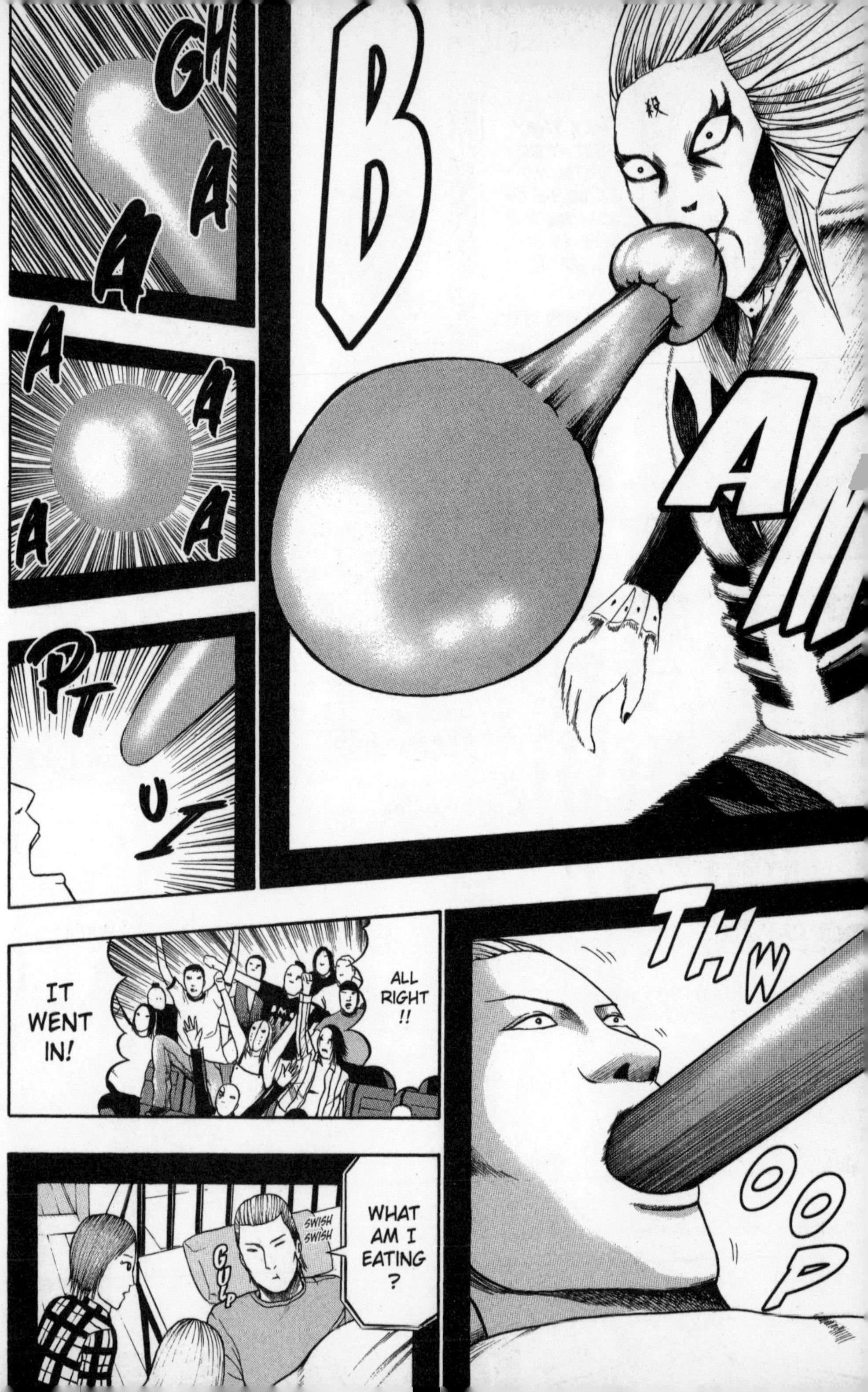

BD
A
GHAAA
AAAAA
PTUI
THWOOOP
ALL RIGHT !!
IT WENT IN!
WHAT AM I EATING ?
SWISH SWISH
GULP

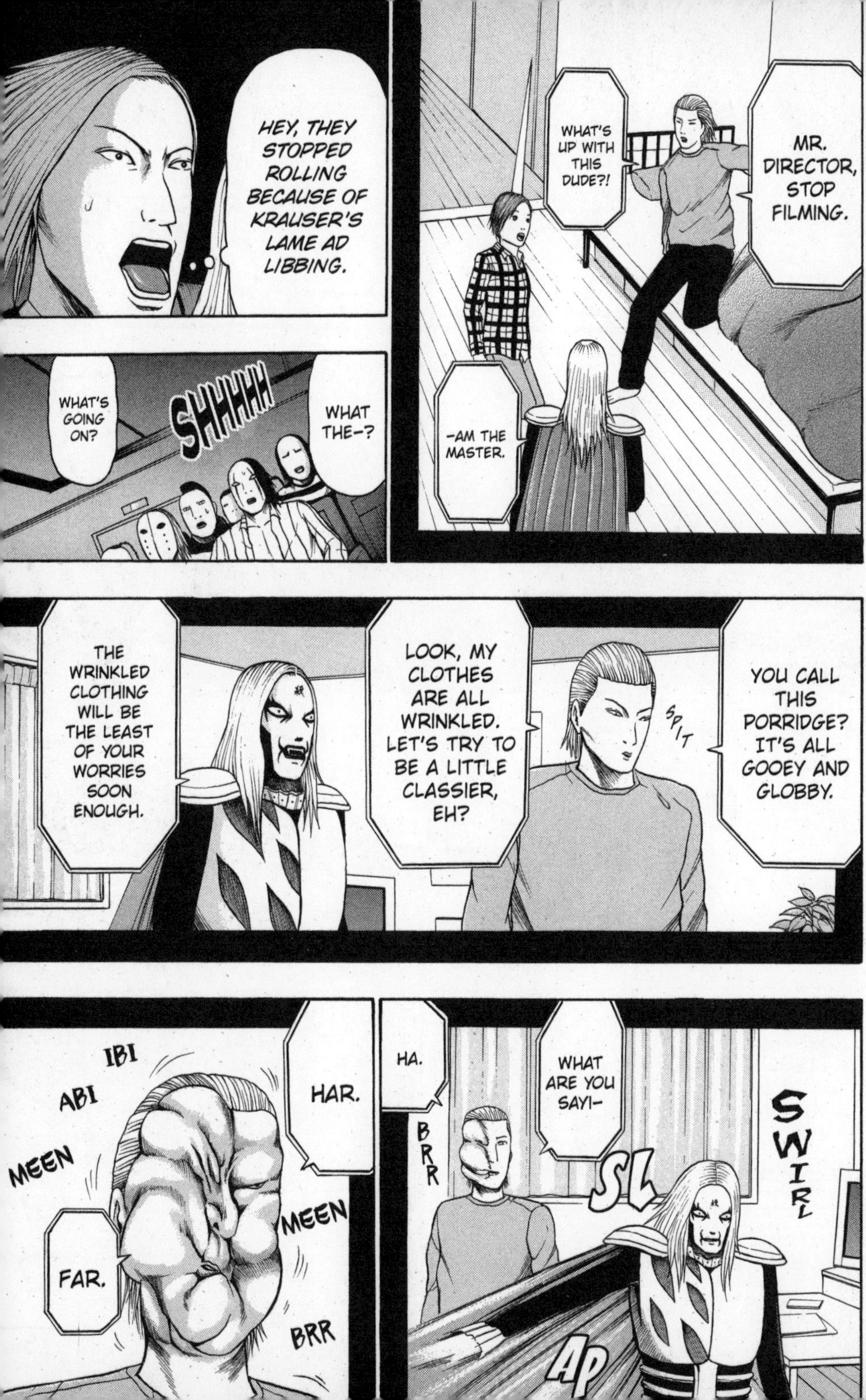
MR. DIRECTOR, STOP FILMING.
WHAT'S UP WITH THIS DUDE?!
-AM THE MASTER.
HEY, THEY STOPPED ROLLING BECAUSE OF KRAUSER'S LAME AD LIBBING.
WHAT THE-?
SHHHHH
WHAT'S GOING ON?
YOU CALL THIS PORRIDGE? IT'S ALL GOOEY AND GLOBBY.
SPIT
LOOK, MY CLOTHES ARE ALL WRINKLED. LET'S TRY TO BE A LITTLE CLASSIER, EH?
THE WRINKLED CLOTHING WILL BE THE LEAST OF YOUR WORRIES SOON ENOUGH.
SWIRL
WHAT ARE YOU SAYI-
SL
AP
BRR
HA.
HAR.
IBI
ABI
MEEN
MEEN
FAR.
BRR

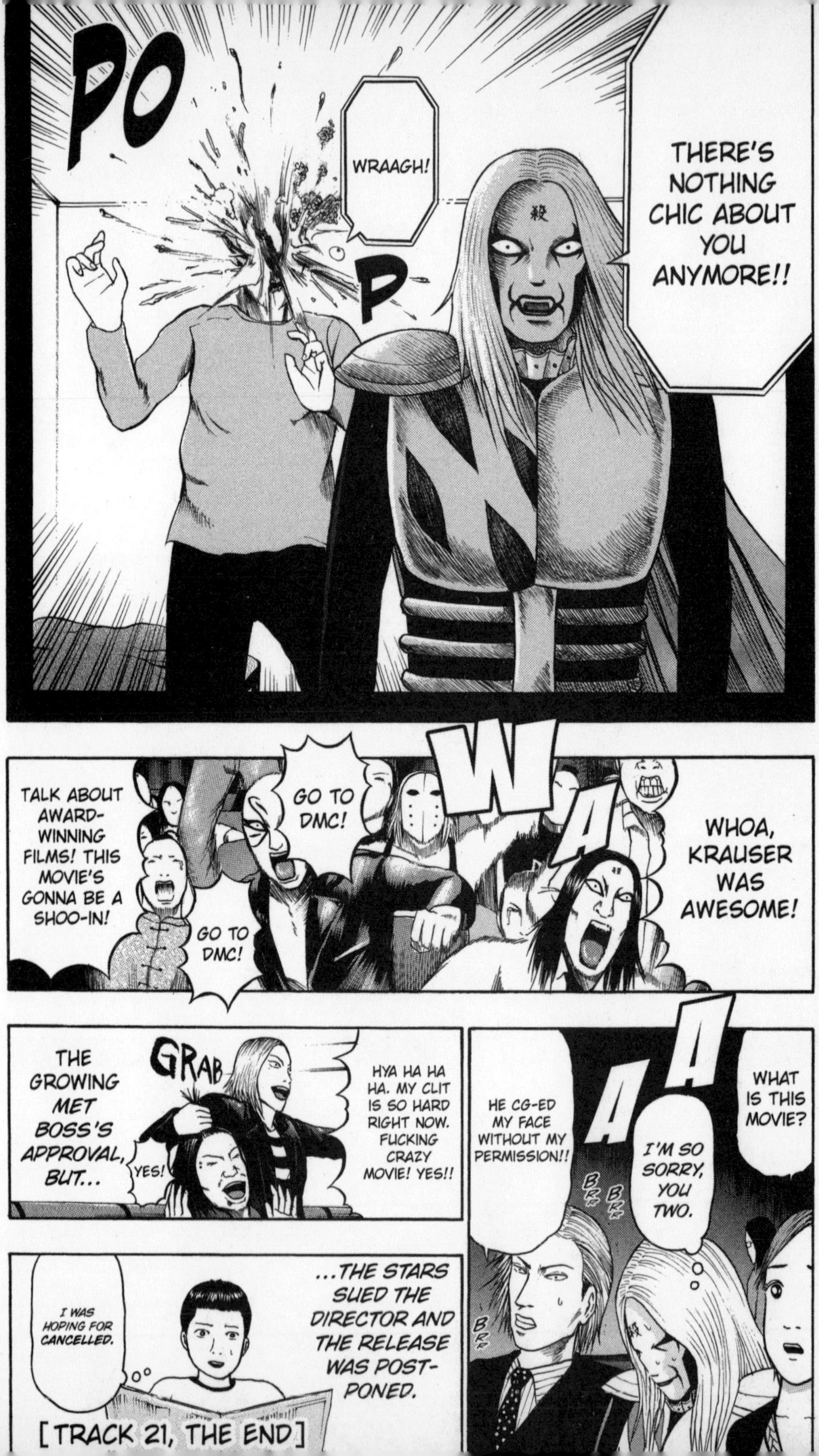
THERE'S NOTHING CHIC ABOUT YOU ANYMORE!!
WRAAGH!
POP
WHOA, KRAUSER WAS AWESOME!
WA
GO TO DMC!
GO TO DMC!
TALK ABOUT AWARD-WINNING FILMS! THIS MOVIE'S GONNA BE A SHOO-IN!
AA
A
WHAT IS THIS MOVIE?
I'M SO SORRY, YOU TWO.
HE CG-ED MY FACE WITHOUT MY PERMISSION!!
BRR BRR BRR
HYA HA HA HA. MY CLIT IS SO HARD RIGHT NOW. FUCKING CRAZY MOVIE! YES!!
GRAB
YES!
THE GROWING MET BOSS'S APPROVAL, BUT...
...THE STARS SUED THE DIRECTOR AND THE RELEASE WAS POST-PONED.
I WAS HOPING FOR CANCELLED.
[TRACK 21, THE END]

DMC LEXICON

 ## AWARD-WINNING FILMS

It is not uncommon for movies to win awards at film festivals and at film-specific awards ceremonies. Winning an award is often the highest form of distinction that a piece of cinema can receive. If you rent an award-winning movie along with your porn, no one will doubt that you won't only be watching porn.

Usage: I rented that award-winning movie too, so look, just spend the night with me! I won't do anything, I promise!

デトロイト・メタル・シティ

Detroit Metal City

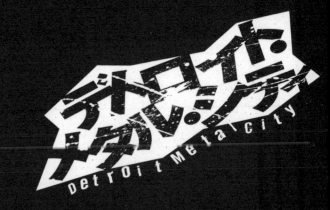

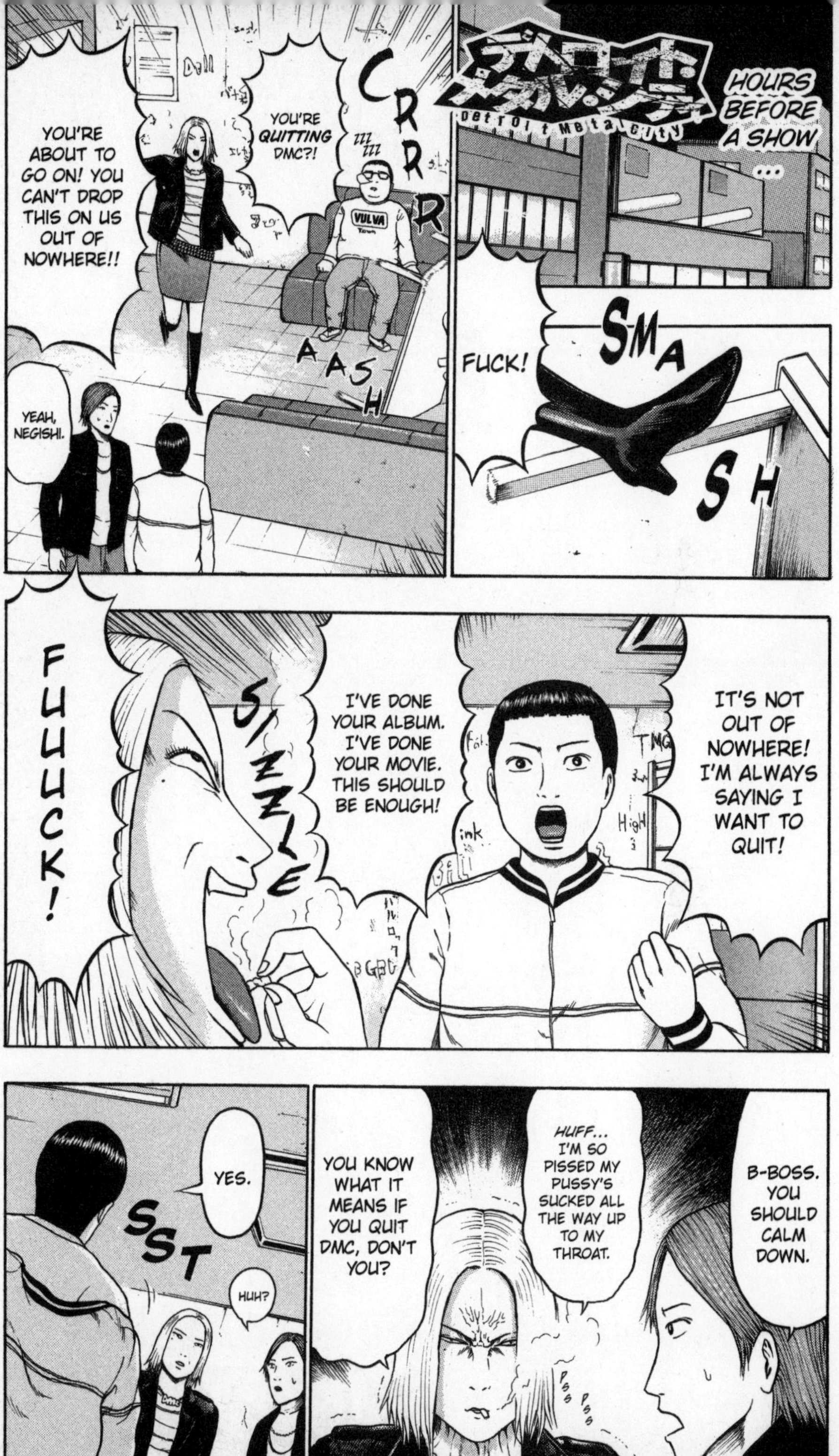
Detroit Metal City
HOURS BEFORE A SHOW...
SMASH
FUCK!
YOU'RE QUITTING DMC?!
CRRR
YOU'RE ABOUT TO GO ON! YOU CAN'T DROP THIS ON US OUT OF NOWHERE!!
AASH
YEAH, NEGISHI.
IT'S NOT OUT OF NOWHERE! I'M ALWAYS SAYING I WANT TO QUIT!
I'VE DONE YOUR ALBUM. I'VE DONE YOUR MOVIE. THIS SHOULD BE ENOUGH!
SIZZLE
FUUUCK!
B-BOSS. YOU SHOULD CALM DOWN.
HUFF... I'M SO PISSED MY PUSSY'S SUCKED ALL THE WAY UP TO MY THROAT.
PSS PSS
YOU KNOW WHAT IT MEANS IF YOU QUIT DMC, DON'T YOU?
YES.
SST
HUH?

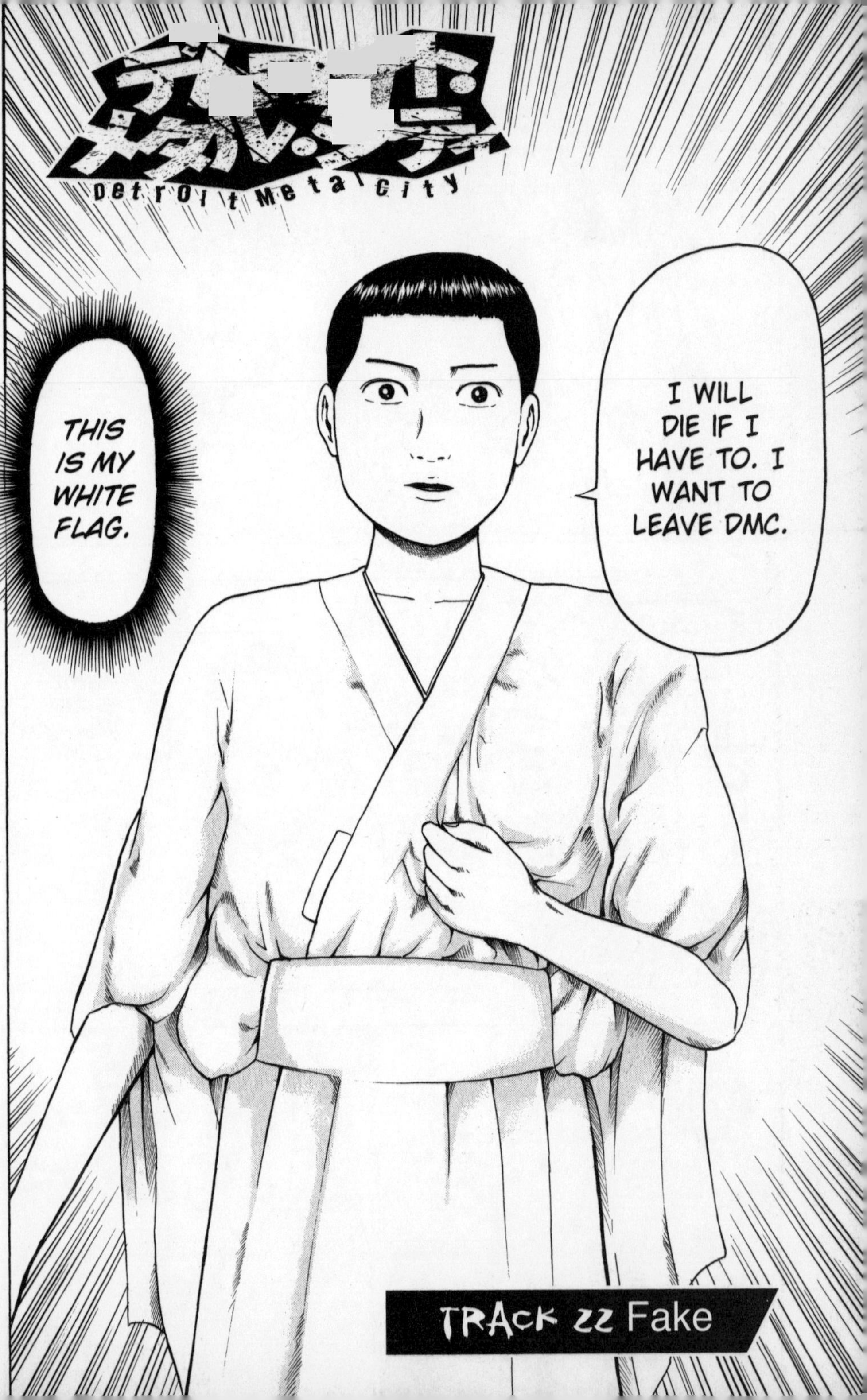
Detroit Metal City
I WILL DIE IF I HAVE TO. I WANT TO LEAVE DMC.
THIS IS MY WHITE FLAG.

TRACK 22 Fake

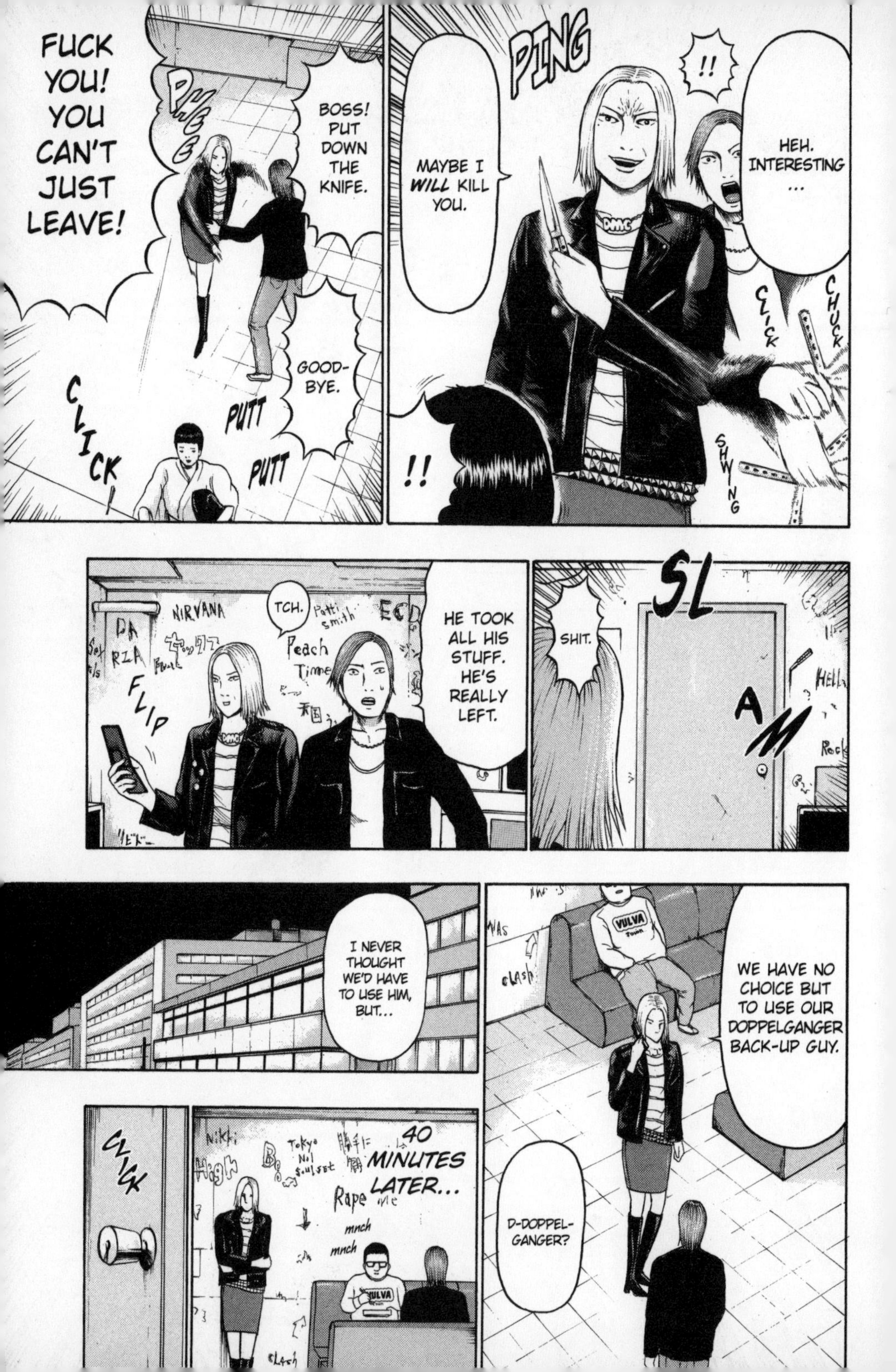
!!
PING
HEH. INTERESTING...
MAYBE I WILL KILL YOU.
CLICK
CHUCK
SHWING
!!
BOSS! PUT DOWN THE KNIFE.
FUCK YOU! YOU CAN'T JUST LEAVE!
GOOD-BYE.
PUTT
PUTT
CLICK
SLAM
SHIT.
HE TOOK ALL HIS STUFF. HE'S REALLY LEFT.
TCH.
FLIP
WE HAVE NO CHOICE BUT TO USE OUR DOPPELGANGER BACK-UP GUY.
D-DOPPEL-GANGER?
I NEVER THOUGHT WE'D HAVE TO USE HIM, BUT...
40 MINUTES LATER...
CLICK
mnch
mnch

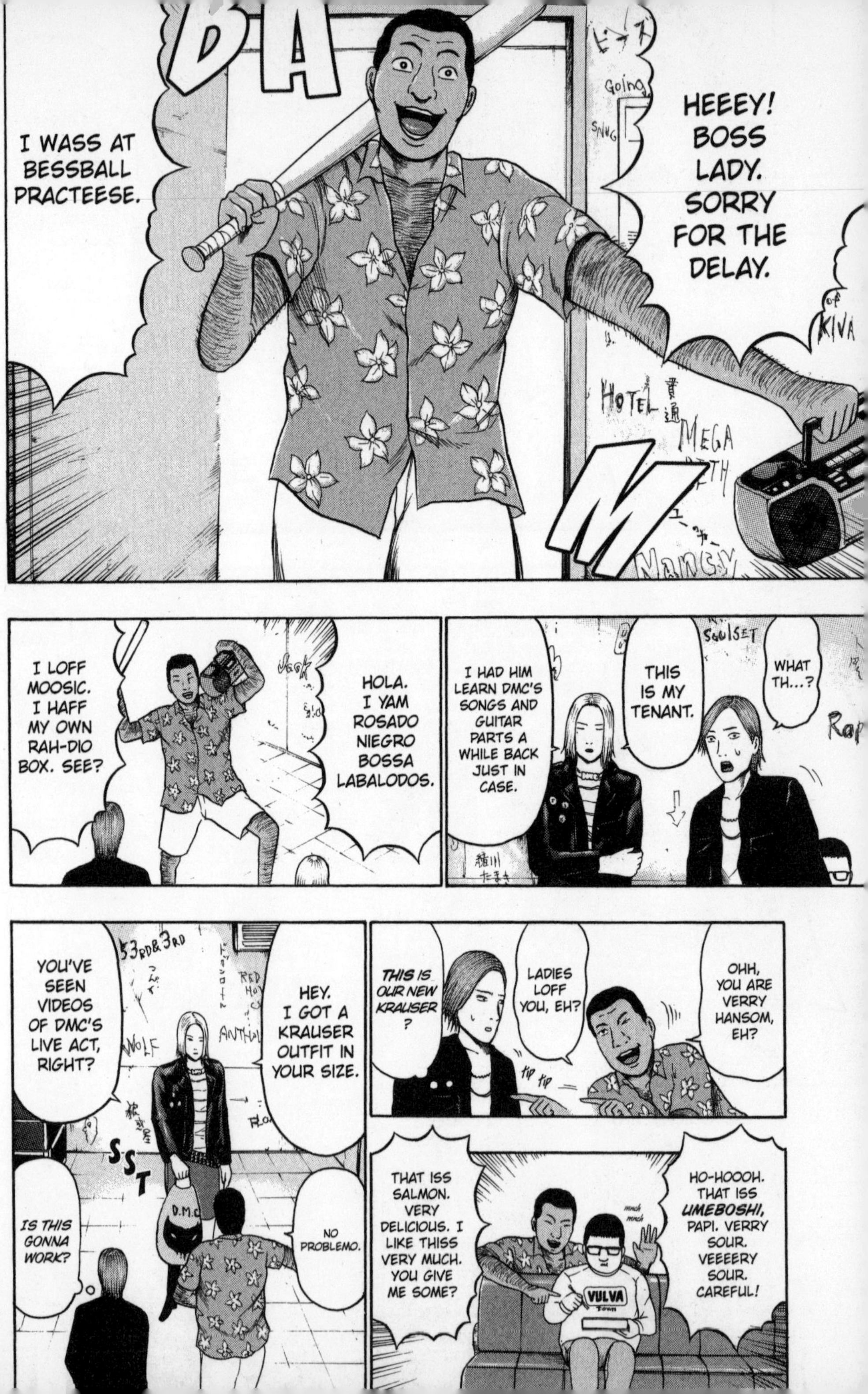

BA
HEEEY! BOSS LADY. SORRY FOR THE DELAY.
I WASS AT BESSBALL PRACTEESE.
M
WHAT TH...?
THIS IS MY TENANT.
I HAD HIM LEARN DMC'S SONGS AND GUITAR PARTS A WHILE BACK JUST IN CASE.
HOLA. I YAM ROSADO NIEGRO BOSSA LABALODOS.
I LOFF MOOSIC. I HAFF MY OWN RAH-DIO BOX. SEE?
OHH, YOU ARE VERRY HANSOM, EH?
LADIES LOFF YOU, EH?
THIS IS OUR NEW KRAUSER?
tip tip
HO-HOOOH. THAT ISS *UMEBOSHI,* PAPI. VERRY SOUR. VEEEERY SOUR. CAREFUL!
mnch mnch
THAT ISS SALMON. VERY DELICIOUS. I LIKE THISS VERY MUCH. YOU GIVE ME SOME?
VULVA
HEY. I GOT A KRAUSER OUTFIT IN YOUR SIZE.
YOU'VE SEEN VIDEOS OF DMC'S LIVE ACT, RIGHT?
S-S-T
NO PROBLEMO.
IS THIS GONNA WORK?

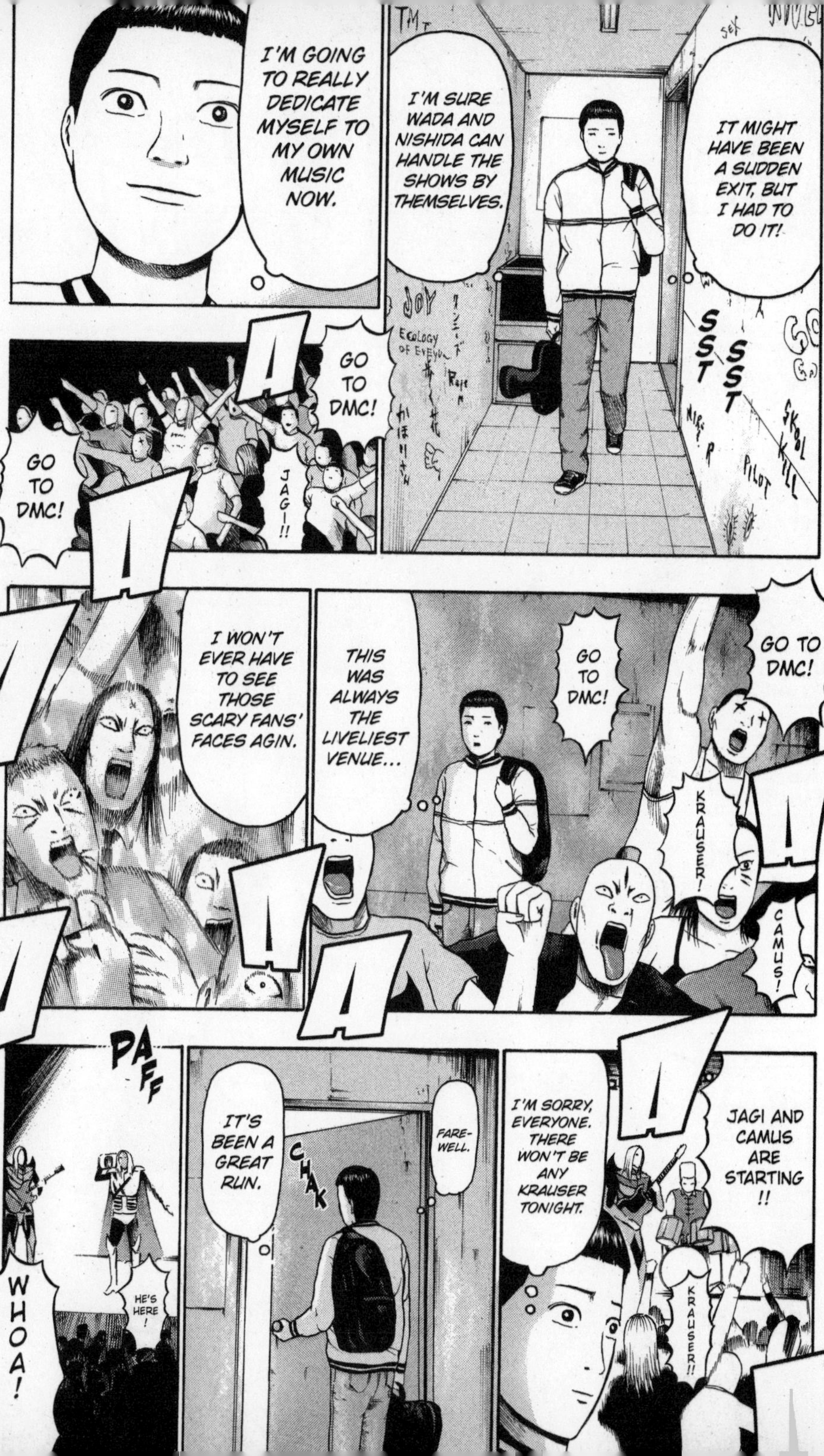
IT MIGHT HAVE BEEN A SUDDEN EXIT, BUT I HAD TO DO IT!
I'M SURE WADA AND NISHIDA CAN HANDLE THE SHOWS BY THEMSELVES.
SST SST
I'M GOING TO REALLY DEDICATE MYSELF TO MY OWN MUSIC NOW.
GO TO DMC!
JAGI!!
GO TO DMC!
GO TO DMC!
GO TO DMC!
THIS WAS ALWAYS THE LIVELIEST VENUE...
KRAUSER!
CAMUS!
I WON'T EVER HAVE TO SEE THOSE SCARY FANS' FACES AGIN.
JAGI AND CAMUS ARE STARTING!!
I'M SORRY, EVERYONE. THERE WON'T BE ANY KRAUSER TONIGHT.
KRAUSER!!
FAREWELL.
IT'S BEEN A GREAT RUN.
CHAK
PAFF
HE'S HERE!
WHOA!

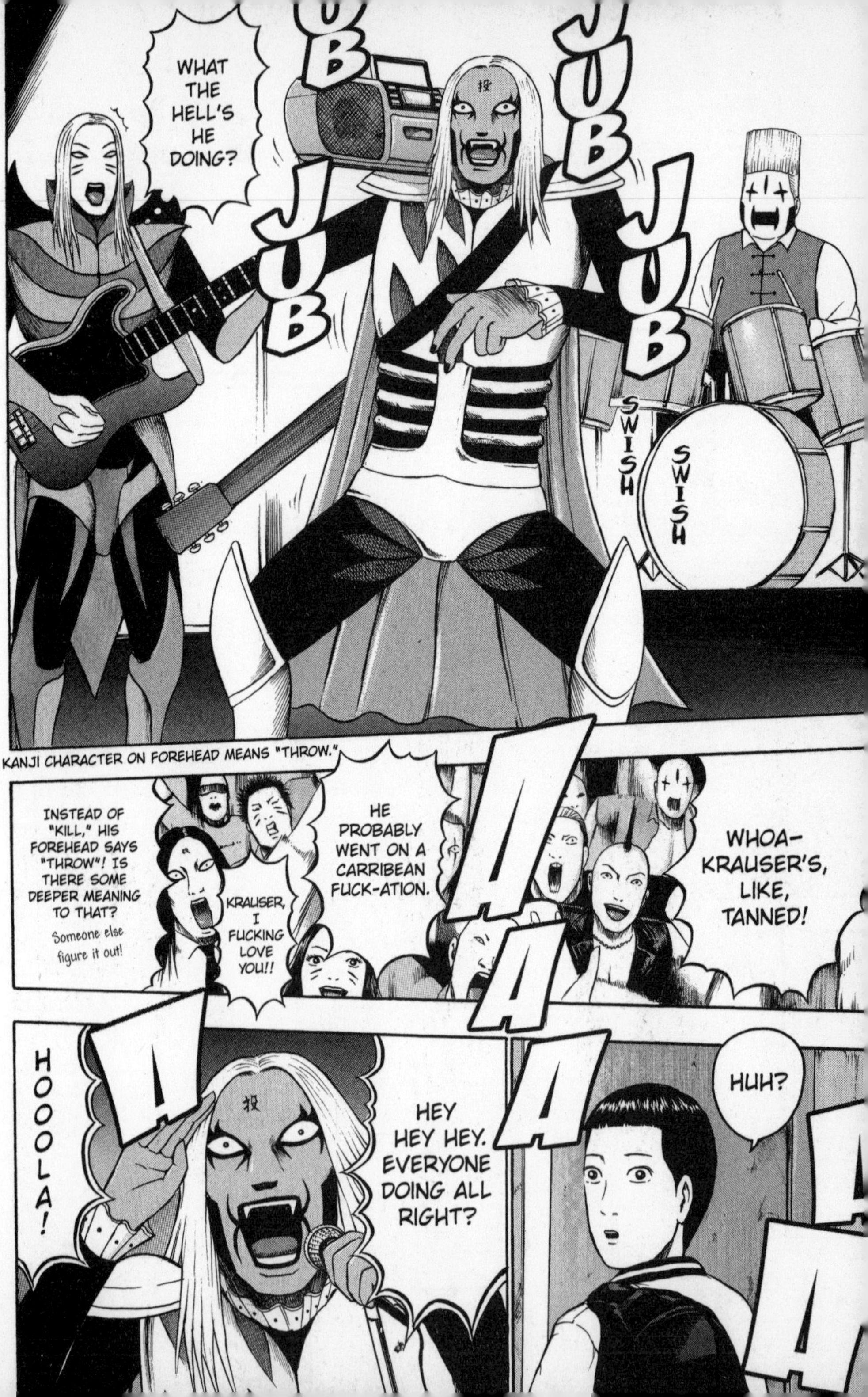
JUB JUB
JUB JUB
WHAT THE HELL'S HE DOING?
SWISH
SWISH
KANJI CHARACTER ON FOREHEAD MEANS "THROW."
WHOA-KRAUSER'S, LIKE, TANNED!
HE PROBABLY WENT ON A CARRIBEAN FUCK-ATION.
KRAUSER, I FUCKING LOVE YOU!!
INSTEAD OF "KILL," HIS FOREHEAD SAYS "THROW"! IS THERE SOME DEEPER MEANING TO THAT?
Someone else figure it out!
AAAAA
HUH?
HEY HEY HEY. EVERYONE DOING ALL RIGHT?
HOOOOLA!

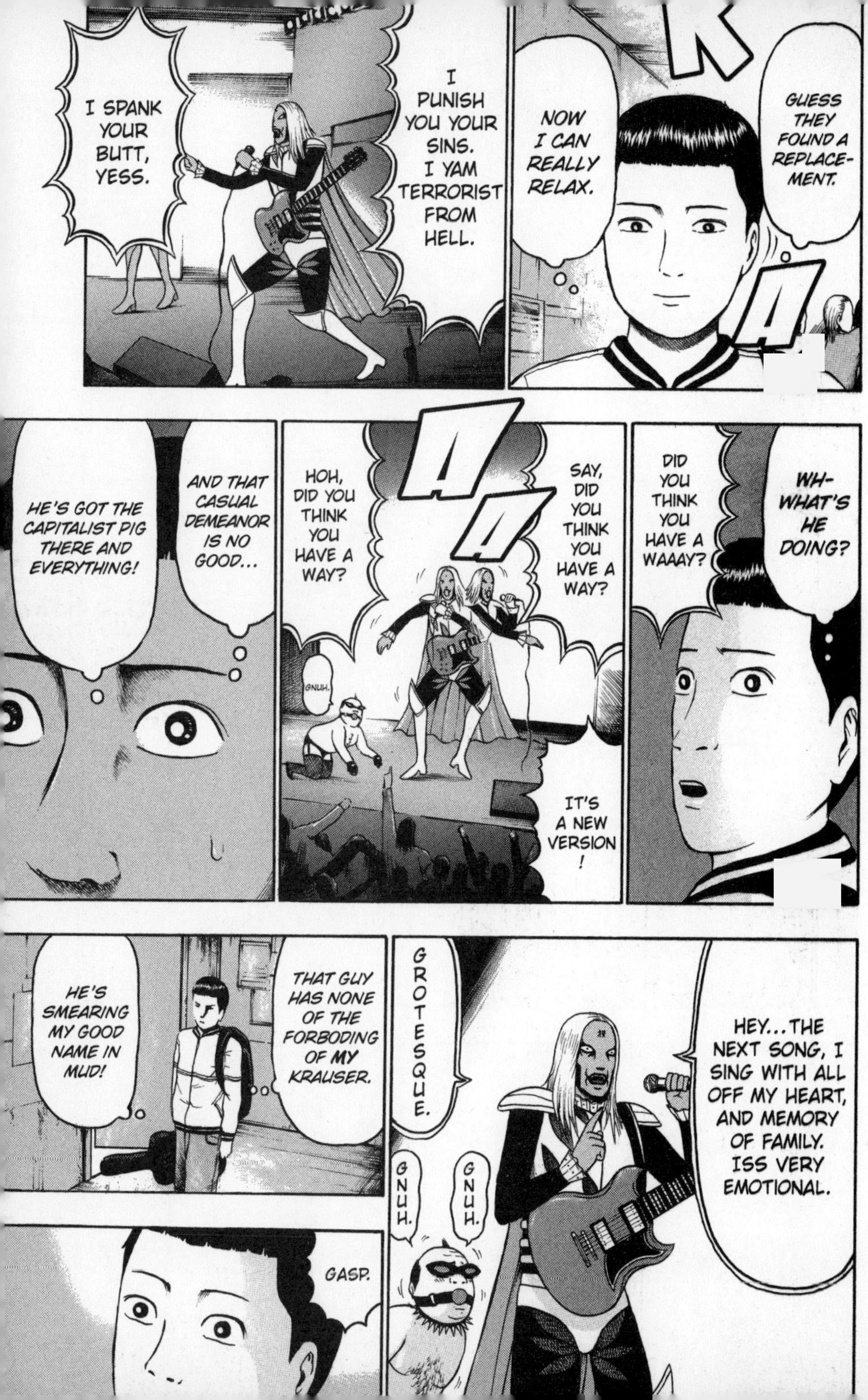
GUESS THEY FOUND A REPLACEMENT.
NOW I CAN REALLY RELAX.
I PUNISH YOU YOUR SINS. I YAM TERRORIST FROM HELL.
I SPANK YOUR BUTT, YESS.
WH-WHAT'S HE DOING?
DID YOU THINK YOU HAVE A WAAAY?
SAY, DID YOU THINK YOU HAVE A WAY?
HOH, DID YOU THINK YOU HAVE A WAY?
GNUH.
IT'S A NEW VERSION!
AND THAT CASUAL DEMEANOR IS NO GOOD...
HE'S GOT THE CAPITALIST PIG THERE AND EVERYTHING!
HEY...THE NEXT SONG, I SING WITH ALL OFF MY HEART, AND MEMORY OF FAMILY. ISS VERY EMOTIONAL.
GROTESQUE.
GNUH.
GNUH.
THAT GUY HAS NONE OF THE FORBODING OF MY KRAUSER.
HE'S SMEARING MY GOOD NAME IN MUD!
GASP.

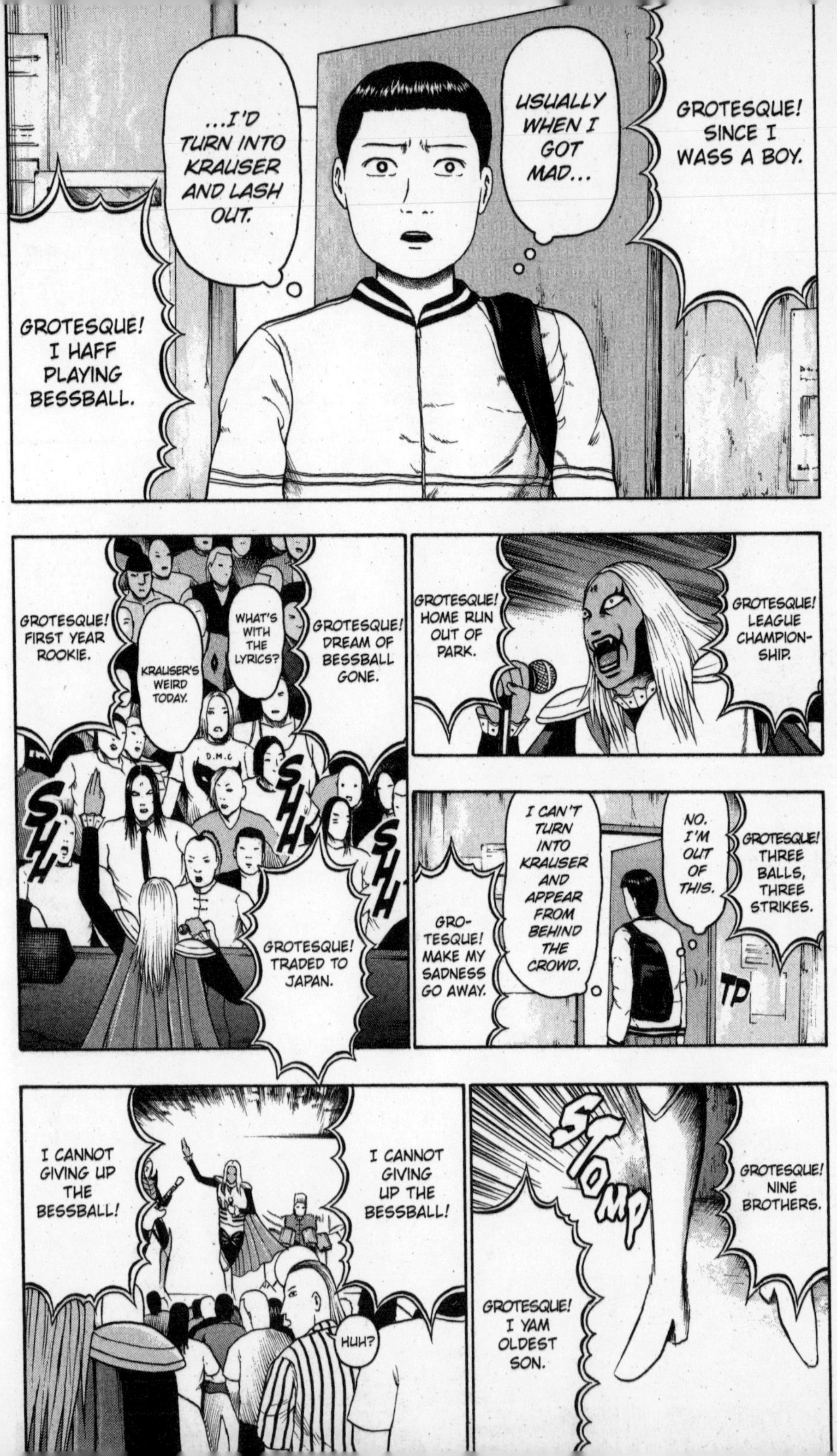
GROTESQUE! SINCE I WASS A BOY.
USUALLY WHEN I GOT MAD...
...I'D TURN INTO KRAUSER AND LASH OUT.
GROTESQUE! I HAFF PLAYING BESSBALL.
GROTESQUE! LEAGUE CHAMPION-SHIP.
GROTESQUE! HOME RUN OUT OF PARK.
GROTESQUE! THREE BALLS, THREE STRIKES.
NO. I'M OUT OF THIS.
I CAN'T TURN INTO KRAUSER AND APPEAR FROM BEHIND THE CROWD.
GRO-TESQUE! MAKE MY SADNESS GO AWAY.
TP
GROTESQUE! DREAM OF BESSBALL GONE.
WHAT'S WITH THE LYRICS?
KRAUSER'S WEIRD TODAY.
GROTESQUE! FIRST YEAR ROOKIE.
SHH
SHH
SHH
GROTESQUE! TRADED TO JAPAN.
STOMP
GROTESQUE! NINE BROTHERS.
GROTESQUE! I YAM OLDEST SON.
I CANNOT GIVING UP THE BESSBALL!
I CANNOT GIVING UP THE BESSBALL!
HUH?

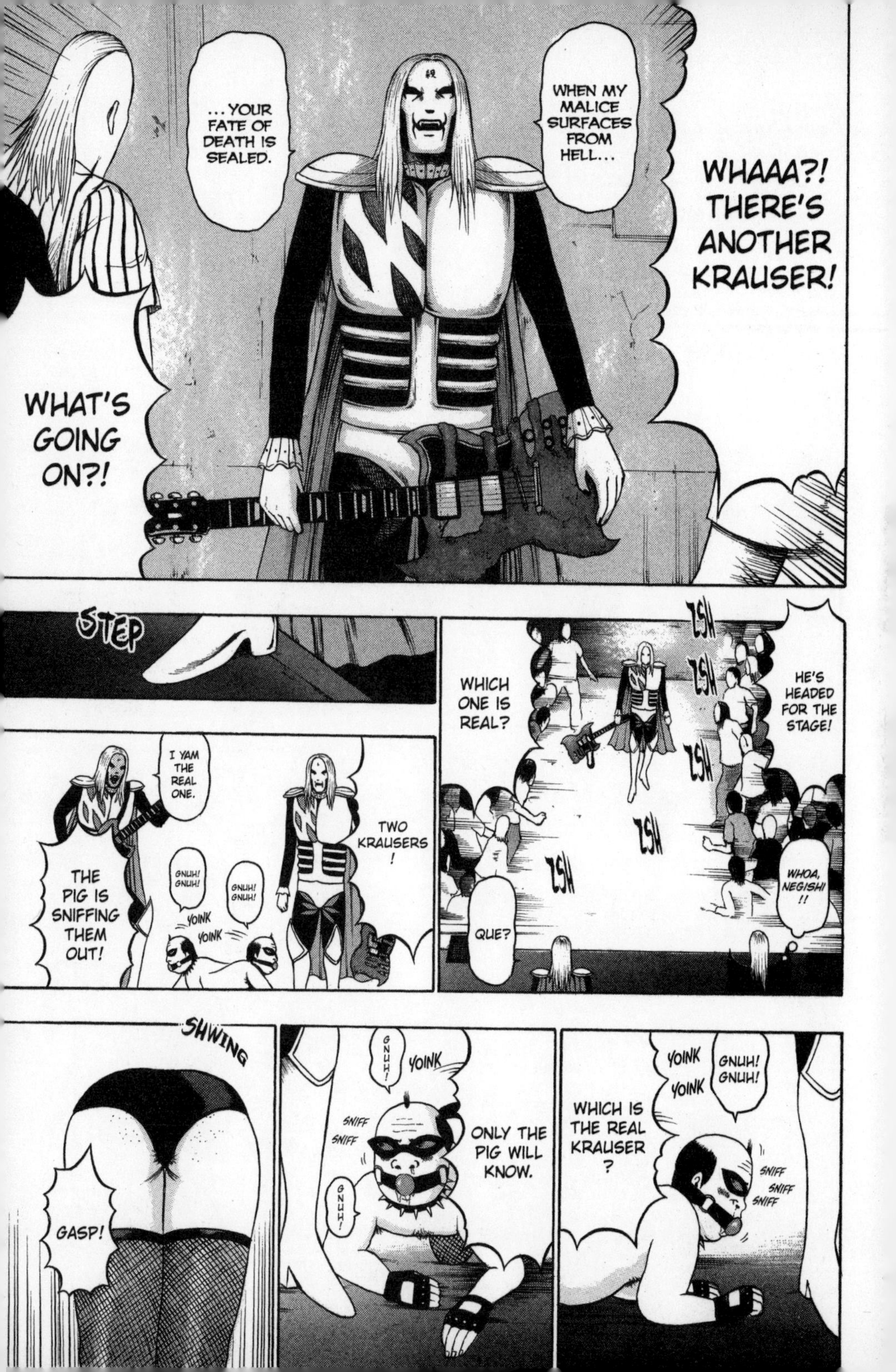
WHAAA?! THERE'S ANOTHER KRAUSER!
WHEN MY MALICE SURFACES FROM HELL...
...YOUR FATE OF DEATH IS SEALED.
WHAT'S GOING ON?!
ZSH
ZSH
HE'S HEADED FOR THE STAGE!
WHICH ONE IS REAL?
ZSH
ZSH
ZSH
WHOA, NEGISHI!!
QUE?
STEP
TWO KRAUSERS!
I YAM THE REAL ONE.
GNUH! GNUH!
GNUH! GNUH!
YOINK
YOINK
THE PIG IS SNIFFING THEM OUT!
GNUH! GNUH!
YOINK
YOINK
WHICH IS THE REAL KRAUSER?
SNIFF
SNIFF
SNIFF
YOINK
GNUH!
ONLY THE PIG WILL KNOW.
SNIFF
SNIFF
GNUH!
SHWING
GASP!

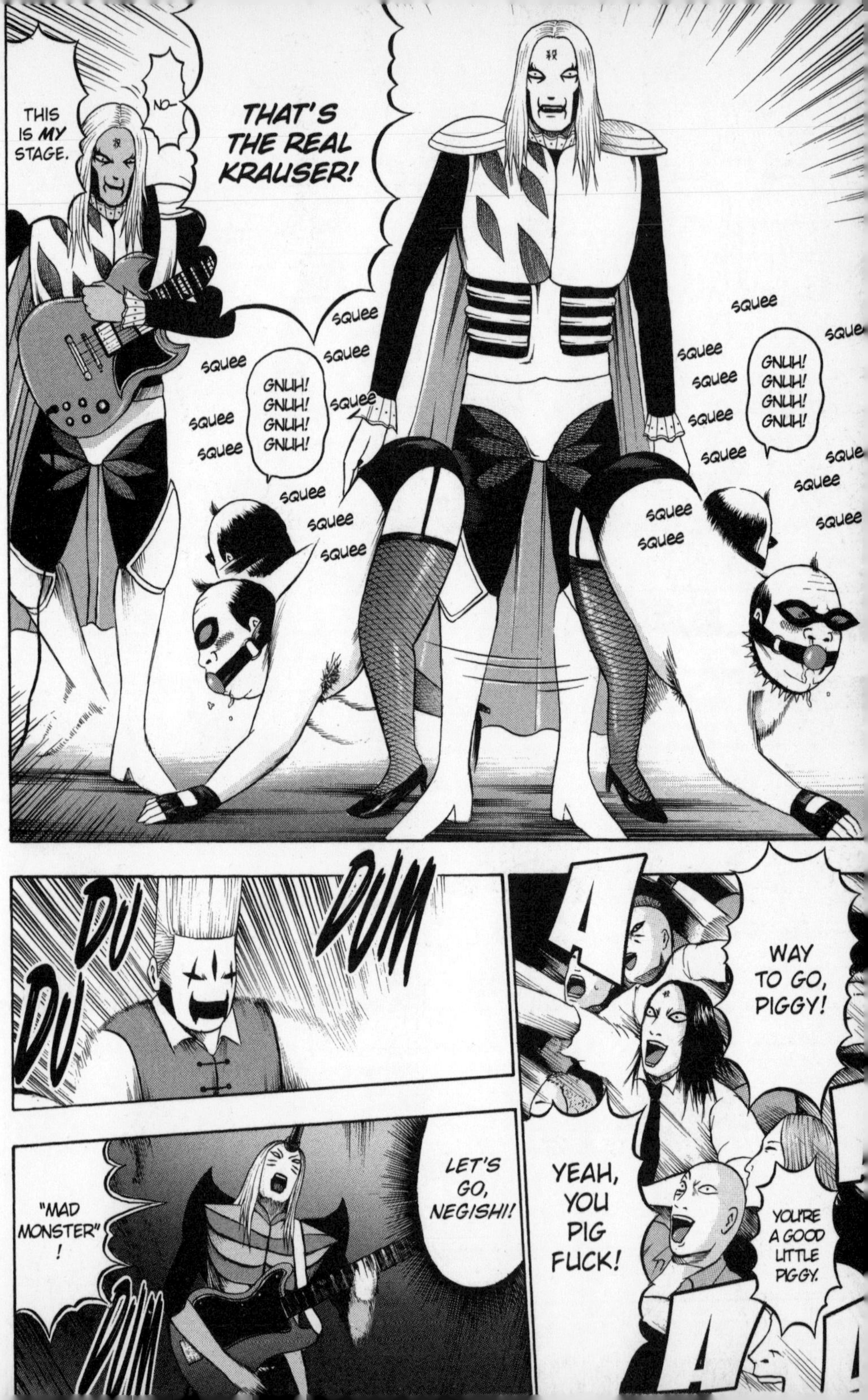
THAT'S THE REAL KRAUSER!
NO—
THIS IS MY STAGE.
squee
squee
squee
squee
squee
squee
GNUH! GNUH! GNUH! GNUH!
squee
squee
squee
squee
squee
squee
squee
squee
squee
squee
squee
GNUH! GNUH! GNUH! GNUH!
squee
squee
squee
squee
A
WAY TO GO, PIGGY!
YEAH, YOU PIG FUCK!
YOU'RE A GOOD LITTLE PIGGY.
A
DU DU
DUM
LET'S GO, NEGISHI!
"MAD MONSTER"!
DUM

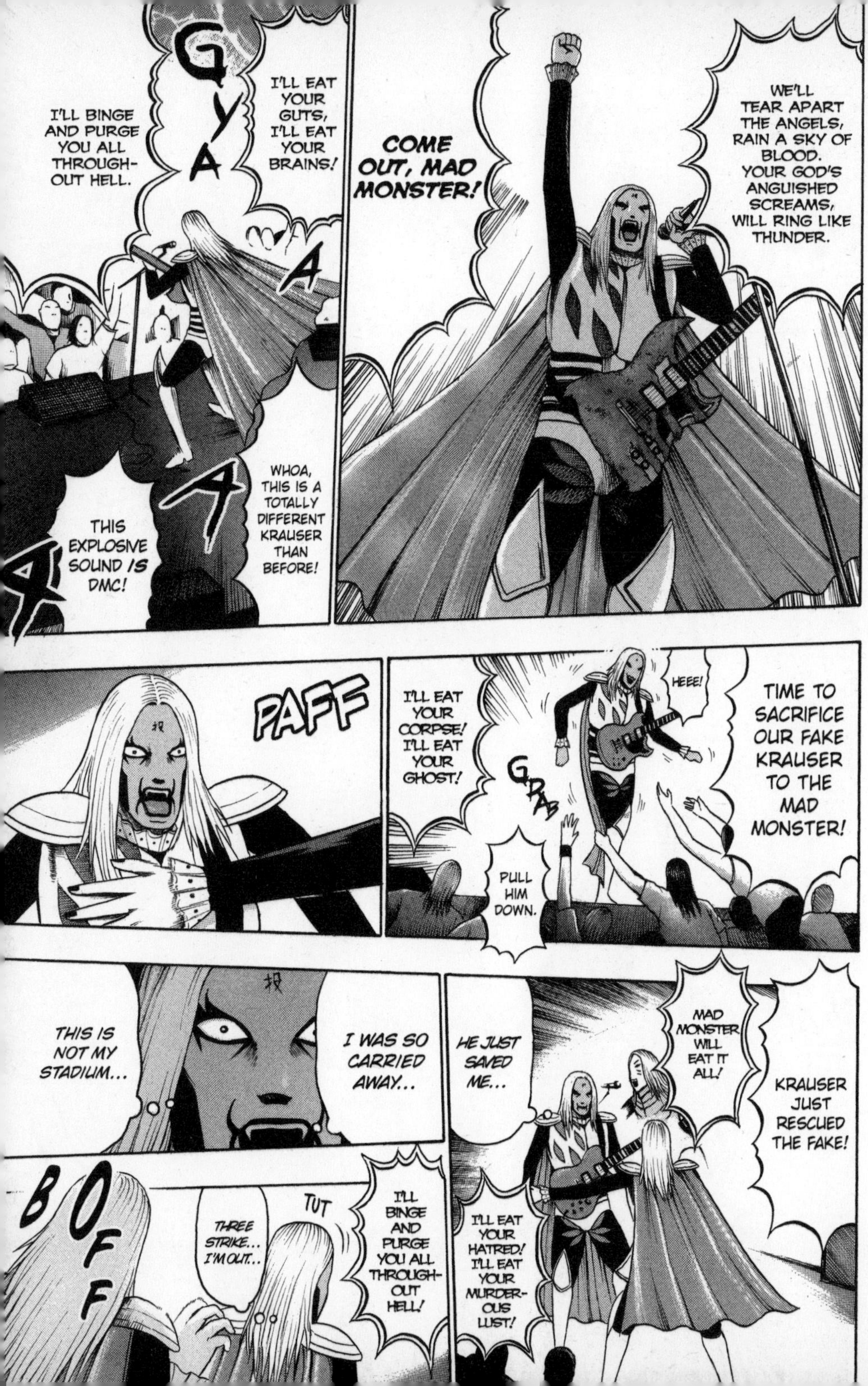
WE'LL TEAR APART THE ANGELS, RAIN A SKY OF BLOOD. YOUR GOD'S ANGUISHED SCREAMS, WILL RING LIKE THUNDER.
COME OUT, MAD MONSTER!
I'LL EAT YOUR GUTS, I'LL EAT YOUR BRAINS!
I'LL BINGE AND PURGE YOU ALL THROUGH-OUT HELL.
GYAAAA
WHOA, THIS IS A TOTALLY DIFFERENT KRAUSER THAN BEFORE!
THIS EXPLOSIVE SOUND IS DMC!
TIME TO SACRIFICE OUR FAKE KRAUSER TO THE MAD MONSTER!
HEEE!
I'LL EAT YOUR CORPSE! I'LL EAT YOUR GHOST!
GRAB
PULL HIM DOWN.
PAFF
KRAUSER JUST RESCUED THE FAKE!
MAD MONSTER WILL EAT IT ALL!
HE JUST SAVED ME...
I'LL EAT YOUR HATRED! I'LL EAT YOUR MURDER-OUS LUST!
I WAS SO CARRIED AWAY...
THIS IS NOT MY STADIUM...
I'LL BINGE AND PURGE YOU ALL THROUGH-OUT HELL!
TUT
THREE STRIKE... I'M OUT...
BOFF

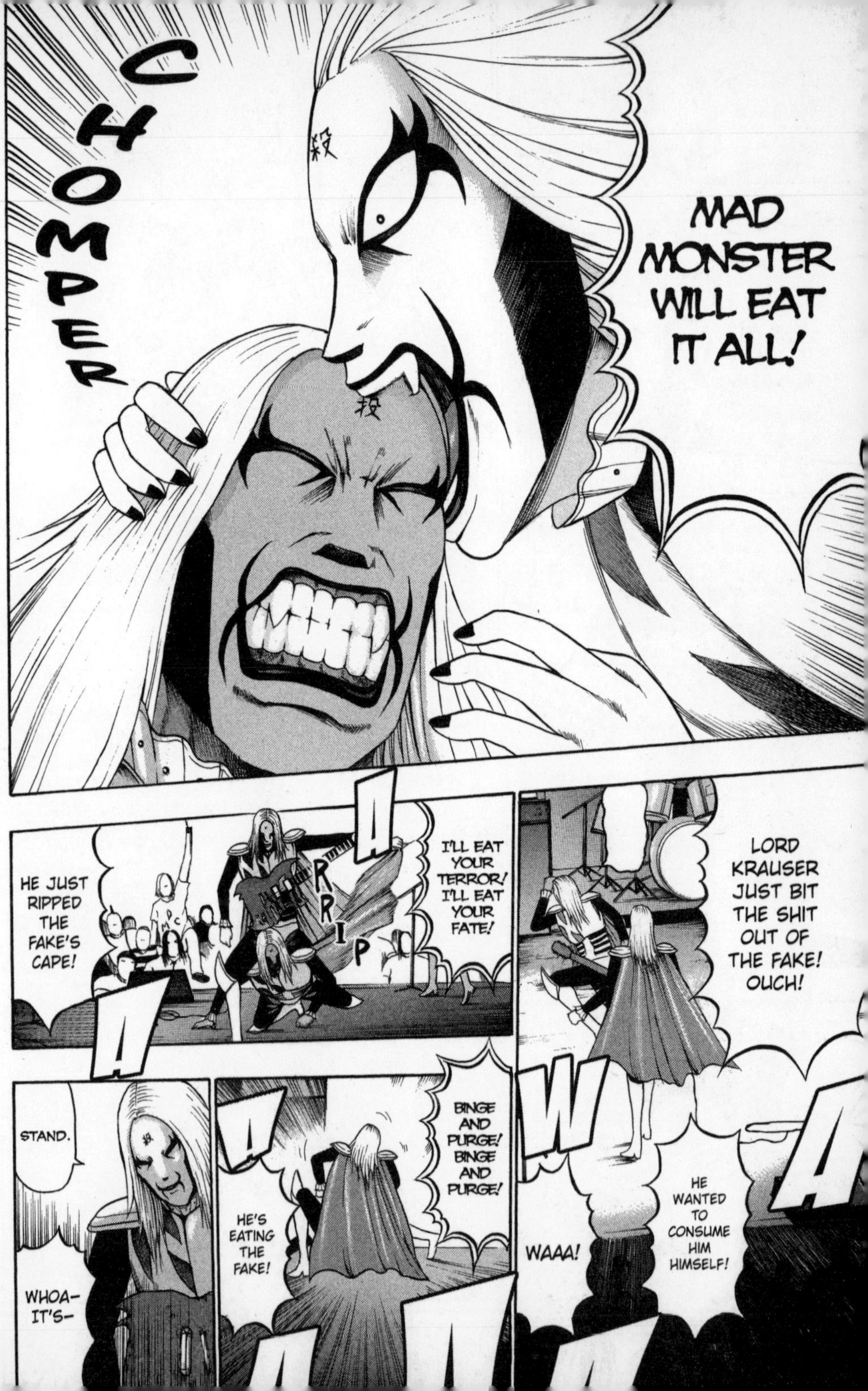
MAD MONSTER WILL EAT IT ALL!
CHOMPER
LORD KRAUSER JUST BIT THE SHIT OUT OF THE FAKE! OUCH!
I'LL EAT YOUR TERROR! I'LL EAT YOUR FATE!
RRIP
HE JUST RIPPED THE FAKE'S CAPE!
HE WANTED TO CONSUME HIM HIMSELF!
WAAA!
BINGE AND PURGE! BINGE AND PURGE!
HE'S EATING THE FAKE!
STAND.
WHOA- IT'S-

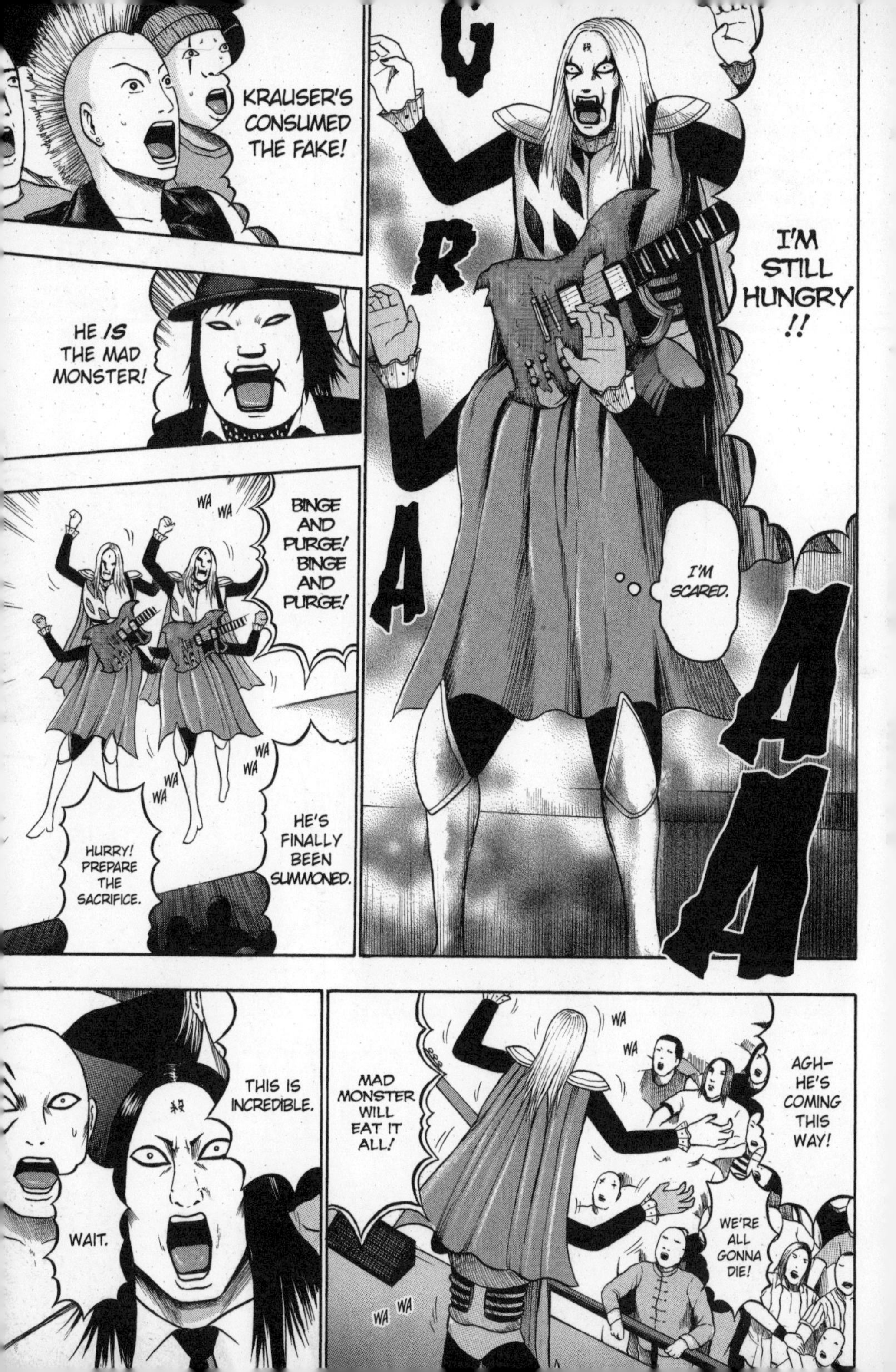
GRAAA
I'M STILL HUNGRY!!
I'M SCARED.
KRAUSER'S CONSUMED THE FAKE!
HE IS THE MAD MONSTER!
WA WA
BINGE AND PURGE! BINGE AND PURGE!
HE'S FINALLY BEEN SUMMONED.
WA WA
WA WA
HURRY! PREPARE THE SACRIFICE.
AGH— HE'S COMING THIS WAY!
WA WA
MAD MONSTER WILL EAT IT ALL!
WE'RE ALL GONNA DIE!
WA WA
THIS IS INCREDIBLE.
WAIT.

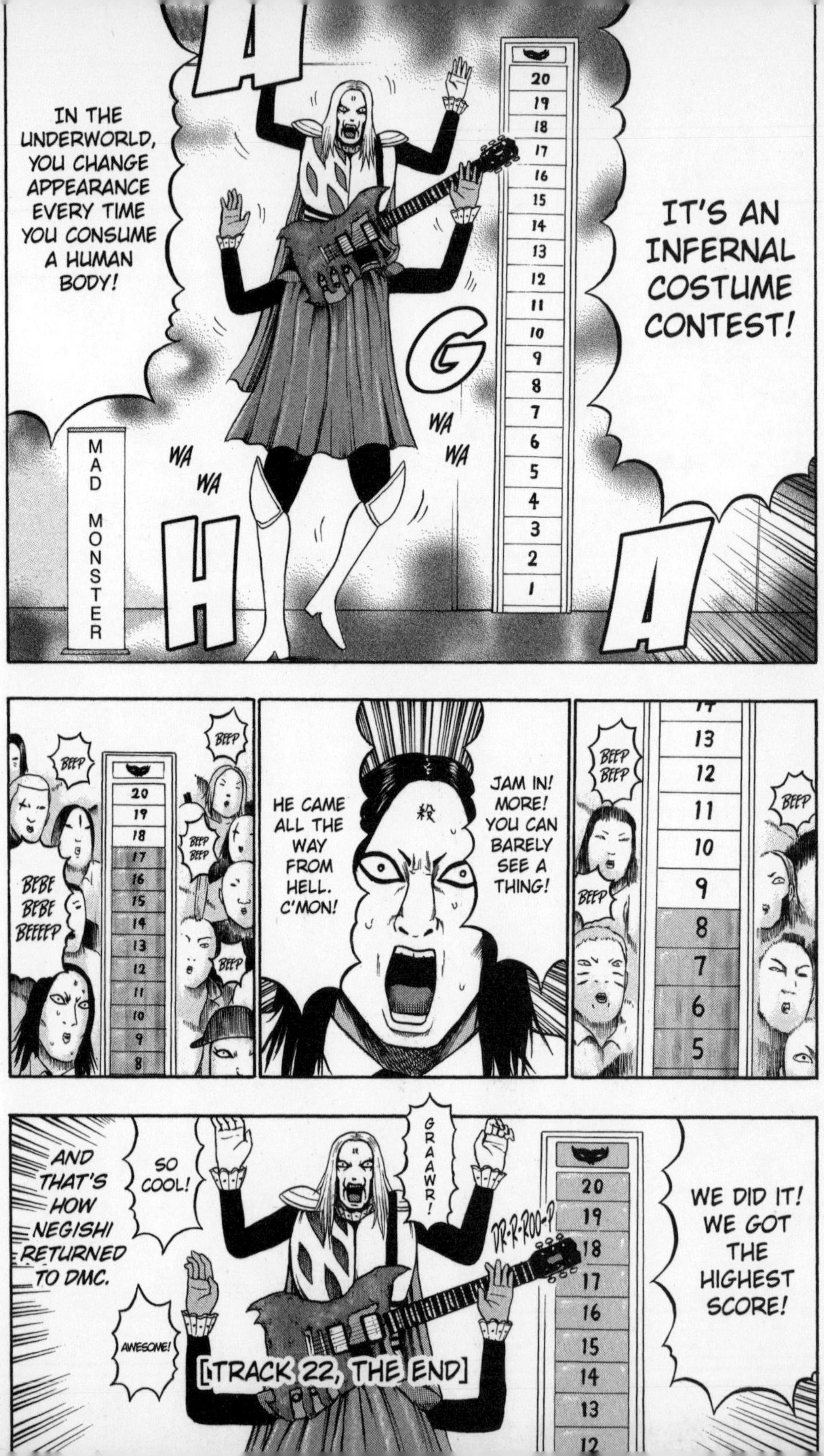
IT'S AN INFERNAL COSTUME CONTEST!
IN THE UNDERWORLD, YOU CHANGE APPEARANCE EVERY TIME YOU CONSUME A HUMAN BODY!
A
G
H
A
WA
WA
WA
WA
MAD MONSTER
20
19
18
17
16
15
14
13
12
11
10
9
8
7
6
5
4
3
2
1
BEEP
BEEP BEEP
BEEP
JAM IN! MORE! YOU CAN BARELY SEE A THING!
HE CAME ALL THE WAY FROM HELL. C'MON!
BEEP
BEEP
BEEP BEEP
BEBE BEBE BEEEEP
BEEP
WE DID IT! WE GOT THE HIGHEST SCORE!
GRAAWR!
DR-R-ROO-P
SO COOL!
AND THAT'S HOW NEGISHI RETURNED TO DMC.
AWESOME!
[TRACK 22, THE END]

DMC LEXICON

DOPPELGANGER

A body double used to stand-in as a person of high ranking. During the warring states period when assassinations were rampant, doppelgangers were a popular safeguard for state leaders. A more modern example of a doppelganger would be Japanese comedian Koriki Choshu. Feel free to look him up online.

Usage: Why is my doppelganger so ugly?

デトロイト・メタル・シティ

Detroit Metal City

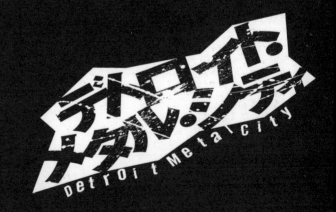

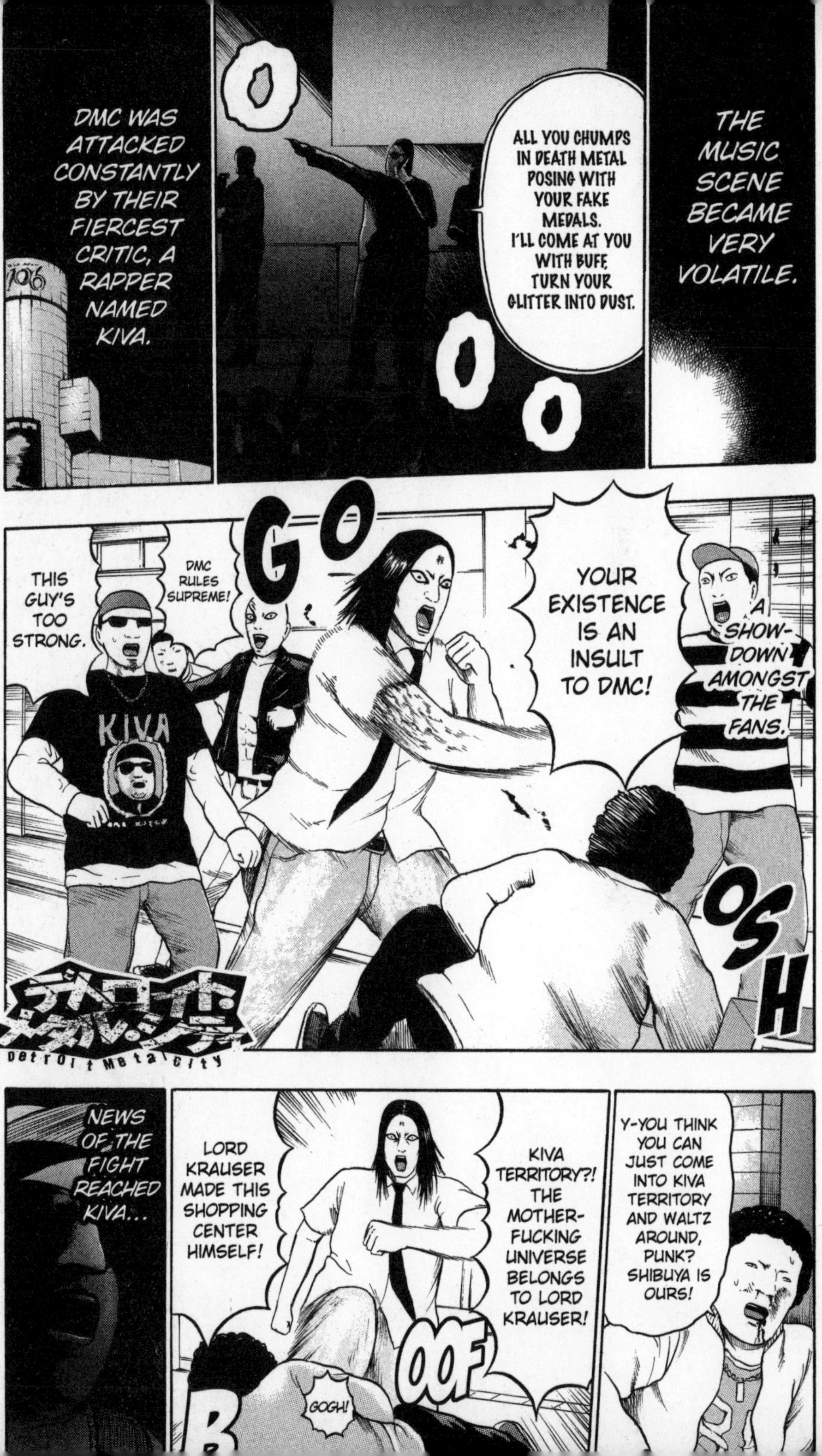
THE MUSIC SCENE BECAME VERY VOLATILE.
ALL YOU CHUMPS IN DEATH METAL POSING WITH YOUR FAKE MEDALS. I'LL COME AT YOU WITH BUFF, TURN YOUR GLITTER INTO DUST.
O
O
O
DMC WAS ATTACKED CONSTANTLY BY THEIR FIERCEST CRITIC, A RAPPER NAMED KIVA.
106
A SHOWDOWN AMONGST THE FANS.
YOUR EXISTENCE IS AN INSULT TO DMC!
GO
DMC RULES SUPREME!
THIS GUY'S TOO STRONG.
KIVA
OSH
H
Detroit Metal City
Y-YOU THINK YOU CAN JUST COME INTO KIVA TERRITORY AND WALTZ AROUND, PUNK? SHIBUYA IS OURS!
KIVA TERRITORY?! THE MOTHER-FUCKING UNIVERSE BELONGS TO LORD KRAUSER!
LORD KRAUSER MADE THIS SHOPPING CENTER HIMSELF!
OOF
GOGH!
B
NEWS OF THE FIGHT REACHED KIVA...

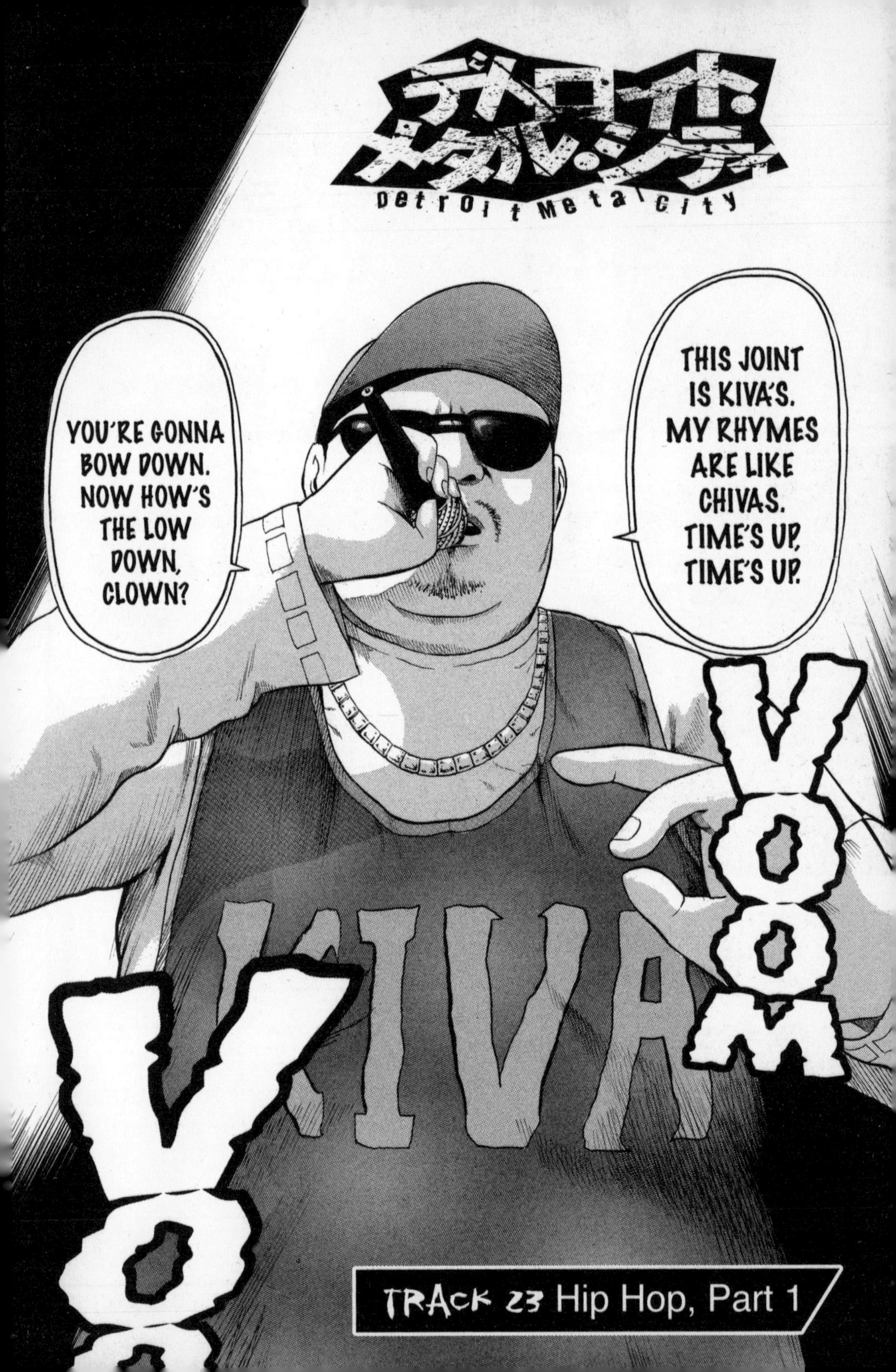
Detroit Metal City
THIS JOINT IS KIVA'S. MY RHYMES ARE LIKE CHIVAS. TIME'S UP, TIME'S UP.
YOU'RE GONNA BOW DOWN. NOW HOW'S THE LOW DOWN, CLOWN?
KIVA
TRACK 23 Hip Hop, Part 1

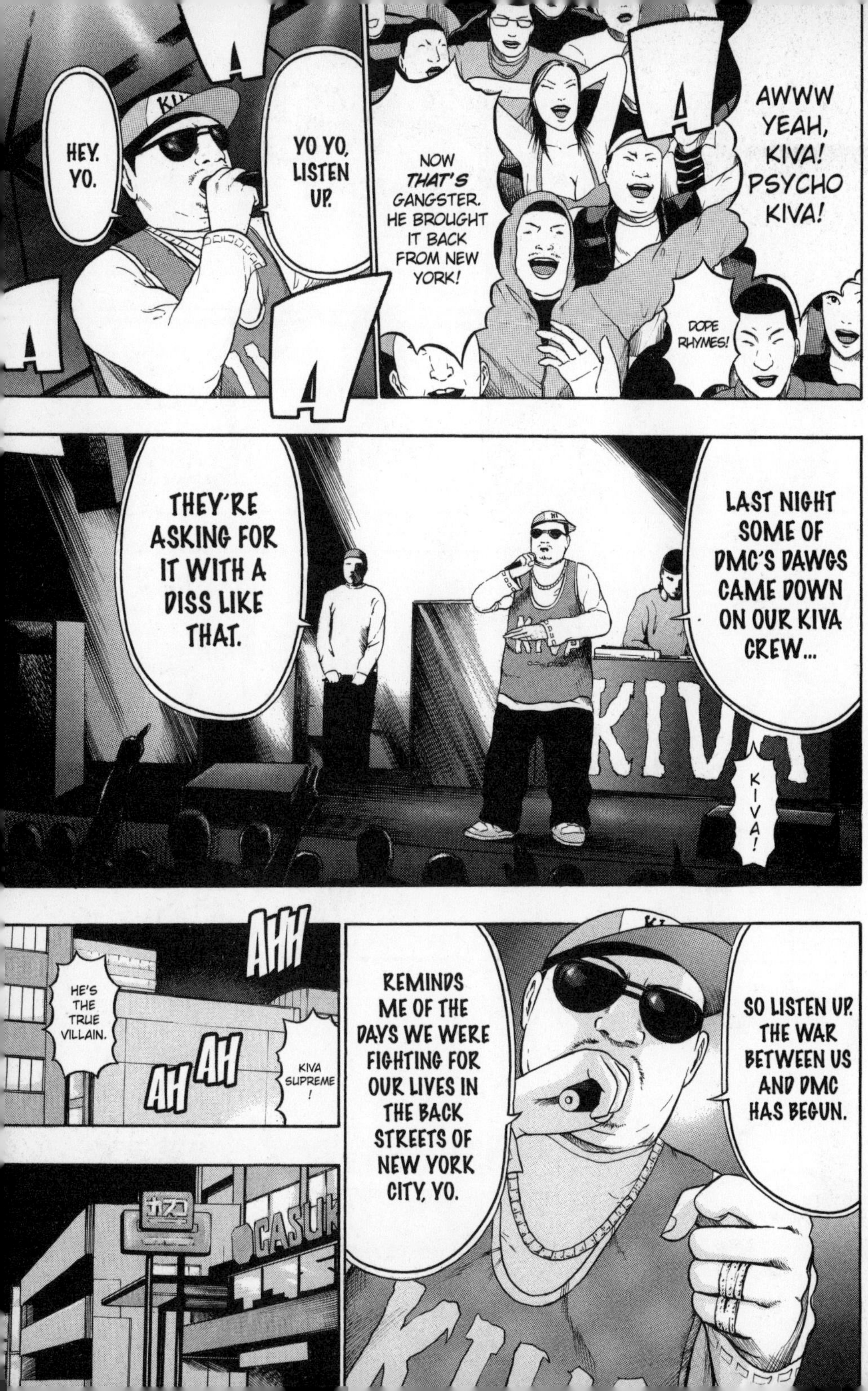
AWWW YEAH, KIVA! PSYCHO KIVA!
DOPE RHYMES!
NOW THAT'S GANGSTER. HE BROUGHT IT BACK FROM NEW YORK!
YO YO, LISTEN UP.
HEY. YO.
LAST NIGHT SOME OF DMC'S DAWGS CAME DOWN ON OUR KIVA CREW...
KIVA!
THEY'RE ASKING FOR IT WITH A DISS LIKE THAT.
SO LISTEN UP. THE WAR BETWEEN US AND DMC HAS BEGUN.
REMINDS ME OF THE DAYS WE WERE FIGHTING FOR OUR LIVES IN THE BACK STREETS OF NEW YORK CITY, YO.
AHH
KIVA SUPREME!
AH AH
HE'S THE TRUE VILLAIN.

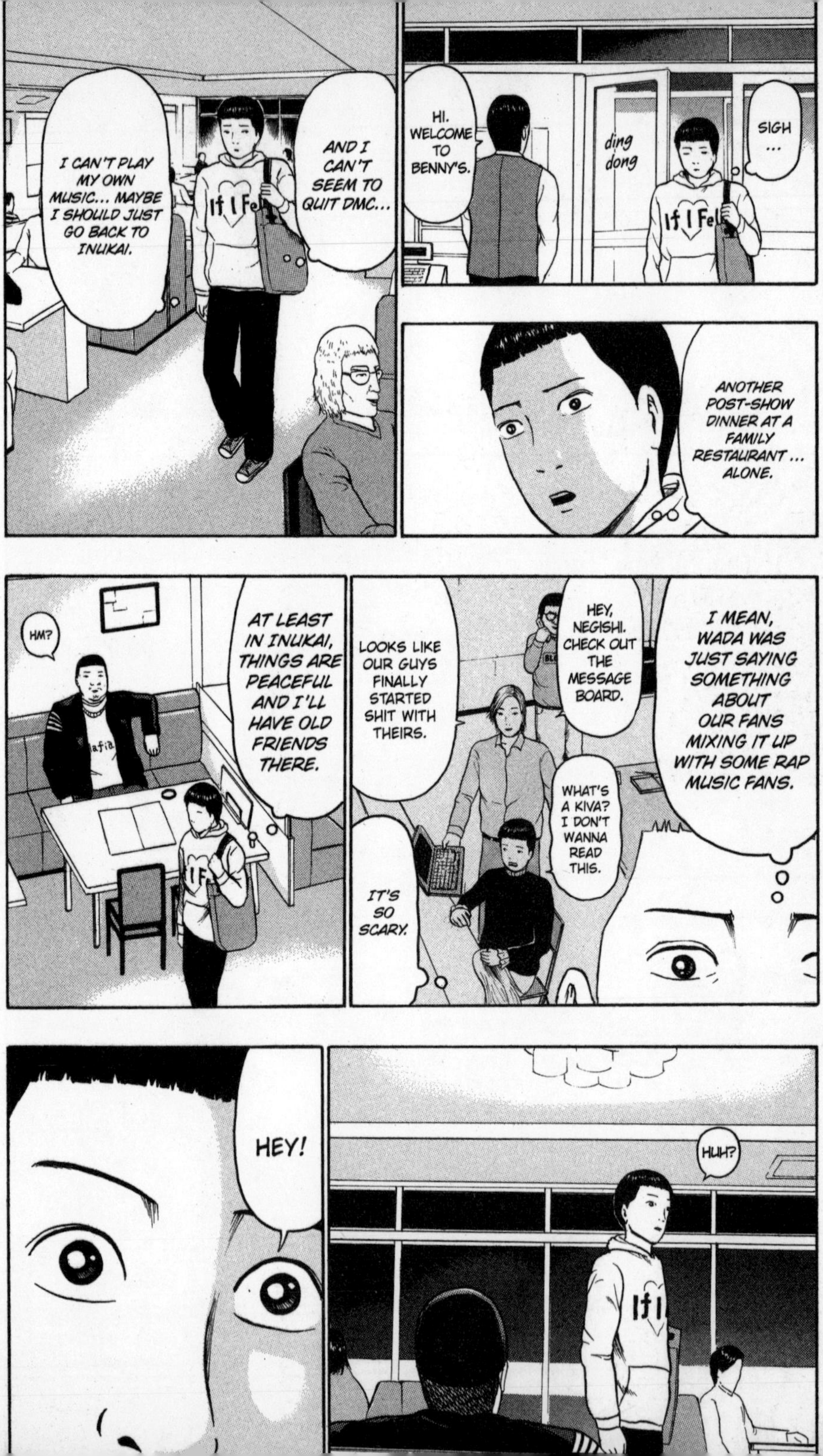
SIGH ...
ding dong
HI. WELCOME TO BENNY'S.
ANOTHER POST-SHOW DINNER AT A FAMILY RESTAURANT ... ALONE.
I CAN'T PLAY MY OWN MUSIC... MAYBE I SHOULD JUST GO BACK TO INUKAI.
AND I CAN'T SEEM TO QUIT DMC...
I MEAN, WADA WAS JUST SAYING SOMETHING ABOUT OUR FANS MIXING IT UP WITH SOME RAP MUSIC FANS.
HEY, NEGISHI. CHECK OUT THE MESSAGE BOARD.
WHAT'S A KIVA? I DON'T WANNA READ THIS.
LOOKS LIKE OUR GUYS FINALLY STARTED SHIT WITH THEIRS.
IT'S SO SCARY.
AT LEAST IN INUKAI, THINGS ARE PEACEFUL AND I'LL HAVE OLD FRIENDS THERE.
HM?
HUH?
HEY!

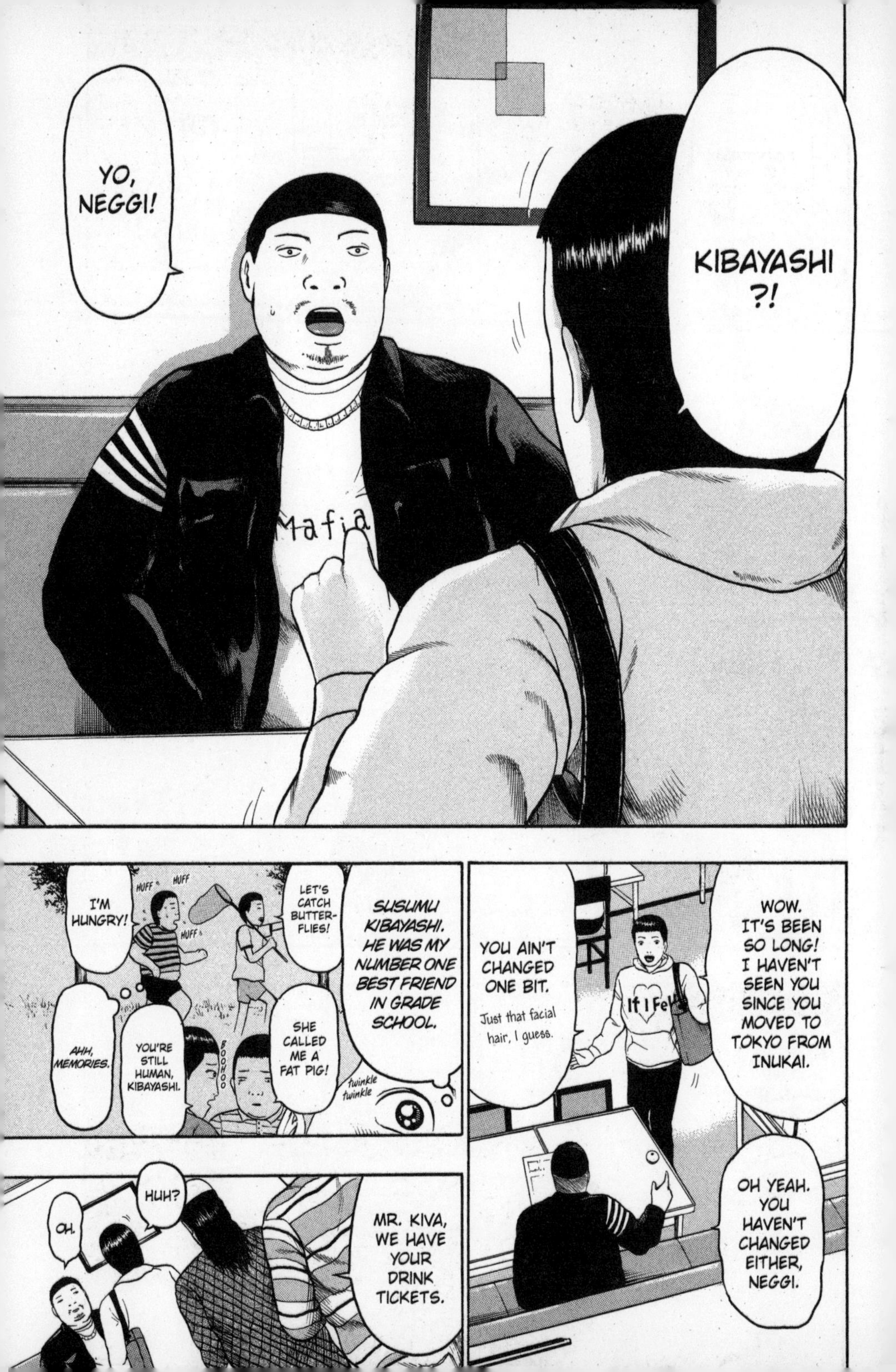
KIBAYASHI ?!
YO, NEGGI!
Mafia
WOW. IT'S BEEN SO LONG! I HAVEN'T SEEN YOU SINCE YOU MOVED TO TOKYO FROM INUKAI.
YOU AIN'T CHANGED ONE BIT.
Just that facial hair, I guess.
OH YEAH. YOU HAVEN'T CHANGED EITHER, NEGGI.
SUSUMU KIBAYASHI. HE WAS MY NUMBER ONE BEST FRIEND IN GRADE SCHOOL.
LET'S CATCH BUTTER-FLIES!
HUFF HUFF HUFF
I'M HUNGRY!
SHE CALLED ME A FAT PIG!
BOOHOO
twinkle twinkle
YOU'RE STILL HUMAN, KIBAYASHI.
AHH, MEMORIES.
MR. KIVA, WE HAVE YOUR DRINK TICKETS.
HUH?
OH.

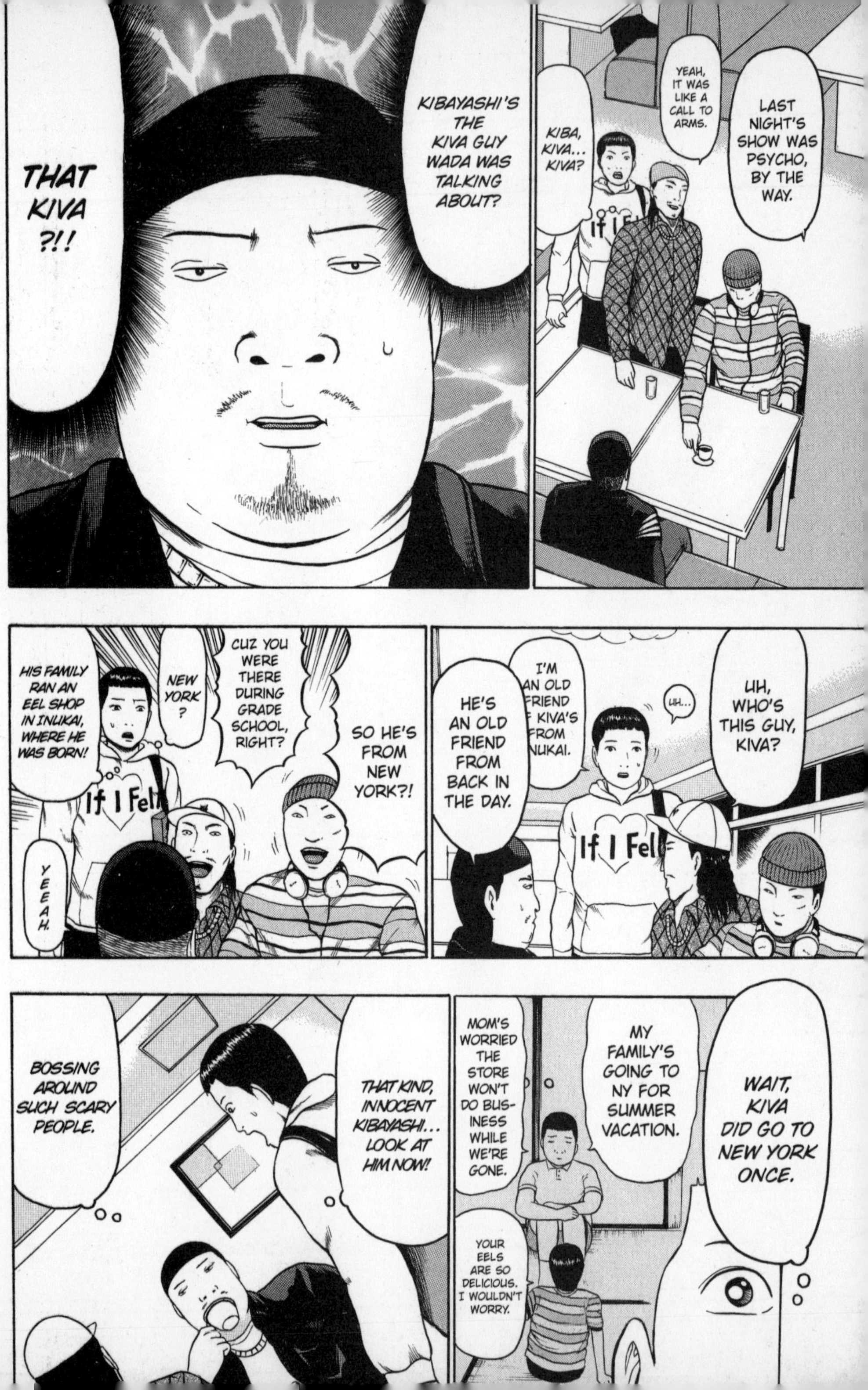

LAST NIGHT'S SHOW WAS PSYCHO, BY THE WAY.
YEAH, IT WAS LIKE A CALL TO ARMS.
KIBA, KIVA... KIVA?
KIBAYASHI'S THE KIVA GUY WADA WAS TALKING ABOUT?
THAT KIVA ?!!
UH, WHO'S THIS GUY, KIVA?
UH...
I'M AN OLD FRIEND F KIVA'S FROM NUKAI.
HE'S AN OLD FRIEND FROM BACK IN THE DAY.
SO HE'S FROM NEW YORK?!
CUZ YOU WERE THERE DURING GRADE SCHOOL, RIGHT?
NEW YORK?
HIS FAMILY RAN AN EEL SHOP IN INUKAI, WHERE HE WAS BORN!
YEEAH.
WAIT, KIVA DID GO TO NEW YORK ONCE.
MY FAMILY'S GOING TO NY FOR SUMMER VACATION.
MOM'S WORRIED THE STORE WON'T DO BUS-INESS WHILE WE'RE GONE.
YOUR EELS ARE SO DELICIOUS. I WOULDN'T WORRY.
THAT KIND, INNOCENT KIBAYASHI... LOOK AT HIM NOW!
BOSSING AROUND SUCH SCARY PEOPLE.

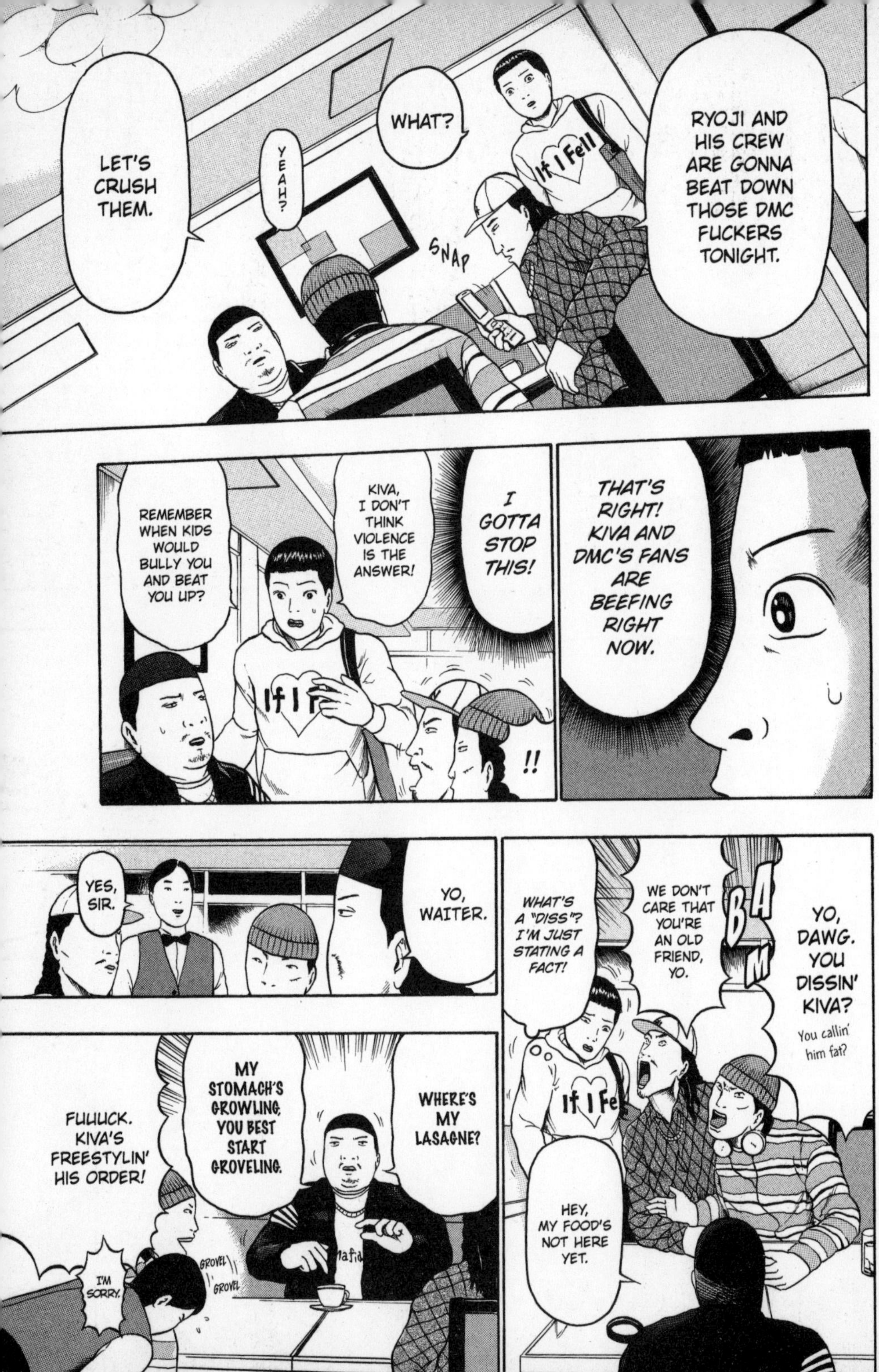
RYOJI AND HIS CREW ARE GONNA BEAT DOWN THOSE DMC FUCKERS TONIGHT.
WHAT?
YEAH?
SNAP
LET'S CRUSH THEM.
THAT'S RIGHT! KIVA AND DMC'S FANS ARE BEEFING RIGHT NOW.
I GOTTA STOP THIS!
KIVA, I DON'T THINK VIOLENCE IS THE ANSWER!
REMEMBER WHEN KIDS WOULD BULLY YOU AND BEAT YOU UP?
!!
YO, DAWG. YOU DISSIN' KIVA?
You callin' him fat?
BAM
WE DON'T CARE THAT YOU'RE AN OLD FRIEND, YO.
WHAT'S A "DISS"? I'M JUST STATING A FACT!
HEY, MY FOOD'S NOT HERE YET.
YO, WAITER.
YES, SIR.
WHERE'S MY LASAGNE?
MY STOMACH'S GROWLING, YOU BEST START GROVELING.
FUUUCK. KIVA'S FREESTYLIN' HIS ORDER!
GROVEL GROVEL
I'M SORRY.

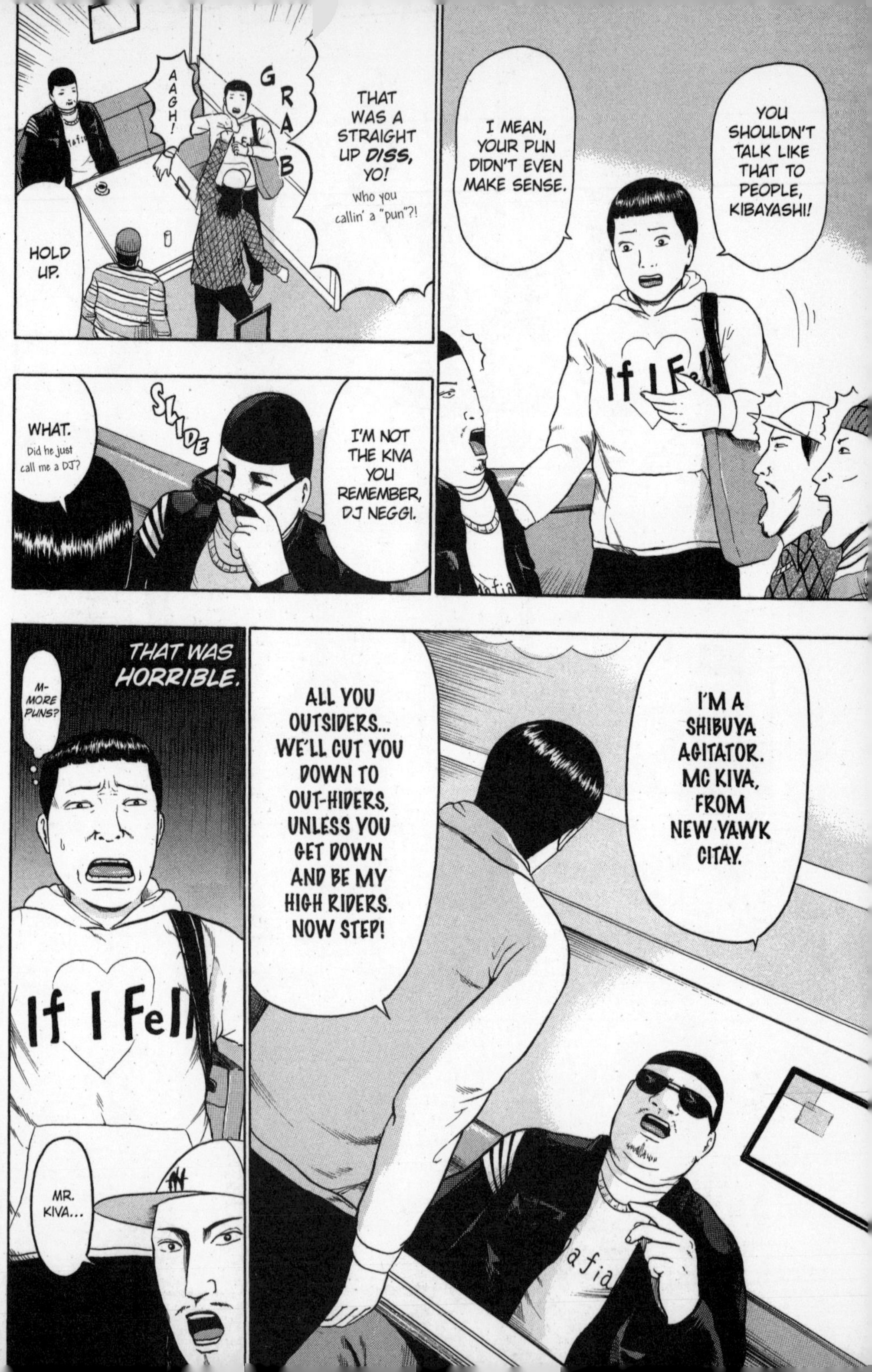
YOU SHOULDN'T TALK LIKE THAT TO PEOPLE, KIBAYASHI!
I MEAN, YOUR PUN DIDN'T EVEN MAKE SENSE.
THAT WAS A STRAIGHT UP **DISS,** YO!
Who you callin' a "pun"?!
GRAB
AAGH!
HOLD UP.
I'M NOT THE KIVA YOU REMEMBER, DJ NEGGI.
SLIDE
WHAT.
Did he just call me a DJ?
I'M A SHIBUYA AGITATOR. MC KIVA, FROM NEW YAWK CITAY.
ALL YOU OUTSIDERS... WE'LL CUT YOU DOWN TO OUT-HIDERS, UNLESS YOU GET DOWN AND BE MY HIGH RIDERS. NOW STEP!
THAT WAS HORRIBLE.
M-MORE PUNS?
MR. KIVA...

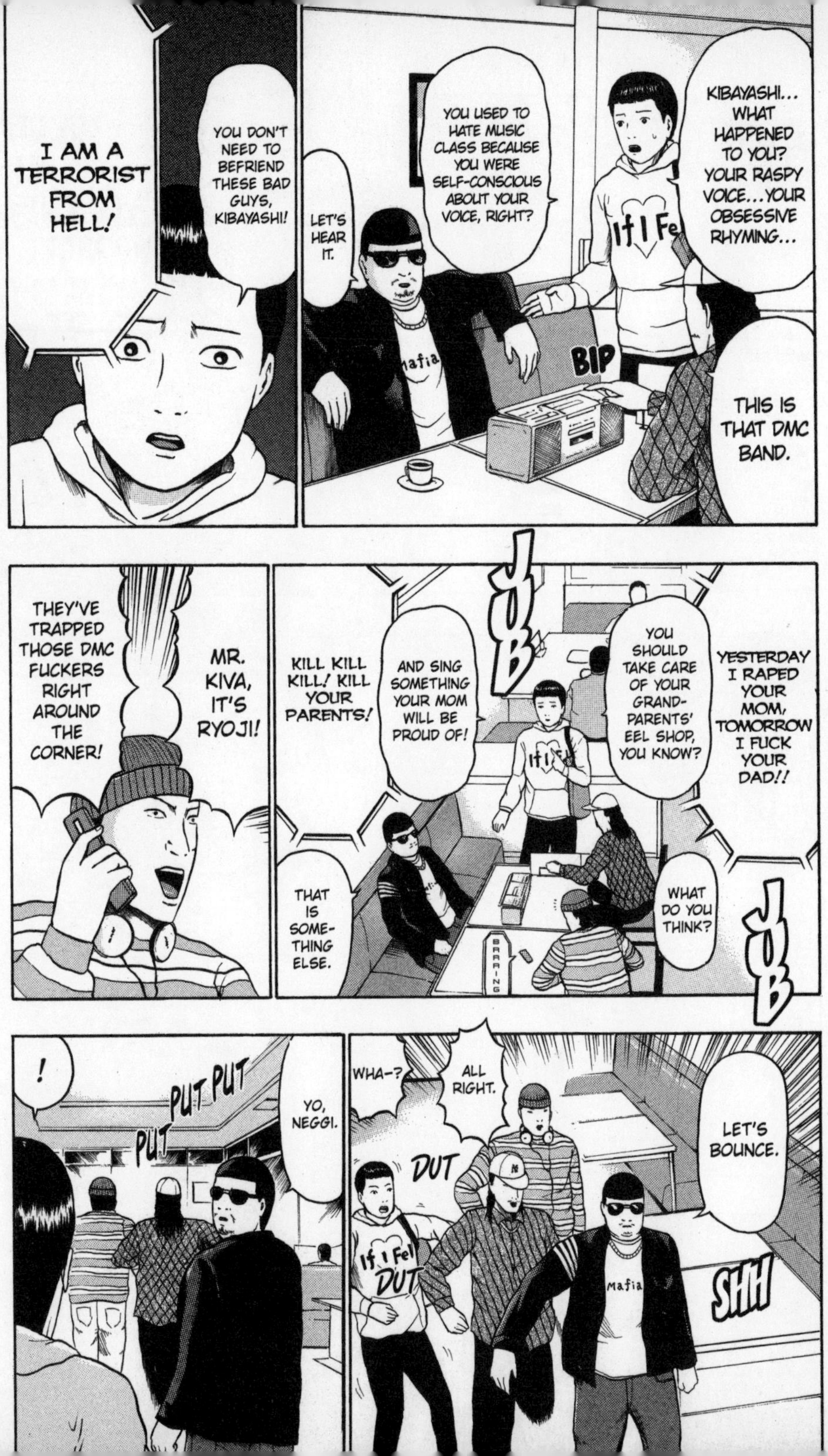
KIBAYASHI... WHAT HAPPENED TO YOU? YOUR RASPY VOICE...YOUR OBSESSIVE RHYMING...
YOU USED TO HATE MUSIC CLASS BECAUSE YOU WERE SELF-CONSCIOUS ABOUT YOUR VOICE, RIGHT?
LET'S HEAR IT.
BIP
THIS IS THAT DMC BAND.
YOU DON'T NEED TO BEFRIEND THESE BAD GUYS, KIBAYASHI!
I AM A TERRORIST FROM HELL!
JUB
YESTERDAY I RAPED YOUR MOM, TOMORROW I FUCK YOUR DAD!!
YOU SHOULD TAKE CARE OF YOUR GRAND-PARENTS' EEL SHOP, YOU KNOW?
AND SING SOMETHING YOUR MOM WILL BE PROUD OF!
KILL KILL KILL! KILL YOUR PARENTS!
JUB
WHAT DO YOU THINK?
THAT IS SOME-THING ELSE.
BRRRING
MR. KIVA, IT'S RYOJI!
THEY'VE TRAPPED THOSE DMC FUCKERS RIGHT AROUND THE CORNER!
LET'S BOUNCE.
ALL RIGHT.
WHA-?
DUT
SHH
DUT
YO, NEGGI.
PUT PUT
PUT
!

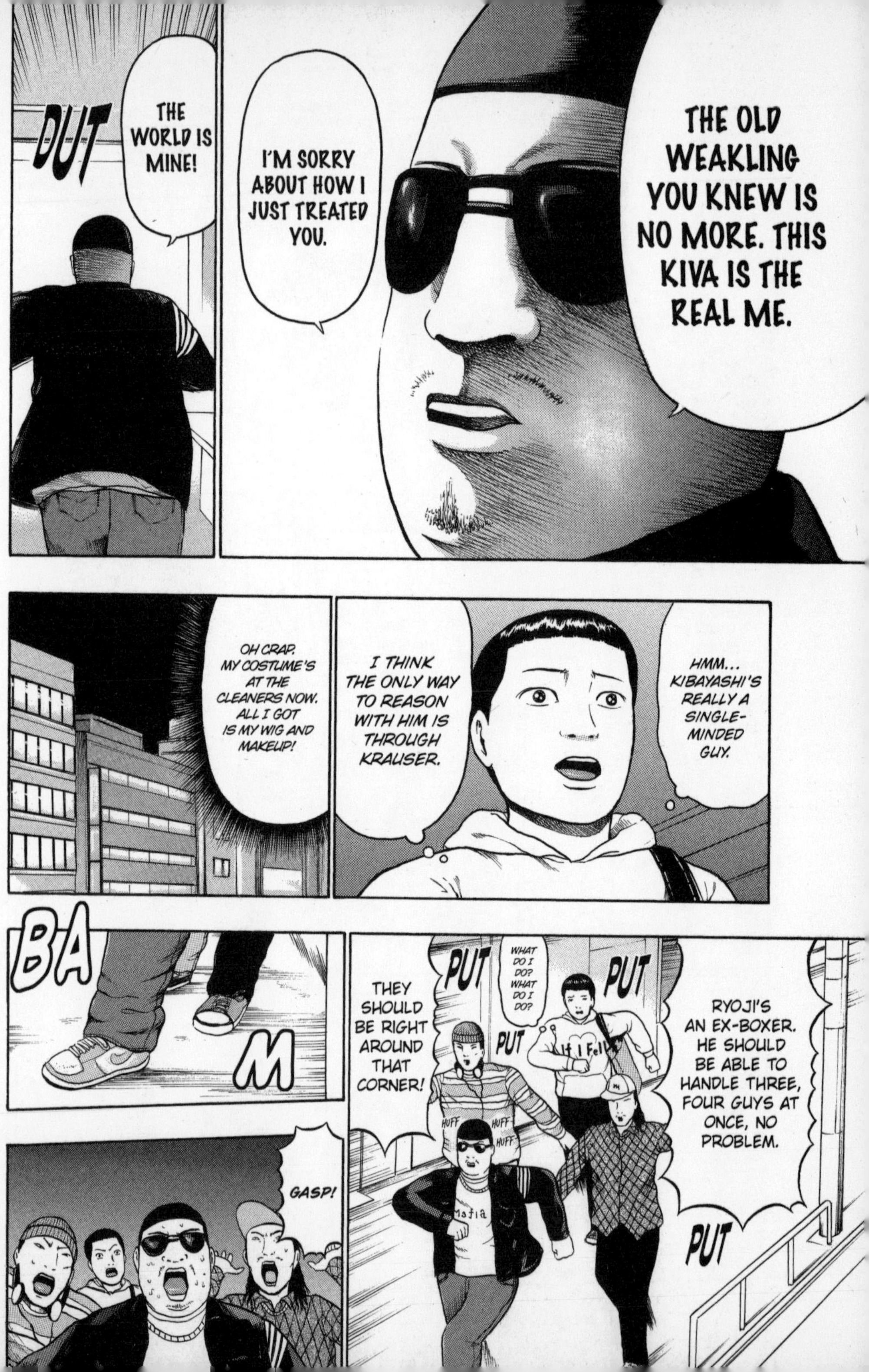
THE OLD WEAKLING YOU KNEW IS NO MORE. THIS KIVA IS THE REAL ME.
I'M SORRY ABOUT HOW I JUST TREATED YOU.
THE WORLD IS MINE!
DUT
HMM... KIBAYASHI'S REALLY A SINGLE-MINDED GUY.
I THINK THE ONLY WAY TO REASON WITH HIM IS THROUGH KRAUSER.
OH CRAP. MY COSTUME'S AT THE CLEANERS NOW. ALL I GOT IS MY WIG AND MAKEUP!
RYOJI'S AN EX-BOXER. HE SHOULD BE ABLE TO HANDLE THREE, FOUR GUYS AT ONCE, NO PROBLEM.
PUT
WHAT DO I DO? WHAT DO I DO?
PUT
PUT
THEY SHOULD BE RIGHT AROUND THAT CORNER!
HUFF
HUFF
HUFF
Mafia
PUT
BA
M
GASP!

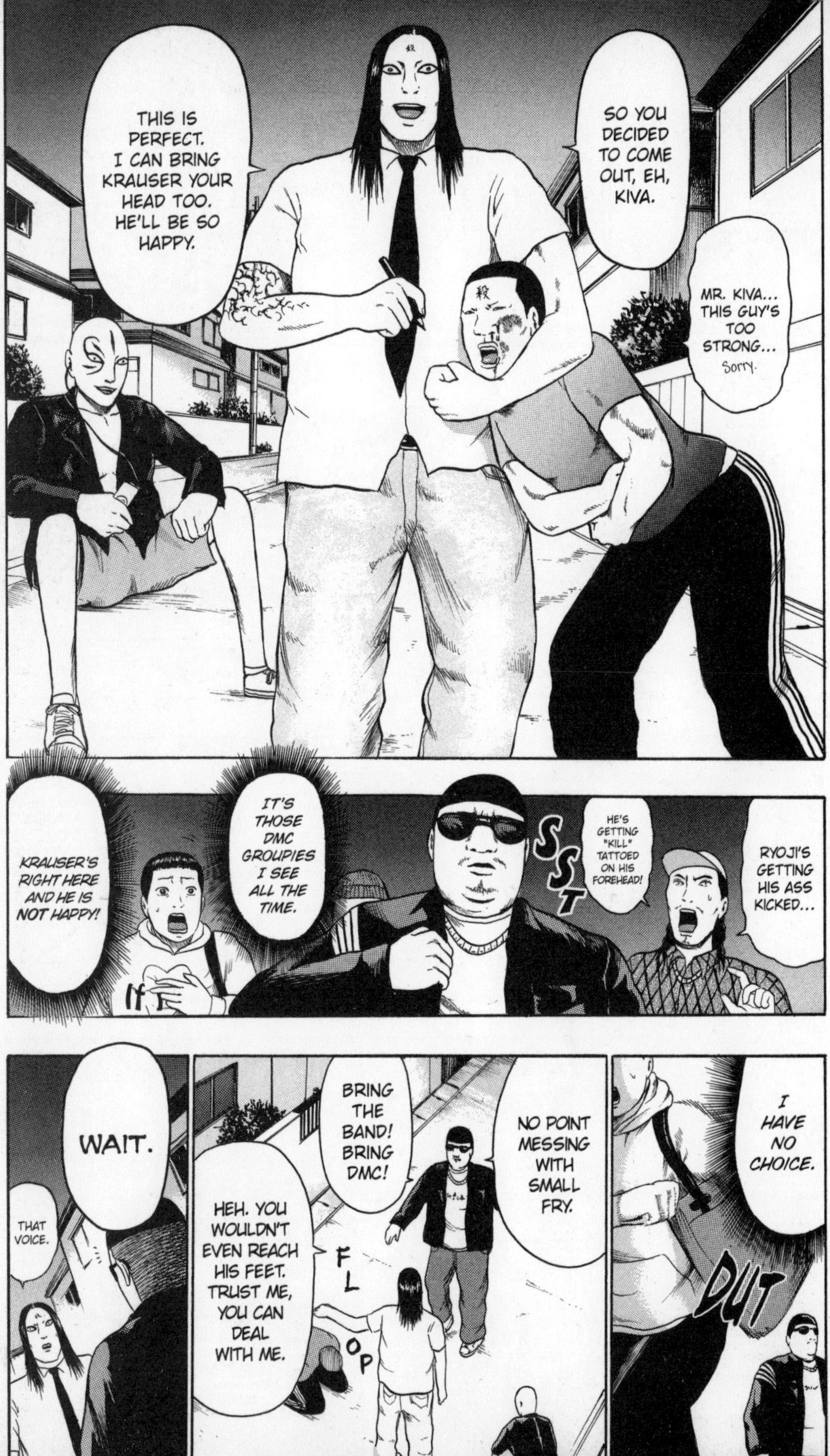

SO YOU DECIDED TO COME OUT, EH, KIVA.
MR. KIVA... THIS GUY'S TOO STRONG... Sorry.
THIS IS PERFECT. I CAN BRING KRAUSER YOUR HEAD TOO. HE'LL BE SO HAPPY.
RYOJI'S GETTING HIS ASS KICKED...
HE'S GETTING "KILL" TATTOOED ON HIS FOREHEAD!
SST
IT'S THOSE DMC GROUPIES I SEE ALL THE TIME.
KRAUSER'S RIGHT HERE AND HE IS NOT HAPPY!
I HAVE NO CHOICE.
DUT
NO POINT MESSING WITH SMALL FRY.
BRING THE BAND! BRING DMC!
HEH. YOU WOULDN'T EVEN REACH HIS FEET. TRUST ME, YOU CAN DEAL WITH ME.
FLOP
WAIT.
THAT VOICE.

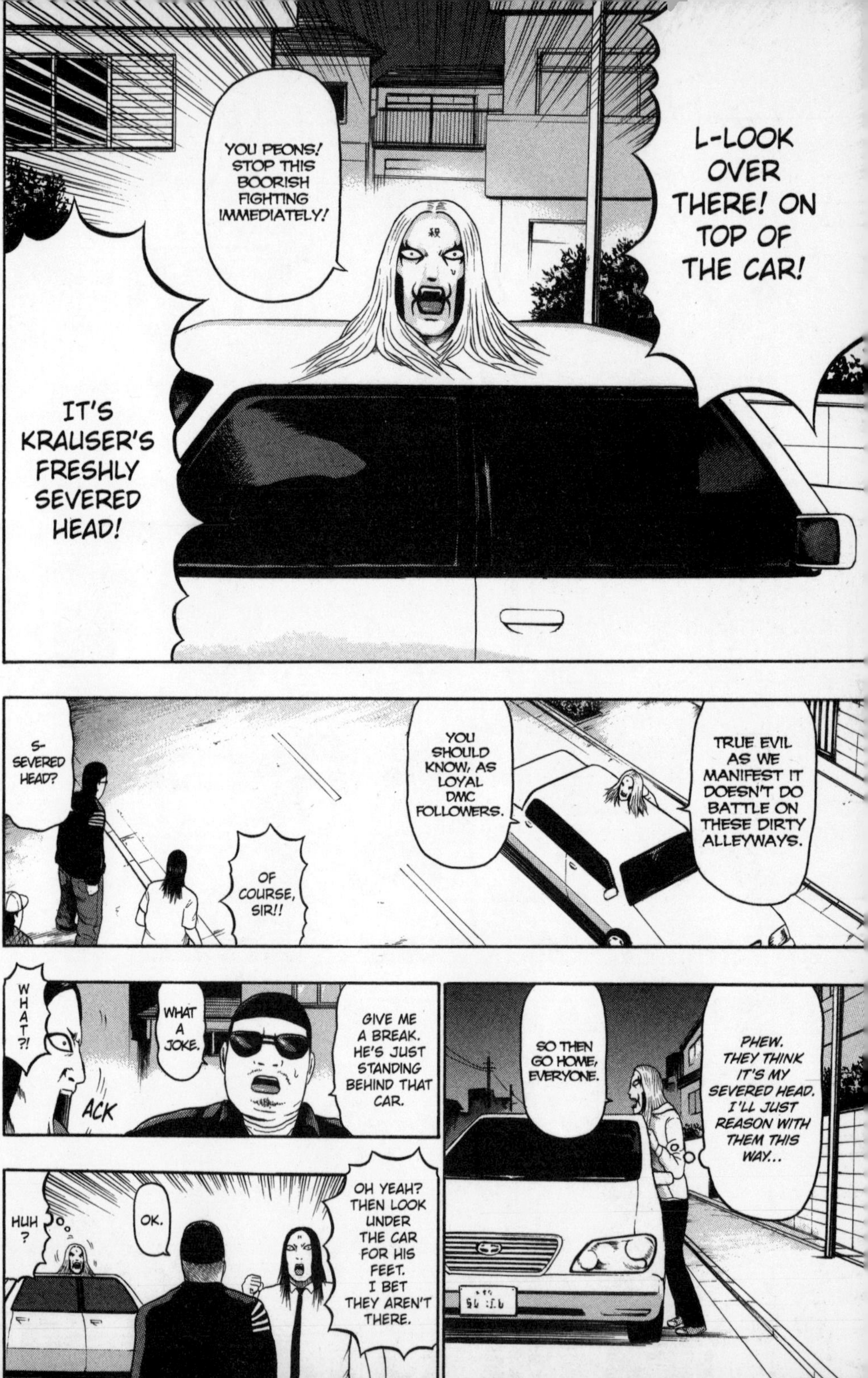
L-LOOK OVER THERE! ON TOP OF THE CAR!
YOU PEONS! STOP THIS BOORISH FIGHTING IMMEDIATELY!
IT'S KRAUSER'S FRESHLY SEVERED HEAD!
TRUE EVIL AS WE MANIFEST IT DOESN'T DO BATTLE ON THESE DIRTY ALLEYWAYS.
YOU SHOULD KNOW, AS LOYAL DMC FOLLOWERS.
OF COURSE, SIR!!
S-SEVERED HEAD?
PHEW. THEY THINK IT'S MY SEVERED HEAD. I'LL JUST REASON WITH THEM THIS WAY...
SO THEN GO HOME, EVERYONE.
GIVE ME A BREAK. HE'S JUST STANDING BEHIND THAT CAR.
WHAT A JOKE.
WHAT?!
ACK
OH YEAH? THEN LOOK UNDER THE CAR FOR HIS FEET. I BET THEY AREN'T THERE.
OK.
HUH?

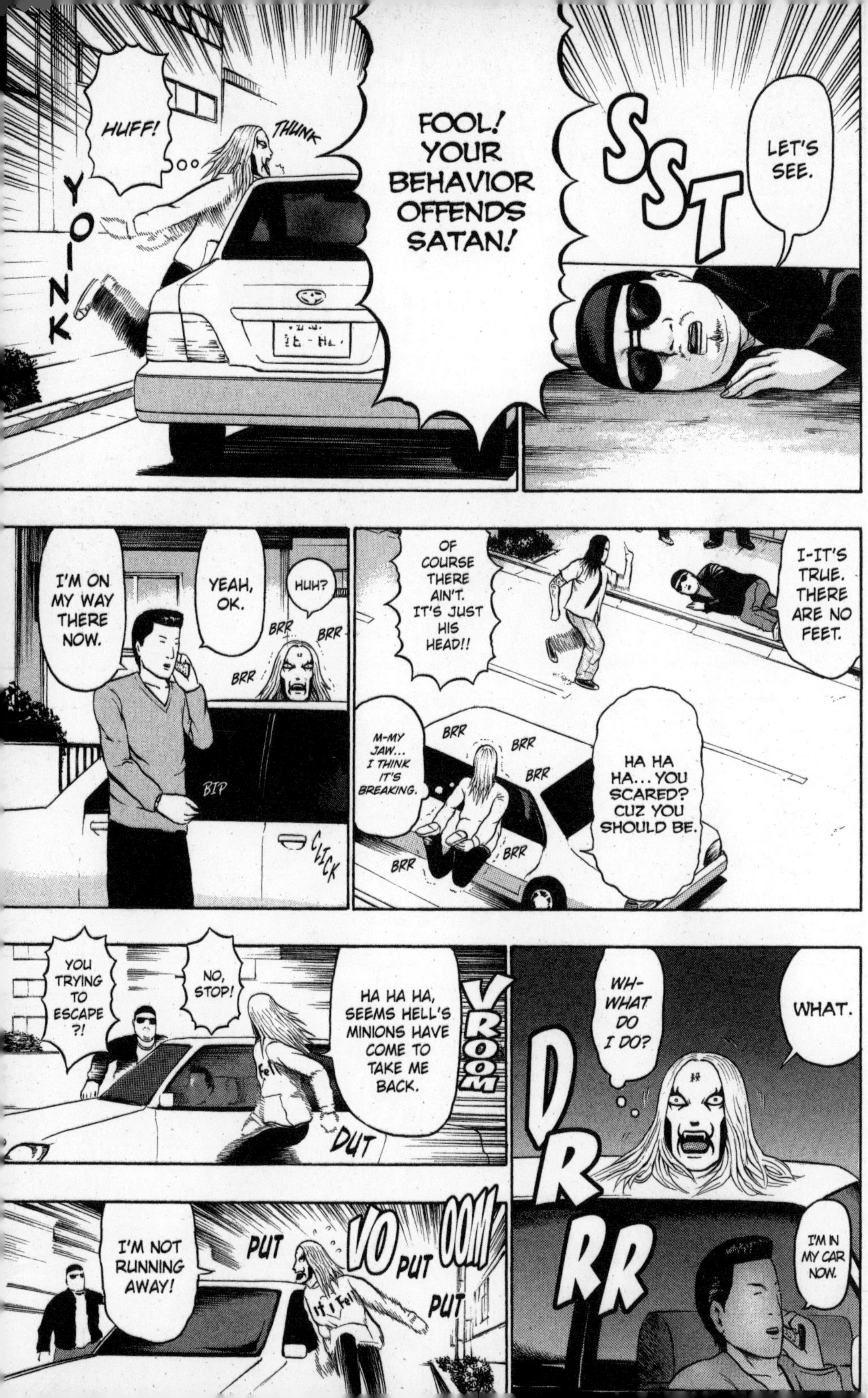
LET'S SEE.
SST
FOOL! YOUR BEHAVIOR OFFENDS SATAN!
THUNK
HUFF!
YOINK
I-IT'S TRUE. THERE ARE NO FEET.
OF COURSE THERE AIN'T. IT'S JUST HIS HEAD!!
HA HA HA... YOU SCARED? CUZ YOU SHOULD BE.
BRR BRR BRR BRR BRR
M-MY JAW... I THINK IT'S BREAKING.
HUH?
BRR BRR BRR
YEAH, OK.
I'M ON MY WAY THERE NOW.
BIP
CLICK
WHAT.
WH-WHAT DO I DO?
DRRRR
I'M IN MY CAR NOW.
VROOM
HA HA HA, SEEMS HELL'S MINIONS HAVE COME TO TAKE ME BACK.
NO, STOP!
YOU TRYING TO ESCAPE?!
DUT
VOOOM
PUT PUT PUT
I'M NOT RUNNING AWAY!

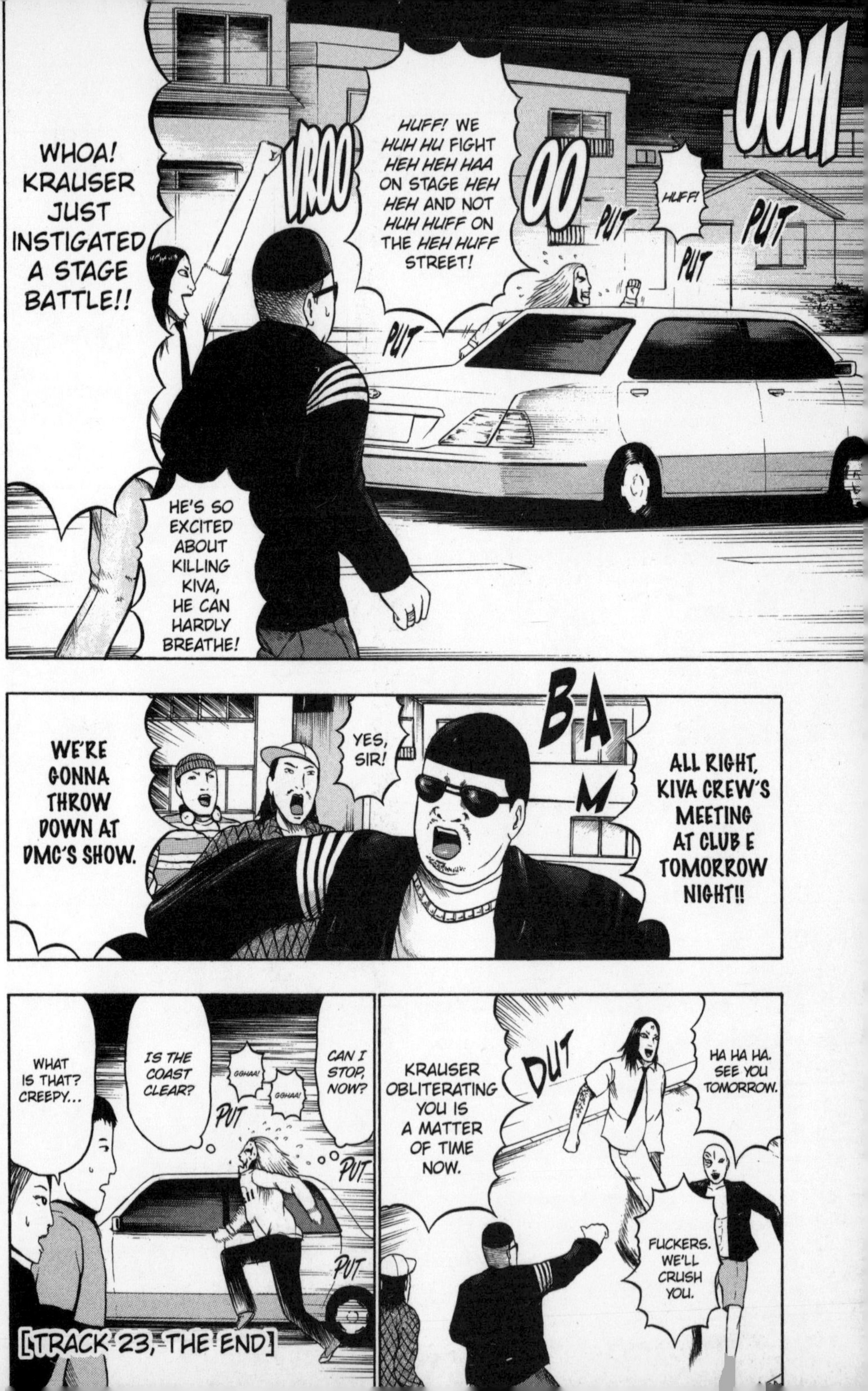
OOM
HUFF!
PUT
PUT
OO
PUT
HUFF! WE HUH HU FIGHT HEH HEH HAA ON STAGE HEH HEH AND NOT HUH HUFF ON THE HEH HUFF STREET!
VROO
WHOA! KRAUSER JUST INSTIGATED A STAGE BATTLE!!
PUT
HE'S SO EXCITED ABOUT KILLING KIVA, HE CAN HARDLY BREATHE!
ALL RIGHT, KIVA CREW'S MEETING AT CLUB E TOMORROW NIGHT!!
BAM
YES, SIR!
WE'RE GONNA THROW DOWN AT DMC'S SHOW.
HA HA HA. SEE YOU TOMORROW.
DUT
KRAUSER OBLITERATING YOU IS A MATTER OF TIME NOW.
FUCKERS. WE'LL CRUSH YOU.
CAN I STOP, NOW?
GGHAA!
GGHAA!
IS THE COAST CLEAR?
PUT
WHAT IS THAT? CREEPY...
PUT
PUT
[TRACK 23, THE END]

DMC LEXICON

 RAP

A rhyming style popular with people in hip hop. They say some neat things, but it's a bunch of bad one-liners strung together when it comes down to it. No one laughs. Moreover, it's called "freestyle" when you improvise your rhymes and "diss" someone. Many of the practitioners are middle-aged management types who can't stand their annoying subordinates.

Usage: Don't call it RAP. It's SHUT your tRAP. Heh heh.

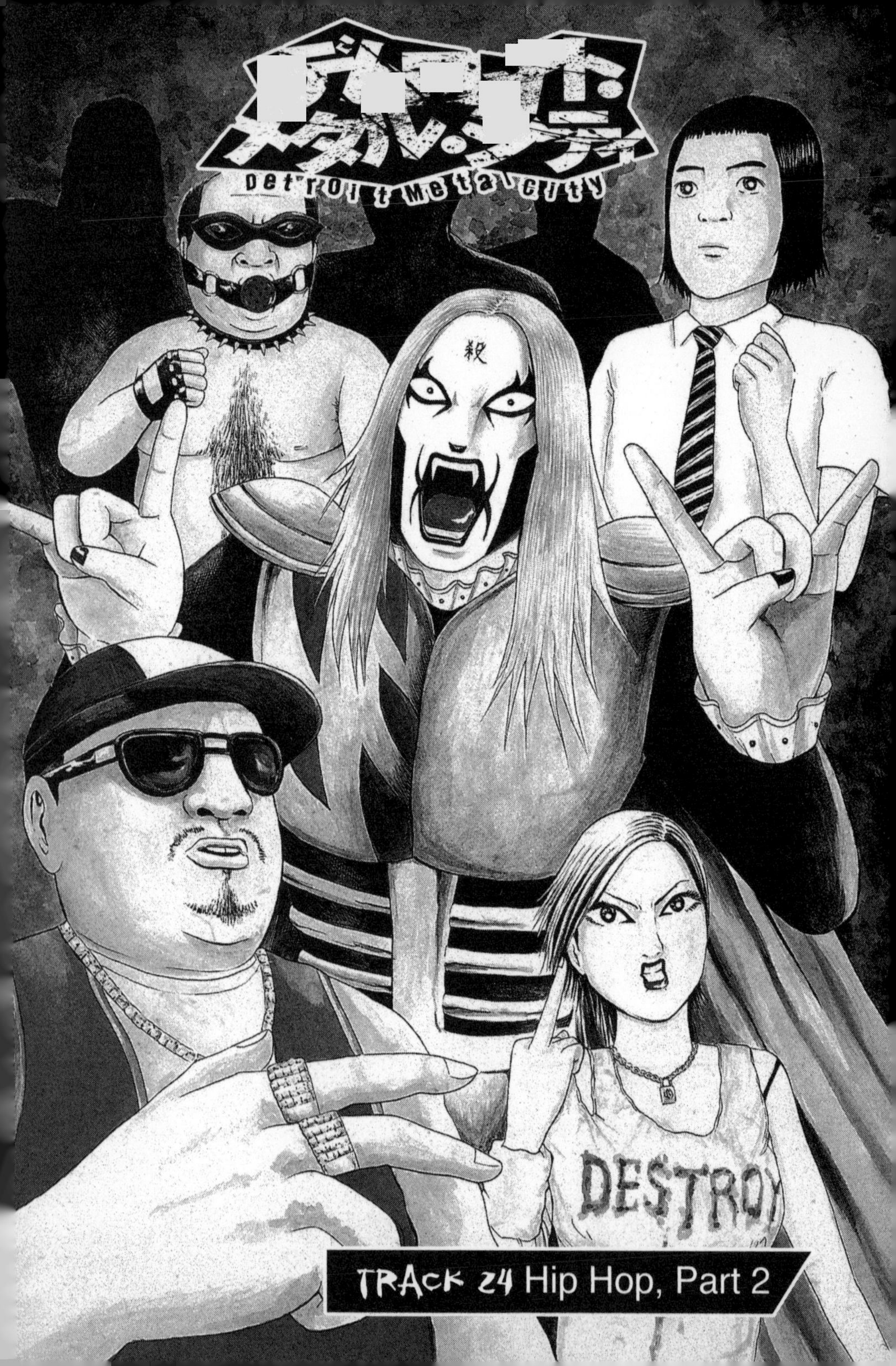
Detroit Metal City
殺
DESTROY
TRACK 24 Hip Hop, Part 2

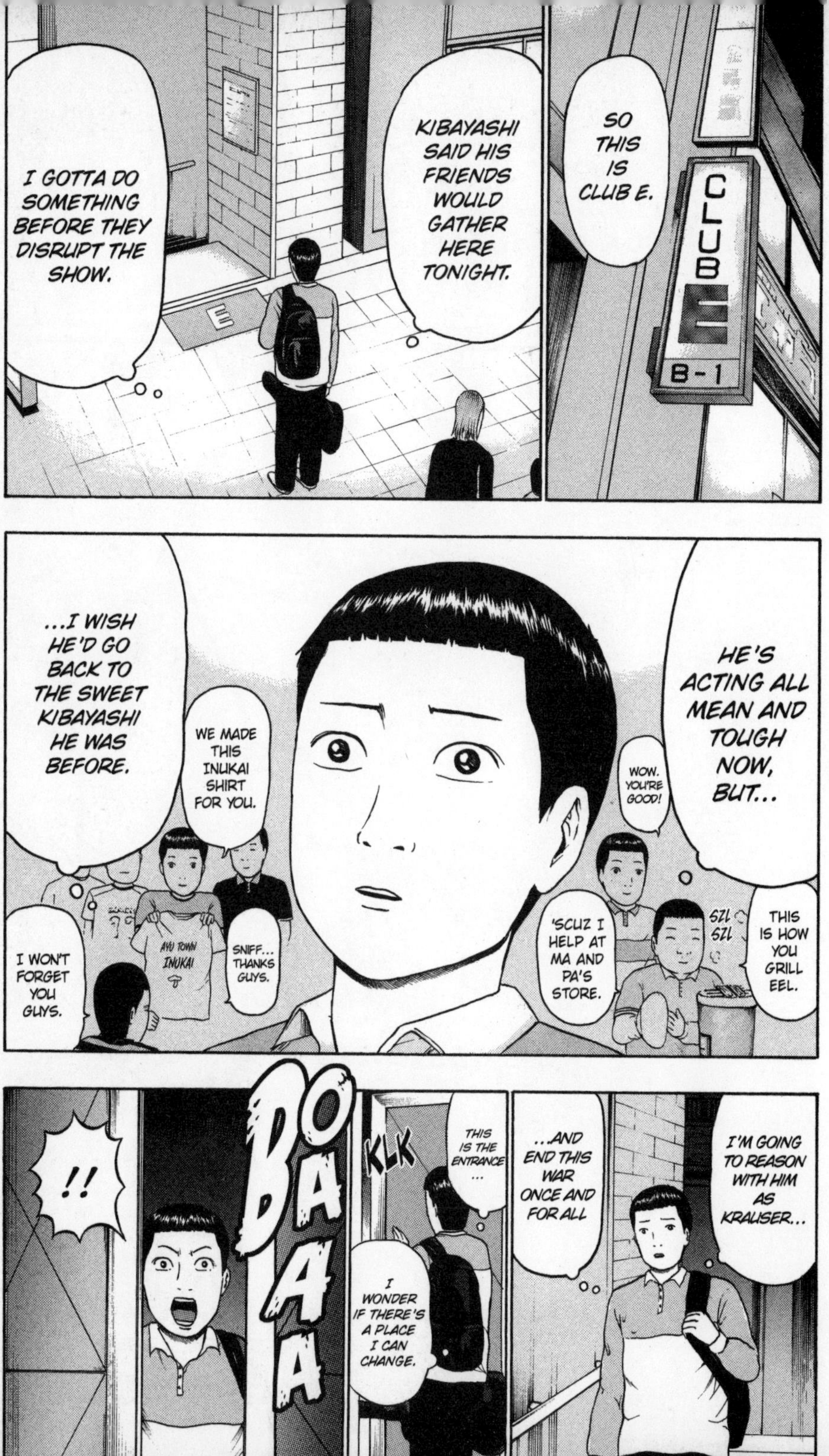
SO THIS IS CLUB E.
CLUB E
B-1
KIBAYASHI SAID HIS FRIENDS WOULD GATHER HERE TONIGHT.
I GOTTA DO SOMETHING BEFORE THEY DISRUPT THE SHOW.
HE'S ACTING ALL MEAN AND TOUGH NOW, BUT...
WOW. YOU'RE GOOD!
THIS IS HOW YOU GRILL EEL.
SZL SZL
'SCUZ I HELP AT MA AND PA'S STORE.
...I WISH HE'D GO BACK TO THE SWEET KIBAYASHI HE WAS BEFORE.
WE MADE THIS INUKAI SHIRT FOR YOU.
AYU TOWN INUKAI
SNIFF... THANKS GUYS.
I WON'T FORGET YOU GUYS.
I'M GOING TO REASON WITH HIM AS KRAUSER...
...AND END THIS WAR ONCE AND FOR ALL
THIS IS THE ENTRANCE...
KLK
I WONDER IF THERE'S A PLACE I CAN CHANGE.
DOBAAAA
!!

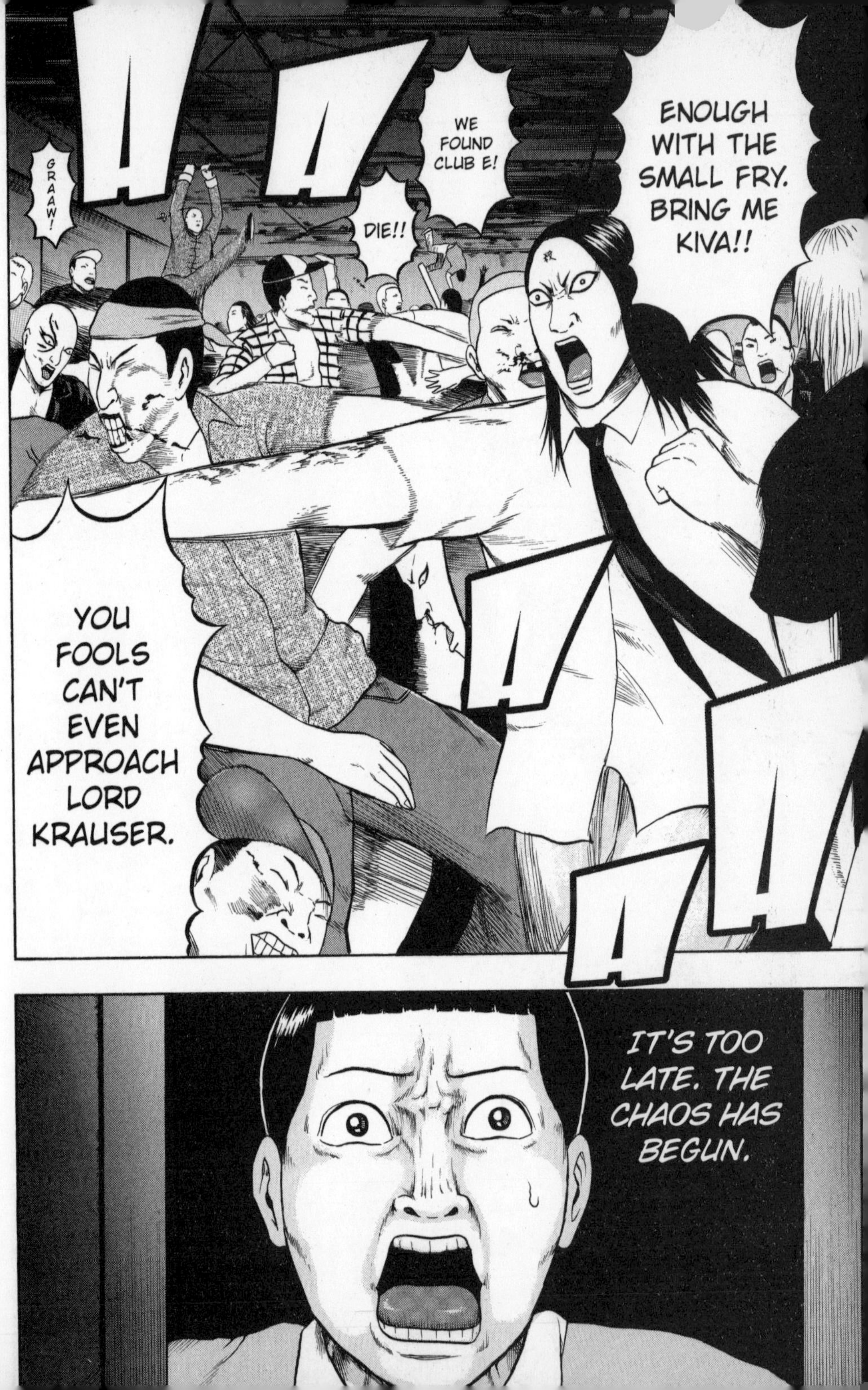
ENOUGH WITH THE SMALL FRY. BRING ME KIVA!!
WE FOUND CLUB E!
DIE!!
GRAAAW!
YOU FOOLS CAN'T EVEN APPROACH LORD KRAUSER.
IT'S TOO LATE. THE CHAOS HAS BEGUN.

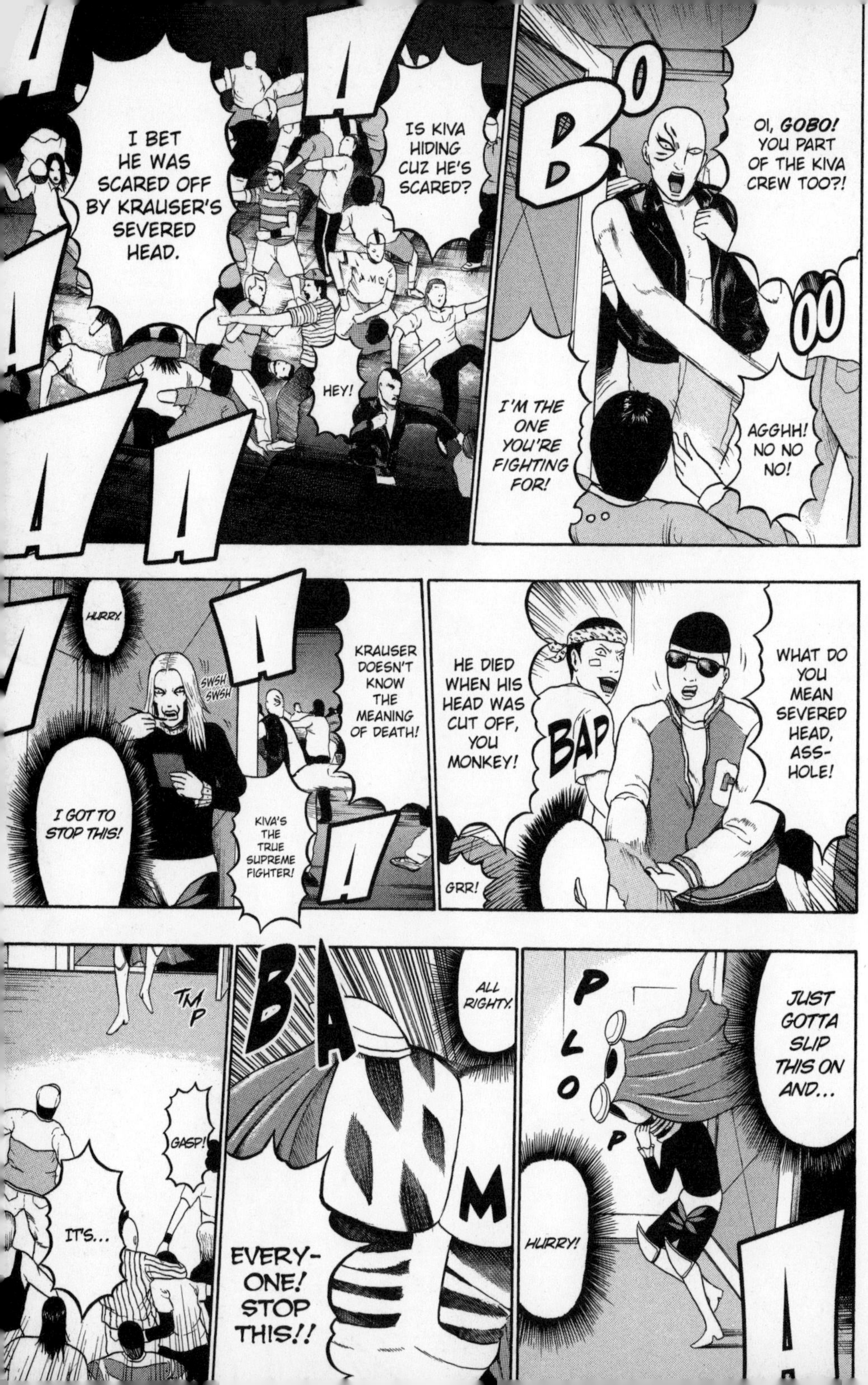
BOOOO
OI, GOBO! YOU PART OF THE KIVA CREW TOO?!
AGGHH! NO NO NO!
I'M THE ONE YOU'RE FIGHTING FOR!
IS KIVA HIDING CUZ HE'S SCARED?
I BET HE WAS SCARED OFF BY KRAUSER'S SEVERED HEAD.
HEY!
WHAT DO YOU MEAN SEVERED HEAD, ASS-HOLE!
HE DIED WHEN HIS HEAD WAS CUT OFF, YOU MONKEY!
BAP
GRR!
KRAUSER DOESN'T KNOW THE MEANING OF DEATH!
HURRY.
SWSH SWSH
KIVA'S THE TRUE SUPREME FIGHTER!
I GOT TO STOP THIS!
JUST GOTTA SLIP THIS ON AND...
PLOP
HURRY!
ALL RIGHTY.
BAM
EVERY-ONE! STOP THIS!!
TMP
GASP!
IT'S...

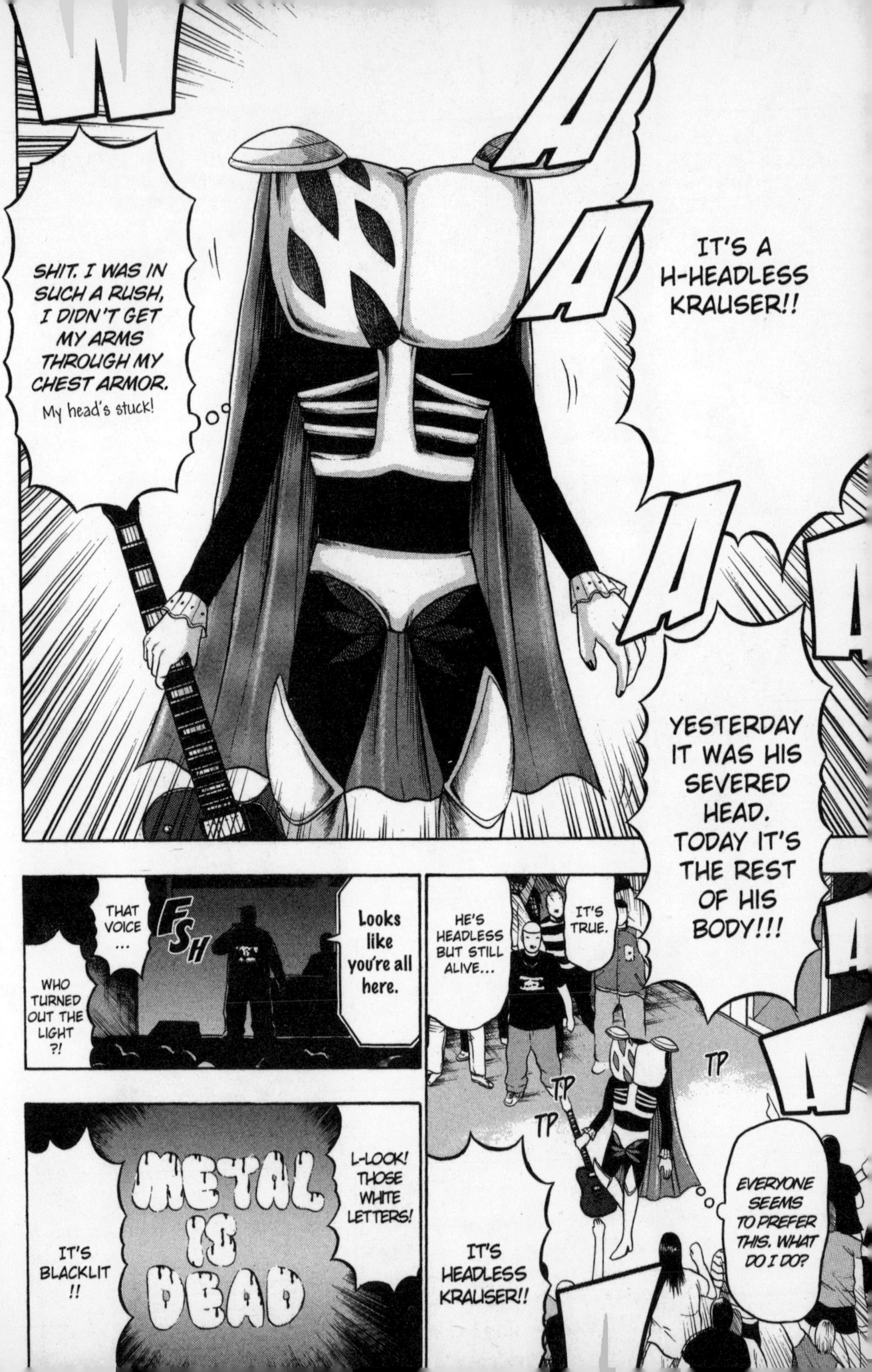
WAAAAAAA
IT'S A H-HEADLESS KRAUSER!!
SHIT. I WAS IN SUCH A RUSH, I DIDN'T GET MY ARMS THROUGH MY CHEST ARMOR.
My head's stuck!
YESTERDAY IT WAS HIS SEVERED HEAD. TODAY IT'S THE REST OF HIS BODY!!!
IT'S TRUE.
HE'S HEADLESS BUT STILL ALIVE...
TP
TP
TP
EVERYONE SEEMS TO PREFER THIS. WHAT DO I DO?
IT'S HEADLESS KRAUSER!!
Looks like you're all here.
FSH
THAT VOICE...
WHO TURNED OUT THE LIGHT?!
L-LOOK! THOSE WHITE LETTERS!
METAL IS DEAD
IT'S BLACKLIT!!

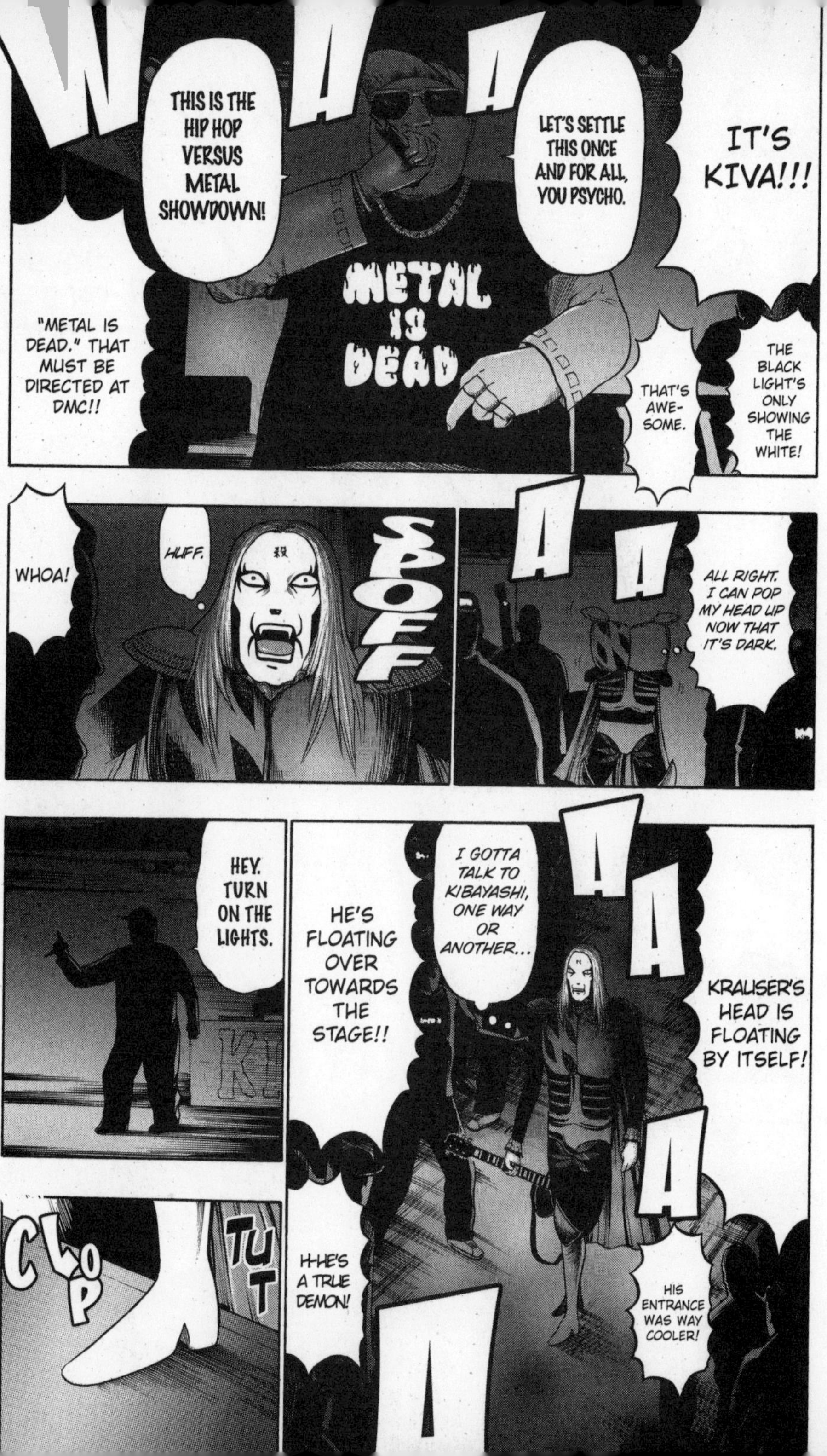
W A A
IT'S KIVA!!!
LET'S SETTLE THIS ONCE AND FOR ALL, YOU PSYCHO.
THIS IS THE HIP HOP VERSUS METAL SHOWDOWN!
METAL IS DEAD
THE BLACK LIGHT'S ONLY SHOWING THE WHITE!
THAT'S AWE-SOME.
"METAL IS DEAD." THAT MUST BE DIRECTED AT DMC!!
A A
ALL RIGHT. I CAN POP MY HEAD UP NOW THAT IT'S DARK.
SPOFF
HUFF.
WHOA!
A A
KRAUSER'S HEAD IS FLOATING BY ITSELF!
I GOTTA TALK TO KIBAYASHI, ONE WAY OR ANOTHER...
HE'S FLOATING OVER TOWARDS THE STAGE!!
A
HIS ENTRANCE WAS WAY COOLER!
H-HE'S A TRUE DEMON!
A
HEY. TURN ON THE LIGHTS.
TUT
CLOP

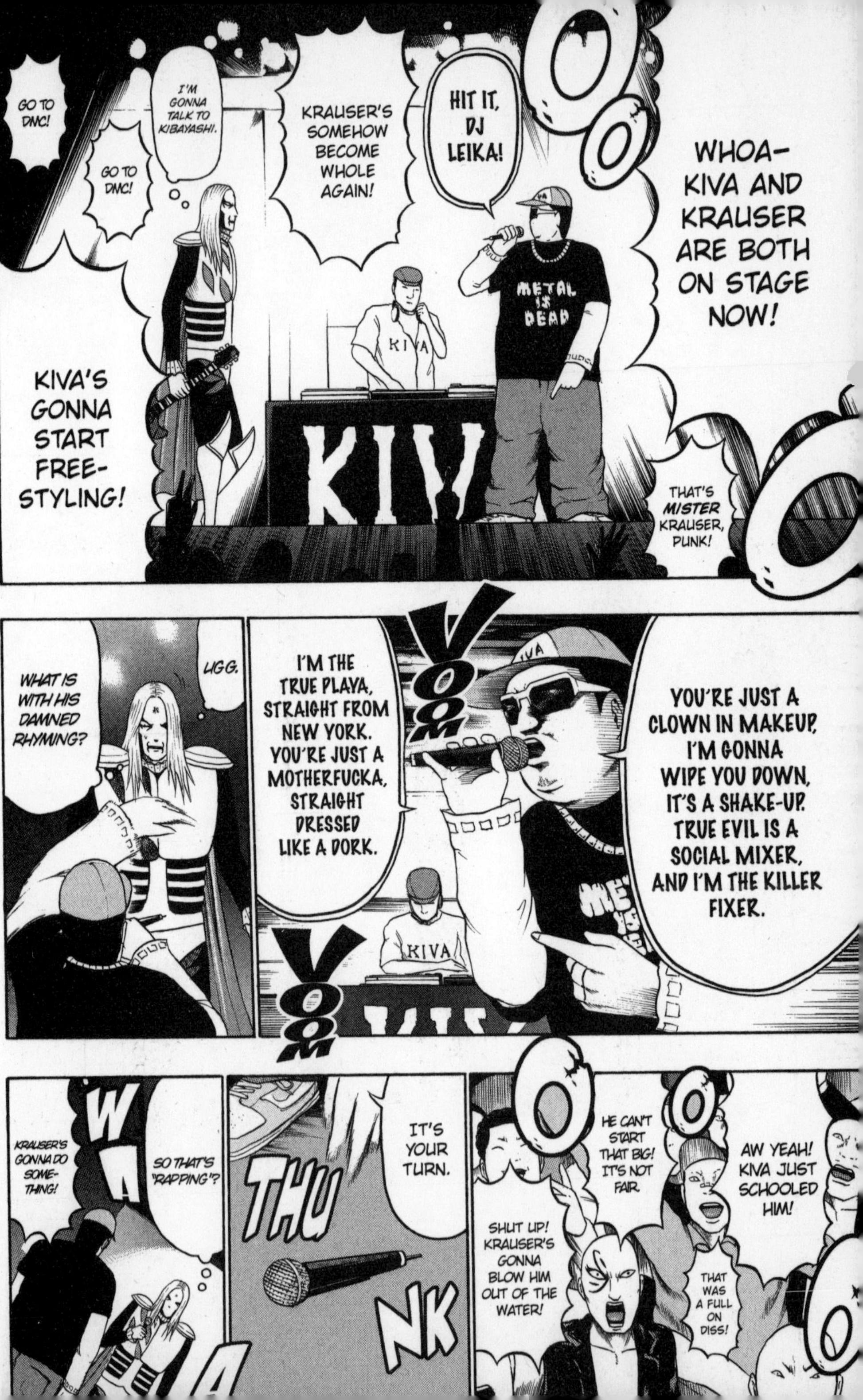
WHOA- KIVA AND KRAUSER ARE BOTH ON STAGE NOW!
HIT IT, DJ LEIKA!
KRAUSER'S SOMEHOW BECOME WHOLE AGAIN!
I'M GONNA TALK TO KIBAYASHI.
GO TO DMC!
GO TO DMC!
METAL IS DEAD
KIVA
KIV
THAT'S *MISTER* KRAUSER, PUNK!
KIVA'S GONNA START FREE-STYLING!
YOU'RE JUST A CLOWN IN MAKEUP, I'M GONNA WIPE YOU DOWN, IT'S A SHAKE-UP. TRUE EVIL IS A SOCIAL MIXER, AND I'M THE KILLER FIXER.
VOOM
I'M THE TRUE PLAYA, STRAIGHT FROM NEW YORK. YOU'RE JUST A MOTHERFUCKA, STRAIGHT DRESSED LIKE A DORK.
VOOM
KIVA
UGG.
WHAT IS WITH HIS DAMNED RHYMING?
AW YEAH! KIVA JUST SCHOOLED HIM!
HE CAN'T START THAT BIG! IT'S NOT FAIR.
THAT WAS A FULL ON DISS!
SHUT UP! KRAUSER'S GONNA BLOW HIM OUT OF THE WATER!
IT'S YOUR TURN.
THUNK
WA
SO THAT'S "RAPPING"?
KRAUSER'S GONNA DO SOME-THING!
A

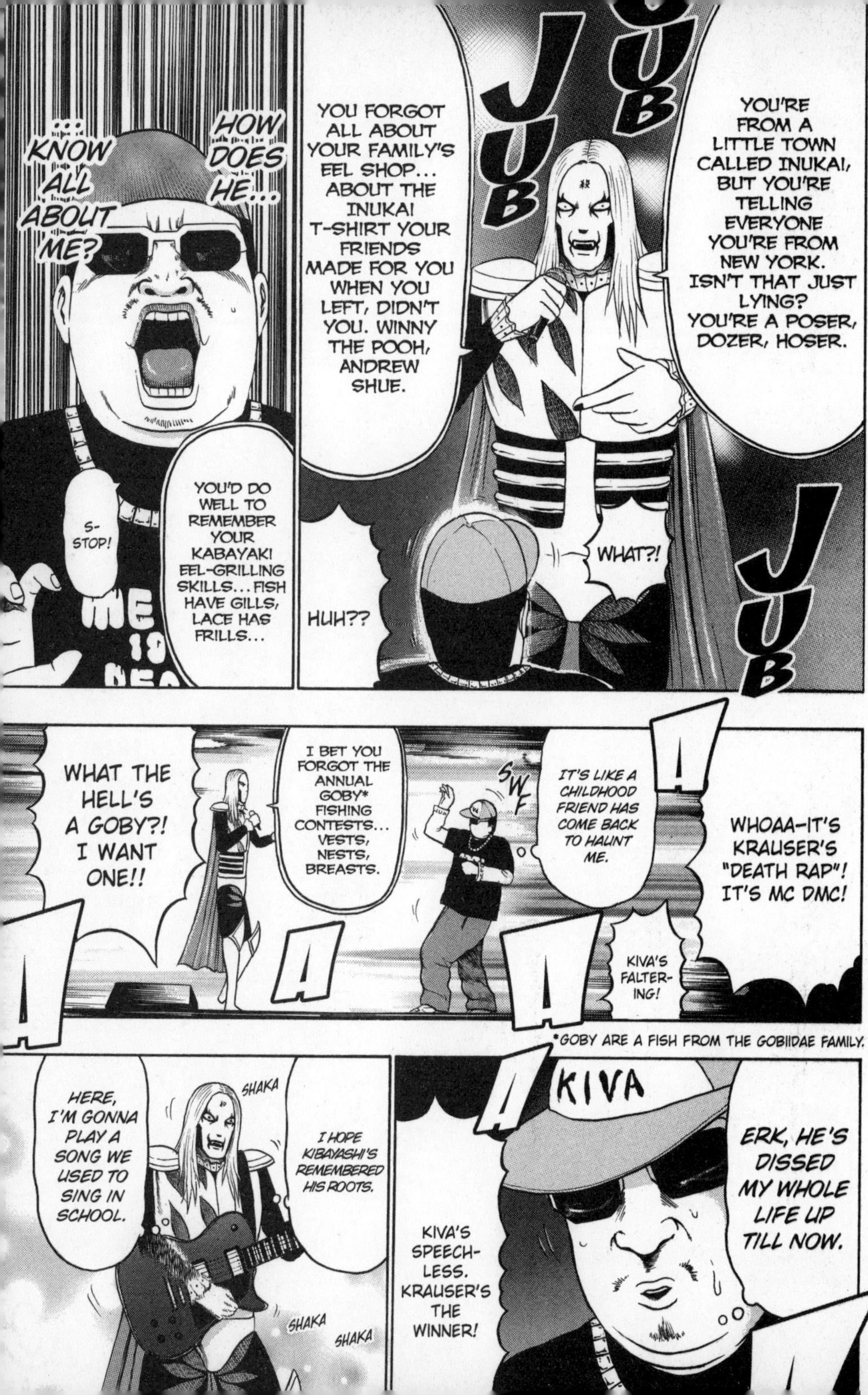
YOU'RE FROM A LITTLE TOWN CALLED INUKAI, BUT YOU'RE TELLING EVERYONE YOU'RE FROM NEW YORK. ISN'T THAT JUST LYING? YOU'RE A POSER, DOZER, HOSER.
JUB JUB
YOU FORGOT ALL ABOUT YOUR FAMILY'S EEL SHOP... ABOUT THE INUKAI T-SHIRT YOUR FRIENDS MADE FOR YOU WHEN YOU LEFT, DIDN'T YOU. WINNY THE POOH, ANDREW SHUE.
JUB
WHAT?!
HUH??
JUB
HOW DOES HE...
...KNOW ALL ABOUT ME?
YOU'D DO WELL TO REMEMBER YOUR KABAYAKI EEL-GRILLING SKILLS... FISH HAVE GILLS, LACE HAS FRILLS...
S-STOP!
A
WHOAA-IT'S KRAUSER'S "DEATH RAP"! IT'S MC DMC!
IT'S LIKE A CHILDHOOD FRIEND HAS COME BACK TO HAUNT ME.
KIVA'S FALTERING!
SWF
I BET YOU FORGOT THE ANNUAL GOBY* FISHING CONTESTS... VESTS, NESTS, BREASTS.
WHAT THE HELL'S A GOBY?! I WANT ONE!!
A A A
*GOBY ARE A FISH FROM THE GOBIIDAE FAMILY.
A
KIVA
ERK, HE'S DISSED MY WHOLE LIFE UP TILL NOW.
KIVA'S SPEECHLESS. KRAUSER'S THE WINNER!
I HOPE KIBAYASHI'S REMEMBERED HIS ROOTS.
SHAKA
HERE, I'M GONNA PLAY A SONG WE USED TO SING IN SCHOOL.
SHAKA
SHAKA

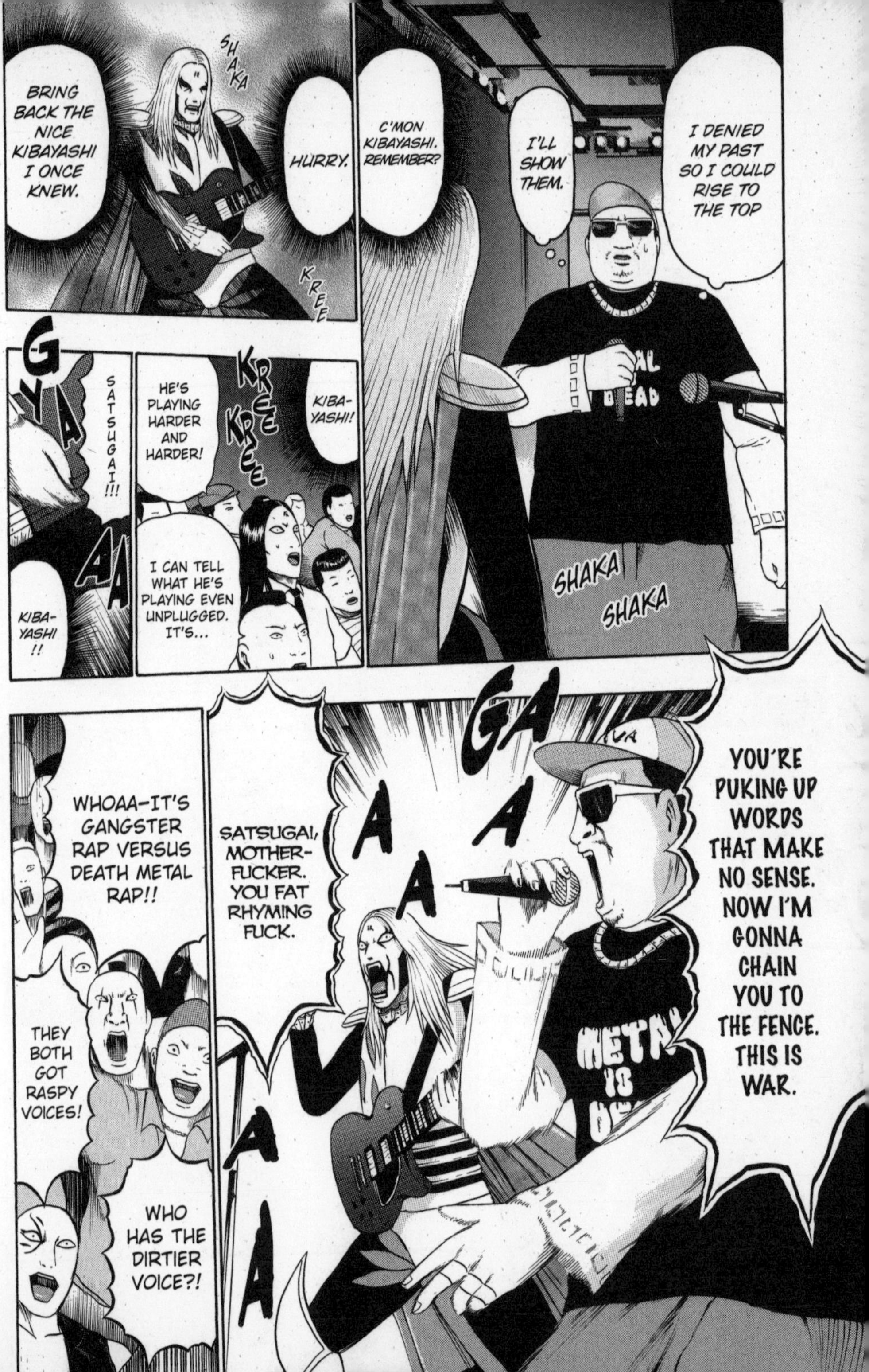
I DENIED MY PAST SO I COULD RISE TO THE TOP
I'LL SHOW THEM.
C'MON KIBAYASHI. REMEMBER?
SHAKA SHAKA
SHAKA
HURRY.
BRING BACK THE NICE KIBAYASHI I ONCE KNEW.
KREE
KIBA-YASHI!
KREE KREE
HE'S PLAYING HARDER AND HARDER!
I CAN TELL WHAT HE'S PLAYING EVEN UNPLUGGED. IT'S...
SATSUGAI!!!
GYA
AA
KIBA-YASHI !!
YOU'RE PUKING UP WORDS THAT MAKE NO SENSE. NOW I'M GONNA CHAIN YOU TO THE FENCE. THIS IS WAR.
GAAAA
SATSUGAI, MOTHER-FUCKER. YOU FAT RHYMING FUCK.
AAA
WHOAA-IT'S GANGSTER RAP VERSUS DEATH METAL RAP!!
THEY BOTH GOT RASPY VOICES!
WHO HAS THE DIRTIER VOICE?!

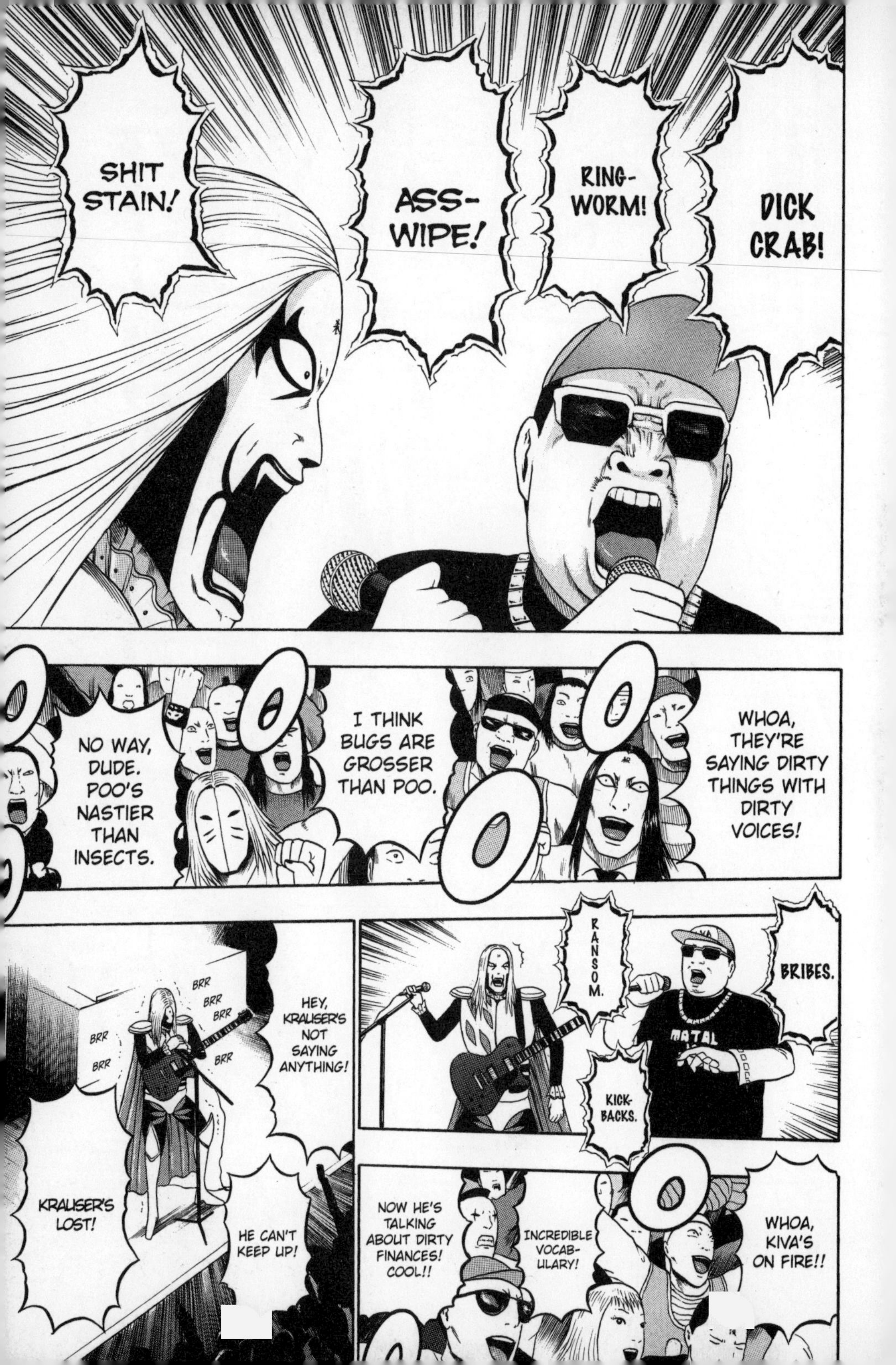
DICK CRAB!
RING-WORM!
ASS-WIPE!
SHIT STAIN!
WHOA, THEY'RE SAYING DIRTY THINGS WITH DIRTY VOICES!
I THINK BUGS ARE GROSSER THAN POO.
NO WAY, DUDE. POO'S NASTIER THAN INSECTS.
BRIBES.
RANSOM.
KICK-BACKS.
WHOA, KIVA'S ON FIRE!!
INCREDIBLE VOCAB-ULARY!
NOW HE'S TALKING ABOUT DIRTY FINANCES! COOL!!
HEY, KRAUSER'S NOT SAYING ANYTHING!
BRR BRR BRR BRR BRR BRR
HE CAN'T KEEP UP!
KRAUSER'S LOST!

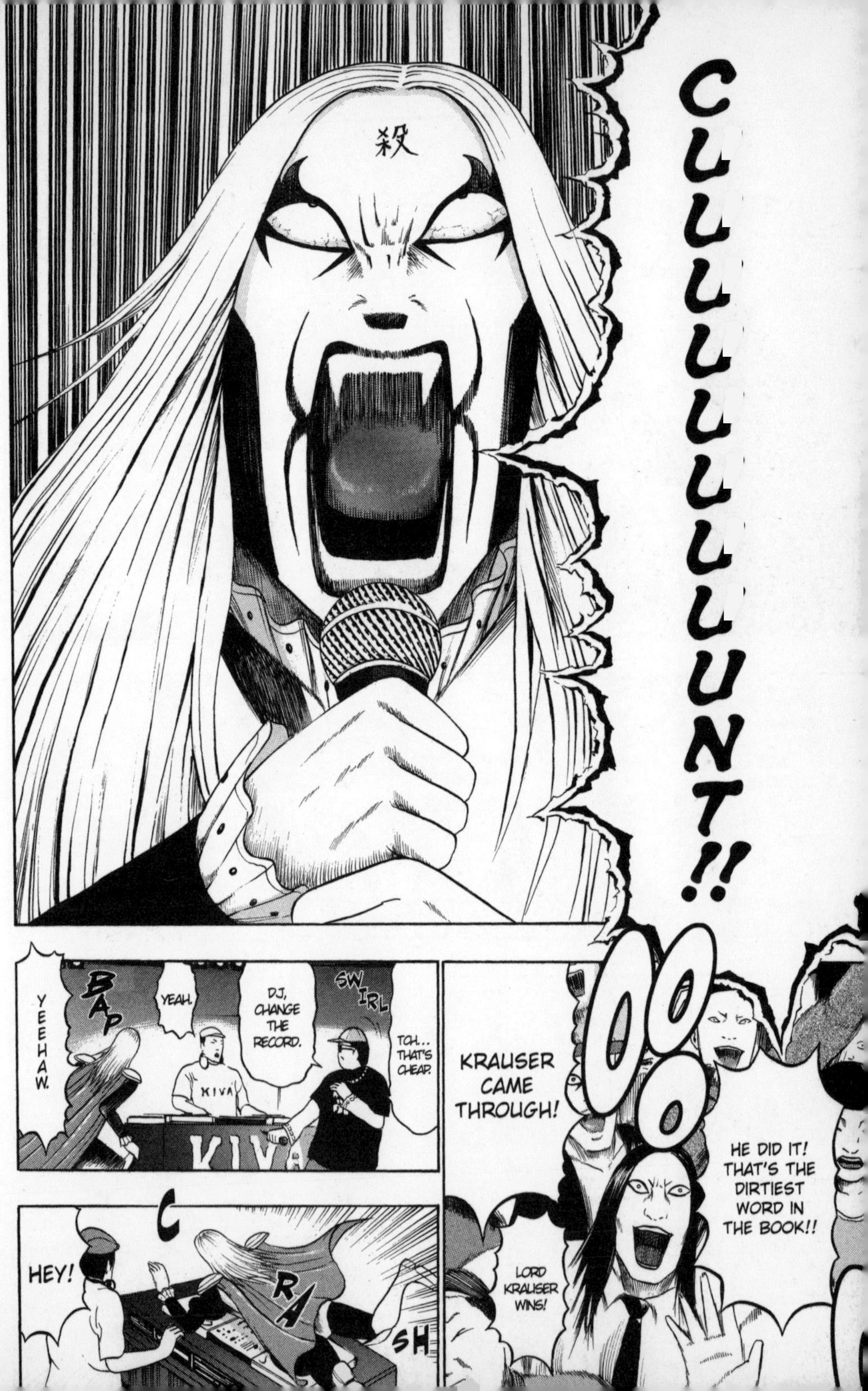
CULLLLLLLLLLUNT!!
OOOO
KRAUSER CAME THROUGH!
HE DID IT! THAT'S THE DIRTIEST WORD IN THE BOOK!!
LORD KRAUSER WINS!
SWIRL
TCH... THAT'S CHEAP.
DJ, CHANGE THE RECORD.
YEAH.
BAP
YEEHAW.
KIVA
CRASH
HEY!

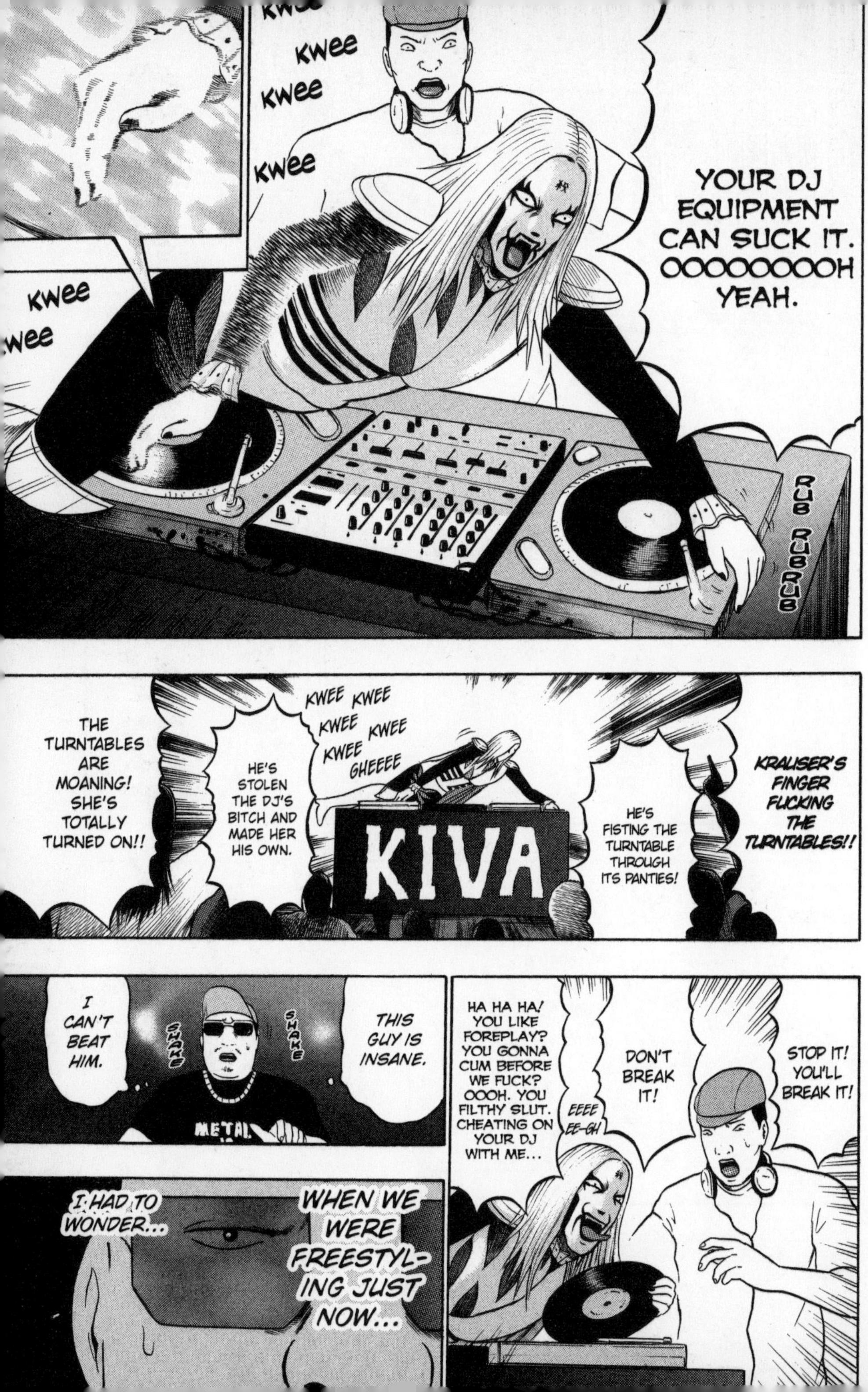
YOUR DJ EQUIPMENT CAN SUCK IT. OOOOOOOOOH YEAH.
RUB RUB RUB
KWEE
KWEE
KWEE
KWEE
WEE
KRAUSER'S FINGER FUCKING THE TURNTABLES!!
HE'S FISTING THE TURNTABLE THROUGH ITS PANTIES!
KWEE KWEE KWEE KWEE GHEEEE
KIVA
HE'S STOLEN THE DJ'S BITCH AND MADE HER HIS OWN.
THE TURNTABLES ARE MOANING! SHE'S TOTALLY TURNED ON!!
STOP IT! YOU'LL BREAK IT!
DON'T BREAK IT!
HA HA HA! YOU LIKE FOREPLAY? YOU GONNA CUM BEFORE WE FUCK? OOOH. YOU FILTHY SLUT. CHEATING ON YOUR DJ WITH ME...
EEEE EE-GH
THIS GUY IS INSANE.
SHAKE
SHAKE
I CAN'T BEAT HIM.
METAL
WHEN WE WERE FREESTYL-ING JUST NOW...
I HAD TO WONDER...

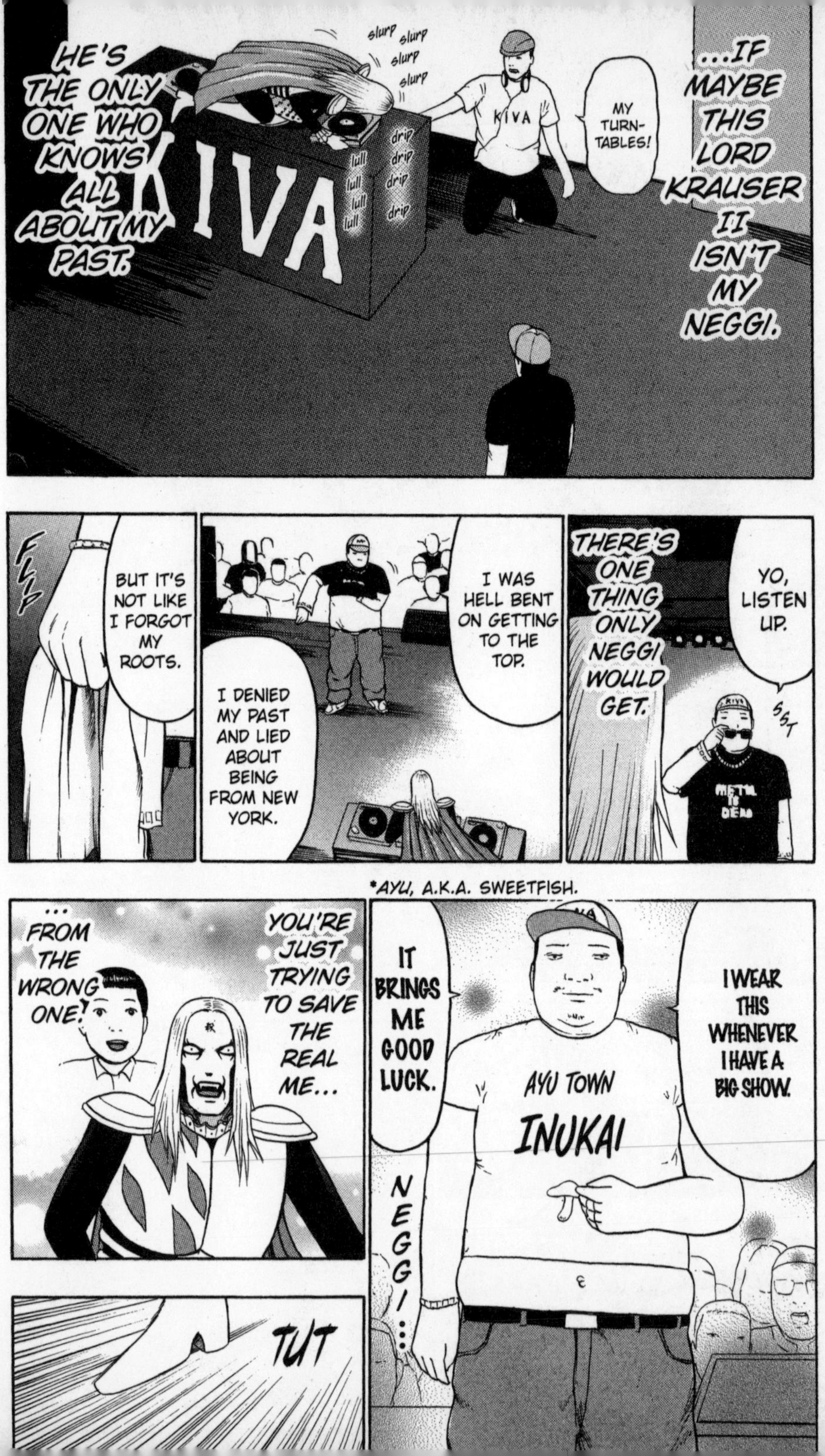
...IF MAYBE THIS LORD KRAUSER II ISN'T MY NEGGI.
MY TURN-TABLES!
slurp slurp slurp slurp
drip drip drip drip
lull lull lull lull
HE'S THE ONLY ONE WHO KNOWS ALL ABOUT MY PAST.
YO, LISTEN UP.
SST
THERE'S ONE THING ONLY NEGGI WOULD GET.
I WAS HELL BENT ON GETTING TO THE TOP.
I DENIED MY PAST AND LIED ABOUT BEING FROM NEW YORK.
BUT IT'S NOT LIKE I FORGOT MY ROOTS.
FLIP
*AYU, A.K.A. SWEETFISH.
I WEAR THIS WHENEVER I HAVE A BIG SHOW.
AYU TOWN INUKAI
IT BRINGS ME GOOD LUCK.
NEGGI...
YOU'RE JUST TRYING TO SAVE THE REAL ME...
...FROM THE WRONG ONE!
TUT

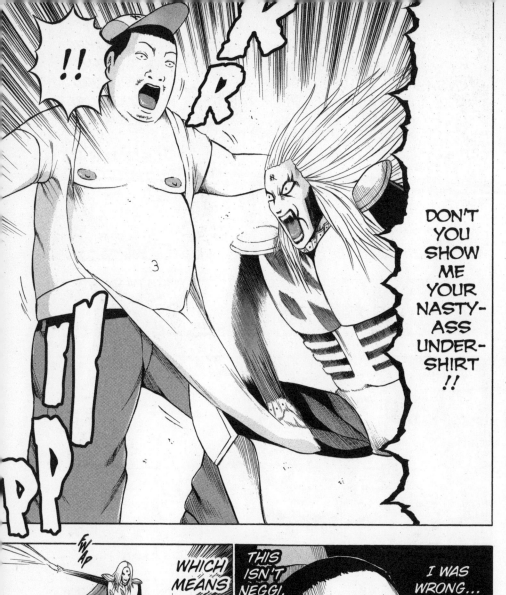

!!
RRIPP
DON'T YOU SHOW ME YOUR NASTY-ASS UNDERSHIRT!!
I WAS WRONG...
THIS ISN'T NEGGI.
WHICH MEANS...
FWAP
THIS IS A TRULY EVIL PERSON.
THUNK
KIVA'S COLLAPSED!!

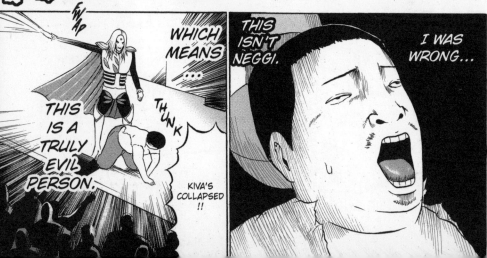

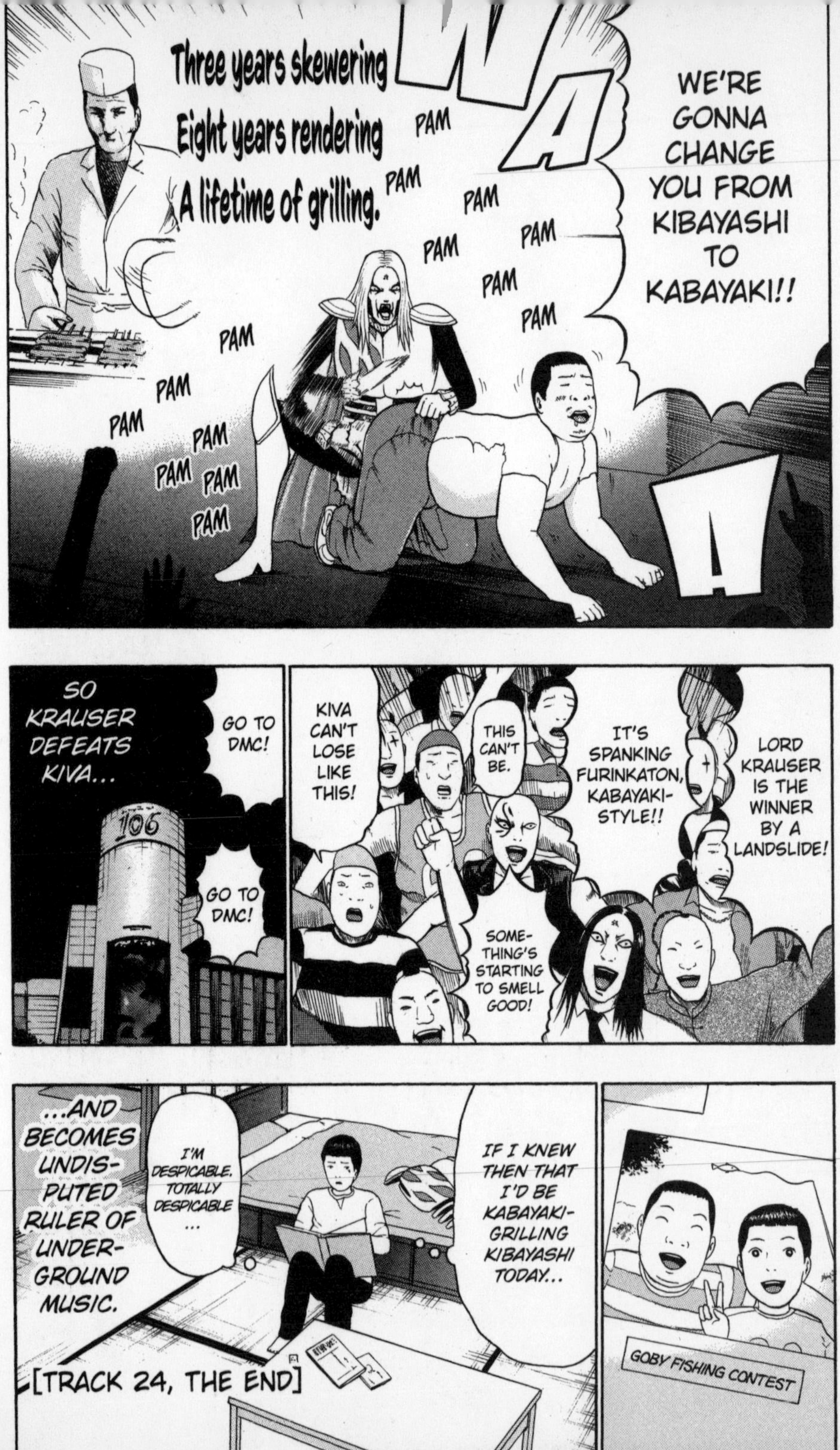
WE'RE GONNA CHANGE YOU FROM KIBAYASHI TO KABAYAKI!!
WA
Three years skewering
Eight years rendering
A lifetime of grilling.
PAM PAM PAM PAM PAM PAM PAM PAM PAM PAM PAM PAM PAM PAM
A
LORD KRAUSER IS THE WINNER BY A LANDSLIDE!
IT'S SPANKING FURINKATON, KABAYAKI-STYLE!!
THIS CAN'T BE.
KIVA CAN'T LOSE LIKE THIS!
SOMETHING'S STARTING TO SMELL GOOD!
GO TO DMC!
SO KRAUSER DEFEATS KIVA...
106
GO TO DMC!
GOBY FISHING CONTEST
IF I KNEW THEN THAT I'D BE KABAYAKI-GRILLING KIBAYASHI TODAY...
I'M DESPICABLE. TOTALLY DESPICABLE...
...AND BECOMES UNDISPUTED RULER OF UNDERGROUND MUSIC.
[TRACK 24, THE END]

DMC LEXICON

KABAYAKI

A process of grilling whereby you strip the eel from its spine, pierce it with skewers and grill it with barbeque sauce over charcoal. A kabayaki without sauce is a "white bake." You can grill sea eels as well as freshwater eel, but it's good to kabayaki someone who's being fresh with you.

Usage: You wanna dive into Tokyo Bay or get kabayaki-ed?!

デトロイト・メタル・シティ
Detroit Metal City

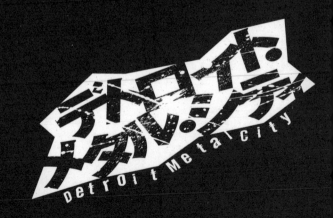

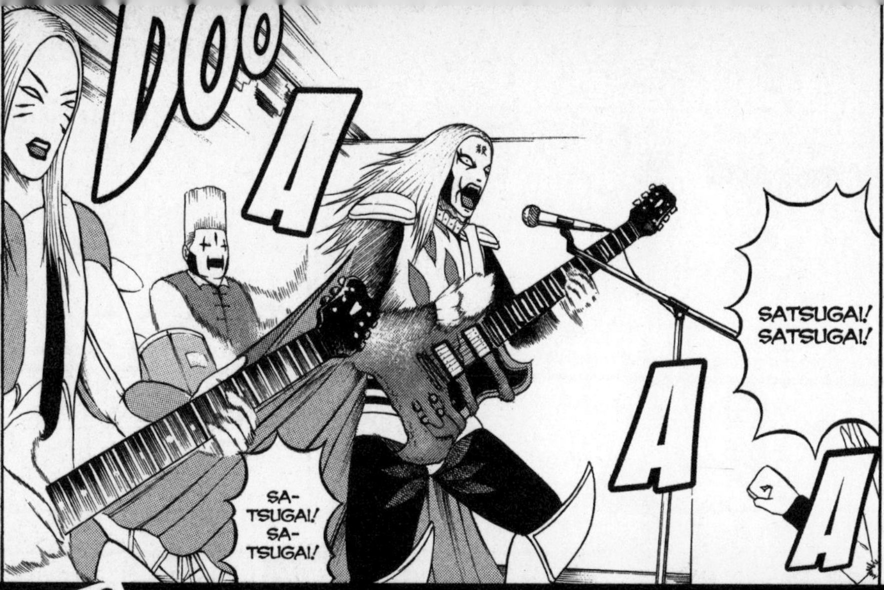
DOOOA
A
A
A
SATSUGAI! SATSUGAI!
SA-TSUGAI! SA-TSUGAI!

BONUS TRACK Detroit Moe City

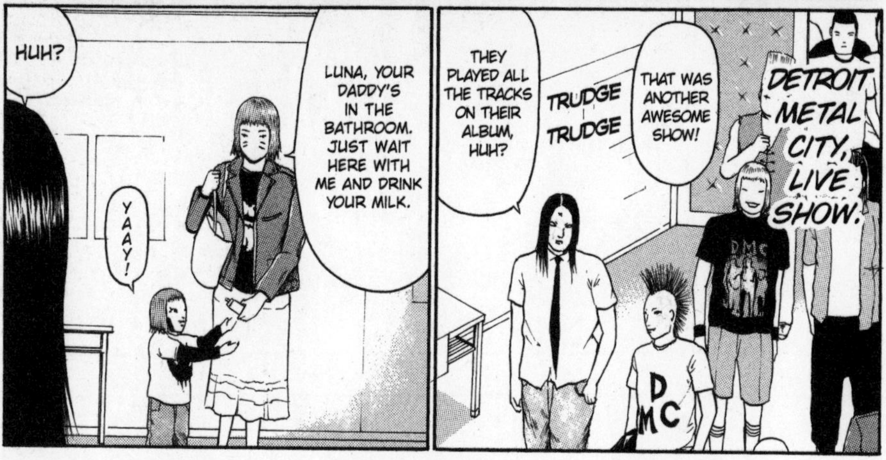
DETROIT METAL CITY, LIVE SHOW.
THAT WAS ANOTHER AWESOME SHOW!
TRUDGE TRUDGE
THEY PLAYED ALL THE TRACKS ON THEIR ALBUM, HUH?
DMC
DMC
LUNA, YOUR DADDY'S IN THE BATHROOM. JUST WAIT HERE WITH ME AND DRINK YOUR MILK.
YAAY!
HUH?

FOREHEAD: SHACHU

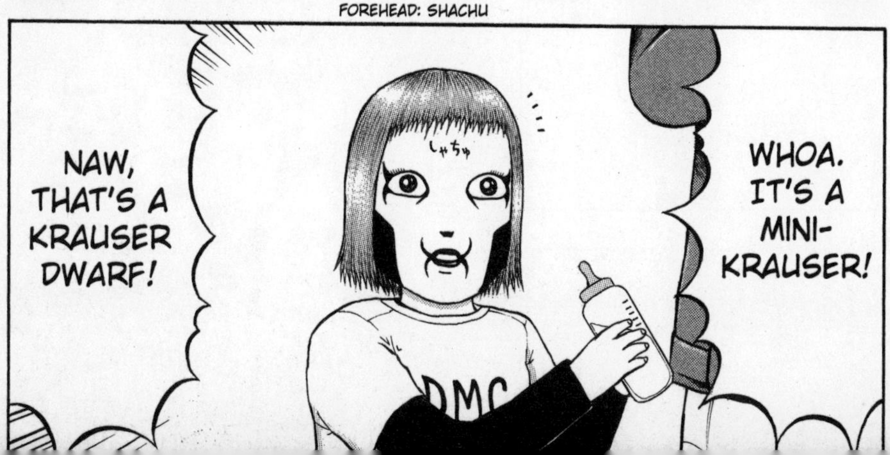
WHOA. IT'S A MINI-KRAUSER!
NAW, THAT'S A KRAUSER DWARF!
DMC

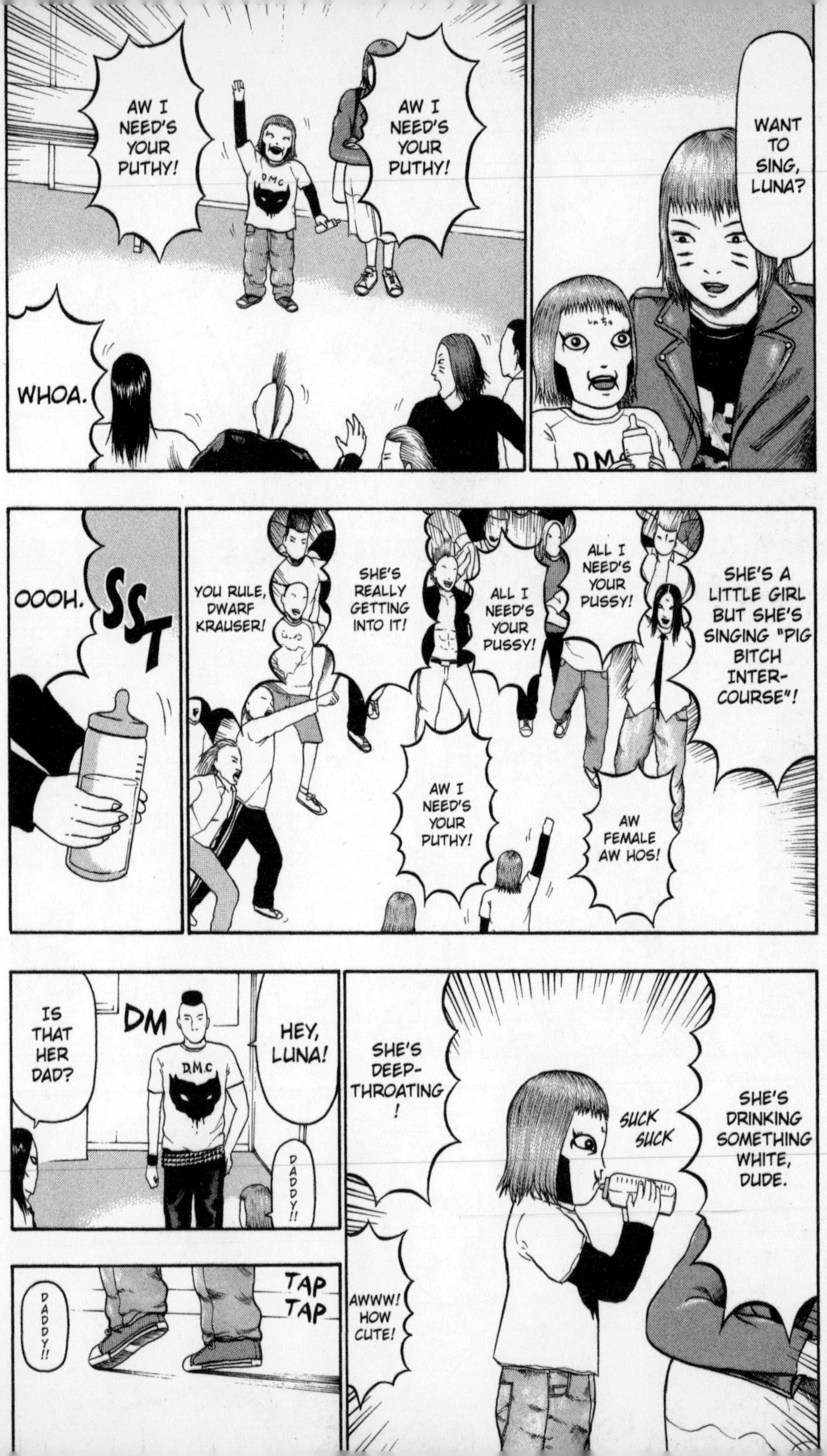
WANT TO SING, LUNA?
AW I NEED'S YOUR PUTHY!
AW I NEED'S YOUR PUTHY!
WHOA.
SHE'S A LITTLE GIRL BUT SHE'S SINGING "PIG BITCH INTER-COURSE"!
ALL I NEED'S YOUR PUSSY!
ALL I NEED'S YOUR PUSSY!
SHE'S REALLY GETTING INTO IT!
YOU RULE, DWARF KRAUSER!
AW FEMALE AW HOS!
AW I NEED'S YOUR PUTHY!
SST
OOOH.
SHE'S DRINKING SOMETHING WHITE, DUDE.
SUCK SUCK
SHE'S DEEP-THROATING!
AWWW! HOW CUTE!
HEY, LUNA!
DM
IS THAT HER DAD?
DADDY!!
TAP TAP
DADDY!!

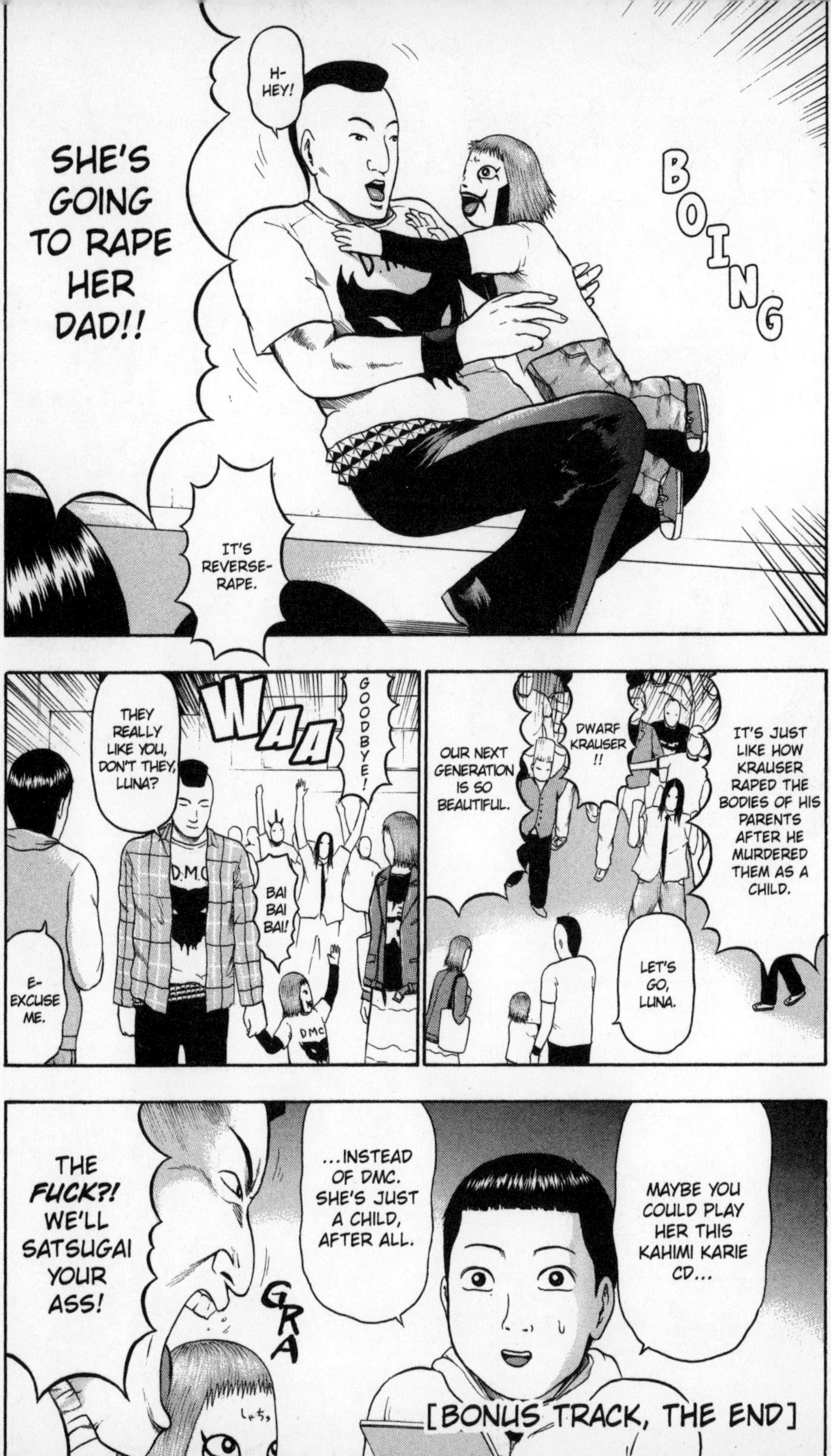
BOING
H-HEY!
SHE'S GOING TO RAPE HER DAD!!
IT'S REVERSE-RAPE.
IT'S JUST LIKE HOW KRAUSER RAPED THE BODIES OF HIS PARENTS AFTER HE MURDERED THEM AS A CHILD.
DWARF KRAUSER!!
OUR NEXT GENERATION IS SO BEAUTIFUL.
LET'S GO, LUNA.
GOODBYE!
WAA
THEY REALLY LIKE YOU, DON'T THEY, LUNA?
BAI BAI BAI!
E-EXCUSE ME.
MAYBE YOU COULD PLAY HER THIS KAHIMI KARIE CD...
...INSTEAD OF DMC. SHE'S JUST A CHILD, AFTER ALL.
GRA
THE FUCK?! WE'LL SATSUGAI YOUR ASS!
[BONUS TRACK, THE END]

Detroit Metal City
VOLUME 2

STORY AND ART BY KIMINORI WAKASUGI

ENGLISH ADAPTATION Annus Itchii
TOUCH-UP ART & LETTERING John Hunt
DESIGN Courtney Utt
EDITOR Kit Fox

VP, PRODUCTION Alvin Lu
VP, PUBLISHING LICENSING Rika Inouye
VP, SALES & PRODUCT MARKETING Gonzalo Ferreyra
VP, CREATIVE Linda Espinosa
PUBLISHER Hyoe Narita

Detroit Metal City by
Kiminori Wakasugi

First published in Japan in 2006 by
HAKUSENSHA, Inc., Tokyo.
English language translation
rights arranged with
HAKUSENSHA, Inc., Tokyo.

Printed in the U.S.A.

Published by VIZ Media, LLC
P.O. Box 77010
San Francisco, CA 94107

VIZ Signature Edition
10 9 8 7 6 5 4 3 2 1
First printing, September 2009

PARENTAL ADVISORY
DETROIT METAL CITY IS RATED M FOR MATURE AND IS RECOMMENDED FOR MATURE READERS. THIS VOLUME CONTAINS PROFANITY AND CRUDE HUMOR.

RATED M FOR MATURE
ratings.viz.com

VIZ media
{ www.viz.com store.viz.com }

LOVE MANGA?
LET US KNOW WHAT YOU THINK!

OUR MANGA SURVEY IS NOW
AVAILABLE ONLINE. PLEASE VISIT:
VIZ.COM/MANGASURVEY

HELP US MAKE THE MANGA
YOU LOVE BETTER!